Beyond Music

Beyond Music

Maestros in Conversation

Interviewers

Geeta Sahai
Shrinkhla Sahai

Foreword by

Meeta Pandit

NIYOGI
BOOKS

Published by
NIYOGI BOOKS
D-78, Okhla Industrial Area, Phase-I
New Delhi-110 020, INDIA
Tel: 91-11-26816301, 49327000
Fax: 91-11-26810483, 26813830
email: niyogibooks@gmail.com
website: www.niyogibooksindia.com

Editor: Gita Rajan
Design: Shashi Bhushan Prasad

ISBN: 978-93-83098-98-9
Publication: 2015

Printed at: Niyogi Offset Pvt. Ltd., New Delhi, India

To all those unheard talents,
forgotten artistes and true artistes

CONTENTS

FOREWORD 9

INTRODUCTION 11

Dr Gangubai Hangal 17
Vocal

Pandit Ravi Shankar 27
Sitar

Vidushi Shanno Khurana 39
Vocal

Ustad Sabri Khan 49
Sarangi

Vidushi Dhondutai Kulkarni 57
Vocal

Vidushi Girija Devi 67
Vocal

Dr N. Rajam 73
Violin

Pandit Jasraj 87
Vocal

Dr Prabha Atre 97
Vocal

Vidushi Shanti Hiranand 117
Vocal

Pandit L.K. Pandit 133
Vocal

Pandit Debu Chaudhuri **141**
Sitar

Pandit Shiv Kumar Sharma **157**
Santoor

Pandit Hariprasad Chaurasia **165**
Flute

Vidushi Savita Devi **175**
Vocal

Ustad Amjad Ali Khan **183**
Sarod

Pandit Bhajan Sopori **199**
Santoor

Pandit Vishwa Mohan Bhatt **211**
Mohan Veena

Pandits Rajan & Sajan Mishra **225**
Vocal

Vidushi Shruti Sadolikar **237**
Vocal

Pandit Ajoy Chakrabarty **253**
Vocal

Ustad Mashkoor Ali Khan **263**
Vocal

Dr Arawind Thatte **271**
Harmonium

Ustad Shujaat Khan **283**
Sitar

Ustad Wasifuddin Dagar **301**
Vocal

GLOSSARY **309**

INDEX **319**

Foreword

I remember as a child I was often taken to classical music concerts, listening to great maestros, at times tagging along with my father, Pandit L.K. Pandit, to their houses or artistes visiting our home in Gwalior and Delhi, both. I had been with them as a child, and now as a practising musician. I always thought that I knew them pretty well, their inner world. But this book *Beyond Music—Maestros in Conversation* by Geeta Sahai and Shrinkhla Sahai—is a pleasant surprise. Through the book I came to know several incidents, facts and their thought process, closely. It goes to the credit of both the writers that the maestros bared their soul in the free-wheeling conversations that not only talk about music as an academic subject but also foray into sensitive issues pertaining to the growth of *musicians* as *maestros.*

This book is the product of a passion of the authors for music in all its forms. I have known few people with a passion for music and for interviewing maestros, as strong as that of the book's authors. I came to know Geeta Sahai nearly ten years ago when she interviewed me. It was one of the most in depth interviews that I ever faced. It was exhaustive to visit my real self and also very satisfying, to get an opportunity to share my deepest thoughts on so many aspects of music and life. During my visit to Radio Gandharv's studio (24 X 7 Hindustani classical music station on Worldspace Satellite Network) in Delhi, I met and interacted with Shrinkhla Sahai. I was amazed at her musical knowledge, zest for doing new things, researching and putting knowledge in a most innovative manner on the radio. Indian classical music needs people like Geeta and Shrinkhla who know how to reach out.

Both the authors succeed in bringing about that same knowledge, clarity and passion for music to this book. As I turned page after page of the book and read interviews one after the other, it was as if each interview opened a new window into the life of an artiste. For instance, in his interview my father and guru, Pandit L.K. Pandit revealed, 'I used to sit in the central park at Connaught Place for hours in the evening and do my practice ... there was no one to rent a house to a *gaanewala*.' One can imagine the pain that he must have gone through at that point of his life. Only the authors could have inspired the artistes to revisit their painful, hidden memories!

These twenty-five interviews are mirror to the inner trials and tribulations of an artiste. With the focus being on life and challenges of the musical world, the lucid language and various musical perspectives make the book thought provoking and an interesting read. It offers students, researchers and connoisseurs' deep insights into the rich and diverse world of Hindustani classical music.

Retrospectively speaking, Hindustani classical music has, over the centuries, survived and maintained its sanctity. The explanations and critical explorations that maestros have revealed in their interviews deepen our understanding of traditional music, its heritage, the musical trajectory, *gharana*s and above all the continued importance of our traditional music in the present high-tech, hurried world. In fact, these interviews unravel new ideas and illuminate grey areas of Hindustani classical music. Some of the important questions, like time classification of ragas or the relevance of *gharanas* have also been debated and maestros have come up with their candid views.

I am confident that this book with its long list including most of the revered names of today's musical fraternity like late Pandit Ravi Shankar, late Vidushi Dr Gangubai Hangal, late Vidushi Dhondutai Kulkarni, would certainly be useful and offer an exceptionally rich experience for musicians, music lovers, researchers and music students.

I am honoured and grateful for this opportunity to pen my thoughts.

I wish the authors, with whom over the years I have developed a special bond, best of luck in their endeavour.

Thank You.

Meeta Pandit
New Delhi
15 February, 2015

Introduction

Music is a universal language. So it is generally believed. Yet, the vocabulary of Hindustani classical music has a niche circle of connoisseurs. Seeing an artiste on stage and experiencing their music is just the tip of the iceberg. It takes years of training, skill, discipline and *riyaaz* to master the grammar of the art form that appears to be an effortless master stroke to spectators and listeners. The truth is that behind the syntax and emotion of each *taan*, *murki*, *gamak*, *alaap* and *pukar* that leaves devoted listeners spellbound, there is a deep-rooted ideology and perspective on music and life. This compilation of interviews with maestros of Hindustani classical music is an endeavour to share those aspects through the musicians' own words and to present a kaleidoscope of their unknown world.

Hindustani classical music has a spectrum of sub-genres within vocal and instrumental styles ranging from *dhrupad*, *dhamaar*, *khayal*, *thumri*, *dadra*, *tappa* and more. These have evolved over time and musical aesthetics have been heavily influenced by sites and modes of production and reception of music. At the turn of the twentieth century, the royal court was the main system of patronage for classical music. While *dhrupad* and *khayal* were accepted as the respected genres performed by male musicians, forms like *thumri* and *dadra* were associated with courtesans and relegated to the realm of petty entertainment. These women musicians faced social ostracisation for a major part of the twentieth century. Even today, these forms are most often categorised as 'semi-classical' music though many musicians disagree with this nomenclature. 'I do not consider *thumri* semi-classical. I think *thumri* is a form of pure classical music and I am fighting for it to be recognised as such,' says Vidushi Savita Devi. Somewhat similar are the views of Vidushi Girija Devi, '*Thumri* is like a garden having various flowers. The singer plucks flowers of different hues and fragrances and makes a bouquet of different ragas. Of course one has to see that the combination of ragas is acceptable. We cannot sing *thumri* without having a knowledge of *khayal.'*

Here we must point out that while we use the commonly accepted term 'Hindustani classical music' throughout this book, many performers and scholars prefer to use 'North Indian classical music,' and often musicians associate their *gayaki* to a particular *gharana.*

Gharana, or a musical style, is the foundation of the unique features on which most artistes have built their individual signatures. *Gharana* literally means household and denotes a formally structured system of musically and socially distinct singing styles. An important aspect of Indian classical music, *gharana* signifies a musical lineage, a socio-cultural position and musical ideology. The names of *gharana*s are linked to their geographical origins, for instance Gwalior *gharana,* Jaipur-Atrauli *gharana*, Agra *gharana*, Patiala *gharana*, Kirana *gharana*, Banaras *gharana,* and so on. While some musicians associate the purity and authenticity of classical music largely on the premise of the traditional roots of their style in a particular *gharana*—'Each *gharana* is unique. For example, in Agra *gharana gayaki* they used to start with *madhya laya* and *alaapchari, bol-baant* was characteristic to Agra *gharana*, while in Kirana *gharana* the emphasis is on the notes, *behlava*; so you see each *gharana* has something special and unique,' says Pandit Jasraj. But there are many who find the concept of *gharana* irrelevant in the contemporary context when there are myriad influences and assimilations—'Society has undergone change, our perspective has changed and that reflects in our music as well. Technological exposure has blurred all distinctions between *gharanas*,' opines Pandit L.K. Pandit. Again Pandit Ajoy Chakrabarty feels, 'See, even earlier this concept of *gharana* was archaic. It had no meaning. Four artistes belonging to one *gharana* will sing differently. Music depends on one's individuality, thinking, values, culture and humanity. Of course, a basic line of thinking is maintained in a *gharana*. In that way *gharanas* are important.'

These are some examples of the debates and discussions that are alive and in circulation today in the world of music. In these interviews, we have raised pointed questions connected with such issues and musicians have candidly expressed their views. Today, the circumstances of presenting music have completely altered. As pointed out by veteran artistes in this volume, the disappearance of royal patronage after Independence: ('Earlier, during the era of *nawabs* and kings, there was complete state patronage. An artiste had to just concentrate on his music. For all the twenty-four hours of the day he was busy thinking or composing music.' Pandit L.K. Pandit), the emergence of radio as a medium and the current dependence on corporate sponsorship, drastically transformed musical styles.

The impact of globalisation and commercialisation are also much-debated topics. 'One must change as per the place and environment. One has to adapt to change. We, classical musicians cannot live in our ivory tower. The distance between the artiste and the audience must decrease,' feels Pandit Vishwa Mohan Bhatt. On the contrary some feel that classical music is an abstract art and 'is not the music of masses. It is the product of a more deliberate aesthetic shaping process. A lot of thinking and experimentation has gone behind its formation. To expect classical music to become as popular as film music would be wrong' (Dr Prabha Atre). Disagreeing with such notions was the view of Pandit Jasraj, who says, 'I just don't agree with those people who are suggesting that classical music is not for the masses. If music is not for the masses then how can you call it music?'

The most controversial and debated topic has been the day-part time classifications of the ragas. While some maestros feel that the time classification theory is no longer required, others disagree. 'It is our tradition, there is a reason behind it and we should definitely follow it' (Dr Gangubai Hangal). 'I see changes happening ... personally, I do not like listening to evening or night ragas in the morning ... but after forty-fifty years it [doing away with time classification theory] might happen' (Dr N. Rajam).

Initially many musicians were hesitant about sharing their inner world, their untold struggle—'But my music says everything I want to express, why talk!' It was slightly difficult to convince them of the relevance of in-depth interviews for preserving music history as well as generating more ideas and dialogues about music. It was pertinent for us to go beyond music to unravel the mystic and the mundane aspects in their respective musical experiments. We were adamant to bring to a large audience their articulations, their thoughts, the process of music making, learning and teaching, and the trials and tribulations of their life journey.

We also knew the importance of making their invisible world accessible to the non-initiated listener who is intrigued and interested in music yet is intimidated by the idea of classical music. While voicing for the changes and the current growing popularity of the World music or Fusion music, Dr N. Rajam opines, 'Any art form should not be static. If it is static, it ceases to be an art form. It has to constantly grow, evolve. Change is necessary. But to change for the sake of change is not healthy. We cannot just overlook or bypass all the musical rules and regulations, made by our ancestors. We cannot just negate all those points and bring about change. No, that is not good. While keeping in mind those points, changes should be brought about; but not blindly.'

Hindustani classical musicians have often lamented about the diminishing audience interest in classical music in India and the absence of knowledgeable *rasika*s as in the earlier times. This compilation is also an attempt at bridging that gap between the layman who thinks 'I don't understand classical music' and the musician who feels an absence of appreciative listeners. The lacunae in integrating music education as part of school curriculum and the absence of media support are issues raised by many musicians in this book. In this context, we believe, it is critical to think and talk about music, to engage with the polemics and politics of music as an essential aspect of society. We see this book as one of the ways of opening and inviting music lovers into that conversation.

As the fields of ethnomusicology, cultural studies and performance studies are in their nascent stage and emerging fast, the locus of research in these disciplines has also shifted from the technical aspects of music alone to encompass the cultural and social aspects. This volume presents an overview of the Hindustani classical music world in the first decade of the twenty-first century and therefore is an important link in the trajectory of music history and research—the history of an oral tradition of transmission of knowledge.

It is our humble attempt to expand the boundaries that accompany the realm of classical music to a global community that wants to know more about the stars of the musical firmament. For many, who might not even be familiar with the musical styles within the classical genres, this might be a route to engaging with the music by first encountering the human side of these larger-than-life personalities. And that aspect is truly universal and humbling.

Last but certainly not the least—these interviews were recorded for the purpose of radio broadcasts on the first and only 24-hour Hindustani classical music station, Radio Gandharv, on WorldSpace satellite Network. These interviews were conducted between 2003 and 2009. The radio station closed down in December 2009 and since then we have received numerous requests from listeners, musicians and enthusiasts to make the interviews accessible in some way.

During the interviews we always sought to go beyond the stage persona of the musician and delve into his/her thoughts and experiences, to have an interview that was intense and fun. And, it was not easy at all to get an artiste to articulate his art. Each interview was preceded with intensive research on the maestro's musical style, *gharana*, life, choices and interests. Conversations would often meander across issues in music to struggles of life, professional success and personal vicissitudes. The personal bonds formed across the studio table have been the most precious gift for us. Sometimes, the interviews happened at the artiste's residence or in a guest house when they were visiting Delhi for concerts.

The content of the interviews varies from exhaustive perspectives on issues of classical music like the relevance of *gharana*s, day-part-time theory, the categories of 'classical' and 'semi-classical,' globalisation and its impact on classical music to personal histories, lineage and gurus, struggle and successes as well as fun facts about their other interests and dreams. It was indeed heartening to see the artistes in a lighter vein, whether it was the fun-filled banter between father and son Pandit Vishwa Mohan Bhatt and Salil Bhatt, or a priceless passing chuckle as Dr Gangubai Hangal reminisced about defeating Pandit Kumar Gandharva in a game of cards and sat with us to compare slipper sizes of her tiny feet. It was moving to listen to Vidushi Savita Devi sharing memories about her mother, Vidushi Siddheshwari Devi, or Vidushi Shanno Khurana's emotional voice while narrating the horror of Partition. It was heartening to see and experience perfect bonding and respect between Pandits Rajan and Sajan Mishra. It was indeed so very overwhelming to see maestros opening up their hearts. Such invaluable 'on-air' moments were cherished by listeners. We were touched by the emotional outpourings of the listeners after the broadcast of each interview.

All these interviews are of great archival value. This compilation presents a few of the recorded interviews of some of the biggest names in the world of Indian classical music. Many of them have been responsible for putting Indian classical music firmly on the global map through the last century like late Pandit Ravi Shankar, Pandit Jasraj, Ustad Amjad Ali Khan, Pandit Hariprasad Chaurasia, Pandit Shiv Kumar Sharma, Dr Prabha Atre and Pandits Rajan and Sajan Mishra. Legends like late Dr Gangubai Hangal, Ustad Sabri Khan, Pandit L.K. Pandit, Vidushi Shanno Khurana and Vidushi Shanti Hiranand have lived through another era which is accessible to most of us today through anecdotes only. Their personal memories converge with music history to create an intricate saga of changing socio-cultural patterns that influenced aesthetics. We recorded the interview with Dr Gangubai Hangal intermittently across five days at her home in Hubli during her ninety sixth birthday celebrations. That was her last in-depth interview. Icons like Vidushi Girija Devi, Pandit Ajoy Chakrabarty, and Ustad Wasifuddin Dagar have become synonymous with genres of *thumri, khayal* and *dhrupad* while maestros like Pandit Vishwa Mohan Bhatt, Ustad Shujaat Khan and Pandit Arawind Thatte have explored new frontiers with instruments and experimented with various genres. Veterans like Pandit Debu Chaudhuri, Dr N. Rajam, Pandit Bhajan Sopori, and others are storehouses of knowledge. By bringing all of these together in a singular collection, this book gives an overarching view of the music scenario in the last four to five decades and maestros who have made invaluable contributions to classical music today. At the same time we must mention that it is by no means a definitive list since a quite a few well-known musicians of the genre have not been featured here. We do accept and believe that their contribution in the field is inarguably important and on some later date we may bring out a sequel to this book.

We hope this volume would enthral *rasika*s, researchers, artistes, critics and enthusiasts alike. We also hope that it would expand the scope and reach of classical music and ignite further discussions and conversations.

V O C A L

Flowing with the 'Musical Breeze'

DR GANGUBAI HANGAL

(5 March, 1913–21 July, 2009)

We had heard her name since childhood. And it was a dream come true when she herself rang up and invited us, 'Beta aa jao ... bas.' We immediately decided to visit her native place—Hubli—to know and understand the most respected, revered musician and the hidden woman behind that childlike laughter.

Little did we know that it was going to be *Ajji's* last interview!

We had met her a few days after her 96th birthday in Hubli and the news of her death on 21 July, 2009 brought back a kaleidoscope of memories—the disarming warmth of her smile, her childlike enthusiasm, and the refrain of her famous *bandish* in Raga Jogiya 'Hari ka bhed na payo.'

It was a priceless moment as she reminisced about her camaraderie with guru-*bhai* Pandit Bhimsen Joshi when he used to accompany her to the station after the day's lesson in their younger days or when she laughed about winning a card game with Pandit Kumar Gandharva. Her eyes brimmed with tears while remembering her dear daughter Krishna who was her constant shadow and she waved away all questions about her struggles with a smile.

Born in 1913, Gangubai Hangal is known as one of the five gems of Dharwad—a district in Karnataka (The other four gems are—Pandit Basavaraj Rajguru, Pandit Mallikarjun Mansur, Pandit Bhimsen Joshi and Pandit Kumar Gandharva) that is the birthplace of a galaxy of classical musicians.

We were apprehensive that we would not be allowed much time with her but her grandson Manoj Hangal dispelled these doubts, 'People admire and adore her and want to pay respects to her. The fact is that she is not just my grandmother, she is Gangubai Hangal. She has a standing in the world that goes way beyond this home and family. The whole world is her family.'

From her humble beginning she rose to become Honorary Music Professor in Karnataka University and achieved several other laurels and awards. She also wrote her autobiography—*The Song of My Life.*

Behind her iconic status is the negotiation of caste-gender-region identities and her struggle from a marginalised lower-caste *gaanewali* to social and state recognition. And now there's Dr Gangubai Hangal Music and Performing Arts University, established on 14 February, 2008. It is the first music and performing arts university in South India. It began its first session in 2010–2011.

(8 April, 2008)

Interviewer:

Ajji tell us something about your childhood. Your mother was also a vocalist. How did your musical journey start?

Gangubai Hangal:

My mother was a Carnatic musician. I used to listen to her. On my way back from school I used to stop at a small shop where they used to play gramophone records. I would stand there and listen to Hindustani music—a *bandish* that I still remember from those days is '*Radha bolo mukh se.*' I was so enchanted with Hindustani music that I started singing lines from those compositions. Noticing this, my mother decided that I should learn Hindustani music and in order to find the right guru for me she sold off our house in Dharwad and shifted to Hubli.

Interviewer:

How old were you at that time?

Gangubai Hangal:

I was only twelve.

Interviewer:

Didn't you ever ask your mother to teach you Carnatic music?

Gangubai Hangal:

Of course I did. She taught me a few *kritis*. But she used to tell me I'm too young to learn both Carnatic and Hindustani. She said, 'You don't have the maturity right now to keep both the styles apart, if you learn both you'll make a *khichdi* of it!' She stopped singing—Carnatic music—so that my *taleem* in Hindustani won't get affected. She sacrificed a lot for me. She was so young, only thirty-five, when she passed away in 1932.

Interviewer:

How did she die?

Gangubai Hangal:

She had an operation and her stitches broke. She was there with me in our rough and tough times, but she didn't live to see my achievements ...

Interviewer:

Who guided you after your mother's death?

Gangubai Hangal:

I was shattered when she passed away. For days I did not feel like picking up the tanpura. It was as if my music went away with her. But my uncle Ramanna was always there by my side. He would accompany me on the tabla and encourage me to do *riyaaz*. Another well-wisher of our family, Dattopant Desai, also motivated me to return to music to get over my grief. Gradually I began to participate in devotional music programmes, organised on weekends, and in the music programmes on occasions like the birth of a baby. Small honorarium from these shows was my only source of livelihood at that time.

Interviewer:

You were quite young when you sang at a Congress session in Belgaum in the 1920s ...

Gangubai Hangal:

Yes, it was in 1923 I think. A group of us, students, were taught an invocatory song at school and taken to the session. Mahatma Gandhi was sitting in front of us. That session was significant for another reason. That was also the first time I saw Pandit Sawai Gandharva and heard him sing and later on in life he became my guru.

Interviewer:

At that time there were lot of restrictions and prejudices regarding caste. Being from a lower caste did you feel scared?

Gangubai Hangal:

Yes, I was apprehensive that after the song at the Congress session they would send me outside to eat separately. But thankfully that didn't happen and I ate with everyone. Often in school I would hide when teachers passed by because I thought they would tell me to sit separately. My friends would ask, 'Gangu, what happened? Why are you hiding?' I would say I don't want to be sent outside! Things are very different now. But when I was a child, we were looked down upon because of caste. I remember sometimes I used to collect mangoes from the gardens of large houses and the residents used to chase me away calling me '*gaanewali ki ladki*.' But why think about all these things now? I have got so much love and respect in life with the grace of God. I am happy now.

Interviewer:

It is quite a distance from Hubli to Kundgol. What difficulties did you face while travelling from your place, Hubli to your guru's place in Kundgol, everyday?

Gangubai Hangal:

I had to travel by train to his village in Kundgol everyday. I would take the morning train at 5:30 am and return by the last train at 9:30 pm.

Interviewer:

What was his method of teaching?

Gangubai Hangal:

He would make us work on one raga, one *bandish* till he was satisfied we were doing it properly. He would teach us and tell us to practise the *taans*, *paltas* and go into the next room. But he would be listening from there. I used to be in tears sometimes because it was so tiring to repeat the same phrases again and again but he would tell me to stop only when he thought I had learnt it properly.

Interviewer:

Pandit Bhimsen Joshi is your guru-*bhai* and you both used to learn together. What are your memories of that time?

Gangubai Hangal:

Bhimsen used to live there at guruji's place in Kundgol. He used to learn music and do all the housework. There was a water problem in the area and he used to go to the well to get water for guruji's use. He used to ask me to get a bigger pitcher so that he could fill more water! He used to accompany me to the station sometimes, carrying the lantern and on the way we used to discuss the raga, the *bandish*, how the notes have to be struck.

Interviewer:

You also met Ustad Abdul Karim Khan once ...

Gangubai Hangal:

Oh yes! I was a child at that time. Actually Khan Sahib had heard and appreciated my mother Ambabai's rendering of Tyagaraja *kritis*. He was also deeply interested in the notation system. My mother was very quick with notations and she used to preserve each *bandish* I learnt in the notation form so that I could memorise it. This system caught Khan Sahib's attention. Once I sang in front of Khan Sahib. He gave me his blessings and said, '*Gala achha hai, khoob khana aur khoob gana*.' (You have a good voice, eat well and sing well).

Interviewer:

Do you remember your first concert?

Gangubai Hangal:

In Bombay every year for one month there were recording sessions for His Master's Voice. Many people used to come. Once a gathering was organised in Goregaon. I remember it concluded with a recital by Menakabai Shirodkar. She was a great singer! She left by the 2:00 am train. But the rest of us were to take the local train at 5:30 am. So the people asked the rest of us to sing till then. I refused because it is disrespectful to sing after a senior musician has sung. But they said, 'She had come to perform for the concert. But we all are *ghar ke log*.' So everyone sang for ten minutes. Then I was invited for a music conference at Kolkata. Jaddanbai (mother of actress Nargis) recommended me to the organisers. I was so scared, Kolkata is so far. The organisers saw me—a tiny, young girl and thought I won't be able to sing. So before the concert they kept a rehearsal to test whether I could actually sing. They were surprised by my voice and *gayaki*!

Interviewer:

So being small-statured had its disadvantages ...

Gangubai Hangal:

It still does! (*Points to her feet*) See ... I never get footwear for my size! (*Laughs heartily*)

Interviewer:

That's a peculiar problem! But then after your tonsillitis operation your voice changed completely. It was in complete contrast to your tiny stature. People began to comment that your voice is, 'More manly than the best male voice.' Did such comments disturb you?

Gangubai Hangal:

(*Laughing*) Yes that happened, people used to think a man is singing, but it never hurt me. Actually the tonsillitis was giving me a lot of trouble. Often during concerts my throat would start aching and I wouldn't be able to do justice to my music. I consulted many doctors and this was the only way out. They warned me that my voice quality might change. But it was not possible to go on singing with a tonsillitis problem.

Interviewer:

What was the reaction of the audiences to this sudden change?

Gangubai Hangal:

I never took criticism regarding my 'manly' voice to heart. In fact, there were many funny instances. Once I told an acquaintance to tune in to my broadcast on All India Radio at 8:30 in the morning. When I asked her later whether she liked it, she replied hesitatingly that when she tuned in a man was singing and she thought I had told her the wrong time by mistake. It was so funny and she was so embarrassed when I told her that the voice she heard was actually mine! See as long as you have your *sur* and *bhaav* at the right place, nothing else matters.

Interviewer:

Your name in the earlier record labels is mentioned as 'Gandhari Hangal'. How did that happen? Did you ever think of changing your name for the purpose of recording?

Gangubai Hangal:

Not at all! Actually in the first few records, the music company published my name as 'Gandhari Hangal' or 'Gangubai Hublikar' since I belonged to Hubli. But my uncle Krishnappa insisted that there was no reason for this. Since my ancestors are from Hangal, he felt I should retain that name and pride in my lineage. Then there was some confusion. When I discussed this with the HMV people in Bombay they said since the record had already been published with that name, changing the name now might affect the sale of records. So, it was decided that if the name had to be changed then why not adopt a completely different name. The next suggestion was 'Gandhari Hangal', since Gandhari is my birth name. But on All India Radio my name was always announced as 'Gangubai Hangal' and that is how people started recognising me.

Interviewer:

Which ragas are close to your heart?

Gangubai Hangal:

There are so many. It is difficult to choose but I have a special attachment to morning ragas, those ragas that have *komal sur* (flat notes). The *komal dhaivat* in Raga Bhairav is soul-stirring. I also love Todi, Jogiya.

Interviewer:

What are your views about the time theory of ragas?

Gangubai Hangal:

It is our tradition, there is a reason behind it and we should definitely follow it. As a child I used to listen to a lot of gramophone records. Of course I did not own any. There was a shop where harmoniums used to be repaired. It was owned by Shripadrao Tamhankar and he was a harmonium player himself. He used to sell gramophone records as well. I used to spend hours listening to the records at his shop. But he was a purist. He would not allow me to listen to a particular *bandish* if the raga was not appropriate to that time of the day. He would say, 'This is a morning raga, it's evening now. You can't listen to it now. Come in the morning and I will play it for you.'

Interviewer:

Tell us about the musicians with whom you have shared a special rapport.

Gangubai Hangal:

All of them are special. Kumar Gandharva used to live in the house above mine in Bombay. He was the only other Kannada speaking person around. We used to play cards together. He had a great sense of humour! Ravi Shankar, Ali Akbar Khan, they all used to be there at music conferences. Mallikarjun Mansur used to stay here in this house when he came to Hubli. He would doze off while rocking Krishna's cradle. And Jasraj ... whenever he comes here, we both cry together remembering his elder brother who was a great musician. There are all kinds of experiences in life. Bismillah Khan was so inspiring. Once in a concert I was given only a fifteen-minute slot. I started crying. What could I sing in fifteen minutes? Bismillah patted me on the back and said 'Go ahead, in fifteen minutes you can really touch people's heart with your music.' I was so inspired and I am still thankful to him for that.

Interviewer:

You were also deeply inspired by the legendary vocalist Kesarbai Kerkar. I see that you have safely preserved her photos.

Gangubai Hangal:

Yes! Kesarbai Kerkar was always there in conferences. She was the senior most, everyone was scared of her. I learnt a lot watching and listening to her. I was too scared to approach her though.

Interviewer:

How old were you when you got 'married?'

Gangubai Hangal:

I was fourteen. By the age of twenty I had three children.

Interviewer:

Once when your 'husband' offered civil marriage, you refused. Why?

Gangubai Hangal:

No, that was not possible because he was a Brahmin. How could he marry me? His family was pressurising him to get married to a girl from a respectable family. Eventually that happened. But I used to live with him and we were happy.

Interviewer:

He passed away suddenly when you were away for a concert ...

Gangubai Hangal:

He was very ill. I told him I won't go for the concert as I wanted to stay with him. But we needed the money. He pressurised me to go. While I was singing, he passed away. I came to know about it later. By then it was too late. I still think about it, I was singing, and his last rites were happening. (*Chokes*) My mother, my guru, my husband, they were there with me during hard times but none of them lived to see the recognition

I got. That's the way life is (*says reflectively*). One goes through so many kinds of experiences in life.

Interviewer:

Apart from your daughter Krishna none of your other children learnt music. Why?

Gangubai Hangal:

It's a hard life. Not everyone can go through all the hardships that are a part of taking up music. I didn't want them to struggle like I did. My two sons are well-settled. Krishna picked up music by listening to me. She started singing on her own. My guruji said, 'Her voice is beautiful; she doesn't even need much *kharaj riyaaz.*' She used to accompany me wherever I went for concerts. She didn't even get married so that she could stay with me. A few years ago she passed away. I don't like singing now, not without her. (*Tears welled-up in her eyes*).

(This was the last interview given by Vidushi Gangubai Hangal before her death on 21 July, 2009)

S I T A R

The Man, The Creator, The Genius
PANDIT RAVI SHANKAR
(7 April, 1920–11 December, 2012)

It was a long chase. A proposal for an interview, submitted to his office in New Delhi, was answered after two months. Before the confirmation, several questions were asked: 'What is it about? What is the main purpose? Where will it be published?' Not only this; we were told to 'Send a short questionnaire.'

It was a misty Thursday in February when we arrived at the Ravi Shankar Centre, Chanakyapuri, New Delhi, for the thirty-minute interview the time granted to us. It is Pandit Ravi Shankar's residence as well.

A meditative silence greeted us in the sprawling campus. On the front lawn, the magnetic sound of classical instruments could be heard. We were completely lost within the red stone building. With barely five minutes to spare, we found an arrow marked 'Reception' and were swiftly escorted to a grandly appointed room. It was a huge room. As we arranged our recording equipment, our eyes travelled outside the glass windows–a big veranda, corridors and several rooms. Except the soothing drones of sitar, silence.

In youth, with his classical training firmly in place, Pandit Ravi Shankar decided to explore the hidden alleys of Hindustani and Western music on his own. Uday Shankar, his elder brother, was instrumental in giving him worldwide exposure. Thereafter he wrote concertos, violin-sitar compositions, scored music for films and was inventive within the parameters of pure classical genre. His virtuosity, speed and craftsmanship won audiences all over the world. And who can forget his mesmerising performance at the Woodstock festival, where he played for nearly an hour in pouring rain and held the audience spellbound.

Exactly at 11:00 am, Pandit Ravi Shankar entered the room. Dressed in *churidar*-kurta, his hair grey and thin, his long angular face lit up with twinkling, eyes, piercing but not intimidating, his fragile frame a contrast to the rest of the office, he appeared amiable, focussed and a man of untiring patience.

There was no time to warm up. The creator of many ragas (Rasiya, Mohan Kauns, Gangeshwari, Rangeshwari, Parmeshwari, Pancham Se Gara, Kaushik Todi and others), sat across with a smile on his lips, his gaze direct, waiting, bringing his right ear closer to us. He was wearing his hearing aid.

(16 February, 2005)

Interviewer:

It is remarkable and rather surprising that your father was a barrister, yet all his children entered the creative field. How did this happen?

Ravi Shankar:

My father, though a barrister was trained in classical music. But it was my elder brother, Uday Shankar, who influenced all of us. He began his career as a painter, but changed the course of his life to become a dancer. He travelled widely in America and Europe in the early part of the last century. He formed a troupe that consisted of the other three brothers, me, my mother and some of my cousins, uncles and a few other musicians and dancers. Paris was our headquarters and all this happened in the 1930s. For the next eight years I was deeply involved in this group as a dancer and a musician. It was during this time, around 1935, that my brother Uday Shankar got in touch with Baba Allaudin Khan, one of the greatest musicians India has seen, to tour with us for one year in Europe and America. And it was that meeting with Baba that changed my life. That is how I got attracted to the pure and traditional form of classical music. I was fortunate that Baba agreed to take me as his disciple.

Interviewer:

Baba Allaudin Khan is a legendary figure. We have heard so many stories and anecdotes about the power and depth of his music and his towering personality. Being his disciple you have spent so many years with him and have known him so intimately. Tell us, what kind of a guru was he?

Ravi Shankar:

Well, actually he was like the legendary gurus of long ago that you hear or read about! He was like a traditional rishi-muni, his way of life at the *gurukul* was like that in an ashram of yesteryears. He was extremely strict in his attitude towards music and of course he expected a lot from his students.

Interviewer:

So how many hours of *riyaaz* did you do at Baba's *gurukul*?

Ravi Shankar:

There was a time when I practised sixteen hours a day, twelve to fourteen hours definitely, at the least. Baba was very particular about discipline.

Interviewer:

Baba was such a multifaceted personality. He played many instruments, didn't he? And you wanted to learn sitar! So then, what was his way of teaching?

Ravi Shankar:

Yes. Sarod was the instrument he was known for, but he played every possible instrument you could think of. He was equally at ease with wind instruments like flute and shehnai as he was with pluck instruments or bow instruments like violin and Chandra Sarang (an instrument invented by Baba) and even drums. Strangely enough, he did not play the sitar. Though he was well-acquainted with the sitar, he didn't really ever play it. He belonged to the traditional school of teaching, starting with exercises for hands, teaching songs because, you see, even if you are an instrumentalist you need to know the old *bandishes* and traditional songs to understand the depth of the raga. He often used to play while teaching us so that we could plumb the depth of the raga and improvise as we listened to him. That is how one learns to perform.

Interviewer:

Okay. For a moment let's go back in time. Do you remember your first solo public concert? At what age was that and what were your feelings at that point of time?

Ravi Shankar:

I had been giving public concerts from a very early age, even before I met Baba. And I was doing that without much serious training. I had a knack for picking up the instrument, listening to records and playing the instrument—be it sitar, sarod or esraj. This was the practice that I started with my brother from the age of twelve or thirteen. I performed at many places like Paris, New York ... many other places. But after learning from Baba and coming into the strictly classical field, my first concert was at the Allahabad Music Conference in December 1939.

Interviewer:

So, now, after so many years do you remember the atmosphere at that concert? Were you nervous? What were your feelings as you came on to the stage?

Ravi Shankar:

Oh boy! (*Laughs*) I was so nervous! You can imagine how I would have felt at that time seeing great luminaries sitting right in front of me in the audience ... oh boy ... great maestros like Ustad Faiyaz Khan, Pandit Omkarnath Thakur and many other great and famous people sitting there right in the first row. I was so nervous that at that point I just wanted to cry and run away and hide! But somehow, thanks to Baba's training, the concert went off well and the great Ustads and Pandits present there blessed me. I was overjoyed.

Interviewer:

Can't imagine Pandit Ravi Shankar getting nervous!

Ravi Shankar

But at that time I was a nobody! Certainly not *Pandit Ravi Shankar*! (*laughs*).

Interviewer:

Speaking of your performing career, you started off in Uday Shankar's troupe. What was your role in the troupe?

Ravi Shankar:

Since the age of ten I was performing with his troupe, involved in both music and dance. I was trained in his style of dancing and took part in many of his choreographies. Later, when I was sixteen, I choreographed a whole item myself. That was based on the Kathak style of dance.

Interviewer:

Why Kathak? Are you trained in Kathak too?

Ravi Shankar:

Yes, for a short time in Calcutta. In Kathak, and Kathakali also, under Shankaran Namboodiri, who was Dada's (Uday Shankar's) guru.

Interviewer:

What was your mother's contribution to your musical life? What about your father?

Ravi Shankar:

Not much. It was my brother who guided me. My mother had heard and attended a number of performances by vocalists like Gauhar Jaan,

Zohra Bai and other such famous singers who used to come and sing for the zenana court. So she picked up many *thumris*, *chaitis*, and folk songs. I have a faint memory of her singing lullabies to me. I was four or five years old and we were living in Benaras. To put me to sleep she used to put my head in her lap and sing songs. She had a very sweet voice. Though she had no training, she picked up easily by listening. My father was very well-trained in classical music, especially *dhrupad*, and he could expertly sing the Sama Veda chants in different *gharana* styles. Unfortunately, I never spent much time with my father as he was usually away.

Interviewer:

Your *jugalbandi* concerts with Ustad Ali Akbar Khan were a huge success. What was the understanding between you both and what clicked that created such immortal, mesmerising music?

Ravi Shankar:

Well, I think it was mainly Baba's training. Both of us had that same essence in our music. Along with that, we were very close friends. We were such wonderful friends. I loved him. I still love him. It was this double bond of emotion and training, I think, that really clicked and that, as you have said, helped us create 'mesmerising' music. Later, due to some family problems, we started drifting apart ... also, as creative musicians we started growing individually and when that happens, one is bound to flower out, think in a different manner and create new things in one's own way.

So, musically too, we separated somewhere along the path ... and that *jugalbandi* that had created magic for almost twenty years had slowly started waning. We realised this and decided not to play together.

Interviewer:

Was the separation very bad ... I mean, emotionally?

Ravi Shankar:

It was tormenting.

(At this point he looked reflective, but soon overcame his emotion and looked at us, as if asking, 'Yes, so what's next.')

Interviewer:

Your cross-cultural, global collaborations like the one with Sir Yehudi Menuhin brought about a new wave of music. How did you think about that and how was that experience?

Ravi Shankar:

Yehudi Menuhin was such a great artiste. I have a lot of regard and respect for him. He took such a fancy to Indian classical music, and me personally; he considered me his guru, which was so embarrassing for me. But at the same time, whatever music we played was more or less composed by me within the raga and *taal* framework. All the compositions were performed all over the world, including that famous United Nations concert.

Interviewer:

What about Phillip Glass and George Harrison?

Ravi Shankar:

I haven't really performed with him, but we have cut records where he has played my compositions in his own way. It was an experimental thing that turned out to be very interesting. I have never jammed or played with George Harrison. He was more or less my student. But there was one occasion when he thought he would tour with me and I got together around fourteen musicians who were not so well-known at that time in the West, like Shiv Kumar Sharma, Hariprasad Chaurasia, L. Subramaniam, Sultan Khan and, of course, I already had Alla Rakhaji as my accompanist and Lakshmi Shankar was there too. So I got together all these people for the tour. In the concerts, in the first half we would perform some short pieces and I used to join in at the end with my sitar. Then in the second half it was George performing with his group. We used to conclude with a piece that I had composed, 'I'm missing you O Krishna/Where are you ...' Everyone used to join in this concluding piece.

Interviewer:

Oh, yes, that became extremely popular!

Ravi Shankar:

Yes, the same song I taught the Jazmin group.

Interviewer:

Fusion music has become very popular. What do you think of fusion music?

Ravi Shankar:

Sometimes I find something very interesting. But most of the time I find it is all concocted, you know, putting different sounds together, it comes out a little artificially. These things have been going on for quite some time but most of it I find very gimmicky. Nowadays everyone is trying to break out with something new that sells. The commercial aspect of it has become the main goal.

Interviewer:

You were the first Indian to compose music for an American film. You have also given music for Indian films like *Pather Panchali*, *Godan* and many more. How was the experience of composing for films?

Ravi Shankar:

Yes, I did compose music for *Alice in Wonderland* for the BBC, *Charlie* in Hollywood and also a Swedish film. All these experiences were very interesting and I love composing music for films. I have done many Bengali films and a few Hindi films like *Anuradha*, *Godan* ... But because I am a performing artiste and tour most of the time, I cannot give that kind of time and attention to films. And that is the reason why I could never take it up seriously as a career. But I love giving music in films!

Interviewer:

You are called 'the cultural ambassador' of India. You have popularised Indian music abroad. In your view how receptive is the West to Indian classical music today?

Ravi Shankar:

Well, that is what I have been working towards since the 1950s. I think we have achieved quite a lot in terms of putting Indian music on the global map and creating an audience in the West. This has been beneficial for Indian musicians.

Today, you see, the same people who criticised me earlier, who used to say things like 'Oh, he performs only in the West, not in India,' are themselves flocking to the West to perform. They are reaping the benefits of the work I did.

Interviewer:

But how did you feel at that point of time when you were criticised so scathingly?

Ravi Shankar:

Naturally, I was hurt. There were all kinds of wrong information; misplaced accusations. I was hurt but I had to get through it to reach where I am now. I am glad that I never lost faith in my conviction and mission and I think I have been true to myself.

Interviewer:

Somebody said the tragedy is that most Indian artistes are given their due in India only when they have become famous abroad. Do you think this is true?

Ravi Shankar:

Yes, I have to believe that. If you go back, right from Swami Vivekananda, Gurudev Rabindranath Tagore, Uday Shankar, and many other people ... including myself ... this is how things have turned out. So, it is sad, but true.

Interviewer:

You have performed all over India, which part of India do you find most receptive to Hindustani classical music?

Ravi Shankar:

I feel ... (*thinks for a while*) ... Maharashtra is the most receptive area. Then parts of Karnataka like Hubli, Gadag, Belgaum; and the Bengalis mainly in Kolkata. I think they have been most attracted, interested and appreciative of Hindustani classical music. The reasons for this might be many, historically and culturally.

For a long time in early history our classical music was arrested within palaces and the private *jalsas* of aristocrats. The common man ... the masses never really had a chance to listen to classical music.

This is very different from the tradition of the south, where temples supported musical tradition and popularised music among the masses. In this way classical music reached the common man and that is why people in the south are much more aware and appreciative of classical music.

Interviewer:

Our music is ancient. Hindustani classical music is bound by a time structure and *gharana*. What are the primary characteristics of the Maihar *gharana* today?

Ravi Shankar:

These are just names, like brands. Music is an ever-changing art form. It keeps changing, after some time some more styles will come in, more names ...

Interviewer:

Does that mean you do not believe in the *gharana* system?

Ravi Shankar:

I do, I do. But at the same time, it doesn't have the same importance or sanctity now. Earlier, each *gharana* kept its own particular style, not taking any elements from other *gharana*s. But the whole thing has changed now. With the advent of radio, cassettes, CDs, public performances, the music of a great artiste of one *gharana* also influences the upcoming musicians of other *gharana*s. While musicians might maintain the speciality of their *gharana*, they are bound to be influenced at some level by features of other *gharana*s as well.

Interviewer:

What is the speciality of the Maihar *gharana?*

Ravi Shankar:

You see it is mainly Baba that we think of when we say 'Maihar' because it is there that he settled down and lived and taught till the end of his life. But Baba had hundreds of gurus! He learnt from many people, starting with gurus of folk music, learning folk drums, shehnai, sarod, violin, and more and he emerged as one of the greatest musicians of his era. Our Dada-Guru, Ustad Wazir Khan Sahib, who was in Rampur, was of the direct lineage of Miyan Tansen from the daughter's side and this was the Beenkar *gharana*. But before that Baba had learnt from many other great gurus and I follow Baba's style. I will not call it a mixed style, but it had everything. It was eclectic in every way.

I think I am very lucky, being one of those who had the opportunity to learn directly from Baba. But, basically, I would like to call it 'Maihar-

Senia' *gharana*, because that captures the whole construction of the instrumental training–the alaap, *jod*, and all the speciality of veena, sursingar, rabab and pakhawaj. That whole musical style is the highest one can think of and I consider myself fortunate I learnt it from Baba.

Interviewer:

You play the sitar but many of your disciples play other instruments, so how do you teach them?

Ravi Shankar:

I think each instrument has its own personality, its own advantages and disadvantages, and some talented musicians go further and bring new dimensions to it. I try to give my students–as much as possible–the depth, the feelings of the ragas, new dimensions of *layakari* and things like that. Then most of them shape up as musicians, bringing in their own individuality.

Interviewer:

Do you remember any incident in your performing career that has embarrassed you?

Ravi Shankar:

Well, there are many instances when I have been embarrassed because of audience behaviour ... sometimes in concerts, you know, people sitting in the first row eating peanuts, talking, making noise without any regard for the artiste ... It is very distracting and disturbing.

Interviewer:

What do you do under such circumstances?

Ravi Shankar:

Sometimes I stop playing and tell them to stop these antics. Such things are extremely disturbing.

Interviewer:

Do you think the Western audience is more organised and disciplined?

Ravi Shankar:

Oh, yes! No doubt about it. That is because they have a long history of having concerts in special halls in a disciplined manner, a history of

500–600 years. So they know exactly how to behave. They won't even cough. They sit quietly and listen and it is only at the end of the item with the applause, whether its thunderous clapping or lukewarm appreciation, that the artiste gets to know what the effect of the performance has been. But here in India things are completely different.

Interviewer:

What advice would you like to give to youngsters aspiring to become musicians?

Ravi Shankar:

Ah! That's a tall task! Young people have their problems, I realise that. It has become very difficult for talented young artistes to get programmes and they get lured into compromises because of frustration. Those who are really talented and have got into the groove of our music, I would like to tell them to have a little more patience and keep up the hard work. At the same time, I would request all the big business houses to sponsor as many young artistes as possible ... I would like to request them to promote music, and art also.

Interviewer:

What do you think of your daughter Anoushka's music? How is she shaping up as a performer?

Ravi Shankar:

She is so gifted and blessed that her hand, her mind, everything is so perfectly attuned. The question is time. She has to manage the time factor. She is so gifted that people now want to see her act, to read her books, she is so versatile ... Time will tell. I am extremely proud of her in whatever she does, sitar most of all.

(The office assistant indicated from the door that it was time to wrap up. We requested for a few more minutes but were politely refused. Someone else was waiting. We had to leave)

VOCAL

No Rough Edges in My Music

VIDUSHI SHANNO KHURANA

(23 December, 1927–)

Vocalist Shanno Khurana lives in an elegantly decorated bungalow surrounded with greenery. Situated in one of the posh areas of New Delhi—Defence Colony—it is untouched by the maddening rush outside. Once inside the gate, there's peaceful silence. Her little office, with her photographs, awards and books greets you as you enter. Next to it is the living room, furnished in pastel shades, overlooking a small garden.

When asked how it felt to be destabilised during the 1947 Partition and rebuilding life in Delhi, she answered, 'When Partition happened we left everything behind us in Pakistan. We had to start from scratch here. But we did not go out and complain that we do not have anything. It was a struggle to overcome the Partition tragedy.'

Partition unsettled her family life, but even in that trauma she never let music go by. 'My husband always used to say, "if you leave music now, you'll never be able to sing." His words always encouraged me to do *riyaaz* everyday.'

Determined, she never let music suffer because of the Partition or her household duties. That determination is still so visible on her face. Her grandson, who was present during the interview, often prompted her to narrate incidents and stories from her life that her memory had failed to recollect. 'Oh, yes ...' She would say and recount the incident.

Her elegant mannerisms, exquisite facial features, thoughtful eyes and disarming smile puts any visitor at ease; yet the gentle, confident voice compels one to maintain a respectable distance.

She speaks with a lot of dignity and circumspection and at times, her voice betrays her inner self—'You know there are different types of anger. One is a constructive anger and perhaps that is in me. Through this anger and tension I want to make my music more beautiful.'

(3 November, 2004)

Interviewer:

You began your musical journey somewhere in the 1940s. It was pre-independence and the social milieu was completely different. So, as a woman, what problems did you face while pursuing music?

Shanno Khurana:

As you know during those times girls, particularly from the Punjab were forbidden to sing publicly and to take it up as a profession was taboo. It was looked down upon and one was associated with *kothewali.* But yes I remember a music teacher coming to our place to teach my elder sisters. I was too small at that time. So, music was there at home but not from the viewpoint of taking it up as a profession. Just before Partition I had started broadcasting on Lahore radio. And before that I had learnt from the Gwalior *gharana* maestro for six years. 1947 and the aftermath of Partition was too disturbing. We came to Delhi uprooted and homeless. We settled here in Delhi. My husband was a doctor, a surgeon. I was only twenty or twenty-one years old, and around forty people came and lived with us in the same house. Despite having numerous household duties, I never left music. I was too passionate about it. The relatives were staying with me but I used to find a peaceful corner for myself and diligently continued my *riyaaz.* Even after childbirth I continued with my *riyaaz*. Those were difficult times but I did not give up. Perhaps I could continue with music because my husband used to encourage me. He used to say, 'If you leave music now, then you will never be able to pursue it.'

Interviewer:

You are saying that at the age of twenty-one you came to Delhi so at what age did you get married?

Shanno Khurana:

I was just eighteen.

Interviewer:

So your husband supported you completely?

Shanno Khurana:

Yes, he did and moreover I was so young, I didn't realise that gradually music would become my passion, obsession and then profession.

At that time I had no inkling that I would be able to do something in music.

Interviewer:

Who else was interested in music in your family?

Shanno Khurana:

Well, during that time music was taught to keep daughters busy at home. So masterji used to come to teach my elder sisters and sister-in-law. I was very young so I used to listen to them practise. I do not remember but my father later told me that at the tender age of four I used to shut myself up in a room and practise the same *bandish* that my sisters were learning. I used to bolt the room and practise on the harmonium. So I did not have a musical lineage but perhaps it was god's gift to me that I was determined to learn classical music.

Interviewer:

You are saying that music was not in your family and that you were the first one in your family to take it up professionally. So how easy or difficult was this journey?

Shanno Khurana:

I had to struggle a lot. I started singing and broadcasting on the radio from the age of eighteen but as my musical journey expanded, I realised that I still have a lot to learn. I came to know that the world of music is a vast ocean. I remember when once I sang a raga Multani *bandish* on Lahore radio, Chief Producer Jeevan Lal Mattoo asked me after the live broadcast whether I knew the difference between the *gandhar* of raga Todi and that of raga Multani. I realised then that I knew nothing about music and that I had to learn a lot to understand the finer nuances of classical music. And this effort to understand the finer differences, to have in-depth knowledge still continues. I gradually understood the philosophy behind our *ragadari* system of music, the technique to expand each *bandish* and various other finer points.

Interviewer:

As a child whose music inspired you?

Shanno Khurana:

Well, when I was twelve years old Roshanara Begum's voice really moved me. I am yet to hear a voice like that; so well trained, so very beautiful. Simply arresting. She was my favourite musician.

Interviewer:

Your musical education began with Gwalior *gharana* then Agra and then Rampur-Sahaswan. So how did you bring the essence of all these *gharana*s in your individual singing?

Shanno Khurana:

I have written a book on this subject. See, of all the eight *gharana*s that are well-known today in *khayal gayaki,* the Gwalior *gharana* is the oldest. It started with Tansen. And some of the people, the 'fountainheads' of this *gharana,* went to different places. Some went to Patiala, Agra or Kirana and other places. These people, who settled down at different places, added their individual style to the *gayaki* that they had learnt earlier. Very soon they started having their own followers. Bahadur Hussain Khan Sahib was the direct descendant of Tansen. He settled at Rampur. After him came Inayat Hussain Khan Sahib, who gave birth to the Rampur *gharana*. And my guru, Ustad Mushtaq Hussain Khan Sahib, was not only the disciple but also the son-in-law of Ustad Inayat Hussain Khan. This is how the Rampur-Sahaswan *gayaki* came into being. It began with the Ustad, trained in Gwalior *gharana gayaki,* who after settling in Rampur mixed his own style, understanding and colour into it. And that style came to be known as the Rampur-Sahaswan *gharana*. And you know that our classical music is not static. It keeps on evolving though the roots remain the same.

Interviewer:

So how did you put your individual stamp on it?

Shanno Khurana:

I try to put my emotions into my music. The roots are of Rampur-Sahaswan *gayaki*; I maintain the structure of *Ashtaang gayaki* but the raga and *bandish* that I am singing have my own interpretation—how much *alaapchari* is to be done, which *swar*s are to be emphasised, how much *andolan* is to be given on *swar*s and on which *swars,* how and what kind of *taan* is to be taken—I try filling all these with my musical understanding and colour while maintaining the strict format of the raga. Every raga has its own *rasa*. When I am singing raga Darbari then that grandeur should appear in my singing also within the structure of the raga. I try emphasising the *rasa* of each raga. Besides, I also lay stress on voice modulation.

Interviewer:

You have been an actress also. How has that helped your music?

Shanno Khurana:

You are calling me an actress (*smiles*) but that was a long time ago. I had done a few operas and it was a gift of our classical music. I tried to use the *rasas* of classical music in my opera singing. I modulated my voice according to the theme of the opera. Similarly in classical music, each raga has its own character, its own personality. And that's what I try to depict through my singing. I always try to modulate according to the structure of the raga. It was easier for me to sing in an opera according to the theme of the opera because of my classical music background. I wouldn't have been able to do justice to it without my training in classical music.

Interviewer:

You have learnt from three *gharana*s then why should you be considered to belong to the Rampur-Sahaswan *gharana*?

Shanno Khurana:

Because I got extensive *taleem* from Ustad Mushtaq Hussain Khan Sahib. When I became his *gandabandh* disciple he gave me a 108-beads necklace and told me to practise each *taan* 108 times. You can understand the kind of rigorous training I received from him. While practising I would look at his face, waiting for him to stop me. But he never did so. So serious and rigorous was my training. I did not receive this kind of training in any other *gharana*. And I would like to reiterate that Rampur *gharana* is an off-shoot of the Gwalior *gharana*. Besides, it is in this *gharana* that I spent maximum number of years learning music; and I followed the basic structure of *gharana gayaki* in my renditions.

Interviewer:

How many disciples do you have?

Shanno Khurana:

I have four or five disciples. All of them are dedicated and hardworking. I do not take a single paisa from them as fee. I just want my style of singing to continue. Out of these I have intensively trained one—Maitreyi Majumdar. I have taught her everything. She has started giving performances. Others are still learning but all of them are very promising.

Interviewer:

Do you get time now to do *riyaaz*?

Shanno Khurana:

Nearly two to three hours. But *riyaaz* does not mean sitting with the tanpura. Thinking about music is also *riyaaz;* listening to music and writing about music is also *riyaaz*. Actually it is a continuous process. Music is going on in the mind for twenty-four hours.

Interviewer:

Hardly any concert goes by where you do not sing a *tappa*, yet *tappa* is not included in the category of pure classical music by many critics. Why?

Shanno Khurana:

I know it is extremely uncalled for. I do not know why it has been included in the light classical form. On the contrary I think it is a very difficult form, one needs a lot of voice control and because it is such a difficult form very few people are able to do justice to it. There are hardly any *tappa* singers. And also it is difficult to write *tappa*s in notation. One can only learn a *tappa* from a guru directly, face to face. There are so many *khatke* and *zamzama* that it is impossible to have them in a notation in a book. The language of *tappa* is a mixture of Punjabi and Multani, the language that took birth in the Indus Valley. It is believed that it originated in the 15th and 16th century from the folk songs of the camel riders of Punjab. They used to sing it. Afterwards it was developed as a form of classical music by Miyan Ghulam Nabi Shori or Shori Miyan, a court singer of Asaf-Ud-Daulah, the Nawab of Awadh.

Interviewer:

So you think *tappa* should be included in pure classical?

Shanno Khurana:

Absolutely. There is no doubt about that. It is a very beautiful form and it should be preserved.

Interviewer:

You organised a festival in 1995 on rare ragas. What prompted you to do so?

Shanno Khurana:

Musicians and organisers are apprehensive about presenting rare ragas. In 1995 I decided to hold a festival of rare ragas because I felt musicians should have musical social concern and responsibility too. The thing is that if we don't take care of some ragas we lose them. There's no point in just presenting same ragas time after time, concert after concert, collecting cheques and forgetting all about the cause of music. So in 1995 I organised an all-women musician festival. But for this I really had to work very hard as I was both performer and organiser. As an organiser I had to collect funds also and this was extremely difficult.

Interviewer:

Why did you think of organising a festival of women musicians only?

Shanno Khurana:

I had struggled in my life. I had seen how difficult it is for a woman, belonging to a non-musical family to get a platform. So I wanted to provide a platform to women who wanted to take music as a profession and not just as a hobby. Let me tell you that with women the struggle is first within the family. First the family has to accept and then one has to battle with co-musicians. They have doubts. They feel, why should an outsider enter their secure fort. In my case people used to think that I am settled and financially comfortable then why am I entering the music arena? They do not understand that art is not connected to money, not even remotely. It is the urge, the inner urge, the need to create, to do something. As I said, when the Partition happened we left everything behind in Pakistan. We had to start from zero here. But we did not go out and announce that we do not have anything. To overcome the Partition tragedy was a struggle. When we, me and my husband, came to Delhi we went to meet Nirmala Joshi. She was the Chairperson of Sangeet Natak Akademi and her father was a medical practitioner, Dr Joshi. She asked me what I planned to do in music. And at that time I had not thought about it. She offered me a job in Sangeet Bharti, an institute that she had just started. She told me to teach music twice a week for it would encourage girls and women to join it. So I started teaching on a salary of ₹75/- per month and at that time Kapilaji ... Kapila Vatsyayan ... was learning Kathak from Achchan Maharaj. During those times girls had to fight social stigma to learn music and dance. Unfortunately Delhi at that time had no environment for classical music. Only small *baithaks* used to happen. So, I started thinking about how classical music can reach people. I thought opera is a good way of making classical music reach the masses. The first opera I did was *Heer Ranjha*. It was in Punjabi; I gave the music, based on folk music and also played Heer's character. After this I did *Sohni Mahiwal*. Though it was again in Punjabi, I blended a few classical ragas. And then I did *Jahanara*—an Urdu opera. This was the first opera in Urdu. In this I made compositions based on sixty ragas. It was produced by B.V. Karanth. People really liked this opera. All this was a challenge for me. I just wanted to encourage the audience to come closer to classical music. But this effort was looked down upon by classical musicians. I had to listen to many snide remarks, like, 'Oh, she does opera ...' Had I been doing it in the West it would have been highly respected. But I did not care for such remarks. I continued with both—classical music and opera. I did *Sohni Mahiwal* while I was a disciple of Ustad Mushtaq Hussain Khan Sahib. He came to see the performance and his son also sang a *tappa* in the opera. He was very impressed by my efforts. As a guru he told me to continue doing it.

Interviewer:

What kind of a person and guru was Ustad Mushtaq Hussain Khan Sahib?

Shanno Khurana:

As a guru, he was strict but as a person very generous. One day I was practising raga Kaunsi Kanhada. Suddenly he stopped me and asked,

'Do you sing *ghazal*?' I replied, 'No.' Then he asked me, 'Why?' So I told him that my father had forbidden us to sing *ghazals* as it talked about romance. He kept quiet for a while and then said, 'Why, can't you love God? Can't you fall in love with *swars*?' His words gave me a new insight. I realised the true essence of music.

Interviewer:

Why am I feeling that there's lot of anger inside you?

Shanno Khurana:

Any work that you want to do, there's a challenge in it. And unless you have anger inside you, it is impossible to face the challenge. You know there are different types of anger. One is a constructive anger; perhaps that is in me. Through this anger and tension I want to make my music more beautiful. Through this anger I want to draw the attention of people towards our culture—music, dance and theatre. To give back to society what we owe, sometimes we have to become aggressive. Not the type of aggression that will kill music. I have seen some dancers, who are so very aggressive and this aggression is depicted in their performance. I have seen some vocalists so aggressive in their daily life that it comes out in their music. And I am trying to avoid this. Because if your music is aggressive, then where is peace, serenity, creativity and beauty? So we have to constantly find a via media, a combination of all the *rasas*—*shant, bhakti, bhayanak, krodh*—in our music. We have to find a balance of all these *rasas*. I want my music to be smooth, to have no rough edges. I want to round off everything, a bit of everything, as a complete whole, not disjointed. Classical music is inward looking. It gives peace and I want my music to offer that. Music, for me, is a way to reach God.

The Strains of Nostalgia
USTAD SABRI KHAN
(1927–)

Sarangi nawaz Ustad Sabri Khan had anecdotes and memories to share. And with his memories one is bound to get transported into that era. You name a musician and he has accompanied that musician. Not only that, he has an interesting story to share.

'I have accompanied most of the artistes—Bade Ghulam Ali Khan Sahib, Amir Khan, Mallikarjun Mansur. I have accompanied even *dhrupad-dhamar* artistes like Aminuddin and Moinuddinn Dagar, Rahimuddin Khan. Mallikarjun Mansur was very selective in taking a sarangi accompanying artiste. If he ever felt unhappy with the sarangi player then he used to scold him right on the stage itself. It is my good fortune that he liked my playing. As there was no telephone at that time he would often come to my place with a list of programmes where he wanted me to accompany him. I am really fortunate that a vocalist of his calibre always preferred me to accompany him on the sarangi.'

Entering his house is like visiting a *gurukul*. Disciples keep coming and their soft whispers can be heard from the other room.

His son and disciple, Kamal Sabri, sarangi player, joins us and sits next to him, often prompting him to remember the sequence of events. The other three sons—Sarvar Sabri, Jamal Sabri and Gulfam Sabri and grandson, Suhail Khan (son of Farzana, Ustad Sabri Khan's daughter) have all been his disciples.

The impact of old age is noticeable in his voice. Words often get jumbled up but the memories are fresh, clear and alive. When he talks about his youth ideal—Ustad Ghulam Sabir Khan, he gathers all the emotions of youthful buoyancy.

Like his simple house in Asiad Village, Delhi, Sabri Khan is unimposing. He is generous and a goldmine of experiences and stories. Often while narrating an incident he would break into a chuckle. Even though he is past eighty, he considers himself a student of music, 'Music is very vast.'

Often during the course of the conversation he would recline on the settee, trying to remember a *bandish* associated with that particular incident and the personality.

(*25 April, 2007*)

Interviewer:

How did your fascination for sarangi begin and why did you think of becoming a sarangi player?

Sabri Khan:

Actually sarangi was played at home. My grandfather, Haji Mohammad Khan Sahib used to play it and my father, Chhajju Khan learnt it from him. As a child, when I used to listen to it, the very sound of it used to move me. My grandfather noticed my interest in sarangi and told me to learn it. He gave me a very small sarangi, marked *sa re ga ma pa dha ni sa* on it with white mud. I started practising on it and for any mistake I made, he used to get angry. Actually he was very short-tempered. He wanted me to be at his beck and call and do *riyaaz* as per his wish. When he used to go for his morning namaaz, he used to carry a wooden cane. As I used to get up late in the morning, he would beat me on the legs, right on the bone with his cane. With his beating I used to get up screaming. And I was only seven years old then.

Interviewer:

So, what about games? Didn't you feel like playing?

Sabri Khan:

No, I used to go out to play but only when grandfather had left for namaaz. I liked sarangi but not at the cost of my playtime. I liked playing with my friends but I was very frightened of grandfather too. I was scared of his anger. If I were playing and he caught me doing so I was a goner. Right there on the playground he would start beating me and the thrashing would continue till we reached home.

Interviewer:

What about school?

Sabri Khan:

I used to go to school. At that time schools used to begin at 10:00 am in Moradabad. Many great tabla players and vocalists belonged to Moradabad.

Interviewer:

Many maestros belonged to Moradabad but Moradabad did not get established as a *gharana*. Why?

Sabri Khan:

People who belonged to Moradabad left the city and went to different places. So when they formed a *gharana* it came to be known by that area's name, like Bhindi Bazaar *gharana*. Now see, Ustad Chhajju Khan belonged to Moradabad. His other three brothers—Nazeer Khan, Shuja Ali Khan and Mubarak Ali Khan were all born in Moradabad. All four of them went to Mumbai and stayed at a place called Bhindi Bazaar. Many people became their disciples and so when it came to naming a *gharana*, it was named after the place where they were staying. Hence Bhindi Bazaar *gharana* got its name. Though I feel it should have been called Moradabad *gharana*. Similarly in the case of the tabla, Moradabad was home of many maestros like Ustad Maseet Khan and his son Ustad Karamatullah Khan and the great tabla player Ustad Ahmedjan Thirakwa. There were many *beenkars* also who belonged to Moradabad. But unfortunately none of them took the name of the city of their birth, Moradabad. Had they taken the name of Moradabad, the city would have been quite famous. But I am taking its name and I strongly say that Moradabad is a *gharana* that gave birth to many top-class musicians.

Interviewer:

So it was your grandfather who initiated you into music?

Sabri Khan:

Yes, at the age of seven. My grandfather Ustad Haji Mohammad Khan took me under his wing. I used to practise for seven to eight hours everyday. Later I learnt from my father Ustad Chhajju Khan, uncle Ustad Laddan Khan and my other grandfather Ustad Allan Khan. Ustad Laddan Khan was my mother's sister's husband and a great sarangi player.

Interviewer:

How did you come to Delhi?

Sabri Khan:

My father brought me to Delhi. My father was very learned. He studied *farsi* (Persian). Besides being a sarangi player he was into business as well. He was a contractor. Even my grandfather was a businessman. He was into the business of wheat grains and ghee.

Interviewer:

So it can be said that you are the first one to become a professional musician in your family?

Sabri Khan:

Yes, that's true. My father and grandfather were musicians and had many disciples but their livelihood was not dependent on music. And because they were into business, they did not become court musicians. Otherwise at that time most of the musicians were court musicians in the courts of Maharaja of Baroda, Nawab of Rampur or Maharaja of Patiala. But my father and grandfather did not feel the necessity of becoming court musicians, though they did stay for sometime in the court of the Nawab of Rampur.

Interviewer:

You were one of the first sarangi players to give international sarangi concerts. So, which were those countries?

Sabri Khan:

There are some places where I introduced sarangi for the first time in 1968, like Europe, America. For one year I was the visiting professor in Seattle University in 1981–82. But before that I had been on a four-months tour. People were impressed by the sound of the sarangi. They used to say that, 'It's a human voice.' And it was a perfect description of the instrument that was also called '*sau-rangi*', meaning an instrument with hundred hues. I think it has many more colours than a hundred because in India we have different kinds of music. You go to Haryana, Bengal, Rajasthan, Maharashtra, every place has its own musical form and many classical styles, like *dhrupad, khayal, tarana, thumri, dadra, tappa, kajri, chaiti, ghazal, geet, bhajan,* etc. As we have so many languages and dialects, so do we have varied forms and styles of music. And sarangi can play all types of music; it accepts all genres of music. This is the specialty of the sarangi. Whatever comes out from your voice, the sarangi can reproduce that. That's why the instrument is often compared with the human voice.

Interviewer:

Is there only one kind of sarangi?

Sabri Khan:

No, no, there are different kinds of sarangi. There is the Sindhi sarangi, the Jogiya sarangi and each kind of sarangi has its own unique structure and even the number of strings vary. I will tell you a very interesting story which has been told to me by my elders. There was Hakim Jalinoos who while passing through a forest noticed the corpse of a monkey. The dried intestines were visible. Curiosity pushed him to touch the dried intestines. When he touched and plucked them it created a peculiar sound. He was so captivated by the sound that he thought of using the intestines as strings. Even now some sarangi strings are made out of the intestines of a goat and this sarangi has thirty-five to forty strings with three main playing strings.

Interviewer:

How and when did you join All India Radio?

Sabri Khan:

At the age of thirteen or fourteen I went to give my audition in Alipore. I couldn't clear the audition. Then at the age of fifteen I went to All India Radio, Delhi. They needed a sarangi player in the Carnatic music orchestra. I was taken on a salary of ₹50/ per month. So, at the age of sixteen, in 1942, I started working in the All India Radio. I was on contract for a year as a Staff Artiste. At that time there were different units. Krishnaswamy was in-charge of Carnatic music orchestra. Because of the language problem I used to commit mistakes so I was made to sit right at the end. But later on Swamy learnt Urdu and started giving me notations in Urdu. When I saw that he learnt the language for my sake, I felt bad and decided to learn his mother tongue. After learning I asked him to give the notations in his language. This made me perform better and I was also given a salary raise. It was now increased to ₹75/ per month. In 1945 Carnatic section moved to Madras (now Chennai) and I joined the Delhi unit of All India Radio in 1946. The business of contract renewal continued for some more years. Actually the contract renewal practice existed till Madam Indira Gandhi became Information and Broadcasting Minister. She changed it. Henceforth she made fifty-eight years as the retirement age and our contracts were drafted accordingly. I retired in 1989 after having a really enriching and varied experience of playing as a soloist, an accompanying artiste, playing in the orchestra and also in a variety of musical forms and styles at the AIR.

Interviewer:

You have accompanied most of the artistes. What is the requirement for being a good accompanying artiste?

Sabri Khan:

The first requirement of an accompanying artiste is to keep his mind, eyes and ears open to understand the style of the vocalist. As there are so many *gharana*s in our music system and every artiste has his own style, it is necessary for a sarangi player to first understand the style of the singer. How can he do that? By playing softly, just following the vocalist. I have accompanied most of the artistes—Bade Ghulam Ali Khan Sahib, Amir Khan, Mallikarjun Mansur—I have accompanied all top artistes. I have accompanied even *dhrupad-dhamaar* artistes like Aminuddin and Moinuddin Dagar, Rahimuddin Khan Sahib. Mallikarjun Mansur was very selective in taking a sarangi accompanying artiste. If he ever felt unhappy with the sarangi player then he used to scold him right on the stage itself. It is my good fortune that he liked my playing. As there was no telephone at that time he would often come to my place with a list of programmes where he wanted me to accompany him. I am really fortunate that a vocalist of his calibre always preferred me to accompany him on the sarangi. I accompanied Kishori Amonkar and also her mother, Mogubai. May god bless Kishori Amonkar; a very nice person and extremely talented artiste. After accompanying so many artistes let me tell you that accompanying is very difficult, more difficult than playing solo. It is an art. One learns it with experience. If one is a soloist, it is enough to know a few ragas but as an accompanying artiste one must know many, many ragas because all artistes have their own repertoire. The interpretations of ragas and the knowledge of different *taals* are very essential. So, accompanying is a very difficult art; to be a good accompanying artiste, apart from knowledge and talent, one must also have great presence of mind.

Interviewer:

Who has been your inspiration?

Sabri Khan:

Ghulam Sabir Khan, Ambalewale. He was a great accompanying artiste. Every vocalist used to ask for him. I became very curious to understand his style. Often I would come to the studio early in the morning to listen to his accompaniment of various artistes. As the broadcast was early in the morning at 7:00 am, often he would be drowsy. Even though he was drowsy, his fingers were his eyes. They just followed the singer. He was a colourful sarangi player and very fond of dressing up in different costumes. Once even a security guard at the studio was taken in by his high ranking military uniform. (*Laughs, while remembering that incident*) Later, when Ghulam Sahib was recording in the studio that guard peeped inside and realised his mistake. It was too hilarious. (*He laughs aloud*)

Interviewer:

You have seen different eras—saw your elders, your own youth and now the younger generation. So how has the thinking of musicians and music evolved over the years?

Sabri Khan:

During those times, children were forced to learn music. But now it all depends on the individual; and it is not necessary whether one belongs to a musician's family or not. A person has the freedom to decide whether he wants to follow in the footsteps of his elders or not. I would like to say that the younger generation should never feel that they have mastered the art of playing the sarangi. It is a difficult instrument. One has to work hard on it. Even now I feel that I do not know anything; I am still learning.

Interviewer:

What about your disciples?

Sabri Khan:

I have disciples all over the world. And all of them are doing well. At the University of Seattle, America, along with the sarangi I also taught the flute. All my disciples, whether in the sarangi or flute or sarod or vocal, are doing well.

V O C A L

Echoes of the Bygone Era

VIDUSHI DHONDUTAI KULKARNI

(23 July, 1927–1 June, 2014)

It was in 2007 that we saw Dhondutai Kulkarni, disciple of the most enigmatic personality of Hindustani classical music—Kesarbai Kerkar, for the first time, at a concert. People like her are nowhere to be found now in the music world. She belonged to the music world of bygone era—simple and traditional, puritan till the last breath.

Speaking Hindi with a Marathi accent, Dhondutai did not hesitate to voice her views on her last guru, Kesarbai Kerkar, 'Initially her voice was not captivating; even her breath was short. But Alladiya Khan Sahib worked hard on her voice. Now everybody talks about voice culture but actually what Alladiya Khan did to Kesarbai's voice was the real voice culture.'

Born in a Brahmin family, it was her father Ganpatrao who was the motivating force behind his daughter's arduous musical journey. He not only encouraged Dhondutai, but was always standing like a rock behind her, protecting her as well as showing her the right path to the ideal guru.

Starting at the age of five, her first guru was Ustad Nathan Khan (nephew of Ustad Alladiya Khan), followed by Ustad Bhurji Khan (son of Ustad Alladiya Khan), Vidushi Lakshmibai Jadhav of Baroda (disciple of Ustad Hyder Khan), Ustad Azizuddin Khan (grandson of Ustad Alladiya Khan) and then her search for the guru ended after becoming Vidushi Kesarbai Kerkar's sole disciple in 1962. At that time Kesarbai Kerkar was seventy-two years old.

A few years later, in 1965, Kesarbai Kerkar announced her retirement but Dhondutai continued learning from her till 1971. And the programmes that her guru was getting were passed on to the disciple. 'Kesarbai encouraged me and started sending me for the concerts. She also offered me her diamond jewellery to wear because she felt that I should look my best on stage.'

With her death on 1 June, 2014, the fragrance of the good golden era also passed away.

(4 September, 2008)

Interviewer:

Dhondutaiji you belong to a Brahmin family where singing was taboo, yet you became a musician. How did this happen? Who supported you?

Dhondutai:

My father was deeply interested in music but because of his family responsibilities, he couldn't proceed with his passion. He learnt from various teachers. He also learnt the tabla but couldn't excel in that either. He did not get the guidance of a good maestro. So, he decided that I must have a proper guru to learn music properly. And in Kolhapur, the only good singer was Ustad Alladiya Khan.

Interviewer:

So he encouraged you and took you to Ustad Alladiya Khan?

Dhondutai:

Yes. But I learnt under various gurus and all of them belonged to the Jaipur-Atrauli *gharana.* After having learnt from various gurus, finally I came to Kesarbai Kerkar, who was the most special disciple of Ustad Alladiya Khan. She was my fifth guru. When I was five years old I was taken to Nathan Khan, Ustad Alladiya Khan's brother's son. But he said that I was too small to learn. His view was completely unlike today's trend, where young children are taught music. But at that time no guru taught a boy or girl before he/she was ten to fifteen years old. The other thing was that gurus were reluctant to teach girls. So he refused. My father hit upon an idea. He approached his friend, whose voice was very good, to learn from Nathan Khan. He took his friend to Nathan Khan and told Khan Sahib to teach his friend and not to bother about the fee for he would make the payment. Khan Sahib started teaching that friend of my father. But when he came to know the truth that through that friend it was I who was getting music education, he agreed to teach me. But he used to teach me only for fifteen minutes in a day because I was too small. I was just five years old then. My hands were too small and the vocal chords had not developed. And because the *gayaki* of this *gharana* is very forceful and strenuous, it was not advisable to strain my vocal chords. Stressing vocal chords at that tender age could have strained my voice and there were chances of losing my voice forever. Singing is an exercise for the throat and only if that exercise is done properly can it enrich the voice, otherwise it can destroy the voice for all times. Unfortunately, not realising this, many gurus spoiled the voices of their disciples. My father knew this. So I was given *taleem* only for fifteen minutes.

Interviewer:

How many years did you learn under Ustad Nathan Khan?

Dhondutai:

For nearly three years. What happened was that film actress Durga Khote took him to Mumbai. And I was left with no tutor for there was no other guru in Kolhapur belonging to the Jaipur-Atrauli *gharana* at that time. But on the basis of whatever he taught me I started giving programmes on All India Radio at the age of eight. I used to sing one raga for ten minutes.

Interviewer:

How did you become Ustad Bhurji Khan's disciple?

Dhondutai:

Bhurji Khan Sahib was the youngest son of Ustad Alladiya Khan. Alladiya Khan Sahib had three sons—Nasiruddin, Manjhi Khan and Bhurji Khan. Nasiruddin had left singing and gone to his village and Manjhi Khan died quite young. Only Bhurji Khan was carrying on his father's tradition. He was teaching Shobha Gurtu's mother, Manekabai Shirodkar. But Mumbai's climate did not suit him, so he came to Kolhapur. Secondly, he was supposed to sing for thirty minutes everyday at the Mahalakshmi temple in Kolhapur. So my father used to take me there to listen to his music. My father requested him to teach me. He didn't refuse directly because he realised my father's devotion. However, he looked at me and perhaps had doubts whether I would be able to understand whatever he would teach me. So he asked for ₹50/ as his fee. The year was 1936 and ₹50/ was a fortune. Very few people used to get this salary. My father did not feel bad. He continued taking me to the temple to listen to his singing. And when I attained the age of thirteen, Bhurji Khan himself came to our house and said that he would teach me. And then he told my father, 'At that time I asked ₹50/ because I knew you would not be able to afford it, but she was so small and seeing your respect and devotion, I couldn't refuse point blank. Give me whatever you can as my fee. I'll not say anything but I'll teach your daughter.' It was 1940 and that very day I started learning from Bhurji Khan Sahib.

Interviewer:

So, for how many years did you learn from him?

Dhondutai:

For ten years, till 1950. He passed away in 1950.

Interviewer:

Then you became Kesarbai's disciple?

Dhondutai:

No, not immediately. Bhurji Khan had prepared me so well that people often used to say that as Ustad Alladiya Khan has Kesar, Bhurji Khan has Dhondutai as his Kesar. I had started giving programmes on radio. Though I was giving performances frequently, somewhere I started feeling that I should delve deeper into the *gharana gayaki*. My father was also quite keen on it. For seven years I stayed in Hyderabad. My maternal uncle had his chemist shop there. So I stayed in Hyderabad for seven years, gave performances in All India Radio, Hyderabad. Roshan Ali of Bhindi Bazaar *gharana* and Rauf used to sing *thumri, ghazal*, etc. They were both very good singers. They used to give me many programmes at All India Radio. During that time the environment at the radio station was completely different from what it is now. Radio gave me a lot of programmes and money for which I am really grateful. At the age of twenty I became an 'A' grade artiste on radio. I am really thankful to AIR for this.

Interviewer:

So, how did you reach Kesarbai Kerkar?

Dhondutai:

Eventually, I got the Ministry of Education scholarship. I was supposed to learn under the same *gharana* in which I was trained. Right at that time Lakshmibai Jadhav resigned from her position as the artiste of Baroda State. She came to Kolhapur. So I started learning from her in the morning and in the evening from Ustad Alladiya Khan's grandson, Azizuddin Khan or Baba, as I call him. We, my father and

I, had heard about Kesarbai but we also knew that she didn't teach. But I do remember that even as a child I dreamt about learning music from Kesarbai.

Interviewer:

What was it about her that fascinated you?

Dhondutai:

She was very famous. Her name was known to everybody. I do not know with what destiny she was born but she was very well known and even now her name echoes everywhere. Recently, Geeta Mehra, belonging to a rich family of Ahmedabad, released four CDs of Kesarbai's music. As you know earlier *mehfils* were organised by rich, aristocratic people only. And Kesarbai was a favourite of these people. She used to be so very busy, performing. These organisers secretly recorded her music. Secretly, because she never let anybody record her music. And these people have a large number of her recordings. So, recently four CD pack of her music was released and it was immediately sold out. So great was her singing that people still love to listen to her voice and singing. Her stature was so strong and powerful that even male singers were frightened of her. I remember expressing my desire to learn music from Kesarbai, though I hardly understood music at that age. I do not know why I used to say it, but I used to say it. So what happened was that she had been refusing to take any student. Many singers tried to become her disciple, but she refused everyone. Even we thought that as she does not teach anyone, it would be useless to approach her. But once she had gone for a concert. After the concert, the Editor of the newspaper *Loksatta* asked her, 'Your music reminds us of Ustad Alladiya Khan, but after you, who is there to carry forward this tradition?' So she replied, 'If somebody is ready to work as hard as I did, then I am ready to teach.' This statement was published in the newspaper. At that time I was in Jabalpur, Madhya Pradesh with my brother. I want to tell you that I've not got married, so I used to live with my parents, my brother. After her statement got published in the newspaper, Azizuddin Khan Sahib told me to write a letter to Kesarbai. According to him I was the most suitable person to become her disciple and that I knew how to handle gurus. So I sent a letter to Kesarbai. And Kesarbai replied to me, 'Even after learning from so many gurus, you still feel that you want to learn something from me, it is remarkable. I like this attitude of yours. Age is fast catching up with me, so I do not know whether I'll be able to teach you the way one is taught in our *gharana*. However, you come to Mumbai.'

Interviewer:

So, you came to Mumbai alone or with Azizuddin Khan Sahib?

Dhondutai:

My father and I came to Mumbai but, yes, we called Azizuddin Khan Sahib also. We sold everything at Kolhapur. The day we came to Mumbai, that very day there was a performance by Kesarbai at Birla Matoshree Sabha. Azizuddin Khan went to meet her in the green room. He told her about me and immediately she called us in the green room. Baba put forth a condition that she must let me sit on the tanpura behind her. She literally glared at him, but agreed. As soon as I entered the green room, she gave me one of her famous scrutinising looks. Had it been some other girl, she would have made an exit, out of sheer fear. But I was not nervous at all because I knew Bhurji Khan had laid my foundation very well. I was confident. And more than me Baba had confidence in me.

Interviewer:

Which year did you become her disciple?

Dhondutai:

In the year 1962. At that time she was seventy-two years old. And I remained her disciple till 1971. She became very ill after that.

Interviewer:

After learning from so many gurus what prompted you to become her disciple?

Dhondutai:

Many people ask me this question. It was not to learn rare ragas. I had a good repertoire already. But you see her voice was very bad initially and her breath was very short. It used to break after one or two *sur.* But Alladiya Khan Sahib worked hard on her voice. I wanted to know that voice culture technique, which changed the texture and style of

Kesarbai's voice completely. Now voice culture has become the buzz word. Every second person claims to be a good voice culture teacher but the real voice culture was done by Alladiya Khan Sahib on Kesarbai Kerkar's voice. And I needed to know that voice culture. I wanted to know how Alladiya Khan made her voice as famous as 'voice of the queen.'

Interviewer:

So you wanted to learn the technique of voice culture?

Dhondutai:

Not only voice culture technique but also about how to present a raga, how to present oneself on stage and how to win over the audience.

Interviewer:

What difference did you find in the teaching style of Bhurji Khan and Kesarbai Kerkar?

Dhondutai:

When I was learning under Bhurji Khan, I was completely raw and was very young also. He had to teach me the basics of classical music. Often he taught one raga for two years. I learnt nearly twenty to twenty-five ragas from him. And when I reached Kesarbai, I was quite mature. I think an artiste gets ready for performances only by the age of forty. The singing of a youth is completely different from the singing of a forty-year old. When I came to Kesarbai I was mature. In our *gharana* a lot of importance is given on preparing the voice to scale through two *saptak*s (octaves) from *mandra saptak* to *taar saptak*. So, in the morning from 5:00 to 7:00 she made me do voice *riyaaz*. She also took me to Lonawala for one month to do *riyaaz*.

Interviewer:

She didn't teach her daughter. Why?

Dhondutai:

Her daughter became a doctor. She wanted her daughter to study and do well in studies. You see, Kesarbai suffered a lot during her younger days. She got respect and adulation much, much, later. Secondly, the daughter had seen her mother working so hard. She didn't want to lead that kind of a life and was not keen on learning music. And this is the truth that people who are keen to enjoy life, cannot pursue music and arts. It requires a lot of self motivation, dedication and abstinence from so many pleasures of life.

Interviewer:

Kesarbai Kerkar was known to be a very temperamental person. How did you cope with her moods?

Dhondutai:

Some artistes are like that but I knew about her temperamental nature and always took care of her likes and dislikes. So, she was very happy with me. Not once did she get angry with me, rather she was so happy with me that she started sending me for concerts. And she wanted her student to be the best in everything. So, often she would force me to wear her diamond jewellery for concerts. But I used to tell her that whatever she had taught me, was in itself a rare diamond for me. I really had to work hard to convince her about it. Finally I just took the earrings and used to wear them.

Interviewer:

Every guru wants his lineage to continue. You taught Namita Devidayal, thinking that she is your 'little Kesar' but because of so many external factors, she couldn't fulfil your dream, how did you feel?

Dhondutai:

Of course I felt very bad. I had a lot of hope from her, but ... anyway now I've a few other disciples, like Manjiri. She learnt and has gone to America. I have heard that she is teaching in America. Then there's Vasant Karnad, brother of Girish Karnad, he stays at Dharward and is doing very well, then there's one small girl, Rutuja who is learning right now from me and I have great hopes from her. I think she will blossom into a great artiste. I am very optimistic. Whosoever comes to me, I teach them. But this is also true that nobody is going to dedicate their entire life to music, the way I did. So now I teach each student a different set of ragas so that after me they can all come together and present shows.

Interviewer:

You did not marry. Do you feel that you missed out on something in life?

Dhondutai:

No, I don't regret. Actually my temperament is different. I never ever thought about having my own family, home, husband, etc. My sister and brother's children are like my own children. From the very childhood I devoted my life to two things—music and spiritualism. I am made like that. Well, all my students are like my own children. They come whenever I call them.

Interviewer:

Don't you feel lonely?

Dhondutai:

No. On the contrary, I don't like staying with too many people.

Interviewer:

Any piece of advice for young musicians?

Dhondutai:

My father taught me music so that I gain knowledge. I was not encouraged to learn music so as to get name and fame. Never. It was for knowledge. To me knowledge is of utmost importance. But now most youngsters learn music to attain instant name and fame. This is not correct. And these young people do not have the right path in front of them. They are directionless. I hope they find the right track and get a direction in their lives. And if they are educated properly at home and by gurus, then they will learn faster than us. They are so bright and talented. I always tell people that don't run after glamour, name or fame. That is not true success. That is just a part of success. Try to have knowledge as much as possible. But perhaps times have changed. My thinking has become outdated (*Laughs*). But I do think that this kind thinking will soon pass off, die and a better world would soon emerge ... Now, at this juncture of my life, whatever I have ... thoughts, music, everything ... I want it to reach the people.

A Remarkable Musical Journey

VIDUSHI GIRIJA DEVI

(8 May, 1929–)

We caught her while she was on her way to a concert in New Delhi. Staying in one of the five-star hotels, where in the evening she was supposed to participate in a concert, she welcomed us with her warm smile and quickly wrapped up her discussion with her disciple. Shorn of all make-up, her skin glowed with peace and contentment and her grey-green eyes had a mystical twinkle. Enthralling audiences with her immaculate and sensitive *gayaki* for more than sixty years, Girija Devi, lovingly titled *'Thumri* queen,' loves poetry, and is the most revered veteran of *purab-ang gayaki*. Her repertoire includes *khayal, thumri, dadra, tappa, chaiti, kajri*. But *thumri* is her first love. 'It is like a garden ...' she feels.

Girija Devi's father, Ramdeo Rai, a zamindar, initiated her into classical music. It was he who took her to gurus like Pandit Sarju Prasad Mishra and Pandit Shrichandra Mishra. She was just a five-year-old then. She gave her first broadcast at the age of twenty in 1949 from All India Radio, Allahabad.

This marked the beginning of Girija Devi in the arena of Hindustani classical music. After this broadcast, Girija Devi never looked back.

With her unshakeable faith in the power of musical evocation, 'Our music is divine. It is therapeutic,' her music epitomises *bhakti rasa* and *shringar rasa.*

With age catching up, Vidushi Girija Devi has reduced the number of concerts she gives. 'I will sing as long as I have something new to give to my listeners ...' With these words she got up to relax before the evening concert.

(*14 February, 2004*)

Interviewer:

Girija Deviji, how and at what age did your music *taleem* begin?

Girija Devi:

I was only five years old when my *taleem* began in Benaras. My father was a zamindar. To educate my brothers and sister, he moved to Benaras from the village. I was born in Benaras. My father liked classical music. He used to practise, so maybe listening to him from childhood I too grew passionate about classical music. And I liked it so much that instead of going to school, or studying, I got completely immersed in it. Then later on, after many years, radio came into our lives and I heard well-known musicians, like Ustad Faiyaz Khan Sahib, Pandit Omkarnath Thakur, Kesarbai, Siddheshwari Devi, Rasoolanbai. It was not that the *gayaki* of only one maestro impressed me. I liked the *taans* of one singer, the *aakaar* of another, the *bol banav* or *sargam* of a third and so on. I tried assimilating the musical fragrance of each and everyone in my little musical doll's house. So I cannot take any particular name.

Interviewer:

Whose influence is predominant in your *gayaki*?

Girija Devi:

See, first of all my two gurus, Pandit Sarju Prasad Mishra and later Pandit Shrichandra Mishra. Whatever they told me I followed blindly. Later on, along with my husband I used to meet litterateurs and tried amalgamating music and literature. Now if we just say the phrase, like *Aaj aavan ki baat ...* it will not have that much of an impact but on the other hand if we add a word and say *aaj aavan ki baat kahi* or *suni,* etc, it will leave an impression on the listeners. I love decorating words with music. Take for instance the line *Ras ke bhare tore nain.* It suggests the Lord's eyes being a repository of emotions. I imagine a hundred *gopi*s or devotees of the Lord seeking attention in the eyes of the Lord. Some see in Him a tinge of jealousy. Others perceive a hint of pride or carefree abandon. Others see only divinity; some see the playfulness of Krishna. I use notes to suit the mood of the sentiment so that a single line can be sung to at least twenty-five different interpretations. We, my husband and I, thought about it. Actually my husband influenced me a lot in this aspect. Also, if you see Ma Saraswati, she has a veena in one hand and a book in the other—*veena-pustaka dharini*—so I thought music has to have the backing of good lyrics. Without a powerful lyrical content it will not be meaningful and will not leave an impact. That's why I love literature and of course, music is my life.

Interviewer:

You represent *Purab Ang gayaki*. What are its salient features? How is it different from other *gayaki angs*?

Girija Devi:

Purab Ang gayaki is not only *chaiti, thumri, hori*. It is *chaturmukhi gayaki*. I am talking about Benaras. In *purab ang* one is taught *chaturmukhi gayaki*. It has *dhrupad-dhamaar, chhand-prabhand, khayal, tarana, sadra, tappa, tap-khayal* and then we have *thumri,* followed by folk music—*chaiti, hori, jhoola, kajri, baramasa* and then we have *purvi dadra* and above all, there's *dhrupad.* During Tansenji's time *dhrupad* came into being, and then certain features of *dhrupad* were included in *khayal*. In our *gharana* we do not take *murki* or *taan* in *vilambit*. It is taken in *drut*. In a way, my guru-*gharana gayaki* is very peaceful and sober; there is no display of musical extravaganza. And if we indulge in it then there has to be some novelty. There's no repetition in my guru-*gharana*. My guruji said, 'Perform as long as you are able to give something new to music. Don't ever bore your listeners or yourself with repetitions.'

Interviewer:

Now-a-days you don't do much *khayal gayaki* ...

Girija Devi:

(*Promptly*) No, no, I always begin my concerts with a *khayal.* Without having a raga base, it is not possible to sing *thumri.* There has to be a raga base. And till you learn 200-odd ragas, it is not possible to sing *thumri*. Let me explain this differently. See, *thumri* is a garden, a bouquet of different flowers. The *khayal* is similar to a ploughed field sown over with a crop of wheat or paddy. The harvest will yield only rice or wheat as it has a set pattern of growth and works much like a machine. It cannot produce another crop at harvest time. But *thumri* is like a garden having various flowers. The singer plucks flowers of different hues and fragrances and makes a bouquet of different ragas. Of course one has to see that the combination of *ragas* is acceptable. We cannot sing *thumri* without having a knowledge of *khayal.*

Interviewer:

So you always begin your concerts with a *khayal*?

Girija Devi:

Yes. Always. And people listen to it. They like it because they get a completely different fragrance. I sing exactly according to the *Shastra* (musical text) and the way I have been taught by my gurus. I have not changed anything, so it gives a completely different colour to my singing. I teach my disciples also in the way I was taught. First I teach them *alankar,* open the window of ragas to them, then teach them *raga-alaap, drut khayal,* etc.

Interviewer:

What do you like singing—*khayal* or *thumri*?

Girija Devi:

I like *shant bhaav* (peaceful renditions). I do not like *uchhal-khood* (too much of ornamentation and musical acrobatics). Whatever I can sing with devotion, *bhakti- bhavana,* I give importance to that.

Interviewer:

You are witness to the changing demographic patterns of listenership. So what changes have you noticed over the years?

Girija Devi:

Earlier listeners had time. As there was no modern technology, listeners used to come to the concert with a relaxed mind. But now people are always in a hurry. Now they do not have time to sit through long hours in a concert. They want everything instantly. While earlier, listeners enjoyed listening to the *raga vistaar* (raga exploration) of one raga for an hour—one artiste used to sing for two to three hours—now in three hours there are four to five artistes. Times have changed. We are living in the times of 'instant coffee.' Moreover, now people avoid travelling after nine at night. Returning at ten at night is quite risky for girls. And it is a reality. Nothing can be done about it. But the crux of the truth is that earlier people were at peace, now people are terrorised.

Interviewer:

Had you not been a singer, what would you have become?

Girija Devi:

(*Laughs aloud*) Had I not been a singer? Well never thought about it. But I love my family, doing household chores; I just love cooking and welcoming guests and I enjoy listening to other artistes, whether it's folk music, *thumri* or *khayal*. Now because of age I am not able to attend that many concerts but earlier I was always eager to go to concerts by other artistes.

Interviewer:

What do you like most—painting, nature, reading or travelling?

Girija Devi:

I like natural beauty—sea, mountains. I like wandering in the mountains, amidst the natural beauty.

Interviewer:

Nearly five decades, Girija Deviji, a long musical journey. If you were to look back, how would you analyse your life—the losses and achievements?

Girija Devi:

I don't feel that I have lost anything in life. In my life's journey I've just gained and gained. I have a rich bank balance of emotions, experiences that I shared with my elders and now with youngsters. It is all deposited in my very personal emotional bank. Life's experiences have enriched me. God has given me everything, so much that now I think I should relax, sit and just observe, otherwise, you know, the abundance of love, happiness may spill over, upturn and overflow (*says with a gentle laugh*).

Interviewer:

Any particular piece of advice for youngsters?

Girija Devi:

I just want to tell them that the present musical scenario is momentary. It is not going to stay. But classical music or folk music is here to stay. It has been there since ages and we have to preserve it. If we, the older people, do not go to listen to youngsters then they will be demoralised. So we must encourage them. We have to preserve our music. Our music is unique in the world. In our music, one phrase can be expressed in many ways. It can be sung in different ways for fifteen to twenty minutes. We do not sing according to the notations. Yes, we do learn classical music according to the notations but to explore the *raga* fully, we have to use our own talent and our creative reservoir. We continuously improvise. The beauty of our classical music is improvisation.

Interviewer:

You have been felicitated with so many prestigious honours—Padma Shri in 1971, Padma Bhushan in 1989 and Padma Vibhushan in 2004. How does it feel to be so precious?

Girija Devi:

Definitely good, but I want to point out that mere awards do little good. They are just like decorative pieces in our sitting room. The government should give medical or travelling allowance or income tax rebate, etc. Artistes devote their entire life for the cause of art and music. They should be given some rebate in various spheres of life. And secondly, you see when we recommend somebody, giving a certificate of merit to a young talented boy or girl, it is not taken into account by All India Radio. They are given B grade or are often declared unsuccessful in the audition. Why? Who are these people who seem to know more than us? If we, who have been decorated with State honours, have no say, our recommendations are not valued in our own field, then why are we being awarded? I would like the government to look into it. I would request the government to do away with such unjustified practices. This is being unfair to young talent.

VIOLIN

Bringing Gayaki Ang on the Violin

DR N. RAJAM

(Ram Naomi Day, 1930–)

Dr N. Rajam's violin has been titled the 'singing violin.' She worked hard, did research and practised for long hours to 'manipulate' the bowing technique in such a way that it appears as if we are listening to a human voice not the violin. As one of the few violinists whose musical creations are both popular and critically acclaimed, she can afford the luxury of being selective in accepting limited invitations for performances. Her ability to transport her audiences to a different world, to bring tears to their eyes, makes her feel contented that her music touches and inspires people around. 'I am happy that my music is bringing smiles on so many faces.'

We talked to Dr Rajam on a Sunday afternoon in the lush campus of IIT, New Delhi. The interview took place in the guest house, with repeated interruptions by the thundering sound of passing airplanes, engulfing the otherwise peaceful surroundings. Despite the intermittent but loud atmospheric punctuations, she steered the conversation to a very intimate kind of lec-dem. Without any hesitation she demonstrated on her 'singing violin' the differences between Carnatic and Hindustani classical music, and played a perfect hostess.

Born in Chennai in a musical family to Vidwan A. Narayana Iyer, her training in Carnatic music began with her father when she was three years old. Later she became the disciple of Musiri Subramaniam Iyer. But it was Hindustani classical music that attracted her. Quite ignorant of the stature of Pandit Omkarnath Thakur, she heard his recordings at her friend's place.

The music was so powerful that it made young Rajam dream about becoming his disciple. And soon the day came when her dream became a reality. 'It was just destiny,' she reminisces.

Under the tutelage of *Sangeet Martand* Pandit Omkarnath Thakur, Dr Rajam underwent extensive training. Inspired and encouraged by her great guru, she experimented by bringing *gayaki ang* on the violin. She undertook a research project–Comparative Study of Carnatic and Hindustani Styles. 'Both the systems trace their pattern to the same parent. Bifurcation came from 12th century onwards. Earlier, even in Carnatic music there was time classification,' she points out in her thesis. With time, both the sisters (Hindustani and Carnatic) meandered through different musical paths, chartering different trajectories, and scholar Rajam's research gave a new dimension and direction to violin playing in Hindustani style. She revolutionised the art of violin playing.

Dr Rajam spoke in perfect, Sanskritised Hindi.

(18 November, 2007)

Interviewer:

Dr Rajam, you have been giving concerts for the last fifty to fifty-five years and now you are giving concerts along with your granddaughters. So how does it feel?

N. Rajam:

I cannot tell you how happy I feel. When for the first time we performed as a three-generation concert (I, my daughter Sangeeta and my granddaughters Ragini and Nandini), people from all over the world rang me up saying that they were extremely delighted to see us on the stage.

At many places we perform as three generations, first my granddaughters, followed by my daughter and I concluding, the musical evening. And at times all four of us perform together.

Interviewer:

How do you teach them? As their grandmother or as their guru?

N. Rajam:

You know, I am a very strict guru. While teaching I am just their guru and the children understand this very well. They realised it long ago that while taking music lessons *nani ke saath khilwar nahin chalega* (One cannot play around with *nani* when music lessons are on), otherwise I am just their *nani*.

And that's how music should be taught. Many parents complain that children do not learn from them. My question to them is don't you help them in studies, aren't you strict with them there? Then why can't they learn music from you? The thing is one is not serious about music; for if you want it to happen, it will happen.

Interviewer:

You learnt from your father, initially.

N. Rajam:

Yes, I started learning at the age of three. That is the tradition in our family.

Interviewer:

So what kind of a guru was he?

N. Rajam:

He was a very strict guru, a hard task master. Compared to my father we are all quite lenient. My father used to be a terror. Nonetheless, whatever I am today, it is all because of my father. It was only violin and violin practice at home. Nothing else was more important than *riyaaz*. Nobody was allowed, not even my girlfriends, and of course there was no question of boyfriends at that time. We were not even allowed to read magazines.

Interviewer:

So how many hours of *riyaaz* were you doing?

N. Rajam:

Six hours, daily. Before going to school, I used to practise for two-and-a-half hours and after returning from school for about three hours. Then, for sometime during the evening. Besides this, being the only daughter with four brothers, I helped my mother in the household chores too.

Interviewer:

What about the other siblings?

N. Rajam:

My father taught everybody. My elder brother, T.N. Krishnan, is a Carnatic musician. But others did not take it up as a profession. My father was equally strict with them too.

Not only did my father teach us, but our children also. He taught my daughter Sangeeta, and Krishnan's children Viji and Sriram and my other brother's daughter, Kala.

Interviewer:

Violin only?

N. Rajam:

Yes, violin to all of us.

Interviewer:

After learning Carnatic music from your father you were initiated into Hindustani Classical music by Kelkarji. So how did that happen?

N. Rajam:

You know, my father was in Bombay (Mumbai) in the early 1920s. He was in a government job but music was his passion. He was a very good violin player. He did extensive research on the violin and discovered the new technique of bowing. As music was everything to him, often he would go to the Pandit Vishnu Digambar Paluskar institution in Mumbai, give recitals and interact with musicians. I do not know how and why but he always wanted one of his children to be a Hindustani Classical musician.

Interviewer:

So how did it happen?

N. Rajam:

Well, that's also a very interesting story. When I finished matriculation, I was only fourteen years and three months old. To take admission in college one had to be fourteen and a half. And this meant that I was not eligible to take admission, meaning wastage of one year. This was not acceptable to father. To him wasting even one minute was unpardonable. So he told me to join Benaras Hindu University as there was a provision there for girl students to appear as private candidates. He told me to take Hindustani music as one of the subjects.

By that time I already had ten years of rigorous training in Carnatic music, had also accompanied M.S. Subbulakshmi. Soon I started accompanying vocalist, L.R. Kelkarji on the violin. He used to sing and I used to play those ragas on the violin.

After a while I appeared for the entrance examination at Benaras Hindu University, cleared it and joined the university. I stood fifth in the university in intermediate. And Benaras was the place where my guruji, Pandit Omkarnath Thakurji lived.

Interviewer:

And Kelkarji was the disciple of one of the students of Pandit Omkarnath Thakurji. So everything was moving according to providence.

N. Rajam:

Yes, you know everything was destined in such a way that I was sure to meet guruji.

Interviewer:

So how did you approach Pandit Omkarnath Thakurji?

N. Rajam:

During the intermediate examination which spread over a month I went to meet guruji. But before this meeting, while I was learning from Kelkarji, a friend of mine made me hear some rare recordings of Pandit Omkarnath Thakurji. In that record there were ragas like Malkauns, Deshkar, Neelambari. And when I heard the recordings of guruji, though at that time I didn't even know him, I decided that if I have to learn Hindustani Classical then I would like to be his disciple. It became my dream to become his disciple. And later on everything fell into place.

For intermediate I went to Banaras and Parur Sundaram Iyer, father of M.S. Gopalakrishnan, was a good friend of Pandit Vishnu Digambar Paluskarji and quite close to guruji. He had given a letter of recommendation to me to be given to Pandit Omkarnath Thakurji. I went to meet guruji with this letter. He read it and then asked me, 'Have you got your violin?'

The moment I said yes, he told me to play something. That was my test. So whatever I had learned for intermediate examination, I played. He was sitting on a swing. Perhaps he saw a devoted student with a passion for music in me. He said, 'So you want to learn? Fine.' And immediately accepted me as his disciple. I could see my dream turning into reality. He was delighted to know that I had endeavoured learning through his records.

Interviewer:

Were you not frightened of him? Because it is said that he was short tempered and a strict disciplinarian.

N. Rajam:

Forget being frightened! At that time I couldn't speak Hindi at all and only a few words of English. I only knew Tamil. But after seeing my devotion for music he accepted me as his disciple. Yes, it is true that he was very short tempered. But I was fortunate, thanks to God, he never shouted at me. He was a father figure to me and loved me too much. I was the youngest amongst all his students, just sixteen years.

Interviewer:

How and when did you think of bringing *gayaki ang* on the violin?

N. Rajam:

Here I would like to say one thing. I had learnt Carnatic music first and in Carnatic music there is no instrumental style or vocal style. Whatever the instrument might be—veena, flute, violin—everybody plays the vocal style. This was my background. When I came to the north and started learning music, I came to know that Hindustani Classical music has two styles; the instrumental, *gatkari* style is different from the *gayaki*, vocal music style. And the instrument that I play, the violin, is a bow instrument, and in a bow instrument we get continuity of tone. The instruments that have continuity of tone are suitable for *gayaki ang*.

My guruji, Pandit Omkarnathji, used to take a raga, explain the nuances of that raga and then would sing a phrase and tell me to play it on the violin. So like this he would sing a phrase and I would play it on the violin. I was expected to play it exactly like his singing. I could play the notes but to reproduce the emotions, the *bhaav,* I really had to work very hard. He used to guide me constantly, where to emphasise, where to glide over lightly, etc. In this way he trained me and I always tried copying his powerful, emotion-packed genre.

So emotionally powerful was his *gayaki* that tears used to well-up in the eyes of the listeners. To reproduce his style on the violin was very difficult. Despite having the best technique and base of Carnatic music it took me nearly fifteen years to become competent in his style, to bring his emotions, life and spirit onto my music. I had to work on each phrase and at times I used to practise one phrase for months to bring elements of his style on my violin. Today, whatever I am is all because of my guruji.

Interviewer:

You have researched on north Indian and south Indian styles. So what has been your conclusion?

N. Rajam:

Here I would like to tell you that violin in south Indian music is 300 years old. Lot of research and development had taken place. When

I came to guruji I had already learnt to play the violin, with all its ramifications and development.

But all this was not enough to reproduce guruji's technique, his usage of *kaku* (volume variation); and you know this touches the heart immensely. To learn his technique I had to do a lot of research and practice. In Hindustani music *taan* is sung. But I was lacking in this area, despite having learnt the most evolved violin technique playing. To play *taans* on the violin I had to do a lot of research. I really had to work very hard. Today I have the technique to play all genres of Hindustani Classical music—*khayal, dhrupad, thumri, tappa, natya sangeet*.

Interviewer:

So what changes did you bring about in the violin?

N. Rajam:

You see, music is such a thing that it is very difficult to explain it in words. It has to be demonstrated (*while demonstrating she explains*). My technique is *gayaki ang,* meaning vocal style. Bowing has to be manipulated in such a way that it appears as if we are listening to a human voice.

I had to develop my technique for *taans* too. And this calls for tremendous control over the fingers. (*She plays it to demonstrate.*)

Interviewer:

What did your guruji think about your music?

N. Rajam:

He had a great liking for the violin. His brother used to play the violin and accompany guruji. M.S. Gopalakrishnan used to accompany him. So, he was quite familiar with the *gayaki ang* on the violin. Later, I started accompanying him on the violin and did it as long as he was alive.

Interviewer:

What was the topic of your thesis?

N. Rajam:

I did my MA in Sanskrit. For my PhD I selected the topic 'Comparative study of Carnatic and Hindustani systems.' It is interesting to note that both the systems trace their origin to the same parent, Bharata's *Natya Shastra*, and Saranga Deva's *Sangeet Ratnakar* but from the 12th century onwards bifurcation began. Though the concepts in both the systems—ragas, *taalas*, compositions, improvisations—are all common, many ragas are common in, but despite such similarities they sound dissimilar. People who like Hindustani classical do not develop a liking for Carnatic music and vice-versa.

Interviewer:

So what is the reason for this dis-similarity in similarity?

N. Rajam:

This is because the presentation is different in both the systems. The same notes are presented in a different way.

Interviewer:

You are saying that the source is same, there are so many similarities in both the systems; yet in Carnatic music we do not have day-part classifications of ragas, where as in Hindustani classical music ragas are sung according to the time classification. What is the reason for this?

N. Rajam:

We do not have it now in Carnatic music. Earlier in Carnatic music also ragas were sung according to the time classification. But when the concert pattern developed, and as concerts were usually happening between 5:00 to 8:00 pm or 6:00 to 9:00 pm, this theory gradually faded away. With the advent of the concert pattern there was no question of adhering to time classification.

Interviewer:

But in Hindustani classical music also concerts happen in the evening, then why is the time classification theory still followed by them?

N. Rajam:

In Hindustani classical music concerts continue through the whole night and at times till the morning hours also. So here artistes get an opportunity to play a variety of ragas according to the time classification. Nonetheless, I see changes happening here too. Now I am going for a recording in the afternoon and I'll play Darbari (*laughs*). But frankly speaking I personally do not like listening to evening or night ragas in the morning.

At least my generation does not feel comfortable listening to morning ragas at night or vice-versa. After all, if ragas had been codified into time boundaries then there's bound to be some reason for it. Gradually, after another forty or fifty years it might happen.

Interviewer:

But similar reasons must have existed in Carnatic music too?

N. Rajam:

Yes, may be. But it changed. One thing more. Earlier, in Carnatic music, raga *vistaar* (raga expansion) was done for two to two-and-a-half hours. But now artistes do it in lesser time because audiences no longer have the patience to sit through for long hours. Now-a-days artistes try giving a bouquet of various hues and shades of classical music in just forty five minutes to an hour. While in the north, artistes still explore the ragas for a longer time. What will happen tomorrow, nobody knows in this wave of fusion music.

Interviewer:

What do you think of fusion music?

N. Rajam:

I don't do it. As of now I am not doing it but we, human beings change, so I cannot say anything about tomorrow, whether I'll do it or not. Only God knows!

Interviewer:

But what do you think of it as a genre? Is it good for classical music?

N. Rajam:

I personally feel that any art form should not be static. If it is static, it ceases to be an art form. It has to constantly grow, evolve. Change is necessary.

But to change for the sake of change is not healthy. We cannot just overlook or bypass all the musical rules and regulations, made by our ancestors. We cannot just negate all those points and bring about change. No, that is not good. While keeping in mind those points, changes should be brought about; but not blindly.

Interviewer:

If tomorrow your granddaughters come out with a fusion album, what will be your reaction?

N. Rajam:

I am their guru. I am teaching them. But tomorrow how they develop their art is up to them. I'll not be able to do anything. After all they have their own thinking, belief.

Interviewer:

When did you think of becoming a performer?

N. Rajam:

You see my training began when I was only three years old and it continued for next ten to twelve years. A child of three or thirteen, at that time, I had no idea about a career or becoming a performing artiste. But my father was very far-sighted. He believed that girls should be taught so that, if need be, they can be self-reliant. I only thought about *riyaaz,* working hard and becoming proficient in music.

Interviewer:

How did you prepare yourself for the stage?

N. Rajam:

I was very fortunate to have Pandit Omkarnathji as my guru. He was not only my guru but a father figure as well. He guided me at every stage of my life. When in the beginning he came for my concerts, and sat in the first row in the audience, he often used to guide from there. He would ask me to play fast bowing. To be able to play fast bowing efficiently I practised a lot on *tarana.*

I learnt a lot about audience psychology while accompanying him on tours. It is a different thing to practise in a closed room and to perform on stage. He taught me how to develop a bond with the listeners. I personally feel that every student should undergo apprenticeship for two years with an established artiste, so as to learn how to present oneself on the stage.

You see, one has to perform according to the audience. In Bengal the audience is the patient and quiet type, while in Punjab, the audience is very vocal. If one is under an apprenticeship, it will be easier to know how to deal with audiences of varying types and nature.

Interviewer:

How was the support of your husband in your musical journey?

N. Rajam:

In this respect I was very lucky. My husband and in-laws were very supportive. Apart from being a performer I also taught at Benaras Hindu University for forty years.

Interviewer:

You were a teacher, a performer, a wife, a mother—so how did you juggle between so many responsibilities?

N. Rajam:

Because of my supportive husband. When I used to do *riyaaz*, he used to look after our daughter, Sangeeta and for concerts, he used to accompany me. I still remember that during the concerts, Sangeeta often used to go off to sleep in the green room. But as soon as the concert was over, she would get up and say, 'It got over? Shall we go?' (*Travels back in time while remembering the incident and laughs*). You see, I was the Dean of Benaras Hindu University, with numerous responsibilities of the administrator, yet I pursued my passion. The truth is I could do it because of my determination and the unstinting support of my family.

Interviewer:

Are you still a visiting faculty member at Benaras Hindu University?

N. Rajam:

It's difficult to travel so much now but they have bestowed on me Emeritus Professorship.

Interviewer:

How many disciples do you have now? And who do you think is the most promising, besides your daughter, Sangeeta and granddaughters—Ragini Shankar and Nandini Shankar?

N. Rajam:

I've disciples all over the world. There's Vicky Richards in America. She is doing very well; my niece, Kala Ramnath is also doing very well. There are many others.

Interviewer:

What are your hobbies?

N. Rajam:

I like reading a lot. Spiritual books, Ramakrishna Paramahansa or any spiritual book. I like the fiction of R.K. Narayan. The book should be gripping, only then I read.

Interviewer:

Have you ever thought about writing your autobiography?

N. Rajam:

Many people suggest it. Maybe one day.

Interviewer:

What does music mean to you?

N. Rajam:

You see, music is a way of life. Everybody is searching for happiness and through music one can achieve absolute happiness. When I hear from people that my music has transported them into a different world or when I see their moist eyes after a rendition, it gives me immense happiness. I feel happy that I am able to bring smiles on so many faces. I am really grateful to God for being so kind to me.

Interviewer:

What do you think about young, upcoming practitioners?

N. Rajam:

Now-a-days, everybody wants everything instantly. They want stage, appreciation, everything very fast. I think they should have patience and perseverance and work hard. If they are really good they will certainly make a mark.

It may take a longer time than a few others who are blessed with the silver spoon, but if you have talent it will certainly come to the forefront.

However, to be on the safer side, one should take up a job and continue following their passion. In my own case, I had taken up a job. I was a lecturer in Benaras Hindu University.

To sustain oneself, a job is necessary as there is no immediate return from the concert arena. It will come, but gradually. One should not lose hope. The main thing to remember, as I said before, is that music gives happiness.

V O C A L

Painting the Canvas of Emotions

PANDIT JASRAJ

(28 January, 1930–)

We got a chance to interview Pandit Jasraj at his friend, Justice Mukul Mudgal's residence in New Delhi, where he had stopped for a day on his way home from a concert in Rajasthan. When we reached there, Pandit Jasraj was sleeping after a tiring journey and tour. We had nearly lost hope after forty-five minutes of wait, thinking that perhaps, 'it's a wrong day.' But his disciple and nephew, Rattan Mohan Sharma gave us company and discouraged any thoughts about postponing the interview, 'It's 5:00 pm and he will soon join us. See, his guests have also started coming.' We became apprehensive. We didn't want to talk to him amidst his followers. Just as we were debating whether to stay back or return, Pandit Jasraj emerged in an orange kurta and dhoti, ushering in an aura of spirituality, so characteristic of his *gayaki* as well. Everybody got up to greet the maestro and sat around him.

He appeared to be touched by their concern and listened to them with untiring patience. Coaxed by his nephew, we ultimately decided to interview him in the midst of his admirers. At ease, often asking for his special tea, he answered while conversing with his 'guests,' enquiring about their well-being and discussing topics related to God, miracles and classical music.

Pandit Jasraj was born in Hissar, Haryana to Pandit Motiram, a classical music exponent. Jasrajji was only four when his father passed away. He received training from his elder brother, Pandit Maniram, and later from

Maharaja Jaiwant Singhji Waghela. Beginning his musical journey as a tabla accompanist to his brother, Pandit Jasraj soon got disappointed with the way tabla maestros were treated. He decided to concentrate on vocal music only. Blessed with a sonorous and meditative voice, smoothly mapping three and a half octaves, Pandit Jasraj gave his first public concert way back in 1952 before King Tribhuvan Vikram of Nepal.

(*2 April, 2005*)

Interviewer:

Panditji, you always start your *bandishes* with a *shloka,* and in all your concerts the atmosphere becomes spiritually charged. How does this happen?

Jasraj:

That's an interesting question. I don't know how it happens, why it happens. But I always start with a prayer to Lord Vishnu– '*Mangalam bhagwan Vishnu* ...' This has been coming down to us through the ages and it's the power of this mantra ...

Interviewer:

So you believe it is this mantra that changes the whole atmosphere; isn't it the power of your *gayaki* as well?

Jasraj:

The mantra makes my *gayaki* what it is. My spiritual guru was Maharana Jaiwant Singhji, a true devotee and he was the one who gave me the vision for this path. The interesting fact is that he was a great musician himself and he was from the same *gharana* that I belong to–Mewati *gharana.*

Interviewer:

Your rendition of the bhajan *Om Namo Bhagwate* has become so popular. What was the creative process behind it?

Jasraj:

This *bhajan* has been written by Shankaracharyaji. An acquaintance, a lady called Prerna Behen Thakur, heard the song and was deeply inspired by it. A true devotee of Lord Krishna, she would get tears in her eyes at the mere mention of his name. One day she came to me and I was so deeply moved by her sincere devotion, *bhakti,* and wondrous love for Krishna that even before she could mention the purpose of her visit I promised her that I was with her in whatever it was she wanted me to do. She wanted to get *Krishna anurag, Shiva anurag,* all of those recorded. Now, I firmly believe that God is behind everything that happens in life, all the people we meet ... even the fact that you are here today and we have met is an indicator of something that is about to happen, there is some cosmic reason behind it. So it was because of her that I sang *'Om*

Namo Bhagwate' and had no clue it would become so popular! Today when I listen to it, I am moved.

Interviewer:

What is the concept behind Jasrangi Jugalbandi? Why did you think of doing this different kind of Jugalbandi with a male and female vocalist?

Jasraj:

Many a time when I heard male and female vocalists singing together, I always felt there was something lacking. There is a pair for everything in nature—like husband-wife, *Shiv-Shakti, Purush-Prakriti*, and these two energies together fulfil one goal, achieve completeness. But when male and female vocalists sing together, one of them always suffers. Why? I asked God that if music is so special then why has one to compromise while singing with the other. Sometimes the female vocalist says she can't sing at a high scale so the male vocalist has to sing from *kharaj* and because of all this they are not able to do justice to their own music. So the answer I got was that the solution to this already exists in the form of '*murchhana*,' In classical music there is *murchhana-bheda—'sapt suran teen gram ikkees murchhana* ...' So the solution already existed and I just tried to give some more thought, direction and depth to the concept.

Interviewer:

But the vocalists sing different ragas in this kind of jugalbandi. What is the reason behind it?

Jasraj:

Exactly! If you take the *shadja* note as *shadja* and sing, it would be one raga. Now if you sing the same combination of notes from *pancham swar* that would be a different raga! So that is why the vocalists would be singing the same note combination, but at different scales and so it would be two different ragas.

Interviewer:

What is your favourite raga?

Jasraj:

Well, it depends on the state of mind at that time. Many a time I had tuned my *swarmandal* before the concert, thinking I would present a certain raga. But when I am on stage I keep the *swarmandal* aside and start with some other raga.

Interviewer:

Today people often say that the concept of *gharana* is obsolete. What are your views on this?

Jasraj:

One thing I want to say is that people who don't give much importance to *gharana* are missing out on something crucial. Each *gharana* has some specialty, something unique, and that is why it became a *ghar*, a *gharana.* For instance, a Commerce college is distinct from an Arts college and they are both different from a Science college. One doesn't question that, but when it comes to *gharanas* in music, why so much scepticism? Try to understand that each *gharana* is unique. For example, in Agra gharana *gayaki* they used to start with *madhya laya* and *alaapchari, bol-baant* was characteristic to Agra *gharana*, while in Kirana *gharana* the emphasis is on the notes, *behlava*; so you see each *gharana* has something special and unique.

Interviewer:

So what is the specialty of Mewati *gharana*?

Jasraj:

In Mewati Gharana, we believe in loving each *swar.* We try to ornament and render each *bandish* as if it were a new-born baby; we are gentle and protective about it. We think of the instruments as mother and father, and for us, music is God. Like a mother takes care of her growing child, in the same manner we approach each raga and develop it. Secondly, the *bandishes* of this *gharana* are mainly on the theme of God, devotion and *bhakti.*

Interviewer:

You don't usually sing *thumri, dadra, chaiti* and such genres in your *gharana*?

Jasraj:

See everything is not for every *gharana*. Those who sing *thumri* are complete musicians themselves. It requires a different thought process.

Interviewer:

You have also revived *Haveli Sangeet*. What was the thought behind that?

Jasraj:

I found something in *Haveli Sangeet* that is not there in present-day classical music. That music is complete in itself. You could call it *pushti-margi sangeet* or temple music ...

Interviewer:

So who was your mentor for this?

Jasraj:

Everyone we come across, everyone we meet teaches us something in some way. In a way, they are all gurus. Now I am learning something from you, so you are also my guru right now! Whoever shows the way, teaches us something, is a guru. There are so many people—kin and disciples of Shri Vallabhacharya, who are my gurus.

Interviewer:

Let's go back in time Pandit ji. How was your childhood? Tell us something about your gurus and the time when you really had to struggle.

Jasraj:

I am struggling even today. In different phases of life our struggle varies. During childhood, it was a different struggle, then when I grew up it was the struggle to reach out to people, now it is the struggle to reach God.

Interviewer:

But what was the struggle in your musical journey?

Jasraj:

All that is the journey of music only! Each musician is trying to reach God through music.

Interviewer:

Who was your first guru?

Jasraj:

I learnt music from my elder brother, Pandit Maniramji and my father, Pandit Motiramji. And there are so many people whom I met in life and learnt something from them about life. Right now also I am learning from the questions you are asking me, something will get stored in the subconscious mind and resurface at some important point in life, maybe in music. My spiritual guru was Maharana Jaiwant Singhji.

Interviewer:

Do you remember anything extremely significant or special that your gurus said; something that you always abide by?

Jasraj:

My father once told my brother, '*Beta*, if someone is ill and cannot come to your concert, but wants to listen to your music, then you must go to him. Don't hesitate to spend your own money, because money doesn't really belong to anybody. Just go and sing for that person. That is *sadhna*.'

Here I would like to tell you a very touching incident. Once I was in Delhi and my wife called. She said she had received a phone call from a girl saying that her brother had cancer and was hospitalised at the Tata Memorial Hospital in Mumbai and that he wanted to meet me, to hear me sing. I immediately recalled my father's words and felt it was my duty to respect my father's wishes. So I went to meet this boy. He was only nineteen or twenty years old and very weak—he couldn't even get up when I entered the ward. I felt so sad but controlled my tears. I didn't want to cry in front of him. He was pleased and grateful that I had come and apologised for not being able to greet me properly. He said, 'When I came to know that I am dying, I had only one wish and that was to meet you. Now I know that since you agreed to come, you will also agree to sing for me. I want to listen to Darbari from you.'

I was overwhelmed with emotion at his words. I tuned my swarmandal for Darbari, calmed myself, closed my eyes and started singing. I sang for forty minutes and when I stopped, he was sitting on his bed. He made another request, 'Pandit ji my last wish is to listen to Niranjani Narayani—Bhairavi.' I sang that *bandish* and because I was meditating on God while singing, when I opened my eyes I saw that the boy was standing on his feet. He did *pranam* to me and said, 'You have fulfilled my last wish. I am not at all sad about death now. I don't have anything to give you; I just have this *mishri* ...' Earlier the doctors had given up hope and had told his parents to come down from Madras because he didn't have much time left. But the very next day, the boy went back to his home in Madras and lived for another two months. It was nothing short of a miracle.

Interviewer:

That is indeed a miracle! There was another such miracle when your elder brother lost his voice and then it was restored ...

Jasraj:

Yes. Now when I think back I feel that was the day when I actually realised and felt the presence of God. I was fourteen years old at that time. I knew which idol symbolised which God, but I don't think I truly understood and believed in God. My spiritual guru consulted many doctors to get a cure for my brother. But nothing happened. Then suddenly one day he announced, 'Pandit ji today your voice will come back. Sing for God; sing for that greater power, that's my only condition.' My brother's voice was in a very bad state, but suddenly his voice came back and he started singing in the most beautiful voice ever. After that he never had any problem with his voice. That day my spiritual guru made me realise that it doesn't matter by what name you call God, what matters is that one has to truly believe in him.

Interviewer:

Coming to the *guru-shishya parampara*, sometimes when we hear your disciples, your image is so visible in their music.

Jasraj:

See, when a child is born, we always think about whether he resembles his mother or father, or any other family members. Why? If an African son is born to British parents, will they digest it? Will they call him their child? Maybe they will doubt the mother or be puzzled. The *guru-shishya* relationship has to be seen in the same light. An emerging musician would definitely resemble his guru. And only when that happens can one say that he is a true *shishya.* If that doesn't happen it means there is some doubt in the mind of the *shishya,* or the guru. Music is magic, and it is very infectious. It gets stored in your sub-conscious mind and when it comes out through the throat it comes out after being trained in the respective *gharana*. Sometimes when you see a good dancer you will see the music in his dance. You can see the *meends, gamak*, the spaces between the notes, through the dance. And the tenderness of the dancer can be absorbed into the throat, into music. So, if a *shishya* has not absorbed the style of his guru, then the question that should be asked is what kind of *shishya* is he? And also what kind of a guru is he, who has not imparted that essence to his *shishya*?

Interviewer:

But what about the music schools that are so prevalent now?

Jasraj:

See, earlier there were *ashrams* where children used to live and study and develop into a complete personality. Now all these things are disappearing. Now there are colleges and in those colleges there are professors and teachers, not gurus. So, now the concept of guru is also disappearing. One needs to surrender completely to a guru.

Interviewer:

Sometimes people say that Hindustani classical music is not for the masses. What do you think about that?

Jasraj:

No, not at all. I just don't agree with those people who are suggesting that classical music is not for the masses. If music is not for the masses then how can you call it music? But you know, this segregation regarding who should come for a classical music session or not, is not at all fair. It makes people feel, 'Oh it's not for the masses so what will we do at this concert?' In this way we make it elite, we isolate it. Being elite is not about clothes, it's about your thoughts. Look at the age group of people in a concert. It starts from eighteen to twenty years and those youngsters are not from any such 'elite class'. They haven't even started earning yet. No one becomes great just because they have money. Our music is for the masses. Earlier when I used to sing and someone sitting in the audience would be showing his feet to me, to the stage, I used to feel offended because to me music was like an offering I was making to God. I used to feel bad thinking that the person was being disrespectful. But now I feel that God resides in each and everyone and if someone is doing that, it's ok, it's their will, after all God is inside them too.

Interviewer:

How do you select your disciples?

Jasraj:

First I try to sense and understand my disciples. Only when I see that they are devoted to music and want it to be their means of livelihood as well, no, no ... don't get me wrong, I don't mean to say that every musician should make it his livelihood. God gives music to everyone. And music is very dear to God. God said to Narad ji, 'I live where my devotee sings for me ...' And that is why our ancestors have gifted this to us and we are gifting it to the next generation. Only those students of music who are serious, devoted and passionate about music become my disciples.

Interviewer:

How do you teach?

Jasraj:

When we start teaching a disciple, we show him the outlines of the *gharana,* like a painter first sketches, draws an outline of the figures. Then we ask the disciple to fill in the colours into that outline with his visualisation but to never step outside the boundary.

Interviewer:

What advice would you like to give to your followers?

Jasraj:

Whether you become a musician or not, always respect your parents, think of them as your God and then see how many people respect you. Love and respect your guru and your parents and you will sail through life smoothly.

VOCAL

Music is My Religion
DR PRABHA ATRE
(13 September, 1932–)

Dr Prabha Atre's voice on the telephone belies her age. She sounds young and lively. And when you meet her, you wonder is this the person who answered the telephone. Her silver crown creates more confusion. From nowhere does she look past seventy years.

Request for an interview was promptly granted, 'Oh, I am coming to Delhi after two days for a day. Perhaps we can meet then.' She came but was extremely busy with her concert. I didn't receive her telephone. I had nearly lost hope thinking that now one will have to go to Mumbai to talk to her. But no, I was wrong. Next day I received her call, 'Well, yesterday we couldn't meet but can we meet just now? My flight is after two hours.' I rushed.

The interview with her was taken on two occasions—first at the airport, in the car and then over the telephone, followed by an email. Forthcoming and straightforward, she has definite views about music and musicians. Though music is her first love, Dr Prabha Atre is a poet and writer too. While talking about music she would occasionally recite verses from one of her poems. Romantic at heart, she laughed at her single status, 'Koi mila nahi na ...!'

Born to Aba Sahib and Indirabai Atre in Pune, with no one in her family into music, she worked hard to create her own space in the field of music. If critics were sceptical about her experiments, she refuted her detractors with her scholarly PhD research on *Sargam* and continued with her musical innovations. She began her career with the All India Radio. After a few years she joined an educational institute. She became Professor and later Head of the Department of Music at SNDT University, Mumbai.

Dr Prabha Atre is not just a musician. She is a thinker, scholar, academician, composer, writer, poet, organiser and founder of institutes. 'It is all connected with music. Music is a multi-limbed tree,' she says, voicing her thoughts in measured tones. Dr Prabha Atre is a private person and doesn't like talking about her private life. She speaks with a typical Marathi accent.

(2 March, 2005/September 2008)

Interviewer:

Prabhaji you are a multifaceted personality. You're a thinker, performer, research scholar, composer, writer and guru. How do you do justice to so many roles?

Prabha Atre:

It is all connected to music. I am not doing anything different. Only my thinking is different. But yes, one needs to have talent to do justice to each role. Not everybody can be a good guru or a composer or do research. But the foundation of all these things is music only.

Interviewer:

How do you take out time for these things? You have performances lined up and then *riyaaz* also ...

Prabha Atre:

I think one doesn't have to sit with the tanpura for two to three hours for *riyaaz*. It is a continuous process. To think is also a form of *riyaaz*. To listen to music is also *riyaaz* and to teach is also *riyaaz*. *Riyaaz* continues throughout the day.

Interviewer:

Who were your gurus? Also, what brought you to music?

Prabha Atre:

See, I do not come from a family of musicians. I do not have any family background of music. Nobody even listened to classical music in my family. Both my parents were teachers. My father was a headmaster in a school in Pune. He insisted that my sister and I should participate in all extracurricular activities of the school. Singing was one of them. But I was not taking regular classes. It was, in fact, my mother's illness that brought music into our house. She used to keep brooding over her illness. To divert her mind, a harmonium teacher was engaged. But after taking four or five lessons she quit music. I continued. I had picked up a few tunes, sitting by her side and started participating in school functions. Perhaps, somebody heard me in school and told my father that since I've a good voice, proper training should be given to me. A friend of my father told him that he knew Sureshbabu Mane. We went to his house where both Hirabai and Kamlabai were also sitting. I was asked to sing something. Now I do not remember what I sang, but it must have been a *khayal*, followed by a *thumri*. He liked it and agreed to teach me.

Interviewer:

For how many years did you learn from Sureshbabu Maneji?

Prabha Atre:

It was for a very short time. Maybe six or seven years. And even in those six years often he was away on tours along with Hirabaiji. He was quite busy. But whatever he taught me was really special. So when he passed away I didn't feel like becoming the disciple of any other maestro. I decided to listen to great maestros and learn by myself ... by listening to them.

Interviewer:

But you became Hirabaiji's disciple also?

Prabha Atre:

I became her disciple because I got the Central Government scholarship. And there was a clause saying that I had to continue my learning in this *gharana*, i.e., the Kirana *gharana* only. So I became Hirabaiji's disciple and she herself was Sureshbabu's disciple. That was the peak period in her career. She used to be away on tour most of the time. I used to accompany her everywhere. So it was again more of listening and learning.

Interviewer:

So can it be said that you're a self-taught musician?

Prabha Atre:

Yes, in a way (*laughs*), just like Eklavya. Anyway, whatever I learnt, though in a short span of time, had depth. Talent is necessary. And one can learn by listening also. Those who sit in front of the guru and learn are fortunate no doubt. Nonetheless, though I may not have had the opportunity to learn for longer durations from my gurus, I did get an opportunity to learn the finer points of music from each one of them—during childhood in Pune from Vijay Karandikar, then from Sureshbabu Mane and then Hirabai Barodekar. In the 1960s, when I was working with AIR, Nagpur, I came in contact with Shrikant Bakre, a senior student of Ustad Amir Khan. Our diverse discussions exposed me to Khan Sahib's style. This brought major changes in my musical thinking also. I am equally indebted to Noorjehan, Roshanara Begum and more particularly to Bade Ghulam Ali Khan Sahib for my *thumri*. Although I have not learnt from Khan Sahib directly, my *thumri* has its roots in his style. And this is the impact of listening to good musicians.

Interviewer:

Since nobody from your family was in music, how did you think of becoming a musician, especially after being a science and law graduate?

Prabha Atre:

Neither my parents nor I had planned things this way. I think I was destined to be a musician. Everything that happened took me to music. People started liking my music and they also offered remuneration for it. I think temperamentally I was most suited to music. Instead of dissecting frogs or defending criminals, I thought singing was much better. After my college education, I joined All India Radio in 1960. I resigned from there in 1970 and took to singing as a full-time career. However, my interest in the academics of music led me again to join the SNDT Women's University in Mumbai in 1979. I worked there as professor and Head of the Post-Graduate Department of Music and Research till 1992. I believe that a good performer needs to study and experience music from different angles.

Interviewer:

When and where was your first public performance? Were you nervous?

Prabha Atre:

My first public performance was in Pune. In Maharashtra, we have a tradition of celebrating Ganesh festival for ten days. It was there that I first sang ... around 1945. Yes, I was nervous in the beginning. But when I saw the audience appreciating ... openly saying '*Wah, Wah*,' I gained confidence.

Interviewer:

One finds a lot of influence of Carnatic music in your music. Have you had any formal training in Carnatic music? What made you give full-fledged concerts on Carnatic ragas in Hindustani style?

Prabha Atre:

I was exposed to Carnatic music when I was working with the All India Radio, Mumbai. I was very much impressed by their *gamakas* and *sargam* rendition. I wish I had some formal training in Carnatic music. It would have made my understanding of it easier.

Hindustani and Carnatic music are the two main styles of Indian classical music. The concepts of raga and *taal* are the same in both the styles; the two systems differ in their approach to these concepts. Their difference lies mainly in the ornamentation—the *gamaka*s—oscillating the notes in a peculiar way and also in the treatment, arrangement and presentation of the musical material (*sahitya*, *alaap*, *taan*, *sargam*). Naturally the resulting structures are different. The languages used in the two systems are also different. The listeners of Hindustani music find it difficult to appreciate Carnatic music because of the ample use of *gamaka*s (note oscillations) with which they are not familiar. The steady notes in Hindustani music stand out against *gamakas* in Carnatic music. The problem of conditioning of the mind to a particular system is seen in the listeners of both the systems. My attempt is to introduce these stylistic nuances of Carnatic music through specially-composed *bandishes* in *khayal*, *tarana* and also in *dadra* and bhajan. Care has also been taken to select ragas from Carnatic music which have no parallel scales in Hindustani music: for example Hindustani Malkauns resembles Carnatic Hindolam, but Carnatic Kirwani has no parallel in Hindustani music. My attempt is not a transposition in totality of Carnatic ragas and Carnatic style to Hindustani music. It is an attempt to introduce Carnatic nuances into Hindustani style. And I am very happy to see that audiences of both Carnatic and Hindustani music appreciate my effort.

Interviewer:

What is the significance of the *gharana* system now when there is so much of exposure?

Prabha Atre:

See ... what is important is that one should have a good base in music. Once the student imbibes significant features of one style, he automatically gets a good foundation for further development and creativity. Only then is it appropriate for him to get exposed to other styles. But the basic foundation must always be prepared by learning under one teacher. This is where I believe is the significance of the *gharana* system.

Interviewer:

Do you feel that adhering to a *gharana* restricts an artiste's creativity?

Prabha Atre:

I don't think a *gharana* necessarily cramps an artiste's style; but at the same time one shouldn't shut oneself from other *gharana*s. There is a lot to learn from exposure to other styles as well. When I was young, the main source for listening to music was the All India Radio. Very few gramophone recordings were available and there used to be fewer live concerts. There was very little exposure to music of other artistes. The only source was the guru and most gurus did not allow their disciples to listen to other musicians. There was no choice, except adhering to the system. Today artistes have more exposure, more freedom. My guru however was very generous and broadminded. He allowed me to imbibe from other styles. I have learnt many things by listening to great artistes, as I said earlier.

Interviewer:

What are the distinct musical qualities of the Kirana *gharana*?

Prabha Atre:

The style is characterised by a note-by-note unfolding of the raga structure, thereby exploring minute details of the structure. The notes have peaceful movements in the *taal* structure. Each note is dipped in emotion and as such, involves even a common listener in music-making. The essence is serenity with sweetness. And the sweetness of tone creates a general soothing effect on the mind. The voice straightaway touches the heart. One need not know *shastra* to enjoy Kirana *gharana*'s music. In a way, the style of Kirana *gharana* is withdrawn and introverted. There is nothing showy or sensational.

Interviewer:

How would you describe your music?

Prabha Atre:

The base of my style is very much Kirana, but it has a modern context. My thinking has been enriched by practically every kind of music—Indian to non-Indian, from all over the world. Secondly, because of my strong academic background, training and experience, I do not accept anything blindly in the name of tradition. Objectivity, analytical ability, selectivity and modernity are some of the things that one can notice in my music. I look for tonal beauty and my notes are invariably charged with emotion. I can also say that I try to bring in variation in tonal texture in addition to variation in volume to project emotional content; there is ample use of *kan swaras* and smooth glides in the formation of phrases. In addition to all this, I like to explore new, uncommon, simple, but aesthetically beautiful phrases, in the context of the raga structure and specific forms such as *khayal*, *thumri*.

Interviewer:

So one can say that your interpretation of the raga is on the basis of tradition, logic and novelty and there is a proper balance between tradition and modernity?

Prabha Atre:

Yes, and also that I maintain design and clarity at any speed in *taans* and that I've a special love for *sargam* phrases and my singing has strong affinity towards Carnatic music—*ragas*, *gamakas* and *sargam*. I try and see that every phrase is rich aesthetically and emotionally and that complementary literary themes are used in *bada* and *chota khayal* in the same raga to maintain the mood of the raga.

Interviewer:

Which is your favourite raga?

Prabha Atre:

If I am practising a raga I sing it in all the concerts for several months, after which I don't sing it for a long time. So, that becomes my favourite raga for that period. But yes, I always enjoy singing Yaman. Not only because it is beautiful in itself but also because I have very fond memories of myself as a young student of music. This was the first raga I learnt from my guru Sureshbabu Mane.

Interviewer:

Classical music is traditional. Can it be contemporised?

Prabha Atre:

You see, it depends on each individual singer. The singer has to update himself continuously and relate his singing to the contemporary scene. Although Indian music encourages blind imitation of tradition, it also expects one to go beyond this stage and put one's stamp as a creative artiste different from one's teacher and/or contemporaries. Sufficient insight and maturity are necessary for this.

Interviewer:

How did your experience at All India Radio help you as a vocalist? Do you miss leaving it?

Prabha Atre:

I loved my job at the AIR. It got me involved with different types of music—from folk, film, light to Carnatic music. It also gave me considerable exposure to Western music. Secondly, as radio is purely a microphone media, I realised the importance of voice culture and acoustics in tonal quality. Thirdly, it gave me an opportunity to conceive and produce new programmes, opportunity to learn the techniques of recording and editing. The required technical equipment and other facilities were easily available and I could experiment without any difficulty. I do miss working on these areas, but then, one looks for variety in life and betterment of oneself. After working for ten years, I opted for being an independent singer.

Interviewer:

You are a professional singer, what made you take up academic work?

Prabha Atre:

See, academic study stimulates thinking. Thinking about different aspects of music stimulates creativity in performance. Blindly following tradition leads to stagnation. Research helps me to look at music with open eyes. It makes me examine critically and objectively various things that are offered in the name of tradition and also helps me to seek in terms of our own times, the new meaning appropriate to what has come from tradition. An academic background also helps in giving a broader perspective of the subject. In case of music, it relates to psychology, sociology, philosophy, physiology, physics, acoustics, aesthetics, poetry, etc. Thus, music needs to be studied and understood from different angles. Only then can one have a complete experience of music. PhD has helped me to reduce the gap between a performer and a theoretician.

Interviewer:

Why did you choose *Sargam* for your doctoral thesis?

Prabha Atre:

The credit goes to you all, our music critics (*laughs*). Most of the critics, especially in Maharashtra state, objected to the use of *sargam* in vocal music for reasons best known to them. This made me think about the different aspects of *sargam*—its origin, its development, its utility in training, its potential in bringing variety in musical material and enriching overall expression of stage performance, its various styles of rendering, its ability to get adapted to various genres including film music, fusion, and the like.

Interviewer:

What do you think of critics and criticism?

Prabha Atre:

Critics play an important role in shaping public opinion about an artiste and his art. It is a sad situation that with just a working knowledge of music and good writing skills, anybody can become a music critic today. We don't realise that music criticism is a serious discipline and needs a special training. Ideally, only serious, academically oriented candidates should be employed by the media. Unfortunately, the importance of serious criticism is realised by few. Authority, sincerity, sense of responsibility, awareness of changing times, practical experience, honesty and objectivity are some of the things one looks for in criticism.

Interviewer:

Performers generally do not like to teach. But you took up a job at the SNDT University. Why? What changes did you bring about when you became Head of the Music Department at SNDT?

Prabha Atre:

I joined SNDT University because of my strong interest in the academic side of music. Also, I honestly feel that teaching makes performance a conscious activity. It makes me think about the practical as well as theoretical aspects of music. One has to be clear in one's mind about the why and why not in music, in order to be able to satisfy probing questions of the modern generation. The content of what is taught and performed and its relevance to tradition on the one hand and the changing times on the other has to be constantly reviewed. In a way, a performer is also a teacher. He or she teaches the masses how to listen and what to listen. And cultivates their taste indirectly. Performing and teaching are complementary.

The syllabus I prepared was comprehensive. It dealt with almost everything in Indian music as well as topics related to Indian music at exposure level. In addition to classical, light-classical and light music, it included folk music, film music, Maharashtra's theatre music, Carnatic music, Western music, World music and other topics related to music like psychology, sociology, philosophy, religion, physiology, physics, acoustics, aesthetics, poetry, cultural history, and so on. Since there was no written material available on the respective topics, I had to meet and discuss with experts in the field, read relevant books and prepare notes for the students. I was also able to persuade some faculty members to write books on subjects like psychology of music, sociology of music, etc. By reading theory one cannot understand the nuances or learn to sing Carnatic music. So I managed to get Carnatic musicians who taught *kriti*, *tillana* and *javali* compositions to our students. But to prepare material on world music or ethnomusicology was the most difficult task. The Indo-American Fellowship programme helped me to undertake courses in Ethnomusicology at the University of California, Los Angeles, US. I had collected some recorded music and books in consultation with the faculty there. All this came in very useful. Probably SNDT University was the first to offer a course in ethnomusicology.

Interviewer:

Should there be standardisation in the content-structure and teaching methods of Hindustani music as it is in Carnatic music?

Prabha Atre:

Personally I feel that it should be standardised. There should be formal structure for any new student aspiring to learn music as it is in Carnatic music. The understanding of note positions, their combinations and *laya* (tempo) are the basic things a student has to learn in the beginning before he actually starts working on raga and *taal*. Once he is equipped with this material it should be left to the guru and the potential of the student. At present, I am working on the standardisation of the material to be taught to a beginner which will help him or her understand *sur* and *laya* and also improve his or her voice range, thinking and skills.

Interviewer:

Has the guru-*shishya parampara* changed? Are you happy with your students?

Prabha Atre:

See, the old guru-*shishya* relationship does not hold good any more. Today, the guru is not the only source of knowledge as he or she was some years ago. The advanced technology has converted music into a saleable commodity. One can see markets flooded with a large variety of music—audio/video cassettes/CDs. Then, there are scholarly books on the theoretical aspects of music. For practical training there are music classes and academic institutions offering courses and degrees in music. By using these aids, a talented student can achieve a certain level without going to a guru. There was a time when a student had to go in search of a good guru. But now we, gurus, have to go in search of a good and faithful student (*laughs*). Now the main objective of the learner is to gain quick returns, fame and money by performing on radio, TV channels, bringing out recordings, giving stage performances, etc. I know people who take names of famous gurus under whom they have not even learnt—learning one or two compositions is not learning in the real sense—just to promote themselves. They do not mention the real guru's name, even if that guru has slogged for years to mould the student. It is quite hurtful. If a student cannot bring any credit to the guru, the least he/she can do is not to hurt the real guru. On the other hand there are teachers also who exploit students. I am aware of that also. I think there should be honesty and integrity on both sides.

Interviewer:

Why is classical music not popular?

Prabha Atre:

We must realise that classical music is an abstract art and is not the music of masses. It is the product of a more deliberate aesthetic shaping process. A lot of thinking and experimentation has gone behind its formation. To expect classical music to become as popular as film music would be wrong. Also, to be able to appreciate classical music, one must understand the musical meaning of music—the meaning of pure sound and rhythm patterns. To do this, one needs background, study and contemplation. The common man has no patience for this. He naturally turns to light music, which is word oriented, rhythm dominated and less of pure musical improvisations. This music is simple, full of emotions, has catchy beats and is easy to identify. Besides, classical musicians tend to give more stress on the theoretical aspects, on the technique, thereby making music dry and lifeless. They forget that theory is to guide the progression; and technique is only the starting point. Classical music has to identify itself with life, with nature, with the known and the 'unknown.'

Interviewer:

What is the future of classical music?

Prabha Atre:

I have no doubt that classical music will always be there in some form. It represents purity, beauty, divinity and unity. It has that abstract quality which makes it comprehensive, covering both the known and the 'unknown.' Today's most popular form—*khayal*, representing classical vocal music has been changing and adapting itself to meet new situations, to cater to new demands. The new wave of 'free expression' that has entered every field has affected *khayal* also but its fight to survive as a separate aesthetic form is really commendable. Let us wait and see what we get after *khayal*.

Interviewer:

Probably, you were the first female Hindustani classical vocalist who toured extensively in 1971 to give full-length concerts in the West. What made you go abroad?

Prabha Atre:

Pandit Ravi Shankar did commendable work in introducing Hindustani classical music to foreigners. But what they heard was mainly instrumental music. A full concert of vocal music was a novelty to non-Indian audiences then. My attempt was to expose them to the beauty of vocal music, which is the 'soul' of Indian music.

Interviewer:

Which music has influenced your singing? You sing *khayal*, *tappa*, *thumri*, *tarana*, *bhajan*—what do you like most?

Prabha Atre:

Music from all regions. Carnatic music enchants me with its peculiar *gamakas*. Arabic music attracts me with its tonal quality, emotionally charged notes and the complicated twists. Western music provokes me to think in new directions and film music has made me conscious of tonal quality of voice, its texture, clarity of words, their musical pronunciation and effective emotional expression.

I also sing *ghazals* but in private *baithaks* (*laughs*). In 2008, during my 75th birth year, I have released a CD of live recordings of my Marathi *ghazals* wherein a few are also penned by me. It's nice to be able to sing different forms. Each has its beauty, demand, audience. You should know well how to keep them separate musically. Otherwise your *khayal* can become *thum-khayal* a new genre having lot of *thumri* expressions. We already have *tapp-khayal* where a *khayal* rendition is influenced by *tappa*.

Interviewer:

There are very few women music composers in classical and light music. When did you start composing?

Prabha Atre:

It was my need after my guru Sureshbabu Mane passed away. I could not go to others as I was very much attached to Baburao. I could not put anybody in his place. It was a lonely musical journey of search. I wanted to sing ragas I had not learnt. Where to get *bandishes*? Who would have agreed to teach me without making me his *shishya*? So while working in AIR I discovered my ability to compose. Although I composed out of necessity in the beginning, I soon got interested, almost obsessed with composition work. It was a new challenge to my creativity. It is really a great advantage to be able to compose. I think it is necessary to have a composition, which matches with and suits your style and temperament. It is wrong to mutilate somebody else's composition to suit your requirements. Today, I am happy that my very first composition in raga Maru Bihag '*Jaagoon main saari raina* ...' has been immensely popular. Even after thirty-five years this record is selling very well. Almost every music loving family has this recording. This Maru Bihag was different from the established Maru Bihag having two *madhyam*s. My rendition has only *teevra madhyam.* After the Maru Bihag composition, I started singing only my compositions—whether *khayal*, *tarana*, *thumri*, *dadra*, *bhajan* or *ghazals*.

Interviewer:

You also gave the lyrics and wrote books. How and when did you think of writing books?

Prabha Atre:

Yes. See unlike in light music, where one person writes poetry and another composes, in classical music the poet and composer generally happen to be one. I have not learnt Hindi language as such. But I have a flair for it. Maybe this is because music comes first in classical music. I like words which are musical, simple. My attempt is that the meaning of the words should reach the audience without any difficulty.

As for books, there was an increasing demand from music lovers and students to publish my compositions. That made me work on *Swaraanginee* which was first published in 1994. The second edition, in 2006, comprises 200 of my compositions covering *khayal*, *tarana*, *thumri*, *dadra* and *bhajans*.

The second book of compositions *Swaranjanee* published in 2006 has 225 compositions. Both the books are accompanied by CDs in addition to notations so that it becomes easy to learn the compositions. And soon I'll take out the English version of both my books with song-text meaning so that it can reach the non-Hindi music community.

Interviewer:

Who has been your inspiration for writing poetry?

Prabha Atre:

My mother has written poetry for small children. Maybe I have inherited that talent. But I am not a poetess. Poetry is just an extension of my musical expression. *Antahswar*, a book of poems in Marathi was published in 1997. Most of the poems express my musical experiences. It was translated into English by Prof. Susheela Ambike and was published in 2007.

Interviewer:

What do you think of music as a career for women?

Prabha Atre:

The status of women has improved considerably. With the result that our society's attitude towards women in performing arts has also changed. However, there are difficulties of the profession itself. The commercial element which has entered the music world today has also created new problems. Public relations and publicity have become the most important part of the profession. A woman musician surely has problems unless her family members—father, brother, husband, son, friends—help her in PR work or she takes the help of some agency. Secondly, there is no security. One has to be patient, hardworking and be prepared for sacrifice. And thirdly, since the family unit is the primary cell of Indian society and the role of women is still that of a wife and a mother, her career would have to be fitted in along with the duties of home, which calls for quite a bit of compromise. She can only take up this profession and pursue it, if her family supports it.

Interviewer:

How difficult was it for you to pursue this career?

Prabha Atre:

Very difficult. First of all, I do not belong to a musical family. Then, my guru Sureshbabu Mane died early. Hirabaiji also retired from the performing field early for health reasons and most important of all, I had no godfather. Of course, my listeners have always been with me. The words and letters of praise of my listeners are my greatest treasure. I feel encouraged when I see my listeners taking notice of my work in the field. I am very happy with my audience. They have made me 'Prabha Atre, the artiste.'

Interviewer:

You didn't marry. Why?

Prabha Atre:

Just like that, *koi mila nahin na* ... never met anybody ... (*laughs*).

Interviewer:

What has been the contribution of Prabha Atre in the field of Indian classical music?

Prabha Atre:

Many generations of great musicians in the past have poured in their knowledge and experience in the vast ocean of music. My contribution is not even a drop. On the contrary, it is music which has contributed a lot in shaping my life. I am grateful to God for this precious gift. Music has taught me to look for purity, beauty, divinity and unity in whatever I do. It is the best medium to experience, express and share these fine qualities of life and nature around. I do not know about my contribution, but I have been doing various things: preservation and promotion of Hindustani classical music by carrying forward the Kirana tradition, propagation of Hindustani classical music by teaching students all over the world, conducting workshops and giving lec-dems, writing books on the contemporary performances, composing music and the standardisation of teaching material for a beginner in Hindustani music. I have also established the 'Dr Prabha Atre Foundation' to cater to the multifarious activities relating to music in particular and the performing arts in general and am starting 'Swaramayee Gurukul' to bridge the two systems of teaching—traditional guru-*shishya parampara* and institutional—for students aspiring to take up music as a profession. I think all this is just a drop in the ocean.

Interviewer:

But you also organise music festivals like *Sureshbabu-Hirabai Smriti Sangeet Samaroh* and *Gaanprabha* at Mumbai, and monthly *baithak*s at Swaramayee Gurukul, Pune. All this is certainly not a drop in the vast ocean of music.

Prabha Atre:

Hmmm ... (*laughs*)

Interviewer:

What do you consider your most significant achievement?

Prabha Atre:

I sing like Prabha Atre and nobody else. The joy of making good music and passing on the joy to my listeners is what I feel very good about. This identity in the music world, I think, is a significant achievement.

Interviewer:

You are called an avant-garde artiste. Why?

Prabha Atre:

Maybe because my approach is different, different in terms of thinking about musical content and presentation; research work on *Sargam* and open advocacy in its favour by incorporating it in actual presentations since the sixties; use of just the *sthaayi* in the presentation of the *vilambit khayal* and use of complementary themes in the compositions of *vilambit* and *drut khayal*, interpretation of ragas rules on the basis of logic and novelty without deviating from tradition and perhaps because of experiments towards exposing the Hindustani music audience to the stylistic nuances of Carnatic music—helping in further enrichment of Hindustani music.

Interviewer:

In a *khayal* performance what do you achieve by dropping *antaraa* of *vilambit bandish* and reducing it to only a *sthaayi* of one *taal* cycle?

Prabha Atre:

Why not if the purpose of *antaraa* is served by *sthaayi*? Even in arts, survival is through necessity. For novelty's sake, one can also add *sanchari*, *aabhog* or convert it into *ashtapadi*. Secondly, the purpose of *khayal* genre is to project a raga's beauty and convey its musical meaning. The words of the *bandish* colour the notes with their meaning and also obstruct the flow of the phrase. Thus, smaller the *bandish*, fewer the words, and freer the notes from the words and their meaning. From *ashtapadi* to *dhrupad-dhamaar* to *khayal* is a continuous reduction in the length of the *bandish*—8 to 4 to 2 to 1.

Interviewer:

Do you believe in raga-*rasa* and raga-time theories?

Prabha Atre:

I am not a strict follower of these theories. I find them more of a conditioning of the mind. They have been deeply embedded in our psyche due to age-old practice. We have to understand that they have lost their relevance with the passage of time. Today we are away from nature, living in closed walls. Our lifestyle has also changed considerably. How do you then relate raga and time? Secondly, raga is an abstract concept. This abstract is transformed into concrete by providing visuals, associations, meaningful words, etc. The *rasa* experience therefore is not the same for all. It is very much subjective and varies with each performer and listener. Actually it is a fact, that a raga can be performed effectively without knowing its time and so called *rasa*. Raga character is intrinsically related to its musical material and its treatment. Its characteristic phrases and their flow give it its musical identity.

Interviewer:

Have you composed new ragas?

Prabha Atre:

The ragas that I've composed are Apoorva-kalyan, Darbari-kauns, Patdeep-malhar, Shivkali, etc., and also new compositions in traditional ragas because I wanted to communicate something different.

Interviewer:

Your rendering of a few ragas like Maru Bihag, Shyamkalyan, Jogkauns, etc., differs from that of your peers and contemporaries. Can you please share your thought about it?

Prabha Atre:

Raga is an abstract concept in Indian music. It comes into being in a seed form in the creator's mind and keeps growing like a mighty tree, maturing through contemplation, deep reflection and its actual presentation by its creator. It is because of this limitless potential of a raga that every time it comes to life through performance it appears in a new form. The freedom an artist gets in interpreting the raga rules has further made it possible to bring variety in a raga's structural details. But while deviating from the established norms, there has to be pre-thought, good reasoning and logic. Not only that, one has to be consistent while detailing the raga structure.

Yes, some of the ragas that I sing sound different. It is because the way I approach its structure, the way I interpret its rules. But I am aware of what I am doing. It is not taking liberty or acting according to whim. It is a conscious decision, act. For instance, in Maru Bihag, I avoid using *shuddha madhyam* because Maru Bihag can do without *shuddha madhyam* and can still maintain its characteristic features. Similarly, in Raga Shyam-kalyan, I emphasise the *Kalyan ang* without breaking any raga rules. In Jogkauns, I use *komal nishad* like in Raga Jog. The main point is how one presents one's thoughts in actual performance with consistency.

Ragas are also governed by science—*shastra*. I am happy that the 'so called' deviations have been accepted even by the knowledgeable and they have come to stay.

Interviewer:

What is your greatest fear?

Prabha Atre:

Ageing (*says with a smile*). With ageing if I am unable to sing—this frightens me the most. I do not know if I will be able to cope up with such a situation. I only pray to God that he takes me away before something like this would happen.

Interviewer:

Are you religious?

Prabha Atre:

Yes, I believe in God He has given me a precious gift—music. Music is my religion. I worship music.

VOCAL

The Eternal Romantic

VIDUSHI SHANTI HIRANAND

(29 October, 1933–)

She is a loner. She loves being amidst nature. And for hours she can stay alone, looking at the sky.

Maybe these are the qualities that impressed Begum Akhtar and she agreed to have Shanti Hiranand as her disciple in 1957. She remained Begum Akhtar's disciple till 30 October 1974, the day Begum Akhtar passed away.

The veteran vocalist is articulate, frank; and deep in her heart she has accepted the fact that her time has passed. 'But this is how I am; I cannot push myself. I am a traditionalist. I cannot remix songs,' she says, explaining the reason why her music has not been widely available in the market.

Belonging to a rich business family, Shanti Hiranand received all the support from her parents to pursue her passion. They trusted Begum Akhtar and were confident that their daughter was in safe hands. 'And Ammi (Begum Akhtar) never let me do things which she thought my parents would not like.'

With her remarkable memory, Shanti ji could remember days and dates while journeying to and fro in narrating the events of her long association with Ammi.

Being a poetess, Shantiji recited a few lines from her poem—'*yeh thandi hawaein, yeh badal ka jhukna, yeh pedo ke patto se paani tapakna, mere dil ko bhaya hai sawan ka aana ...*'

And if one has to see the respect, adulation, and grief at the loss of one's guru, then one really has to meet Shanti Hiranand. Often the conversation veered towards the one and only legend who rose far above the social marginalisation of the '*baiji*' tag and earned respect and love from all quarters and classes of society. It was one interview which couldn't have happened without discussing Begum Akhtar and her music.

(25 September, 2007)

Interviewer:

You belong to a business family but you took up music. How did you find your passion in music?

Shanti Hiranand:

Good question because even I wonder sometimes how is it that God has placed me in this position when I was not supposed to be there. Yes, my father was in business, belonging to a very rich family. He had settled in Lucknow and I was the third daughter. I don't know, but from childhood I was interested in singing. I just used to sing and whenever I used to go to the shops to buy something, the shopkeepers would always say, 'First sing only then will we give you.'

Interviewer:

You must have been listening to music on the radio?

Shanti Hiranand:

No, no. At that time I didn't even know what singing is. I would just go and sit in functions, marriage ceremonies and all that, wherever singing was happening. And spontaneously I used sing with them. At that time I was just six or seven years old. Even at school I used to sing.

Interviewer:

You were not listening to the radio, you had no tutor, then how did you learn music?

Shanti Hiranand:

It so happened that our family friend, who was a doctor, was deeply interested in music. He heard me singing. So he told my father, 'Hirabhai, this girl has a good voice. Train her.' Now my father didn't know anything about music. He just put me in Music College in Lucknow, where I started going after my classes.

Interviewer:

That means that until you joined music college you did not get any proper training under any guru?

Shanti Hiranand:

That's right. I didn't even know the concept of guru or classical music. There was just something in me, inside, a natural liking for music. I was in the fourth or fifth standard. In the evenings I started going to Music College. I learnt in this college for one or one and a half years. In the meanwhile my father had to go to Lahore on some business trip. And being the youngest daughter, I also went along with him. Now what happened was that in Lahore there was a blind music teacher, Indira Kohli, living near our house. I started going to her to learn music and also for programmes. For five years she taught me. And she taught me well. She introduced me to Lahore Radio. At that time auditions were not done. The programme in-charge heard me and gave me a chance to broadcast. Now that I got an opportunity to broadcast, listening to my own voice on the radio set got me more interested in music. At that time I used to sing *bhajan*s, *geet*s and *ghazal*s. I knew Urdu as during that time it was taught in schools. And then came 1947 and the Partition. During Partition we came back to Lucknow. It was my High School year also. But now I seriously wanted to learn music. So, for the first time I became a disciple of Ustad Aijaz Hussain Khan Sahib of Rampur. Though he was quite old, he used to come to our place to teach me.

Interviewer:

Didn't your family object to it? Certainly during those times girls from good families did not learn music.

Shanti Hiranand:

Quite true. Girls were forbidden to learn music. But luckily in my family there was a lot of emphasis on education. Hence, we were very broadminded, almost Westernised. So I was never disallowed from pursuing music. My routine used to be to go to college in the mornings and in the evenings learn music from Ustadji. Along with this I started giving programmes on All India Radio, Lucknow. I used to sing whatever I was told or given to sing. At that time I did not have much knowledge or understanding. But as I had a good voice I was included in a large number of shows, be it drama or chorus. With praise from all quarters my interest in music deepened.

Interviewer:

How did you meet Begum Akhtar sahiba and how did you become her disciple?

Shanti Hiranand:

As I said I used to go to Lucknow Radio for broadcast. I am talking about 1947 to 1952. She used to come there in her car. At that time it was a small station, unlike nowadays. She used to get down from the car in the porch. And at times I used to see her getting down from the car and admire her. She was always dressed in *garara* with a long plait dangling behind and a starched *dupatta* draped across her shoulders. She used to look so pretty. So one day I asked the people at the station who is she? That's how I came to know her. In fact just then I came to know her name, Akhtaribai a.k.a. Begum Akhtar. That's all I knew. Then I topped in M.A. I have done my M.A in Indian Philosophy. My guide asked me to take up research and at the same time the Programme Executive at AIR, G.C. Awasthi, told me that since I've been singing for so long I should become a disciple of 'some good Ustad.' I told him that I did not know anybody. He told me about Begum Akhtar and in the same breath said that nowadays she does not teach anybody. But he promised to talk to her. Perhaps he called her up and convinced her to meet me just once. So I went to her house. After a while she came out, met me and it was love at first sight.

Interviewer:

Why was she not teaching?

Shanti Hiranand:

Actually she had got married to Barrister Ishtiaq Ahmed Abbasi in 1943-44 on the condition that she will leave her music. And she left music. But in 1950 her mother died. She was very close to her mother and Ammi suffered a nervous breakdown. So the doctors advised Abbasi Sahib that she must have an outlet. Hence she started giving shows on the radio. It was at this time that I approached her, you can say it was my luck. So I met her, she took me inside and told me to sing something. I sang a *bhajan*. She listened to it and said, 'You sing well enough; what would I teach you? Anyway, come tomorrow.' Next day I reached her house. This continued for two to three days. After that she began teaching me. It was as if she just wanted to let flow her pent-up emotions. Mr Abbasi would go to office at 10:00 am and after that just tea and singing–*palta* after *palta*. I used to be with her, the whole day, learning; lunch used to be at 4:00 or 5:00 pm. But there were also days when there was no singing at all. This is how I learnt from her.

Interviewer:

You also started living with her. Isn't it?

Shanti Hiranand:

Yes, yes. She was a very loving person. If she started liking somebody then she would not let that person go away. Both she and Abbasi Sahib had grown very fond of my parents also. She used to address my mother as *bhabhi*. One day she told my mother, 'I am keeping Shanto with me now.' My mother said, 'Sure. Please do so.' So I started staying with her and I stayed with her for days and days, used to travel with her; there was no difference between her and my parents; not even once did I think that she is a Muslim and I am a Hindu. Nothing. She was a very loving person. I used to feel that I cannot live without her; I couldn't see beyond her.

Interviewer:

How did you adjust to the different lifestyle?

Shanti Hiranand:

It so happens that by nature I am a very simple, quiet person. That's why I took up Philosophy as my subject. And I used to write a lot. In my younger days I had written so many letters to God ...

Interviewer:

Which, of course you never posted ...

Shanti Hiranand:

(*Laughs aloud*) ... I wrote poems also ... Now I've started writing songs. So I was that kind. I was always different from my family. They were non-vegetarians and I was a vegetarian, they would go out for movies and I would sit at home. So I never had any problem adjusting. Above all my parents were very supportive, understanding and encouraging. I never had any problems while I was with her. They trusted her, she kept their trust and treated me like her own daughter. But yes, her living style was different. She had many guests at her home, all staying together in the living room only. While at our place everything was spick and span. Waiters were there to serve food, the table was laid properly and so on. All these differences were there but I didn't feel it. There was so much of love that everything else was overshadowed into oblivion.

Interviewer:

When you accompanied her on stage how did you feel?

Shanti Hiranand:

She never sang prepared music. It wasn't that pieces were decided beforehand or practised. No, never. She used to sing whatever she felt like singing at that moment.

Interviewer:

So it was never ever discussed before?

Shanti Hiranand:

No, never. She used to carry one copy, would turn the pages and then ask me, '*Beta,* should I sing this *ghazal*?' Now what would I say? And this used to happen at times on stage or just before going on stage. I used to feel happy and thank God that I know the piece in a particular raga, which she had taught earlier. But on stage, she used to begin it in some other raga. She was amazing. There was no concept of planning in her life, whether it was her concert, her marriage, her programmes or her travel. Never planned anything. For days she would go away from home. Or for days she would stay at home and not meet anybody. Completely secluded.

Interviewer:

How did she live such a compartmentalised life?

Shanti Hiranand:

Now when I reflect and think back about it, I think she was a split personality. There was one aspect that was completely devoted to home, children, family, while the other facet of her personality was completely free-spirited. Love was her staple food for inspiration. The second facet believed in total freedom. When she used to get tired of that freedom and free lifestyle, she would return to her comfort zone, her nest.

Interviewer:

But in all this, seeing the second facet of her personality, how did her husband, Abbasi Sahib feel?

Shanti Hiranand:

What happened was that right at the beginning of her married life, that is after marriage, she left singing altogether. But when she bounced back after a gap of a few years, people just showered love and affection on her. So Abbasi Sahib understood her very well. He first gave her permission to sing on the radio but gradually he realised that she is such a strong personality that he cannot hold her back. He knew that she would do as she wishes. She on the other hand had so much regard for him that she would always tell him, 'You are the one who brought me here, on this platform, otherwise where was I?' In domestic life she would always walk behind him, never ahead. But in her musical life, she was a free bird, a liberal spirit. This was her escape route. Because she could never lead a well-disciplined, planned life. And Abbasi Sahib knew all this.

Interviewer:

How many hours of *riyaaz* did you do with her?

Shanti Hiranand:

First she taught me *paltas*. She used to play the harmonium and I would be on the tanpura. I used to practise for hours and hours. Along with the *paltas* one day she would teach me a *thumri*, the next day a *ghazal*. I could not understand. I could just manage to sing along with her. If one day she sang a *ghazal* in Bhairavi the next time it would be sung in Darbari. So I really had to keep my mind and senses alert and keen so that I could follow her correctly. If I would commit a mistake she would stare at me but if I did well, she would kiss my forehead, right there on the stage; but she never uttered any words of praise. She would always say, '*Bitiya*, there's still scope for improvement.' My *gandabandhan* also she did after many years because to her I was still Hiranand's daughter. In actual sense that guru-*shishya* relationship happened much later. So with her it was like either she used to teach me for hours and hours and sometimes for eight to ten days she wouldn't teach me anything. So whatever she taught me, actually it went to the reserve section of my mind. It was only after her death that I realised that the life-size tree has fallen and that I had no shade. I was so dependent on her. It was only after her death that I started asserting myself.

Interviewer:

So as long as Begum sahiba was alive you didn't give solo concerts?

Shanti Hiranand:

I did. I gave solo concerts in Hyderabad, Mumbai and Amritsar but after seeking her permission. I used to give solos as well as accompany her. But as it happens. when the guru is there the confidence level is less, unlike what is happening nowadays. Now the children are so confident that they surpass their gurus also and go wherever they want to, without seeking the guru's permission. We could not even think about it.

Interviewer:

How many disciples do you have?

Shanti Hiranand:

I have around sixteen or seventeen disciples but now the thing is that I am reliving whatever she had taught me. And it is now that I understand her music, after so many years. Now I understand the meaning of her stresses on words and why, the way she sang, the way she brought *bhaav* into that word, etc. Now I understand the importance of it. At that time I didn't understand, just sang as she was singing or as she told me to sing. And that's how I teach my students. I tell them that the *sargam* of a particular word is this but the way it should be sung is like this because only then it will bring out all the shades of the underlying emotions.

Interviewer:

Why is it that your music is not readily available in the market?

Shanti Hiranand:

There's a reason for it. When I got married, my husband was a scientist. He lived in America for many years.

Interviewer:

You also went to America?

Shanti Hiranand:

No, I didn't. But there were a lot of restrictions. I was told who to meet and who not to meet. Well, now I think I am a person who is very easily taken in by other personalities. He was a very strong personality. But I didn't leave my music. I gave programmes on the radio but didn't do networking, the way other people do. So by the time I got fame as a singer, I was in an era where there were so many younger people already on the scene. My time had passed. and even now I go by the traditional old style. My PR is very poor. For example, many people tell me why don't you remix the *thumris*. But I don't like compromising. They tell me if I remix it, it will give me instant fame. But I never want to achieve that kind of a fame. I have never been greedy for fame. Whatever I've achieved is the result of my hard labour and my faith in my guru. In the music world I am well-known, but I am not a popular artiste. So that's the reason why very few of my albums have been released. I cannot go and ask people. That's not my nature. It's not that I don't know people. I know, but I am hesitant. I am like that. Earlier whosoever sang well was noticed but now there's so much competition, media exposure, and the like that one really has to do aggressive marketing. It is no longer a certainty that if you're a good singer, you will be noticed. Times have changed. But I love music. I always thought that till there is *ras* in my *sur*, it is all right for me and that I should serve the art. I am an artiste who does not believe in instant coffee type creativity for I am not an artisan. For me music is that which ignites emotions, touches others' heart and satisfies my own self. That is music for me. I cannot say how many people believe in this now. But I refuse to compromise. Whatever traditional music I have with me, I believe in that only and it gives me happiness.

Interviewer:

Have you ever sung for films?

Shanti Hiranand:

Yes, I have. But I do not have the voice required for film songs. The pitch of my voice is not suitable for film songs but I can sing certain *qawwali*-like songs. Earlier, during my times, I mean when I was young, the texture of the voice required for film songs was different. Now the trend is for natural voices but as I said, I've passed the age. I sang in C. Ramachandra's film *Naushervan-e-dil* and the other film is *Siddhartha*, a foreign film. I also acted in *Siddhartha.* Then I sang in *Dance of the Wind* as well. I was also approached by Muzzafar Ali. He was planning to make a film on Begum Akhtar. But somehow I didn't want to come out with what all Ammi had told me about her life. Her life was very colourful, fascinating. I mean I didn't want to bring out her private life in the open. So the discussion ended there only.

Interviewer:

But in your book on her, you have been quite open about her life.

Shanti Hiranand:

Only a little bit. But that's not scandalous. She was a person who would be infatuated by someone, but only for a short time; this would give her the needed inspiration and then it would fade out. (*Laughs*)

Interviewer:

I think this is what is called artistic freedom.

Shanti Hiranand:

Perhaps. But the other partner suffers. Abbasi Sahib knew about her 'freedom' and he also knew that every fibre of his Begum sahiba is an artiste. But if I want to become Begum Akhtar today, I cannot. My background is different, quite different. I used to really wonder how she managed to do these things, but then I used to worship her, so I never thought what she did was wrong. Never, never thought that she is wrong. Never thought about ethics. But in my case if I ever wanted to do a similar act, she would be the first to reproach, 'How dare you do this? You're not from this kind of a background. Your mother has given you to me on trust.' That was it.

Interviewer:

What you're saying means that even she understood whatever she was doing wasn't exactly right or moral?

Shanti Hiranand:

Of course. But you know, she used to get so stimulated and moreover she never went into anything serious.

Interviewer:

Do you believe that *thumri-dadra* etc., are light classical forms? Some people are against the usage of word light or semi-classical for *thumri-dadra*.

Shanti Hiranand:

No, it's wrong to call them that. It is one other form of classical music. People call it light because the beat is different. And its beat is in six *matras* or eight *matras* or in *rupak*, which are generally used for *geet* and *bhajan*, etc. But the gayaki, *badhat,* is like it is in *khayal* and it is based on ragas. Lot of importance is laid on words, poetry in *thumri and dadra.* I think it is post graduation to sing 'light classical'. And one can only sing so called 'light' classical after knowing classical (*laughs*).

Interviewer:

How is your music different from that of your guru?

Shanti Hiranand:

The base is hers. How to strike *sa,* how each note is to be expanded, how improvisation is to be done, etc. But now after listening to so many great legends I've started thinking about different *harkats* or *taans.* However, the colour remains that of my guru only. And yes, when I sing people say that they get the essence of Begum Akhtar's singing. And this for me is very precious.

Interviewer:

Why is it that none of Begum sahiba's disciples could touch the same chord of 'greatness' as she did?

Shanti Hiranand:

Yes, it should have been so but it did not happen. It seems ironical. But the truth is that trees under the shade of a big tree do not blossom. You can look around. Bade Ghulam Ali Khan and his son Munawar Ali Khan; then Jasrajji and his daughter; so many others. Yes, a few exceptions can be there. But as a general rule, it does not happen.

Interviewer:

How do you teach your disciples?

Shanti Hiranand:

Just like Ammi. She often used to tell me that don't ever hide anything from your students. Tell them everything and don't ever fear that he or she will surpass you. One always gets whatever is written in one's destiny. So I teach openly, telling my students about every nuance, every finer detail, never hiding anything.

Interviewer:

What is your vision about classical music?

Shanti Hiranand:

Over the years classical music has grown. Now I see younger people eager to learn classical music. Even concerts have gained popularity. Earlier classical music was limited to *darbars* only, but after independence through concerts it reached the masses. Similar is the case with Begum Akhtar. She brought *thumri-dadra* on to the concert stage and brought respectability to it. After *khayal* presentation by a maestro, Begum Akhtar used to present a *thumri-dadra.* It never used to happen like that earlier. Her solo concert shows of *thumri-dadra* also started happening. And then, once classical music reached the concert arena, people developed an interest in it. As their interest grew, shows started happening in fairs and festivals. Once it gained so much popularity, children also started learning. So the taboo that was attached to classical music disappeared. The *baiji* culture also declined, though we should all be very grateful to the *baijis*. Had they not been there, light classical music would have died. And this is a fact. They are the ones who kept it alive.

Interviewer:

In your book, *The Story of my Ammi*, about Begum Akhtar, you have touched upon this aspect.

Shanti Hiranand:

Yes, that's true. She belonged to that strata and wanted respectability which she got after marrying Abbasi Sahib. After becoming Begum Abbasi she attained a stature in society. That's why she kept her promise. She never sang in Lucknow, never.

Interviewer:

She never ever sang in Lucknow?

Shanti Hiranand:

No, never. Only exception was in 1965 during the Indo-Pakistan war when the ladies had organised a programme in the Information Department, where only ladies were present; she sang there.

Interviewer:

But she was singing everywhere else, records were available, so how did not singing in Lucknow help? Rather, the people of Lucknow were denied her music.

Shanti Hiranand:

See, that was his pre-condition. He was very well-known in Lucknow. And maybe it was a mental block, a fear that people will say that his wife is a *gaanewali*. Maybe.

Interviewer:

Shantiji you sing *thumri, dadra, chaiti, kajri, sawan, jhoola* and also *ghazal*. How do you prepare yourself for different genres, particularly *ghazal*?

Shanti Hiranand:

I sing light classical from *thumri ang.* And *ghazal* also I sing according to the *thumri ang*. How? In *ghazal* we select the raga as per the mood of the poetry, like *kiska khayal kaun se manzil nazar mein hain*. Now instead of singing it in Pahadi, it is meaningful to have it in a heavy raga like Darbari. Then importance is also to be given on where to break the words, so that the meaning is not lost. Now if you break *kiska khayal kaun* after *kaun*, then the meaning is lost. So we have to understand this. And in *thumri* also this happens. Like this *thumri—ab ke sawan ghar aaja.* Here also we have to give emphasis on the right words and break at the right moment, variations have to be brought in, to heighten the essence, meaning and emotions of the words in a *thumri.* And in a *ghazal* also we have to do the same thing. We have to bring out the pain and different shades and nuances of each word. The only difference is in the language. A *ghazal* is in Urdu.

Interviewer:

What do you like singing the most?

Shanti Hiranand:

I sing all but yes, I am very fond of Urdu poetry. I get carried away.

Interviewer:

Whose poetry have you sung most?

Shanti Hiranand:

I have sung Ghalib very often and in modern *shayars*, Jigar, I knew him personally, then Shakeel also. I like singing romantic poets. Even in *thumri* I like singing romantic words. *Ang* is the same, *khatke, murkiyan* are taken in both—*ghazal* and *thumri.* In *thumri* we do a lot of improvisations. One word is improvised in different ways while in *ghazal* there isn't that much improvisation.

Interviewer:

Are you romantic by nature?

Shanti Hiranand:

Yes, very romantic. I love to feel things, know them and enjoy them and I love nature.

Interviewer:

What do you do in your free time?

Shanti Hiranand:

I love nature and that's why I go for morning and evening walks. I love reading, swimming and my home, my family is very important to me.

I can sit for hours watching the sky, rather than going out for parties. That's why many people say, 'You are a loner. You'll always remain aloof.' But what can I do? That's my nature. That's me.

Interviewer:

You didn't teach your children?

Shanti Hiranand:

I have only one son. He can't sing, doesn't have the flair for singing. You see my husband was a scientist. He was very fond of Western Classical and Begum sahiba. They were both on very good terms. In fact, it was she who arranged my marriage to him.

Interviewer:

How easy or difficult is it for women to pursue music life-long?

Shanti Hiranand:

Very difficult. Many of them leave it after getting married. Such good voices, but they have to leave because of in-laws, husbands or household responsibilities. In this line, why only in this line, in any art form, one has to take a form of *sanyas*—mentally and physically; and you have to forget about parties, movies and so many other things. One has to give priority to *riyaaz.* Art requires lot of dedication and self discipline.

Revisiting a Lost World

PANDIT L.K. PANDIT

(5 March, 1934–)

Pandit Laxman Krishnarao Pandit lives with his wife in a small two-bedroom apartment in a government colony at Munirka, New Delhi. Minimally furnished, the house exudes overwhelming aesthetic sense with music books and the strains of tanpura. His students visit him regularly. 'I can't ask them to stay here in this small apartment. But yes, if I am granted a place, I'll definitely love to start a *gurukul* and impart musical education the way I was given,' says L.K. Pandit in his baritone voice.

Pandit L.K. Pandit spends a life of solitude and still lives with his memories of the golden period of classical music. He doesn't shy away from recounting tales of the time when *ragas* were considered so precious that one could mortgage them for money—'That was the golden period. Musicians were respected. People would give way if any musician was passing by.' His wife was sitting across the table, and he often looked at her, as if confirming the facts.

Often he receives his vocalist daughter Meeta Pandit's calls, clarifying her doubts about intricacies of music. To him music is life, tradition and soul. It is his strict classicism and refusal to compromise with what is popular that has earned him the reputation of being one of the few true representatives of Gwalior *gharana.* Presenting and elaborating ragas in a traditional *Ashtaang gayaki,* L.K. Pandit would often explain his point by rendering a *bandish.* And like his concert, he concluded the conversation with a *tappa.*

(7 April, 2006)

Interviewer:

Panditji you have seen so many changes in your life, in your musical journey. You have seen the glory of state patronage and after that the changes in musical scenario. So, how has the musical scenario changed?

L.K. Pandit:

Yes, immense changes occurred once state patronage was over. That is a very long story. During state patronage, artistes were really looked after very well—their food, shelter, learning, everything was looked after by the state rulers. They were respected in society. Musicians had a distinct status. All this changed after independence.

Interviewer:

So how did you and your father cope with the changing times?

L.K. Pandit:

See, my father never left Gwalior. Most of the other artistes either went to Mumbai or came to Delhi. But my father never left Gwalior. He lived there till his death. I shifted to Delhi because of my job at the All India Radio. In Delhi I had no place to do *riyaaz*. I used to sit in the central park at Connaught Place for hours in the evening and do my *riyaaz*. I used to practise while walking. This way I made quite a few friends. Even to get a house in Delhi was a problem. No landlord wanted to rent out his premises to musicians. They would call us *gaanewala* and refuse to rent out their premises to us.

Interviewer:

You never thought of settling in Mumbai?

L.K. Pandit:

Never got an opportunity. I had a job here. Going to Mumbai or Kolkata meant leaving the job and restarting all over again, which obviously I thought was not a good option.

Interviewer:

What has been the contribution of Pandit family in Gwalior *gharana?*

L.K. Pandit:

See, Gwalior gharana is one of the oldest *gharanas* of *khayal gayaki.* My grandfather and great grandfather got an opportunity to be associated with musical giants who popularised *khayal gayaki*. It was a completely different period. Let me tell you that as nowadays gold is pawned, at that time it was raga that was pawned by musicians, if they needed money. So, if a musician had pawned raga Malkauns, then he didn't sing that raga till the loan was repaid. Such was the social status of musicians in Gwalior during those times. Music was highly appreciated in Gwalior. It was said that in Gwalior even a child cried in *sur*. Musicians used to earn in thousands while officials' salaries were only ₹20 per month! Court musicians used to ride on the elephant and received their salary in silver coins. And now about your question—contribution of Pandit family—well, the thing is that my forefathers had learnt directly from Gwalior *gharana's* stalwarts. Ustad Nissar Hussain Khan of Gwalior *gharana* stayed at our place till his death. My grandfather learnt directly from him. He had a huge repertoire of *bandishes* which he passed on to the Pandit family only. That's why we say we are the direct lineage of Gwalior *gharana*.

Interviewer:

Ashtaang gayaki is the most important aspect of Gwalior *gharana*. What's so special about this form of *gayaki*?

L.K. Pandit:

There are *asht ang (*eight parts) in *gayaki* and *ashtaang gayaki* involves the systematic eight-fold elaboration of the raga. That's why it is called *ashtaang gayaki.*

Interviewer:

It is not done in other *gharanas*?

L.K. Pandit:

I don't want to compare with other *gharanas*. But as I said Gwalior is the oldest and main *gharana*. *Dhrupad* took birth in this gharana; Raja Man Singh Tomar, *pitamah* (grand old man) of *dhrupad* and Tansen, the most popular musician, belonged to Gwalior *gharana*. Then *khayal* was popularised by Gwalior *gharana*. In fact Gwalior *gharana* has been the fountainhead of all forms of *gayaki*.

Interviewer:

In today's world what is the importance of the *gharana* concept?

L.K. Pandit:

Music and musicians portray society. They are an important aspect of society. Many years ago one could figure out which part of India a person belonged to just by looking at him—whether one is a Maharashtrian or from Punjab or from Uttar Pradesh. But this doesn't happen anymore. So, why segregate music and musicians? Society has undergone change, our perspective has changed and that reflects in our music as well. Technological exposure has blurred all distinctions between *gharana*s. Having said this, the truth is that *gharana*s exist, they have their own importance and they have kept music alive.

Interviewer:

What is the status of classical music in society?

L.K. Pandit:

It is passing through a very bad phase. There's no programme on TV. The radio which used to give twelve shows in a year, now gives only one or two programmes. In this scenario what will artistes do? As a result of this many artistes have stopped passing on the art to their children. Classical music is passing through difficult times.

Interviewer:

What do you think should be done to improve the condition of classical music and musicians?

L.K. Pandit:

We need patronage, be it of society or of the government. Earlier, during the era of *nawab*s and kings, there was complete state patronage. An artiste had to just concentrate on his music. For twenty-four hours he was busy thinking or composing music. You need time to do creation. And that's why that period was the golden period for music. But now there is no such thing. We have corporate sponsorship, but that is limited to a few favourite artistes only. The star system has emerged in the music world too.

Interviewer:

Who created this star system?

L.K. Pandit:

This again is the outcome of societal changes. It is a trend of our ever-changing society. And yes, this decline has also occurred because of the audience. Earlier, the audience might have been lesser in number but the listeners had in-depth knowledge of music. If any musician was not up to the standard, they used to question him. Now the strength of audience might have increased but they lack musical sensitivity—most of the time. They do not understand music. They just come to enjoy and clap.

Interviewer:

There are thousands of ragas but we keep hearing only a handful. Why?

L.K. Pandit:

Yes, there are many ragas like Shankara, Tilang, Jaijaivanti, Durga—we hardly hear them in concerts. On radio one generally hears Todi, Lalit or Ahir Bhairav and not Bhairav because it is difficult to do justice to its notes. So it is either fashion or compulsion.

Interviewer:

What kind of disciples do you have?

L.K. Pandit:

I have many talented disciples. But the thing is that talented students get frustrated when they don't get programmes. There are many hurdles for newcomers. Where are the avenues? Mass media has not supported the cause of classical music. It is just cricket. Honestly speaking, I think, music has more impact than any other form of entertainment. Classical music is not incomprehensible. If one listens to it, he or she will definitely be influenced by the beauty of it. This is creative, cultured art. One has to really nurture it, just like a farmer ploughs his fields and then gets a good crop.

Interviewer:

How many hours of *riyaaz* do you do?

L.K. Pandit:

All the time. When I was a student I just used to do *riyaaz* and study during examination time. I am the first graduate in my family. But I used to study during examination time only, rest of the time it was just music and music.

Interviewer:

At what age did you give your first public concert?

L.K. Pandit:

In my school there used to be a *mehfil* every Thursday. All students were expected to sing in this *mehfil*. I used to go along with my father to all major concerts, particularly to Harballabh festival where I used to sing. My father used to stay there for three days and in those three days he used to give four to six concerts, unlike the present day scenario where artistes give just one concert and earn in lakhs.

Earlier, artistes were devoted to popularising this art and to teach the audience. It was not just to earn money. I am talking about the 1940s.

Interviewer:

How many concerts used to happen earlier?

L.K. Pandit:

There were many concerts, I tell you! There were music circles in Kolkata and Mumbai in the 1940s and 1950s. A week-long programme used to happen and in these seven days my father used to give at least twenty concerts—morning, afternoon, evening, night. Often it used to start at 9:00 am and get over the next morning at 5:00 am. We used to be completely exhausted. My father wouldn't allow me to sleep because it was believed that sleeping is bad for the throat. So I hardly slept for those seven days.

Interviewer:

What kind of a guru was your father?

L.K. Pandit:

Very strict.

Interviewer:

And you?

L.K. Pandit:

One has to be a very strict guru to make disciples learn. There's a lot of thinking process in music, too. Unless a guru is strict, a student will not learn the art properly.

Interviewer:

You sing *tappa* quite a lot. Why is *tappa* not sung so often in concerts these days? And what about *thumri*?

L.K. Pandit:

It is a very difficult art. *Tappa* is extremely difficult to sing, a most taxing form of singing and demands instant, protracted movement up and down the octave. This calls for constant innovation, apart from superb breath control.

And as for *thumri*—the number of *thumri* vocalists have decreased. The popularity of both these art forms has decreased because of the transitions in society—*samajik vyavastha* and of course for *tappa*, as I said, it is extremely difficult to sustain notes in this form. Even trained singers avoid singing it.

Interviewer:

Which is your favourite raga?

L.K. Pandit:

All.

Interviewer:

Which is your favourite *bandish?*

L.K. Pandit:

Many. I sing only those ragas in which I know at least twenty-five to thirty *bandishes*. I have learnt ragas according to the *bandishes*.

Interviewer:

Besides music, what do you like?

L.K. Pandit:

I like hockey. I used to play during my childhood. It was the most loved sport in Gwalior because the legendary hockey player Roop Chand belonged to Gwalior. It was the experience of a lifetime to watch him play ... Oh, my God ... such a great player. He was a great penalty specialist. He never missed it ... wah!

Interviewer:

Did you ever think that your daughter Meeta Pandit would be your family's sixth generation in music?

L.K. Pandit:

That is all because of her talent. I remember when she was two or three years old, Halim Jaffer Khan had come to our place. While playing, this little girl was singing *alankars* and *paltas.* Khan Sahib was surprised. Then he told her to follow him and sing the same notes as he did. She followed him perfectly. He was so happy that he blessed her and said that she will become a singer only. Another time when I had gone to Benaras for the Sankatmochan festival, I had requested the organisers to let my little daughter sing. They agreed. She sang there and immediately impressed the audience. She was only seven or eight years old then. She decided to take up music professionally after the death of my son in 1994. He died in an accident. But to tell you frankly, I never wanted any of my children to become musicians.

Interviewer:

Why?

L.K. Pandit:

We do not have a healthy musical environment now; no longer do we have an interested and discerning audience or good organisers; times have completely changed and it is difficult for me to adjust to the present times. There is no respect for musicians anymore. Earlier musicians were respected. They were VIPs. Secondly, one has to struggle a lot in music. That's why I really did not want Meeta to become a musician.

Interviewer:

As for young people who want to take up music, what advice would you like to give?

L.K. Pandit:

Before going on stage they should first learn properly, do *riyaaz*. Actually music is an art where learning is a lifelong process. Classical music is our priceless legacy. The happiness that we get by listening to classical music cannot be found anywhere else.

SITAR

Unravelling the Musical Truths
PANDIT DEBU CHAUDHURI
(24 June, 1936–)

Devabrata (a.k.a Debu) Chaudhuri lives with his son and grandchildren in a double storey building at Chittaranjan Park, New Delhi. In his *riyaaz* room is kept his precious seventeen-frets sitar which has been his companion for more than seventy years and has been his instrument for creating eight new ragas—Bisweswari, Palas-Sarang, Anuranjani, Ashiqui Lalit, Swanandeswari, Kalyani Bilawal, Shivamanjari and Prabhati Manjari (named after his late wife Manjushree). Sitar maestro, guru and teacher, composer, author, musicologist, academician—former dean of Faculty of Music and Fine Arts at Delhi University—Pandit Debu Chaudhuri has authored the books *Sitar and Its Techniques, Music of India* and *On Indian Music*.

Born and brought up in Kolkata in a large family that hardly had any musical inclinations, young Debu Chaudhuri was encouraged and patronised by one of his sisters-in-law, singer of Rabindra Sangeet. The young boy had his first brush with the sitar at the tender age of four. A major milestone came in the shape of a solo performance in All India Radio, at the age of fourteen. The initial training was under the tutelage of Shri Panchu Gopal Datta and thereafter under the aegis of Ustad Mushtaq Ali Khan who initiated him into the Senia Gharana. In 1960 he shifted his base. He joined Delhi University as a lecturer in the Music Department, and later became the dean of the Faculty of Music and Fine Arts. 'Many students join Music Honours just because they could not get admission in any other course. For them it is just a BA degree,' he remarks on the quality of students that he groomed while he was heading the institute.

Dressed in a white Kurta with a grand *rudraksh mala* adorning his neck, Pandit Debu Chaudhuri's frank and forthright views on issues connected with music and young students seeking admission in Music Honours, leaves one in a contemplative mood.

(18 January, 2005)

Interviewer:

Panditji, what do you think is the larger role of music in society? In the wake of natural or man-made tragedy many concerts are organised to raise funds. Can music be an active force?

Debu Chaudhuri:

Well, we have a very limited role to play. Merely helping on the financial front. There's still a long way to go, to be able to reach those people, who suffer. I think the best thing I could do would be to go to the victims and help them. We can't be sure where the funds go. My heart bleeds when I see such disturbing news. As a musician, as an artiste, our responsibility is limited to performing for a cause and the rest we can only leave to God, hoping and praying that this will reach those in need.

Interviewer:

You said one should actually go to the people in need. Have you ever done that?

Debu Chaudhuri:

Once a concert had been organised in Jalpaiguri in aid of flood victims. There I met them and tried wiping their tears. We cannot bring back those who have died, but for the survivors we can do a lot in terms of resettling them and rebuilding their lives. It was a very touching experience.

Interviewer:

How many concerts do you give in a year?

Debu Chaudhuri:

Well the number of concerts has gone down now since I've crossed seventy. And I also think we should not continue when it's the time to retire. We must make room for the new generation. If you insist on being on the stage, the young will never get an opportunity. Also, this whole matter of 'getting a concert' is a very controversial question to ask ...

Interviewer:

Why is it controversial? Can you explain how it is done?

Debu Chaudhuri:

How do you get a concert, tell me! Who decides whether you should get twenty or thirty concerts in a year or none at all?

This is the tragedy of our country. The organisers say that they invite artistes according to the feedback from the common man about who they want to listen to. This means that only those people who are popular with the public will 'get the concert.' isn't is? And how does the organisers' 'common man' come to know about an artiste?

Interviewer:

Through CDs and albums and concerts.

Debu Chaudhuri:

No common man is ever asked. He's just given a name—'so and so would be performing here at this time.' Now if that 'common man' hasn't heard that name before, if it's a lesser known artiste, he will not get a concert!

This means that even if an artiste is good but if he doesn't have any albums to his name in the market, people are not familiar with his name then he will not get concerts. Does that mean he is not a good artiste? This is why I'm very critical about audience behaviour in this regard. If someone is not in the news, he might not get an opportunity to perform. It's all about publicity.

Interviewer:

So what about those artistes who do not have good PR but are talented? Don't they get depressed and frustrated?

Debu Chaudhuri:

They do! People have to realise that if someone doesn't have good PR it doesn't mean he is not a talented artiste. In fact, it is the moral duty of the media to talk about a cross-section of artistes. But the truth is that the media highlights only those who sell. That's why I'm very unpopular; because I speak the truth. I have no grudges against the great maestros—they are truly great, but let's not forget that there are so many people who are serving the music fraternity and are totally in the shadows. It is our duty to bring them forward!

Interviewer:

But how would we get to know those people when we haven't heard their albums or their concerts, how do we reach out to those deserving people?

Debu Chaudhuri:

This is a wrong concept. In any concert, the first participating artiste is not well-known. The top artiste is always scheduled to perform at the concluding part of the concert. So people deliberately come late, only to hear the top artiste, not the relatively lesser-known artiste who performs at the beginning. By this attitude we are demoralising the younger generation. How will they survive?

Interviewer:

So how about placing the younger artiste right in the middle of the performance schedule rather than the beginning?

Debu Chaudhuri:

That might be a good idea but the organisers would not do so.

Interviewer:

Why? Can't senior artistes like you insist upon it for the welfare of the newcomers?

Debu Chaudhuri:

Here tradition is involved. If the senior artiste has performed, a junior cannot perform after him or her.

The suggestion you have offered is a good one and I support it. But it is up to the organisers to do that. You see I am a performer. I have my own cultural centre called Ustad Mushtaq Ali Khan Centre for Culture and I would definitely keep this view in mind. It is a positive suggestion. But then it should also be explained to the audience that all the artistes who are famous today were newcomers some day. So now my appeal would be to request all the leading musicians of India to help newcomers come up. Many of them are already doing that. I think it is the general tendency of the masses ... but before that let me tell you something I have often said—classical music is not for the masses. Classical music is classical, the word itself denotes classicism. Pop music is popular music. To understand pop music you don't need any lesson. Some may disagree with me. But if you go to the West, any passerby would tell you about Michael Jackson and Madonna. Ask the same person about Tchaikovsky, Bach or Mozart, he would not know. I am giving you this example as a proof of what I am saying. Most people wouldn't even know the proper lyrics of the Michael Jackson song they are humming. So, with pop music you sing and dance and don't need much knowledge about it but if I'm playing Todi in the morning, you have to know how the notes are applied and how that is different from other ragas to appreciate it. The beauty of classical music is that the same note has different shades and colours in different ragas. This is one factor where you need some kind of knowledge and grooming to appreciate.

Interviewer:

In that case, then do you think classical music should be taught at the school level so that young people have enough knowledge to understand and appreciate classical music? So, you think that classical music is for the class?

Debu Chaudhuri:

Yes. Absolutely! I have been advocating this theory for a long time. I suggested this to the government in many forums. Music must be made compulsory from the kindergarten level. I can prove that children who grow up with music would evolve into a different set of people. Their physiological and mental set-up would be very different from others. It is something that changes your character also. And if there is more music, there would be less violence.

Interviewer:

What has been your experience as a teacher? You taught at Delhi University for a long time, how was your exchange with the students there?

Debu Chaudhuri:

My experience is a mixed one. I have been teaching for forty years and have written four books. There would be very few people who have taught for such a long time. At times I was deeply disappointed. My experience is that those who come to these institutions are not always talented.

Interviewer:

Then who are those students? So what do they do after graduating in music? If they were not interested in music and are not talented then what do they do for livelihood after taking the course?

Debu Chaudhuri:

Eighty per cent students joined Music Honours because they failed to get admission anywhere else.

Most of them get married.

Interviewer:

But that would be true mostly for girls. What about the boys?

Debu Chaudhuri:

In Delhi University the percentage of boys in the music course is very less! I haven't been to the department for a long time now, but out of seventy students there would be about seven boys.

Interviewer:

It must be very frustrating for you, to teach students who are not serious about music.

Debu Chaudhuri:

That's why I said I have had a mixed experience. I remember I was the only dean in the faculty who had three tenures. Once a parent came and started arguing with me, 'Why has my daughter not been admitted to the course? She has got 90 per cent!'

I replied, 'She might have got ninety per cent but she has to prove that she is worth ninety per cent. Let her prove even forty per cent and I will admit her. Let her sing *sa re ga ma* ...' She just couldn't sing in tune! Then I asked her why she came here when she can't even do that and she honestly replied, 'I knew I wouldn't get admission anywhere else.'

Interviewer:

What about those who pass out with a degree?

Debu Chaudhuri:

If you see the number of people who pass out from all the universities in India that have a music course, as well as from private institutions, there would be thousands and thousands of people who have a Master's degree in music. But hardly one or two will take up music seriously and evolve into a musician. Frankly speaking, institutions cannot produce performers.

Interviewer:

But then why is the course not scrapped altogether?

Debu Chaudhuri:

You see, the purpose is to have it as a curriculum, to know, to educate. No university would claim to produce performers, not even the professional institutions. All the top musicians you see today, none of them are products of any institution.

Interviewer:

So basically what you are saying is that those who are seriously interested in music should learn with a guru under the *guru-shishya parampara*?

Debu Chaudhuri:

It is fundamentally a *gurumukhi vidya*. That too has its negative side. Still, that is the only way we can learn. At an institution, our purpose is not to create a Tansen, we say we would like to create *Kaansen* (good listener). The University never tells us that we have to create maestros. Maestros are born, not created. In a performing art like music you need to have god-gifted talent.

Interviewer:

How has the *guru-shishya parampara* evolved over the years from your youth to now?

Debu Chaudhuri:

Well, it has lost its charisma these days because of too much publicity, propaganda and institutions all around. It has lost its value in a way. But I am very confident it would never be lost completely. After doing a course from an institution one can at least know how to hold the instrument. Then, if one is passionate about it one can go to a guru. You will see that many degree holders get a job as a music teacher and start teaching but they have never really performed. So, if you have never performed, what will you teach the students, how will you make them performers?

I do believe that theory is an important and integral part of our music but only a part. You can read and memorise and mug up theory, but you cannot mug up talent.

Interviewer:

What is your style of playing? How is your *gharana* unique and different from the other *gharanas*?

Debu Chaudhuri:

Presently, our *gharana* is the only one that is following the oldest system of playing with seventeen frets. This is from the time of Maseet Sen who was related to Tansen. Today also people play the Maseetkhani style. We call our *gharana* 'Senia' because it follows the Senia principle, Tansen's legacy and lineage. But we are carrying this forward with great difficulty. With seventeen frets you do not have *komal ga* and *komal ni*. So when we play ragas that need both the *gandhars* or *nishads*, we have to work very hard. But that helps us to have a habit of playing with the *meend*. Secondly, we are very proud to be following a very old style.

Interviewer:

So, earlier the sitar was played with seventeen frets. When did the change happen because now it is usually played with nineteen or twenty frets.

Debu Chaudhuri:

It happened in the early 1940s, or maybe late 1930s.

Interviewer:

And what was the reason behind it?

Debu Chaudhuri:

It was done for the sake of convenience so that both *gandhar*s and *nishads* are on the fret.

Interviewer:

What innovations did you bring about?

Debu Chaudhuri:

Let me explain. See, in my style I've tuned the first, second, third, fourth, fifth, sixth and seventh strings on the top of the sitar to *'Ma'(F – 'Baaj ka taar'), 'Sa'(C – 'Jod ka Taar'), 'Pa/Ma'(G/F – 'Kharaj',* tuned according to Raga), *'Pa'*(G – steel), *'Sa'(C* - middle octave), *'Sa'(C* - middle octave), *'Sa'(C* - higher octave).

Interviewer:

Fine. When did your rendezvous with the sitar begin?

Debu Chaudhuri:

It's a long story. But to cut that long story short, in my family, nobody was a musician. My mother and elder sister used to love music. In the 1940s my elder brother got married and his wife started going to a music school in Kolkata and the best teachers used to come there. I was about six years old at that time. There was a room for every discipline—*khayal, sitar, guitar, Rabindra Sangeet,* etc. So one day I accompanied my *bhabhi* and while she was in the class I was loitering around. I just happened to peep into the sitar class and the teacher there called me and asked, 'Do you want to play the sitar?' I said yes! That was the beginning. At home they were all against it, 'What do you mean you want to learn music,' they asked. In those days taking up music was a crime! I started crying but next week I again accompanied my *bhabhi*. The same thing happened. Finally my mother told my father, 'Give him a sitar, he is just a child and will not play for long.' I got the tiny sitar but after that I never looked back. That's my story.

Interviewer:

At what age did you come to Delhi?

Debu Chaudhuri:

I was twenty-four.

Interviewer:

You came to study music or ...?

Debu Chaudhuri:

I got a job at Delhi University. I didn't have any money and I cried throughout the journey. I came here and got the job; and that used to pay me ₹200 per month. For accommodation I used to share a small room with three other people and used to have one meal a day. Those were hard times. Whatever I have achieved, it is on my own. People didn't even know the name of my guruji—Ustad Mushtaq Ali Khan. I have struggled all my life to make people know his name and recognise his talent. From childhood I was very obstinate, focussed, had tenacity. I was determined to achieve and attain what I wanted.

Interviewer:

So when and how did you get your first break?

Debu Chaudhuri:

After coming to Delhi I got national recognition at an early age through my broadcast in the All India Radio in 1963. The second break came when I went to America and Europe for the first time in 1966.

Interviewer:

Who invited you for that tour? How did you get it?

Debu Chaudhuri:

There also I had to fight it out. The famous tabla player Faiyaz Khan and I were good friends. He was working with the All India Radio at that time. He had accompanied some musician abroad. He gave me a visiting card, and that card really helped me. I tell him this even today. It was of someone in Paris. I wrote to that person and he invited me. That's how I got the link. The America visit happened because of my brother who is settled in Los Angeles. Meanwhile, I had also started playing a lot in Delhi.

Interviewer:

You have got so many awards—Padma Bhushan, Sahitya Kala Parishad, and many others. How important is it to get awards and accolades?

Debu Chaudhuri:

Awards don't make you a better musician. But it is an impetus, a stepping stone, an encouragement to forge ahead to fulfil your mission. I am still the way I was before I got these awards. And musically I haven't gained anything through them, but I have got satisfaction and recognition for my achievement that I have made it, all by myself. I was nothing. In fact, even today I am nothing.

Interviewer:

That's being very humble ...

Debu Chaudhuri:

But I tell you, in the field of music, it takes many lifetimes to understand and learn and that way I still haven't plumbed the depths of the ocean of music.

Interviewer:

People say each raga is an ocean in itself. Which raga is closest to your heart?

Debu Chaudhuri:

I must tell you that my guru Ustad Mushtaq Ali Khan Sahib had a favourite *bandish* in raga Adana. One day I requested him to teach me that *bandish*. He agreed but on the condition that for one year I would not play anything else, only that *bandish* and that raga. I did that. There are many ragas close to my heart like Yaman, Bageshri, Bihag, Ahir Bhairav, Lalit.

Interviewer:

What is it that makes someone create a new raga or compose a new *bandish*?

Debu Chaudhuri:

You see, if you ask any creator he would never say that he sat down to create something. That doesn't happen. It is spontaneous. I will give you an example. My recent eighth creation is the raga Prabhati-Manjari. My wife's name was Manjushri. After two years of her death, one day I was playing and suddenly this raga came to me.

Interviewer:

And how is this raga different from any other?

Debu Chaudhuri:

It is different in approach, in spirit, in *rasa*. Wherever I played this raga, everybody said it was highly emotional. Some people even wept when I was playing this raga. In the case of a raga I created earlier, I had to justify to people at the All India Radio what was special and different about that raga. There were senior people like Pandit Jasraj, Pandit L.K. Pandit, Dr Sumati Mutatkar, and I had to justify and answer their questions.

Interviewer:

How did you meet your wife? Was she your student?

Debu Chaudhuri:

She was in the first batch at the Faculty of Music and Fine Arts in the 1960s. I was a young teacher at that time. There were only six girls in that batch. I was unmarried and young and maybe that's why I was very popular with the girls at that time. I am popular today also amongst girls ... hahaha ... anyway, she was Bengali and she was attracted towards me. I used to avoid meeting girls during those days. I thought I would not marry unless I became famous. So for six to seven years this continued and ultimately we got married. But she is no more today.

Interviewer:

How was your companionship with her, since she was also a vocalist?

Debu Chaudhuri:

She made a sacrifice. She had done her PhD and had written a book. She used to give me all the support as a wife, as a friend. Without that I couldn't have made my mark. She gave up her career. But whenever I used to go abroad, I used to take her with me. And in the concerts, before I started to play, she would sing.

Interviewer:

When I interviewed your son Prateek he told me that in one of the concerts someone remarked that in fact the singing was better than the sitar! But how did you feel when someone made that comment?

Debu Chaudhuri:

Yes, her music had an appeal. She was not a professional singer but her music had deep feeling. People always enjoyed her music.

I was very happy and proud. I never thought of competing with her. On the contrary I was really happy to have those musical vibes.

Interviewer:

Since she was a creative person herself and gave up a promising career in music, did she ever regret it or feel frustrated? As her husband and guru did you ever feel that she was withdrawing into herself because of that?

Debu Chaudhuri:

No, never. She was very supportive and she said, 'If I also sing then who will look after the family?' So, she made a sacrifice. Whatever I am today, a lot of it is because of her. Otherwise, I would not have become Debu Chaudhuri today, that's for sure.

Interviewer:

Like they say—behind every successful man there is a woman ...

Debu Chaudhuri:

Yes, but we had fights also, many times, some serious, some sweet. I was very popular with girls, maybe because I am an artiste. I used to tell her that if they are giving me so much attention how can I completely ignore them! But she used to say, 'Let them love you, but you can't love anyone else.' I always recite this Urdu couplet—'*Hum aah bhi bharte hain toh ho jaate hain badnaam, woh katl bhi karte hain to charcha nahin hota ...*'

Interviewer:

If given a chance would you like to live a relatively solitary life in the mountains?

Debu Chaudhuri:

I love having people around. But I also like to have my own privacy. And to help people. God has given me this gift—you see many times people come to me and I help them. I don't want them to face the same struggle that I have been through. Nowadays my grand-daughter takes up all my time. So, she's my girlfriend now ... hahaha ... she gives me all her love and affection.

Interviewer:

Coming back to music, who are your most promising disciples today? And how do you rate your son Prateek Chaudhuri's music?

Debu Chaudhuri:

Well, I have thousands of students. But now I am concentrating on five or six only. Three of my disciples are already professors in the Department of Music at the University. Dr Anupam Mahajan, Dr Indrani Chakraborty ... they are all doing well.

Then there are some foreign scholar students, and some students who are learning the guitar.

Well, as a father I would say—good, as a guru I would say—no, not yet. He has to come up. In music, sky is the limit. I would say he has all the potential and understanding and musical sense and he should continue to grow and keep on improving.

Interviewer:

How would you describe your musical journey and experience with audiences?

Debu Chaudhuri:

My only feeling is that earlier—in the 1940s and 1950s—although the audience was limited, they were much better.

Interviewer:

In what way? Do you think they were more disciplined?

Debu Chaudhuri:

Yes, they were much more disciplined and they didn't get carried away by the media. In those days the media was not playing such a major role as it is playing today.

Interviewer:

But don't you think it is a vicious circle—everybody just blames the media!

Debu Chaudhuri:

That is because people pick up certain albums or go to listen to some people because of the media. There are so many examples but I don't want to take names. Just open the paper and see who is being written about and those are the people audiences go to listen to.

Interviewer:

Are you talking of Page 3 celebrities?

Debu Chaudhuri:

Everything. See for yourself—the artistes who perform—their name, photograph is not in the newspapers. So, it is the media that has made some artistes popular amongst the masses and as a result the scenario has changed. I will give you a clear example. Take a list of ten best music festivals of Delhi in a year and in all those ten festivals you will see that most of the artistes' names keep repeating. Why so? Does it mean there are no more artistes in the world? No, it's because they feel it is these artistes whom people will come to listen to. And these artistes become the media's favourites and also of the audience. So, that is the state of affairs. It's a circle. My only wish is that let the audience be more aware of the ragas so that they can appreciate more logically, more substantially. That's how we can improve the standard of our music.

Interviewer:

In such a scenario what advice would you like to give to youngsters who are coming to the music field?

Debu Chaudhuri:

I'll tell them to learn and learn and learn. Don't expect instant results.

Interviewer:

While taking up music as a profession, what points should one take into consideration?

Debu Chaudhuri:

Sadhna, perseverance, practice. Music is a performing art. It is not that you get a degree and get a job. Here talent counts.

Interviewer:

But as you said in the beginning it is not only talent but many other factors also operate and influence success in the music world ...

Debu Chaudhuri:

Yes, that happens. That's why the attitude of the media and the audience has to change. Finally what is needed to become famous is luck.

Interviewer:

And luck is something that we can never really describe or guarantee.

Debu Chaudhuri:

Yes. I just hope that audiences today should develop compassion and encourage those musicians who are talented but not known. One must listen to them, help them come up; for that is the only way we will get more talented people, those hidden talents that remain in the shadows due to lack of support or publicity.

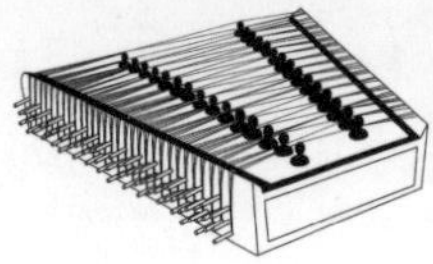

SANTOOR

Strings of the Soul

PANDIT SHIV KUMAR SHARMA

(13 January, 1938–)

The interview was arranged hurriedly. We conducted it a day prior to the official launch of his new album in a five star hotel in Delhi. Dressed in a resplendent sapphire-blue *kurta*, Pandit Shiv Kumar Sharma walked into the lobby and we joined him in his hotel room a few minutes later. In less than thirty minutes we were supposed to complete the interview. There was slight hesitation in the beginning but it soon disappeared as we progressed with the conversation. Though he was in a hurry, he answered each question at length and repeatedly apologised to waiting media persons.

Having started in the 1950s, today Pandit Shiv Kumar Sharma has made the santoor a household name. 'Its popularity can be estimated by the fact that even soaps and restaurants are named santoor,' he says with a mischievous smile. Without compromising on the purity of music, Pandit Sharma's 'un-traditionalist' musical approach brought about experimental albums like *Call of the Valley, Feelings, Mountains, Water, Soundscape*, etc. 'I keep doing experiments in thematic music ...'

Believing that music is food for the soul, he has experimented in different genres. Film music caught his special attention. Along with Pandit Hariprasad Chaurasia he composed haunting melodies for *Silsila, Lamhe, Chandni, Darr.* 'My dream has always been to create that kind of music which makes listeners forget even to clap; there's absolute silence after the performance.'

(17 October, 2007)

Interviewer:

Earlier, santoor was not an accepted instrument of classical music. So, what is its history and how was it eventually included in the concert arena?

Shiv Kumar Sharma:

Santoor is a very ancient Indian instrument. It was never used in Hindustani classical music. The ancient name of this instrument was *Shata-tantri Veena*, a hundred-stringed veena. It was played in Kashmir only.

Before that, there is a mention of it in Sanskrit texts that this instrument was used with the recitation of *Veda mantras*. Later on it emerged as an accompanying instrument for *Sufiana Mausiqi*. But it was never used outside Kashmir and was never used in Hindustani classical music or even played as a solo instrument. My father, Guru Pandit Umadutt Sharma was the first one to think about it. He was the disciple of Pandit Ramdasji of Benaras. By the way, my father was a vocalist who also played the harmonium, tabla and esraj. My *taleem* began with vocal music and tabla.

Interviewer:

How old were you then?

Shiv Kumar Sharma:

I was five years old. It was my good fortune that I got the opportunity to introduce santoor in the arena of classical music. In the beginning I faced many problems. People were not prepared to accept that traditional classical music can ever be played on this instrument. There was a lot of criticism.

Well, anyway, I brought about changes and modifications, tried to evolve a completely different character for santoor. I worked on the tonal quality and playing technique. It took many years.

Interviewer:

Initially you accompanied your father also. Isn't it?

Shiv Kumar Sharma:

Yes, on tabla. I also accompanied Pandit Ravi Shankar when he came to Jammu radio station for the first time to perform. I was booked to accompany him on the tabla.

Interviewer:

So, you brought about changes in santoor so as to play classical music on it and if I am not mistaken, you increased the number of bridges to get a wider range of octaves, and changed the system of tuning and the structural configuration of the strings to allow for more precision on note reproduction?

Shiv Kumar Sharma:

Yes, because in 1955 when I first brought it on stage there was a lot of criticism. There were two kinds of reactions. There were some people who had never heard or seen this kind of an instrument. And the other, knowledgeable people openly said that this instrument cannot be used in classical music. Their reaction made me think about it. In classical music there is a term *meend*. It is used during *alaap*; vocalists use it; it is a way to move from one *swar* to the other, without breaking the continuity of *swars*. This was not possible on the original santoor. So I thought about it. I was left with only two options—either to imitate the already existing instruments like the sarod, sitar or veena, or to experiment and modify so as to retain the individuality of santoor.

The truth is that every instrument has its own technique. A sitar cannot be played like a sarangi or vice versa. So I decided not to copy the technique of other instruments but to experiment. And it took me many years to innovate and give a final shape to the hundred-stringed instrument.

Interviewer:

What modifications?

Shiv Kumar Sharma:

I modified it a little bit. I introduced a new chromatic arrangement of notes and increased the range to cover full three octaves. I also created a new technique of playing. And with that technique I could sustain the notes and maintain continuity of sound. And see, today the santoor is recognised as a classical instrument all over the world.

Interviewer:

When did you first record your solo album?

Shiv Kumar Sharma:

In the 1950s I began playing this instrument and in 1960 I recorded my first solo album. In 1967 I teamed up with Pandit Hariprasad Chaurasia and Pandit Brij Bhushan Kabra. We thought of a theme and came out with the album *Call of the Valley*. This album is still very popular. Today we are in the 21st century and this album was produced in 20th century but it is still very popular.

Interviewer:

You came out with other thematic albums also, like *Elements*, *Soundscapes*, *Feelings* ...

Shiv Kumar Sharma:

Yes, actually I keep doing experiments in thematic music. I have also done *Upnishad Amrut*, verses in Sanskrit then the *Prarthana* series. I have composed music for *Ram Manka*—it has 108 *dohe* through which the entire life story of Lord Ram is narrated.

Interviewer:

In the beginning how many hours of *riyaaz* did you do?

Shiv Kumar Sharma:

See, *riyaaz* is something which cannot be fixed. First you have to know how to do *riyaaz*. And what is the right way to do it. And this can be taught by a guru only. After learning the correct way, it depends on the individual. One can do it for two hours and achieve the same result another person might take four hours to achieve. So, it varies from person to person. But yes, *riyaaz* is imperative. Constantly thinking about music and *riyaaz* are two very important aspects of music. Mere *taleem* is not enough. In the beginning I did *riyaaz* for long hours. Even now I do it.

Interviewer:

Do you get time now?

Shiv Kumar Sharma:

Nothing can be achieved without *riyaaz.* And *riyaaz* is of two types—to do it physically and to think about music, new ideas. And this second type can be done anywhere, it doesn't matter whether you have the instrument or not.

Interviewer:

You have created raga Antardhwani ...

Shiv Kumar Sharma:

It just happened. I do not believe that to be credited for doing something one has to create a raga. I believe that thousands of ragas already exist. And even after dedicating a lifetime to *riyaaz*, we can only master a few ragas, that too, not completely. So, if we cannot play the existing ragas with complete control, what is the point of creating new ragas? I think so. But I also do not consider it inappropriate to create new ragas. I think it is artistic creativity, and one can create new ragas. As about Antardhwani raga, it so happened that my listeners all over the world wanted some specific musical piece for meditation. They wanted that I should play some music in which there is only *alaap*, without tabla so that they can use it for meditation. Many psychiatrists, doctors and yoga centres use my santoor music. Their request made me think about it. And while contemplating I hit upon a scale and that raga I had not heard before. So I recorded it. After recording it I gave that piece a name. As I had done this specifically for people who wanted to use my music for meditation, I named it Antardhwani. Actually later when I heard those *swars* myself I discovered that they (*swars*) had the capability to make one look inward, to introspect. This music inspires you to look inwards. *Antar* means the inner self *dhwani* means sound. *Antardhwani* literally means the sound of the inner self.

Interviewer:

Which is your favourite raga?

Shiv Kumar Sharma:

It is very difficult to say. Often it happens that we play a few ragas for months and months and then for many years we do not play them at all. But I have two *rasas,* two moods, that are my favourites—meditative and romantic. So, I like all ragas which come within the fold of these two moods.

Interviewer:

So do you think that classical music has the power to heal or to bring about a change?

Shiv Kumar Sharma:

I'll say that music has that power. It can be folk music or Western music or symphony or our classical music. There are only seven notes all over the world. Nobody has been able to create an eighth note. Ragas have been created by many maestros but till now no artiste has ever given birth to the eighth *swar*. Each *swar* affects an individual in its own way. It depends on the individual and what he likes.

But it is true that music does heal our mind, body and soul. And if we understand how and which *swar* affects an individual and in which way, if proper research is done on this, then I think music can be used for therapy.

Interviewer:

Our classical music or any music?

Shiv Kumar Sharma:

I think every music, if we know how to use and on whom to use. Maybe for us in India, our Hindustani classical music might be more effective, because we have heard it from the beginning. But in music *agar swar saccha lag raha hai to asar hoga (*if the notes ring true and pure that music will definitely have an impact).

Interviewer:

Is the *gharana* system relevant now?

Shiv Kumar Sharma:

Earlier there was not much exposure, records were not available, even the radio was not there. With time and technological advancement everything changed. Now if something is happening in one part of the world, it can be seen by and known to the rest of the world. There is so much exposure. In this era of technological exposure, the boundaries of *gharana* cannot be maintained. Musicians do get inspired by any good music from any part of the world. While earlier, this was the speciality of the *gharana*s. Each *gharana* maintained its exclusivity. But now it cannot be maintained. Times have changed now.

Interviewer:

Do you have a *gurukul*?

Shiv Kumar Sharma:

No, not a *gurukul*, but I have been teaching for the last thirty years. My disciples are there everywhere in the world. They are doing very well.

Interviewer:

How do you prepare yourself for *jugalbandi* or *tigalbandi*?

Shiv Kumar Sharma:

I hardly do *jugalbandi.*

Interviewer:

With Pandit Hariprasad Chaurasia you have done many such concerts and recordings. What is important in *jugalbandi*?

Shiv Kumar Sharma:

In *jugalbandi* two things are very important—first, there should be proper understanding between the two artistes and secondly, each should understand and appreciate the other's music. And they should play with the spirit that they have to create music together and not be in competition with each other. The feeling of one-upmanship should not be there.

Interviewer:

There appears to be a spiritual ambience when you perform. What are you thinking at that time?

Shiv Kumar Sharma:

Music for me is meditation. Music is a kind of prayer that gives me a spiritual high. It gives me a kind of bliss which I am sharing with the audience. That is my approach to music, and that is how I feel. Maybe when I'm on stage my expressions change, I don't know. Maybe I am looking at someone, my eyes are looking at somebody, but though physically I am sitting there, looking at someone, actually I'm somewhere else.

Interviewer:

Many tabla players have accompanied you, like Ustad Alla Rakha, Pandit Kishan Maharaj, Pandit Anokhey Lal, Swapan Chowdhury, Karamatullaha Khan, Ahmedjan Thirakwa, Samta Prasad and many others. What is it that you look for in a tabla player that energises you as a performer?

Shiv Kumar Sharma:

I have also played with Shafaat, Anindo, Zakir. Every tabla player has his own style. And the only thing that I expect from them, while accompanying me is that they should capture the spirit of my music. I think with Zakir and Shafaat I have played the maximum. And both played with me for the first time when they were just fifteen or sixteen years old.

Interviewer:

Your name has become synonymous with the santoor. Even the instrument is very popular, yet there are not as many disciples of santoor as we have for sitar. Why?

Shiv Kumar Sharma:

I would like to ask how many performers are there of other instruments? Many people can learn it, but how many are performing and of what calibre are they? Think about it. As for santoor, it is just fifty to fifty-five years old, while the other instruments have been here for centuries. So, if we compare it in that light then we would realise that today people know about it, it is included in concerts all over the world. Additionally, its popularity can be judged by the fact that many restaurants have been named after it, a *pan masala* is named santoor, even a soap has been named santoor! (*Smiles*).

Interviewer:

What do you want to convey through your music?

Shiv Kumar Sharma:

To me classical music is not merely for entertainment. Music to me is meditation; spirituality and our classical music are two sides of the same coin. Music should create spiritual bliss for the performer and the listener and it is this essence that I am forever searching for. My dream has always been to create that kind of music which makes listeners forget even to clap; there's absolute silence after the performance.

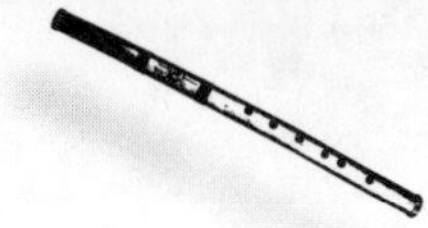

FLUTE

Struggle is necessary

PANDIT HARIPRASAD CHAURASIA

(1 July, 1938–)

The soothing strains of the flute infuse the environment at the Mumbai *gurukul*—Vrindavan. The frequent telephone bells often join in to create a harmony with the musical notes.

Pandit Hariprasad Chaurasia talks without mincing words and is straightforward in expressing his dismay and anger on classical music being marginalised by the policy makers, 'I'll ask them why they have become apathetic towards classical music and musicians ...'

Not belonging to a musical family did not stop him from pursuing his dream and passion.

His father was a wrestler and his mother passed away when he was just four years old. Scared of his father who wanted him to become a wrestler, he did go to the *akhada* to learn wrestling. But with his heart in music he stealthily began to learn music too. And at the age of eighteen, much against the wishes of his father, he joined All India Radio (AIR) as staff artiste. But here also restlessness followed him like a shadow. After a few years of job security, he gave up everything to follow his dream—music.

Pandit Hariprasad Chaurasia is a classicist and traditionalist, and frankly admits that he enjoys experimenting in new creative genres, 'Giving music for the films is my hobby ...'

Modest, speaking in a lyrical way, he listened to each and every word carefully before replying. Often in between he would speak to his disciples about his schedule and music.

Like a cascading stream flowing down the mountain top, his gurukul reverberated with musical notes from all corners.

There was a musical sphere of silence.

(3 March, 2005)

Interviewer:

Tell us about your childhood. Your father was a wrestler, how did you get interested in music and why did you take up the flute?

Hariprasad Chaurasia:

Interest in music happens because of God's blessings. Only a handful of people receive God's blessings to become a musician. I was thus blessed and so I decided to pursue music. For the last fifty to fifty-five years ! am walking on this musical path, and happily pursuing the journey. In fact I think it is because of my training at the *akhada* that I could develop the stamina and lung power required for playing the flute. And as far as my interest in the flute is concerned, it developed while admiring the photographs of Lord Krishna. Whenever I used to see Lord Krishna with the flute I imagined myself playing it. So I got a flute and secretly started playing it and later on I approached a guru to teach me. Today also I want my flute to be a memory of Krishna. It is the symbol of divine love.

Interviewer:

Earlier the flute was basically an instrument for folk music. Has the playing style and structure of the instrument changed with its introduction into classical music?

Hariprasad Chaurasia:

Flute is one of our most ancient instruments. In fact in the *shastra*s it is said that *vani* (vocal music), *veena* (string instruments) and *venu* (flute and wind instruments) are the three aspects of music. Since it is Lord Krishna's instrument it is divine—it seems very simple but actually takes a lot of strength and perseverance to learn. The way the flute is manufactured and the blowing and fingering techniques have changed a lot over the past.

Interviewer:

Who was your first guru?

Hariprasad Chaurasia:

My first guru was Pandit Raja Ramji. He was staying in Allahabad only and I learnt vocal music from him. Later on I became the disciple of Pandit Bholanathji. He belonged to Benaras but was a staff artiste at AIR, Allahabad. Then I joined AIR as a staff artiste in Odisha. But in Odisha

I couldn't find any guru. Luckily, I was transferred to Mumbai where I became the disciple of Ma Annapurna Devi, daughter of Ustad Allaudin Khan, the legendary musician. Her musical knowledge is immense and I think even two to four births is not enough to gain even a little bit of knowledge from her vast musical repertoire. She is so talented. She gave shape to my thinking and my music.

Interviewer:

So, you started with classical vocal music and then shifted to the flute. Why?

Hariprasad Chaurasia:

Yes, I started with vocal music under Pandit Raja Ramji but later, I was enraptured by the sound of the *bansuri* when I listened to the recital of Pandit Bholanathji. So, I became his disciple and started learning the flute. But that does not mean that I stopped singing. An instrumentalist sings through his instrument. You might not have a melodious voice but that doesn't stop you. Just like somebody who is not good looking, doesn't stop dressing up well.

Interviewer:

Annapurna Deviji plays the surbahar. Then how did she teach you flute? Rather how does a guru who is an expert in some other musical instrument teach something quite different?

Hariprasad Chaurasia:

An instrument is a medium between a *kalakaar* (artiste) and his guru. To play an instrument is a different thing. We don't have to learn to play instruments. We take lessons in music from gurus. I wanted to learn her tradition, not how to play the flute. So, a guru can be an expert of any instrument, it is not a hurdle to learning music from that guru on another, different instrument.

Interviewer:

It is generally believed that music is one art that is passed on from generation to generation ...

Hariprasad Chaurasia:

No, no, it is completely wrong. Till one has the blessings of Ma Saraswati, one cannot become a musician. Now see, there are many musicians whose children have not taken up music. For instance Ustad Amir Khan was such a great musician. But nobody in his family is pursuing this art form. In my own family, except my nephew (Rakesh Chaurasia), nobody else is a musician. It is not imperative that if the parents are musicians, so should the children be.

Interviewer:

Is it not more difficult for a person who does not belong to a musician's family? Does that person have to struggle more to establish oneself?

Hariprasad Chaurasia:

Yes, one has to struggle. But then we all have to struggle to establish ourselves. There's satisfaction and joy in struggle also. It gives us strength, self confidence. If one does not struggle, then one cannot enjoy the fruit of one's hard work. It is very necessary to struggle in any field. One, who struggles in life, learns to live and is blessed by God.

Interviewer:

Why did you think of starting *gurukul*s?

Hariprasad Chaurasia:

This is how I have learnt music and this is the way I want to pass it on to my students. In this tradition there is no give or take of money. The guru keeps the disciple at his place and imparts musical education, without taking anything in return. He looks after the disciple like his own child. This has been the *gurukul* tradition. Most of us have forgotten this aspect. So I decided to restart this ancient tradition, here in Mumbai. And with the blessings of God, it is doing quite well. Now I am planning to start such *gurukul*s in Odisha and Uttar Pradesh and also in America and Europe. I want *gurukul*s to be established everywhere, so that all deserving and poor children can benefit from them. So that children can learn music under the guidance of a good guru and pursue their dreams.

Interviewer:

You don't take a fee or is the fee subsidised?

Hariprasad Chaurasia:

I don't take a penny. When I have not given any fee to my guru how can I charge my students? If I want to continue my guru's tradition then I do not have the right to charge anything from my students also. I believe in this.

Interviewer:

Which is your favourite raga?

Hariprasad Chaurasia:

I like all ragas. Whichever raga I play, it becomes my favourite. Depending on my mood, sometimes I like morning ragas, sometimes afternoon or evening ragas or at times night ragas. For every time slot there are beautiful ragas and *ragini*s. Now if I take the name of one particular raga, it will not be fair. If I have four children and say that one child is very dear to me, will it be proper? Every raga has its own essence, hue, shade and emotions. So to take any particular raga's name will not be correct.

Interviewer:

What do you think about the mushrooming music schools?

Hariprasad Chaurasia:

People who have opened these institutes think that this is the only way to do it and that is all they want to do. They want to earn their livelihood through it. So, it is all right for them. But it is a business. They take fee from the students. What I am doing is completely different. I believe in imparting musical education through the *gurukul* method.

Interviewer:

But is it a good trend for classical music?

Hariprasad Chaurasia:

Students who are devoted to music, who want to pursue music, should search for a good guru. They should go and stay with that guru, serve him day and night and learn music seriously. They should be prepared to devote their life for the cause of music. This is my opinion.

Interviewer:

You have given music in films also. What do you prefer doing—giving music in films or giving concerts?

Hariprasad Chaurasia:

I like both. To give music in films is very creative. One has to see the film and accordingly assimilate music to enhance every scene. Also one has to have an idea of who is the target audience in the cinema halls. Keeping these factors in mind, one has to compose music for the film. It is a very different experience and I really learnt a lot and enjoyed it. Classical music is my *dharma* and giving music in films is my hobby.

Interviewer:

What is so special about the Shiv-Hari duo that it enchants everybody?

Hariprasad Chaurasia:

Our heart is one. It appears that we are twins, musically. Whatever he thinks, I come to know and whatever I am thinking he can understand, immediately. It makes quite a lot of difference in the way we work. And we respect each other's views.

Interviewer:

While giving *jugalbandi*s on stage do you discuss with the partner before going on stage or is it impromptu?

Hariprasad Chaurasia:

At times we discuss before going on stage and sometimes we just begin on stage. Suppose it's a concert of many artistes and we have no idea about other artistes and their presentations, raga, *bandish*, etc., then we do not plan. But if only the two of us are in the concert then it is planned in advance. We discuss about the raga and *bandish* and also take into account the type of audience before finalising our piece. I am emphasising on audience because the audience is not the same everywhere. In some places we have a knowledgeable audience that understands the intricacies and in some places it is mixed, so we plan accordingly.

Interviewer:

Where do you think is the audience better—here or abroad? People generally say that abroad the audience is more disciplined and organised.

Hariprasad Chaurasia:

No, no. Human beings are the same all over. We all have two eyes, two ears two hands. We all think alike. Our emotions are the same. But yes, abroad they are more disciplined. If the show is supposed to begin at 6:00 pm, the entrance door closes five minutes before the concert. Nobody is allowed in after that. But here, in India it is not like that. People keep coming even after thirty minutes into the concert. This is something to do with habit. So, I don't blame them. I know if I am performing in India it is for an Indian audience.

Interviewer:

What has been the contribution of your family in your musical progress?

Hariprasad Chaurasia:

Everything is because of them! Unless we have the complete support and well wishes of our family and friends we cannot progress, not only in music but in any and every field. Family support is very vital. It is not necessary that they have to be in the same profession or be with us on stage but they have to understand us, our moods and dreams and encourage us to follow our passion. Only when one has family support, he or she can move ahead, be it music, art, sports, or any other field.

Interviewer:

On what basis do you take disciples?

Hariprasad Chaurasia:

Besides talent I see whether he has any family responsibilities or problems. It would be wastage of time for me as well as for him, if he bows down to family pressure and responsibilities and gives up music after a period of training. This becomes all the more important since I do not take money. Had I been taking a fee it would have been fine for he would have given me money as compensation. But as I do not take money, I expect complete devotion from all my disciples.

Interviewer:

How many disciples do you have?

Hariprasad Chaurasia:

There are many.

Interviewer:

Who are the most promising ones?

Hariprasad Chaurasia:

All are promising. I don't take any disciple till I am satisfied that he is going to carry forward my tradition and that he is devoted. Because I work hard on them and they too have to work very hard. I don't have time to waste; neither do I want them to waste their time.

Interviewer:

There's a general notion that Hindustani Classical Music is very difficult to understand. It has a select audience. What should be done to make it reach the masses?

Hariprasad Chaurasia:

Till a few years back All India Radio was doing a good job by broadcasting various programmes. It really had a very vast network. It used to take music even to people in remote villages. But now it appears that they have become allergic to classical music. This situation is incomprehensible. I have seen the golden period of All India Radio. I am talking about 1952 and since then I have been associated with the radio. I don't understand why and how it has deteriorated. The same system, officers, same building, staff artistes, but its standard has gone down. Nothing is the same now. I don't see art being respected, neither is there any respect for artistes, nor are there any interesting music shows on air waves. Everybody is getting money, they are working, but art has completely disappeared. I want to ask when will art regain its stature. What have we done to merit this treatment? Now we have television also but the AIR is like the grandfather of media. If it's not happening on AIR then what can be expected from television, which is still in its infancy.

Interviewer:

Who is responsible for this apathetic attitude?

Hariprasad Chaurasia:

Who else? It is the government. I am not saying the AIR is responsible. Guidelines for the AIR are set by government officials, Information and Broadcasting Ministry. What do these officers do? Just sit there and sip tea? Why do they make such policies which have ruined our tradition, our culture? There used to be a National Programme, concert programmes, artistes were so involved—where have they all gone? Ministers are there;

the ministry exists. It is not that the ministry has been shut down. Had that happened, I would have understood. I am really very unhappy about it and this pain will remain, because we had all begun our musical life's journey with the radio. Even now I am associated with the radio but I am very unhappy that officers who make policies have scant regard for classical music. I should not blame anybody, but what can one do, times have changed, classical music has lost its sheen with the media and it makes me so unhappy. But I know, this too shall pass.

Interviewer:

What do you want to express through your music?

Hariprasad Chaurasia:

I want to say that in every family, area, colony and country there should be peace and happiness and harmony. Future generations should be healthy and prosperous, away from illness, and they should be blessed with a joyful mind. And only music can bring all this. Music is a medicine that can purify the body, mind and soul.

Interviewer:

What would you like to say to people, any particular advice?

Hariprasad Chaurasia:

I would just like to ask policy makers why have they converted the Taj Mahal of music into a ruined hut? I am very sad about it. What has happened? Why has classical music, our tradition and culture been pushed into the background? That's all I want to ask. Thank you.

V O C A L

Music is Love

VIDUSHI SAVITA DEVI

(7 April, 1941–)

We interviewed Vidushi Savita Devi at her home in New Delhi, where her mother Vidushi Siddheshwari Devi had left behind a great musical tradition. It is in this very house that Savita Devi began her Siddheshwari Devi Academy of Indian Music in 1978, a year after the death of her mother and guru.

Vidushi Siddheshwari Devi groomed both her daughters—Shanta and Savita—to carry on her tradition. But a queer twist of fate unsettled everything. Savita Devi's elder sister, Shanta Devi, who had been accompanying Siddheshwari Devi, suddenly passed away. And Savita Devi married Pandit Kishan Maharaj, against the wishes of her mother. Relations between mother and daughter soured. But fate had something else in store. Her marriage hit a bad patch. She returned to her mother, began her musical journey afresh. Completely devoting herself to music, soon Savita Devi began to accompany her mother in concerts, filling the vacuum created by her sister's untimely death.

Brought up in the *purab ang gayaki* environment, Savita Devi enriched it further with her well-modulated voice. Her *khayal* training under Pandit Mani Prasad helped her create her own style in *thumri*. 'I never thought about it consciously, it just happened ...' The interview often meandered from music to the vicissitudes of life. Every time she tried brushing away tiny dust particles from the various chapters of her life, her eyes welled up with tears.

(2 March, 2005)

Interviewer:

Your book *Maa—Siddheshwari* is a very touching biography. Do you miss her too much?

Savita Devi:

I have expressed myself quite openly in the book. However, there are a few memories which I forgot to include in the book. And there's one particular memory which I would like to share. It is generally believed that with death all ties are snapped. But I do not think so. Even after the death of my mother, I feel her presence everywhere. I often talk to her. You will not believe that I've learnt a few *bandishes* in my dreams from my mother.

Interviewer:

Really? That's intriguing. How?

Savita Devi:

There were certain pieces that Maa had not taught me completely. I often used to think about it and wonder how to complete it. So, it was in my dreams that Maa taught me. I could hear her singing in my dreams and next morning during *riyaaz* I discovered that I knew the *bandish* completely. There's one more instance. My mother was a great devotee of Uddhav, friend of Lord Krishna. She always used to say that there can be no greater *bhakt* (devotee) of Lord Krishna like Uddhav. I was sitting here, in my living room and trying to compose one of the *bandishes* of *Baramasa—Uddhav bhor rahi madhukar jayen.* I roughly recorded it and when later I listened to it I could distinctly hear another voice along with my own. And that another voice was that of my mother, Siddheshwari Devi. Then I made my son listen to that tape. He too confirmed my doubt.

Interviewer:

This is mystical.

Savita Devi:

Yes, but true. In fact, many a time, whenever I have to go for some big concert I always feel that Maa is with me. Once in Benaras I was supposed to perform *jugalbandi* with Ustad Bismillah Khan Sahib. I was very nervous. But while I was practising at Khan Sahib's home, I felt as if Maa was guiding me. That very night I again dreamt about

Maa. I saw my childhood home in Benaras and Maa calling me from the wooden stairs. (*Her voice chokes, eyes become moist*). ... It was purely because of her blessings that the next day's concert went off very well. Even Khan Sahib was very pleased and he blessed me. I believe in mysticism and I always feel her presence around me, protecting me, guiding me.

(*At this point her grandchildren return from school and cling to her.*)

Interviewer:

At what age did you start learning music?

Savita Devi:

Arre bhai, if I say that my lessons in music began while I was in my mother's womb, it would not be wrong. She was giving concerts till the last trimester of the pregnancy. I'll show you one photograph of the concert where all the bigwigs like Ustad Amir Khan Sahib, Ustad Bade Ghulam Ali Khan Sahib, Bal Gandharva, were sitting in the audience and Maa, with me in her womb, was on stage, singing. And as for formal training, I think, it began when I was four or five years old.

Interviewer:

Was she strict?

Savita Devi:

During childhood she taught me lovingly but later on she became very strict. She was stricter with me than with any other student. Any mistake by me was intolerable to Maa. For each mistake the punishment was to practise it hundred more times. She never praised me. Even if somebody would praise me she would always cut them short, 'Yes ... she would do well, if she practises more.' Actually she wanted me to study. She always used to say, *'Sangeet to ghar mein hai ... par vidya!'* So, when I was six or seven years old she sent me away to a boarding school in Benaras. To my mother, education was very important. It was only during summer vacations that I used to travel with her for concerts.

Interviewer:

What about your elder sister, Shanta?

Savita Devi:

Maa taught her. She used to sing very well, but unfortunately she died very young.

Interviewer:

When did you give your first public concert, I mean at what age and how were you feeling at that time?

Savita Devi:

See, though I was put in a hostel Maa had arranged for a music tutor there. He was very strict. I received regular canings from him. Can you imagine that at that tender age he taught me *dhrupad?* I still remember it; you see ... I still remember his cane ... (*laughs aloud*). At the age of seven I sang in my school competition and won a gold medal. And during that time, before Independence, a gold medal was made of pure gold. But Maa was so generous that she gifted that gold medal to my tutor. She was that sort ... caring and sensitive.

Interviewer:

You had music as your subject?

Savita Devi:

Oh, no, no. Actually Maa had categorically told me not to take music as a subject. First I took science, then Sanskrit and then finally I took music, without informing my mother. I started learning sitar from Bimla Nandan Chatterjee. He used to take sitar lessons in the school. And the first song that I played on the sitar was *Jana Gana Mana,* our national anthem. Maa was unaware of my change of subject. She came to know much later, after seeing my results, through a letter from our principal.

Interviewer:

And then you must have got a good ticking off.

Savita Devi:

A little bit, but she was pleased that I passed with distinction. And my logic made sense to her. You see, she had asked me not to learn *gaana,* meaning vocal music, not *bajaana*, instrumental music. So I convinced her that I had not done anything wrong. (*She narrates laughingly*) ... Words, you know ... and their interpretation. Anyway, after this she told me to carry on her tradition and to take music seriously. After a few years I came to Delhi and became a lecturer at Daulat Ram College.

Interviewer:

In between you married Pandit Kishan Maharaj (*At the time of the interview Pt. Kishan Maharaj was alive. He passed away on 4 May, 2008*). Was your mother happy with your decision?

Savita Devi:

You can say it was destiny. Maa was searching for a right match for me. But most of the families were against my singing. So I told Maa that if I will not be allowed to pursue my art, my *kala*, then how could I be happy? During this time I met Kishan Maharaj. He was so handsome, good-looking and pleasant that I was completely swept off my feet. We gave many programmes together. Finally, we decided to get married and when I informed Maa she was very annoyed. She and the other members of the family were against it. But it had to happen, so it happened. As I said, it was destined.

Interviewer:

Then why did you separate?

Savita Devi:

Actually, Maharajji was a very dominating personality. See, I married him, thinking that he will encourage me, not throttle my talent. *Jab aapse aapki kala hi chheeni jaye tab phir aap bhi to marne lagte hain na bhai* (If your art is snatched away from you, you too start dying inside, don't you)! We had many arguments regarding this. I started feeling suffocated. And finally I had to take a decision ... a hard one ... You understand what I am trying to say?

Interviewer:

Yes, yes.

Savita Devi:

Besides this, there were many other domestic misgivings. By this time we had two children also. Responsibility of their upbringing ... no money ... and so many other things, it was becoming chaotic ... and before marriage I had resigned my job at Kanpur Degree College, where I was the Head of Department of Music. So, I went back to my mother and she pardoned me. She helped me financially but how long could I take financial support from my mother? And I didn't want my children to study in some municipal school. Once you get married and have children, then you must take up the responsibility also. *Nahin?* So, I decided to take up the responsibility. I begged Maa for forgiveness. I wrote a letter to her, apologised and requested her to help me. I told her that the future of my two kids was very bleak in Benaras. Maa understood my plight and I came to Delhi. With her blessings I got a job in Daulat Ram College. Thus began my life all over again. After all, how long could I have suffered and jeopardised my children's future. (*She breaks down*). I started writing the biography during that time.

Interviewer:

So you started writing the book, *Maa– Siddheshwari* in the 70s?

Savita Devi:

Yes. This book is an outcome of nearly twenty years of labour.

Interviewer:

In the book you have not mentioned much about your father. Why?

Savita Devi:

Well, he was a retired army personnel. He used to come and stay with us but I had a stepmother and step-siblings too. And most of the time he was away. I wasn't attached to him. He was my father but there was no affection. It was my mother who brought me up, just like I've brought up my children. Kishan Maharaj has not done anything for my children. He is their father, that's all. The responsibilities that come when one becomes a parent have not been fulfilled by Kishan Maharajji. I have brought them up. Similarly my father was there but it was my mother who really looked after my needs and brought me up.

(*The telephone rings. She picks it up and talks about her forthcoming concert.*)

Interviewer:

How many kinds of styles are there in *thumri*?

Savita Devi:

People say there are two kinds of *shaili* (styles)—*Purab ang* and *Punjab ang*. But Bade Ghulam Ali Khan Sahib used to say that there is only one style and that is *Purab ang*, only the presentation differs. The language used is *braj bhasha*. Now, you see one raga sung by different maestros will sound different. The notes are the same but the presentation style of each maestro is different. It bears the signature of each maestro. It is the same in *thumri gayan* also. The same *thumri* sung by Badi Moti Bai or Siddheshwari Devi or Bade Ghulam Ali Khan Sahib will sound different.

Interviewer:

Why it is that *thumri* is still not considered to be a form of pure classical music?

Savita Devi:

I do not consider *thumri* 'semi-classical.' I think *thumri* is a form of pure classical music and I am fighting for it to be recognised as such. You see *thumri* is a language of emotions—*bhaav pradhan.* It is a bouquet of different ragas. But just as a painter has to choose which colour combinations will appear beautiful, so is the case with *thumri.* We have to use an appropriate and rich combination of ragas and *swars.* There is a proper method to it. It cannot be done blindly. The words are very limited in *thumri,* but we convey those very words in different emotions. Like for instance take the words *Jao wahin tum shyam jahan saari rain jaage ho.* It can be improvised in so many ways (*she sings—improvising in different ways and decorates it with layers of emotions.*) You see, one word can be improvised in so many ways. But in improvising we have to highlight the hidden emotions also. That's why it is called *bhaav pradhan shaili.* If there are no emotions in *thumri gayan* then it is mechanical, technical.

Interviewer:

What kind of an institute is the Siddheshwari Devi Academy of Indian Music?

Savita Devi:

I established this Academy after the demise of Maa. It is to primarily impart education in *thumri gayaki.* For the last so many years (The

Academy was established in March, 1978, a year after the demise of Vidushi Siddheshwari Devi) I am running this institute and imparting education in music. I have many students and they are doing quite well. I have also established an award, honouring Maa–*Swar Siddhi*. It is given to artistes, in recognition of their contribution to classical music.

Interviewer:

Your children didn't pursue music. Why?

Savita Devi:

No, they have not taken it up professionally. My elder son, Sanjay, used to play the tabla very well even though he didn't receive any proper *taleem*. Unfortunately he died in a car accident. He was only eighteen. (*Her voice chokes*) I was completely shattered. Even my younger son, Ajay was in that car. He was in the ICU for eleven days. But my elder son died on the spot. It was too devastating. I don't want to talk about it now. (*She starts crying*)

Interviewer:

What is music to you?

Savita Devi:

Music is love. Music is faith. Music is devotion. Music is an offering, a prayer to God. Music makes us reach out to God. Music spreads happiness, peace and unity. It has no boundary. It spreads the message of love and our music, whether of the north or the south, is deep, meditative and it enriches the soul.

SAROD

Music is Universal

USTAD AMJAD ALI KHAN

(9 October, 1945–)

It was a difficult task attempting to meet Ustad Amjad Ali Khan for an exhaustive tête-à-tête. A busy artiste, travelling all over the world, mesmerising everybody with his scintillating strings on the sarod, he was often away on tours. After being informed by his receptionist several times that Khan Sahib is out of the country, one day I heard a modest voice from the other end saying, 'Hello!!!...' I immediately recognised the voice and persuaded him to give us an appointment. 'Okay ... day after tomorrow ... at 11:00 am.'

We reached his bungalow, situated in a posh locality of Delhi. The moment we stepped inside, the aesthetic beauty and artistic grandeur touched a chord. Immediately, Ustad Amjad Ali Khan greeted us. Dressed in an off-white kurta pyjama, his intense, twinkling eyes looked directly at us, as if scrutinising our knowledge of music.

He took us into his place of worship—the *riyaaz* room. A grand portrait of his father and guru, the legendary Ustad Hafiz Ali Khan, stared at us. We were immediately transported to the realm of music. On the right and left side of this portrait were the photographs of the earlier five generations of Ustad Amjad Ali Khan (he is the sixth generation of the Senia-Bangash *gharana*). It was as if Ustad Amjad Ali Khan was telling us, 'I am here, because of them ... my ancestors ...' Not a streak of memory was allowed to fade. And as we gradually inhaled the pure, artistic air charged with emotions, warm feeling and a sense of care, Ustad Amjad Ali Khan left us to adjust our technical gadgets, amidst the awe-inspiring gaze of yesteryear legends. On the small, slightly raised platform were the musical instruments, a part of the family inheritance down the ages.

On stage, always dressed in an immaculately designed kurta, he never forgets to express his gratitude in his soft voice to his danseuse wife, Subhalakshmi, for constantly being his support and strength and of course, for being his dress designer.

The interview lasted for more than an hour. Often during the course of the interview, he would gradually take off on a completely different trajectory. But would soon return, 'Sorry, I had wandered off ... where was I?' Ustad Amjad Ali Khan speaks as if the sentences echo off a printed page, explicit, explanatory and quite absorbing.

(21 July, 2004)

Interviewer:

Khan Sahib you have won innumerable awards, international recognition and have a huge following. How does it feel to be the second Indian to win the Fukuoaka[1] Asian cultural award—a very prestigious Asian award?

Amjad Ali Khan:

I was overwhelmed when I got the telephone call informing me of this award. For a few seconds I thought some divine voice was making the announcement ... Of course it is an honour for our tradition and culture and I hope the next generations would also do their best to preserve the purity and sanctity of Hindustani classical music. I accepted the award in all humility, thinking of my guru, my parents and our ancestors. It is because of them, their blessings that classical music is what it is today. Poets, saint-musicians—like Swami Haridas, Miyan Tansen, Swami Tyagaraja, Muthuswami Dikshitar, Shyama Sastri, Purandaradas, Baiju Bawra—all these legends are still alive in my heart and it is actually these people to whom these awards should be given. I am a tool, a medium ... I accept awards, recognition, on their behalf. It is their *tapasya* and blessings, and the blessings of my guru and father Ustad Hafiz Ali Khan Sahib and my mother Rahat Jahan that I am here today, an artiste ...

Interviewer:

Your mother always stood by you, through your struggles?

Amjad Ali Khan:

As you know, at that time, most Muslim women remained in purdah and my mother was no exception ... a simple woman who remained in purdah throughout her life. It's really sad that no one knows, no one talks or asks about my mother. I really believe that a mother is the first guru of any child.

Interviewer:

Your father was also your guru. How was your relationship with him?

---

1. Fukuoka Award is given to honour the remarkable contribution of individuals/groups/ organisations in preserving and promoting the Asian culture. It is presented by Fukuoka City and Yokatopia Foundation. The first award was given in 1990 and in 1991 late Pt. Ravi Shankar was the first Indian to be bestowed this award under Grand prize category. There are three categories—Grand Prize, Akademic Prize and Arts and Culture Prize.

Amjad Ali Khan:

There was a huge age difference between me and my father. He was the hero of the forties, contemporary to Ustad Abdul Karim Khan Sahib, Ustad Faiyaz Khan Sahib, Ustad Inayat Khan Sahib, Pandit Achhan Maharaj, Ustad Ahmad Jan Thirakwa and Pandit Omkarnath Thakur. So he was an artiste of that generation. Human values were very important to him. He was very generous and forgiving and I really respect that because today these values have lost meaning ... today human beings have become cruel. There is no *tehzeeb* (manners/etiquette/decorum) now amongst people. But to my father, *tehzeeb* was extremely vital. Actually Abba had a certain innocence about him—very helpful, kind, courteous and encouraging. The most beautiful thing about his character was that in whatever condition he was, he would always feel that he had everything. He was satisfied under all circumstances.

Interviewer:

Even though he had to see poverty and hard times?

Amjad Ali Khan:

Yes, I'll share an incident that reveals this side of Abba. In 1960, when he was awarded the Padma Bhushan, he took me with him to the award ceremony. After the ceremony, we went to the Mughal Gardens for tea. There, our first president, Dr Rajendra Prasad, asked Abba, 'Khan Sahib is everything fine? Are you facing problems of any kind?' Now the reality was that we were not very well off at that time, we were living in a rented house; we had hired a scooter or a taxi to go to the ceremony. Many artistes, even at that time, had been given government houses and patronage, so if a statesman of such stature was enquiring about his well-being Abba could have asked for anything. He could have asked for a house. But no ... to him all these things never mattered. Very innocently Abba said, 'You are like the Emperor of India, you must save Raga Darbari. People today are taking too many liberties with Darbari, this really upsets me. If it continues like this Darbari will lose its purity. You must save Raga Darbari because it was created by Miyan Tansen.' As a young boy I was so embarrassed about what my father was saying and wondered whether the president really understood what my Abba was talking about. For a second, even our president was flummoxed. He replied, 'Khan Sahib I'm not sure I understand what exactly you want me to do about this.' Basically Abba, in his innocence, wanted an assurance from the president—he thought the president might be able to pass some legislation in the Parliament about how Raga Darbari should be sung and played! Such was his commitment to Hindustani classical music and he felt it was his duty to preserve and propagate the art. After a while, Dr Prasad said, 'Don't worry Khan Sahib, I'm sure Darbari will remain safe. Is there anything else I can do for you?' Abba thanked him and said he had to leave since it was going to be his namaaz time. Completely oblivious to the protocol that no one can leave before the president, Abba made his way back, with me in tow. Throughout the return journey I had the urge to ask him why he had said all that. But our relationship was more of guru and disciple. I used to address him as 'Abba Sahib' and dared not ask such questions. On reaching home he told my mother like an innocent child that all was well and that the president had given his word that Darbari would be safe. He was so happy, content. It's amazing that people with such pure hearts existed in this world.

Interviewer:

Indeed very touching! Khan Sahib, when you started your musical journey, did you also have to struggle a lot?

Amjad Ali Khan:

Those were difficult times. There was a time when we used to live in a rented house, had to pay ₹250 as rent every month, and we didn't know whether we would be able to pay the rent next month or not. But I didn't run away from those worries. Nowadays in classical music there are two kinds of musicians—those who take care of their future by pursuing a parallel career, they have academic backing. Life becomes safe with a job; and the other kind of artiste is the fakir. This is a different way of life, the fakir doesn't know or care about the future ... two plus two has no meaning for us, music is the only thing that matters, this is the way my forefathers lived. And I too believe in this.

Interviewer:

But how did you deal with this insecurity?

Amjad Ali Khan:

My father used to say, only two kinds of people should pursue Hindustani classical music—the *badshah* (emperor), someone who is rich enough to take care of his needs and can indulge in music, and the fakir (saint), who doesn't care about security or future; for fakirs, music is life and he trusts God. The one thing common between both is that they don't care about the future. That's why if you notice, in the earliest history of Hindustani and Carnatic classical music, all the musicians were actually saints ... Swami Tyagaraja, Swami Haridas and people like them. So maybe, the true fakir and devotee, finds his path and reaches his *manzil* (destination). This is how I saw my father living his life and this is my way of life too.

Interviewer:

So it is a part of the music profession?

Amjad Ali Khan:

Well, I feel embarrassed to say music is my profession, it is not only my profession, it is my passion, my way of life. Only playing music by itself is nothing, it is a complete way of life—how you talk, conduct yourself, move, live, who are the people you meet, and why you meet them. So my life is like an open book. My wife Subhalakshmi, my sons Amaan and Ayaan, we are all like friends, we discuss every point before taking decisions and the common binding factor is that we feel the presence of God and we feel that there is only one religion in this world and that is humanity. Music has no religion, like flowers, water, wind, fire, fragrance and the seven notes or with the flats and sharps—twelve notes, music belongs to everyone. Music is universal.

Interviewer:

So music connects everyone. But even within music, there are many different branches of it in the world, Hindustani music being one of those. Where does Hindustani music stand in relation to the other music genres and styles in the world?

Amjad Ali Khan:

Yes, sometimes people want to discriminate between our music and their music, saying this is Japanese music, this is Western classical, that is pop, but for me *music is music*. I have learnt and understood music not through books but by personal experiences, by the values that my father has given me, by listening to great artistes, by listening to the discussions of great stalwarts about music and by being introspective about music. I make my own decisions about what I want to play, how I want to present music, what I want to express through my music. The search continues.

Interviewer:

Khan Sahib you said 'your music is a search'. So what exactly are you searching for in music?

Amjad Ali Khan:

Once I got the opportunity to pay my respect to Swami Tyagaraja by performing at his *Samadhi* (tomb) at Tanjavur. But the condition was that I had to present a Tyagaraja *kriti* only. So I learnt from a South Indian vocalist. In one of the *kritis*, Tyagaraja asks God whether it is possible in one's lifetime, to understand the meaning of all the seven notes! Imagine, a learned saint like Tyagaraja 'searching' the meaning of seven notes ... he was so humble. So, to understand these seven notes, and then to understand a raga takes a lifetime—each raga, each *taal* is like an ocean! Every time I sit to play a raga, I'm scared of the raga, I don't know whether I would be able to do justice to the purity of the raga ... whether I would be able to experience the deity in that raga. This humility, nervousness is important to me. My father often used to say, 'If you are not able to show the true soul of the raga, then the raga gets restless and it will curse you.' Most musicians perform one raga for long durations. But Abba would play a raga for a relatively short time. Listeners would often coax him to play the composition for a longer time since they were enjoying it, but he would get angry and say, 'I am not here to do an operation of the raga, I want to bring out its beauty, its *roop*, its character.' Till this day I remember his words and it is with these thoughts and philosophy that I want to take my life, my quest forward.

Interviewer:

You performed on stage for the first time when you were six or seven years old. Who was your source of inspiration?

Amjad Ali Khan:

I have three elder brothers. One was in Bhopal, the other in Gwalior, and one cousin of mine, they were all outstanding sarod players. In fact, they were all like gurus to me. But unfortunately, they did not adhere to my father's advice as devotedly as they should have. Now the firstborn, the eldest child, is the one who is expected to be the rightful heir to a musical legacy. For all of Abba's contemporaries, their eldest children were already carrying the mantle of their musical legacy, but there was a vacuum in our home. My eldest brother was too complacent about being the eldest son of a famous father ... he broke away from music, from us ... decided to walk alone. When he went away my father was shattered. That grief, that sadness that I saw on Abba's face, the suffering that he went through, made me promise to myself that I won't ever let him down. For the last ten years of his life he was bedridden, he was not keeping well. During that time I would give him all my earnings. He was a generous man; he made many donations and all this made him happy. Seeing him happy, I was happy. Today when children start earning they often ask their parents where they are spending money and why, but I never asked Abba. I wanted him to feel as if he himself was earning, not me. This gave me a chance to look after him. This is the reason I remained in Delhi. I remember in 1970, when James Beveridge was making a documentary on me, he asked me about my life's ambition and I had promptly replied, 'to look after my parents and serve them.' That was my true feeling. He was amazed. See, I believe that whatever ambition or expectations we might nurture; we simply cannot fulfil them without the blessings of our parents and gurus. We will not be able to achieve our dreams till we serve our parents and gurus. That's why the concept of ambition and career has never really been very significant to me.

Interviewer:

So, you always believed in this and never ever compromised?

Amjad Ali Khan:

No, you see, it is said that our Hindustani classical music has the gait of an elephant—slow, steady and dignified; it is not a horse race. That's what I feel about my life too. I have not compromised in life's philosophy as well as in my music. I am not an entertainer; I am a representative of a long legacy.

Interviewer:

Since you started performing so young in life, what about formal education?

Amjad Ali Khan:

In childhood, I had tutors for each subject who used to come home. In Gwalior, there was a boarding school and family members were keen that I go to this school. Though Abba was keen about my going to school, he also wanted to have me around all the time. He had grown old by that time and moreover he was concerned that I must learn everything from him before anything happens to him. That was the time when I used to wish that my father was younger, I would have had more years to spend with him, to learn, to play and take care of him. So when I grew up I wanted to get married early and have children, so that I would be able to play with them and be with them, like a friend. The worst part of my life's journey was that I could not hear the music of my father's young days. At that time we had shifted to Delhi and all my father's friends advised him that Amjad should be sent to a school. So I was enrolled at Modern School in Delhi.

Interviewer:

How did you find the atmosphere in school?

Amjad Ali Khan:

It was a shock to me—a culture shock. The *tehzeeb* we had learnt at home had no place in the outside world it seemed. I would always address people as *aap* and touch the feet of elders. But in Delhi, in school, these things didn't matter to anyone and my classmates would address me as *tu*. This was totally out of tune with my upbringing and I was shocked the way people talked, addressed, moved in society here! But anyway, with due respect to my school friends, my teachers were very kind and school taught me how to face the world.

Interviewer:

School, studies, games ... did you get time to do *riyaaz* at that time?

Amjad Ali Khan:

Well, I honestly feel that a lot of time is wasted in school because there is hardly any talk about art, culture and tradition. There is only an unnatural competition for grades and marks in subjects and that is why our tradition of education does not really encourage any child to become an artist. They destroy all the artistic instinct in every child. But having said that, I'm really thankful to my school principal. We used to have a sports period for two hours. I requested him if I could go home during that time and do my *riyaaz* instead of playing football since I was not interested in sports at all. He could see my future—he had foresight, vision. I think he had faith in my conviction. He allowed me to leave the school for *riyaaz.* It was a difficult decision for any principal, but Mr Kapoor was a true educationist. And to top it all, he always protected me. I'll tell you a very interesting incident. You see, I was very weak in Mathematics. Strangely, Maths is very important in music, *layakari* involves a lot of Maths, and that I could do easily, but in my Maths paper in school I could never pass. So one day my father asked my principal how my Maths can be improved, and Mr Kapoor good-humouredly said, 'Khan Sahib don't worry, this boy will never pass in Maths and I will never let him fail!' He was very kind, he was keen to encourage and kindle the hope of being an artiste ... *kalakaar* ... in me. Wish we have more principals like him ... hahaha ... But frankly speaking it is my honest wish that all schools should have a period where children are taught about art, culture, values, tradition, how to conduct oneself in life ... *tehzeeb* is very important. I can't tolerate disrespect, *badtameezee* ...

Interviewer:

Talking about education, Khan Sahib you have been taking lecture-demonstrations (lec-dems) here and abroad. How is that experience?

Amjad Ali Khan:

Well, abroad, it is very heartening to know that the world respects Indian culture and tradition so much. Whenever I'm taking such lec-dems I talk about how special and unique Indian culture is. India is the only country where people have the strength and character to touch another person's feet, to respect others, our elders. Realisation of God and reverence towards the guru is given the highest importance in our tradition, our culture.

Interviewer:

You have brought about many innovations in the playing style on the sarod. Tell us about this aspect of your musical quest.

Amjad Ali Khan:

As you know, 'sarod' is actually derived from the Persian word *sarood* that means music, *nagma*, *tarannum*. The earliest sarod was a modification of the Afghani rabab. From childhood I have been listening to the instrument and Abba used to sing and teach me. Now in bow instruments like the sarangi and violin, it is easier to bring out the vocal nuances but sarod is a staccato instrument, it has a pluck, *khaal ka baaja hai*, the drum can be heard. When someone plays the sarod badly it is said jokingly *rui dhuni jaa rahi hai* (playing as if cotton is being carded). My father used to call the sarod a *bepard saaz* ... it doesn't hide your mistakes. It was my desire to be able to sing through my instrument. Today whenever we compare Indian classical music with Western music, we talk of improvisation as the greatest quality of Indian music. Improvisation is fine, but the greatest gift God has given only to Indian music is *meend*—the slides and glides. This is our forte, our precious possession. The world can play staccato music, but the grace and humility of our culture is reflected in that *meend*, which is so unique to our music. This is my personal research and discovery. When we produce that *meend*, it is with the highest grace and humility that we express, it is the most peaceful and pleasing expression I play on my sarod. It is my human feeling. For this, one has to surrender to God and *swar*. After hearing *meend*, Western journalists often write about it as the 'twang' sound. But one has to understand what it is. It is the essence of life!

Interviewer:

You have brought the *khayal gayaki ang* on sarod, so how important is it for a sarod player to be a vocalist as well?

Amjad Ali Khan:

See, earlier in my biographies people used to write that I have developed this *khayal-ang* on sarod. But now, at this age, I want to say that I sing through my sarod; be it *dhrupad*, *khayal*, *thumri*, *dadra*, or folk music, my deepest desire is to sing through my sarod. My effort had always been to be able to play or portray songs on my sarod. This was a taboo for sarod players earlier. In every era, every sarod player has given his best, but in the creative field the sky is the limit. My search, my quest, has brought me where I am today; I am playing the sarod the way I want to play it. The important thing is what does the *Sarod* want to say? Every musician says I play the instrument and I sing, but a musician needs to understand what the instrument wants to say. People lovingly call me 'sarod wizard' and *shehenshah-e-sarod*, but the truth is that I am just a humble servant of the sarod ... the sarod is the emperor; I'm just trying to understand its *mizaaj* (temperament).

Interviewer:

You have in a way simplified the sarod, in the sense that you have taken it to the common people, to the younger generation. But still, today when a youngster wants to learn an instrument, sarod is not very often their first choice, why?

Amjad Ali Khan:

Thanks to the Beatles ... hahaha ... I think it's a syndrome in our country. We have been ruled by the British for 200 years, so there are some latent complexes we have been carrying for ages that have crept into our system.

When Yehudi Menuhin introduced a musician to the world, a sitar player or sarod player, we Indians immediately recognised him ... called those musicians gems of the country. So this has been a kind of *pratha* (tradition) that when Indian musicians are hailed as great musicians abroad, India also accepts them readily, but till then, he is not recognised for his art. Now I also got my first doctorate abroad, from England. But thankfully no pop-star had to introduce me ever! I am proud that first my countrymen encouraged and showered their blessings on me and then people abroad recognised my talent. You are right in pointing out that sarod is not as popular as it should have been, but now we have more communication channels with websites, email, etc. My sons keep telling me about how many people visited our website and this means that exposure is increasing, the world is becoming a global village and more people are getting to know about the sarod. And it's my heartfelt desire that people should recognise the sarod as easily as they do the violin and the guitar.

Interviewer:

Which is your favourite raga?

Amjad Ali Khan:

There are many ragas that the audience love and they are my favourites too like Yaman, Bageshri, Kedar, Hameer and Kamod. But there are certain ragas that are difficult to play on certain instruments. Sarod is technically a very difficult instrument; it doesn't have any frets. Abba used to caution, *Yeh bepard saaz hai, bajaanewala agar dhyan se nahin bajayega to usko beparda kar deta hai!* (Sarod doesn't hide anything. If the instrumentalist does not play it properly, the instrument bares it all!) So there were certain ragas that sarod players were hesitant to play and in my childhood I never heard those ragas on the sarod. Some ragas that are elementary for a vocalist like Bhoopali, Malkauns are very difficult to play on the sarod. When I was a child, Shambhu Maharajji often used to come to our place and during those days I remember playing the tabla in his dance class. So he would teasingly tell me to play Raga Saraswati on the sarod. Now that is a raga that instrumentalists never attempted at that time because of various technical difficulties. His teasing prompted me to think and innovate. On Shambhu Maharajji's first death anniversary, his family invited me to play in his memory, and that day I played Raga Saraswati. It was the first time this raga was attempted by anyone on the sarod.

Interviewer:

You have also created many ragas. So what are your emotions and thoughts when you are creating a raga?

Amjad Ali Khan:

I won't call it creating a raga, ragas cannot be created. I would say I have discovered a raga. Some things are instinctive. I feel every raga has an *atma* (soul). The way spirits surround us, ragas also exist. So sometimes when I am alone, humming something, suddenly I stop and think, 'What is this I'm singing?' It turns out that I've never heard it before, it is something new, then an *atma* can be felt, and it says, 'Do you recognise me?' I say, 'No, I don't.' Then it asks me, 'Will you embrace me, accept me or should I go?' I think it's God's grace that this *atma* has revealed itself to me, I accept it and give it a name and that is a new raga with a name. Scientifically it is said that all kinds of sound and voices exist in this world, it is for us to search and discover.

Interviewer:

Today, what is the future of Hindustani classical music? What do you feel about fusion music that is coming up nowadays?

Amjad Ali Khan:

I think music is of two kinds in this world. One is pure sound, where there are no words, the purest form of music and this means that if you listen to pure sound with full concentration, you receive all the positive effects on your mind and body. It is said, '*Swar hi eeshwar hai*' (Music is God). The second kind is based on language—text, lyrics, story and there is an old saying, 'language creates barriers.' It is through words that you can lie, manipulate, win and lose elections. But *swar* never lies, through sound you cannot lie or deceive anybody. There is yet another kind of music and that is commercial music, there are 'industries' of music that are committed to selling. Here you are tailoring your music according to the choice of the listeners. I am not tailoring anything, I am not compromising. I am just conveying the message of our music that is 5000 years old. Yes, as far as the presentation is concerned, when I am playing in America or France, maybe I think about the presentation aspect so as to keep alive the interest of Western listeners. Whereas while performing in Bengal I have played alone all night, on three occasions. With music, I feel I am connected to every soul, every country, every religion and every song of the world. Music is music and there is nothing to understand in music. Music has to be appreciated and experienced. If there is something you don't understand about music it is only the language. Say when I listen to Pavarotti's music, I don't understand what he is saying, but I enjoy the tone, the sound, the expression of his music. I also enjoy listening to Western classical, Bach and Mozart. But my roots are very strong. I am fortunate that I was born in Gwalior, the land of Tansen where my ancestral house has been converted into a museum.

Interviewer:

You had also started your own music label called Bangash Music. So what kind of music are you promoting under that?

Amjad Ali Khan:

It's basically our archival music; now all our concerts are being recorded digitally.

Interviewer:

Talking of your disciples, apart from your sons who are your other disciples who are very promising?

Amjad Ali Khan:

See, expectations and hopes are high. But I always say that in Indian classical music there's always struggle and there will always be struggle. Only those who can surrender themselves and be dedicated should come into this line. One who wants to know what is going to happen tomorrow should not venture into this line. It is like walking into a dark tunnel, hoping to find sunshine some day. Fortunately, Amaan and Ayaan both showed interest in music since childhood; both think and play differently. Then there are many disciples in different parts of the world. But after teaching so many people, today so many gurus are disillusioned and that experience has been heartbreaking, shattering. There are very few disciples who are the guru's *hamdard* (well-wisher). I realised some years ago that most of my disciples, for whom I did everything, turned their back on me. It was extremely shattering ... I came to know how opportunistic they were and how they have used my name, have exploited my image for their own good. They betrayed me. I taught my disciples like my own children but they broke my trust. It is a grief that I am living with. So today, I teach, but without any expectations. Music institutions with formal training and fee are different. Moreover, that sacrosanct guru-*shishya parampara* has weakened. Today, most of the disciples come to a guru with a hope that the guru would retire soon, thereby they can take his place. There is a saying, *Niyat sabut to manzil aasaan* (Good intentions can make one achieve one's destination). I believe that if your intentions are not right, you can't achieve anything in life. Those who break a guru's heart can never achieve their goal. I believe in this.

Interviewer:

Your family has always stood by you ...

Amjad Ali Khan:

In today's world everyone wants to be alone, everyone thinks they are most important. People are moving away from each other. But we four—my wife and our two children—we live together, we are always together, and this requires understanding and adjustment, and there is no bigger prayer than that. Thinking that the bread earner is the most important person is not true. Everyone is equally important. On sarod we tune nineteen strings, so why can't we tune our own lives too? My life is based on harmony.

Interviewer:

How much credit for your success would you give to your wife?

Amjad Ali Khan:

All the credit! She has contributed so much. And she remains an artiste because she was a performing artiste. I don't agree to it when someone stops performing, people say 'She *was* an artiste.' Any artiste whether he or she performs or not, remains an artiste. For our concerts, she designs the clothes, kurtas, shawls and looks after stage decor, coordination, planning; we always discuss before taking any decisions.

Interviewer:

People often say Hindustani classical music is too difficult to understand. What would you say to them?

Amjad Ali Khan:

There is nothing to understand in music. Music is to be experienced. Music is universal. All systems of music are great. The world would be a much better place with music all around.

SANTOOR

History Revisited

PANDIT BHAJAN SOPORI

(22 November, 1948–)

Fair complexion, long hair, well-chiselled features, full of wit, humour and mixed emotions regarding the history of santoor. That's how santoor maestro, Pandit Bhajan Sopori, comes across. Somewhere deep down he feels that the 'limelight' that ought to have been his prerogative has eluded him. 'I exposed this instrument to the public for the first time. Then in 1959 I played it in Allahabad. It was a seven-day festival. And in front of all the musicians, I, a boy of eleven years, played this instrument. People had not even seen this instrument. They could not even think that classical music can be played on it. ... See I am the person who has brought the santoor back from Central Asia to Kashmir, although it was an instrument of Kashmir.' It was a long interview, delving into discussions on family tradition, music and *Sufiana baaj*.

Pandit Sopori inherited the santoor and *Sufiana gayaki* from his predecessors. Initially he was trained by his grandfather, Pandit S.C. Sopori and later his father Pandit S.N. Sopori became his guru. Even while studying he accompanied saints from place to place. He used to sing and play the santoor. Hardly sleeping for two-three hours at night young Bhajan Sopori was as serious towards studies as he was about music, 'I was always interested in studies. And with the blessings of God I was a very good student throughout my life. All the credit for balancing music and studies goes to my mother. My mother was very particular that along with music I should do well in studies too.'

He obtained a masters degree in English literature, studied Western Classical music at Washington University and also spent a good part of his life with saints. 'The thing with me is that I want to gain as much knowledge as possible. Half of my life has been spent in the company of saints, in the quest for knowledge and truth.'

No wonder, he is conventional, traditional, progressive and a poet, too.

(24 August, 2007)

Interviewer:

You have done masters in two subjects, you write poetry, you are also an organiser of cultural events, besides primarily being a musician and composer. So how do you balance so many different roles?

Bhajan Sopori:

I think it is a gift from God, along with the blessings of our elders. Otherwise it would not have been humanly possible. I was always interested in studies. And with the blessings of God I was a very good student throughout my life. All the credit for balancing music and studies goes to my mother.

Interviewer:

Was she also a musician?

Bhajan Sopori:

No, she was not a musician. On my father's side we have a lineage of dedicated musicians. They really worked hard for the santoor. There is only one santoor *gharana*, and that is ours. There is no other santoor *gharana*. My father was quite strict with me. I was a small child but my father saw to it that I get up early in the morning at 4:00 am and do *riyaaz*, though I might have gone to sleep at 2:00 am only. Mother often used to argue with father but he used to say, 'If he sleeps now, he will keep sleeping throughout his life.' My mother was very particular that along with music I should do well in studies too. It is because of her that both my elder brothers are doing very well in America ... scientists. The eldest one plays the sitar and the one elder to me plays the tabla. But they did not take up music professionally.

Interviewer:

Then how did you happen to take up music professionally?

Bhajan Sopori:

I was considered a child prodigy. I performed for the first time in 1953 and in 1954 my broadcast was featured in the children's programme. I was only six years old. But I was deeply interested in studies also, even now I am. If I get something new to read I am impatient till I have read it. My philosophy in life is very simple—whatever you do in life be convinced about it, be certain about it.

Interviewer:

You have said that one should be certain in life. But you were studying and pursuing music also then towards which field were you 'certain'? Because I think you also appeared for the IAS ...

Bhajan Sopori:

(*Chuckles*) ... Yes, yes. See it's both. That's why I say my mother's contribution has been immense. Musically, my father's side was well established. First my grandfather taught me and then my father took over. My grandfather passed away in 1954-55. And even at that time I was being taught both the styles—*Sufiana shaili* and Hindustani classical. But my mother was very keen that I should do extremely well in studies. She did not want to hear that her child became an artiste because he could not excel in studies. So, I worked hard to complete my studies along with pursuing my passion for music. The thing with me is that I want to gain as much knowledge as possible. Half my life has been spent in the company of saints, in the quest for knowledge and truth.

Interviewer:

Did you live with them?

Bhajan Sopori:

I used to play santoor for them from midnight till early morning, 4:00 am. That is my tradition, though now we hardly have any great saint amidst us. My son also plays for them. So, when I was with saints I saw different facets of life. Now-a-days people are talking about sound therapy. But to really make sound work as therapy one has to know which *swar* will have what effect on different individuals.

Interviewer:

But you do believe in sound therapy and if I am not wrong you practise it also.

Bhajan Sopori:

A little bit, but after a lot of research and experimentation. My association with saints has helped me a lot in all this. You see, *mera bachpan to santon ke beech mein hi beeta hai* (I've spent my childhood in the company of saints). Their contribution in my life and understanding of music is of the same depth as my study of different subjects like metaphysics, logic, maths, literature or psychology and also the study of *raga shastra*, and contemplation. Sound therapy, effective sound therapy can be derived after the study and proper understanding of all these aspects.

Interviewer:

You inherited the *Sufiana* tradition from your family, predecessors, then how did you bridge the difference between *Sufiana music* and Hindustani classical music?

Bhajan Sopori:

Sufiana music is *muqam badh* (a musical mode and set of melodic formulas used to guide improvisation and composition). Earlier *muqam* and raga were often considered one. All compositions are in *taals*, quite difficult ones, and then there are innumerable *taranas*. I feel that *Sufiana* singers have a vast collection of *taranas,* more than what we have in Hindustani classical music. And this is because *tarana* itself is a *Sufi* concept although we do get reference of it here also in our texts. But the word *tarana's* origin can be traced to Persia. And in our music it gets associated with many things. It can be found in *beej mantra* also. That's why many words are entwined with each other. And santoor is that instrument on which *Sufiana* music is dependent. The leader of the group is one who plays the santoor and can sing also and vice-versa. My predecessors were doing this only. In Sopore area there are many *ashrams* for santoor. Sopore is a very rich area, has very fertile soil and is known for many things, such as delicious apples.

Interviewer:

That's why your surname is Sopori?

Bhajan Sopori:

Yes, yes. Sopore is a village in Kashmir. I belong to that area. So when travellers used to come to Sopore, my predecessors used to play classical music but for general people they used to play *Sufi* music only. So my *taleem* was in both Hindustani and *Sufiana* music. I picked up those compositions and accordingly made modifications on the santoor—what will be the position of fingers, wrist, etc, so that it could bring out the requirement and portray the essence of Hindustani *shastriya sangeet* in a rightful manner.

Interviewer:

So what changes did you bring on the santoor? You are the only one who plays *dhrupad ang* on the santoor, so what all changes have you brought about?

Bhajan Sopori:

See, my father started bringing some changes in the playing techniques of santoor in the 1930s. He facilitated *mandra saptak* on santoor. The thing in *Sufiana shaili* is that it is one and a half *saptak—sa re ga ma pa dha ni sa, sa re ga ma pa*. The treatment of music and voice culture is done according to this. And when we talk about Hindustani classical music changes become necessary on the instrument, otherwise how would one play raga Puriya or Marwa or ragas which operate on *mandra saptak,* if it is not available in the instrument. If the instrument could not sustain, had no glides, or no octave variation, then certainly it required some modifications. So I started working towards that. Earlier I used to play santoor with twenty-seven bridges only. Then in 1959 I started making changes on the santoor. I changed one bridge. I asked the person who used to make santoor for me and there was only one family that was making santoor for our family. His family had made santoor for my predecessors also. So I told him to make thirty bridges. Then I did a lot of experimentation. Along with all this I also took the initiative to check each and every santoor going out of Srinagar. My effort was to popularise the santoor outside Kashmir. My only flaw was that I did not boast about it. I was only serving the santoor because this was our tradition. You can verify history also. If classical music is alive in the valley, it is because of the Sopori family.

Interviewer:

When and how did two schools emerge in santoor—one yours, *Sopori baaj* and the other one of Pandit Shiv Kumar Sharmaji?

Bhajan Sopori:

I'll say there's only *Sopori baaj*. All others follow it. Why? Because santoor began with my family. We have 250 years old santoor tradition in our family. Nine generations. So, this is history and not of a person who is the first generation. Secondly, when you listen to my recital then *gana nazar aayega* (it flows like a song). My *alaap* is a song. And this happens because we are all singers. So, it is called *Sopori baaj*. It all depends on how you are presenting it scientifically. After all what is *shaili*? To me *shaili* is that which has emerged out of research and on which further development can be done. If under the name of your *shaili* you say, this is, say for instance, this is jaltarang and through this I interpret raga, then I am sorry, it is not correct. Even according to *shastra* it is not right.

Interviewer:

What is *Sopori baaj*?

Bhajan Sopori:

Sopori baaj is a *shaili* of classical music which present raga according to the raga-*ang*. The problem arises when somebody operates within the set pattern and thinks that that's the only right way to do it. I am not criticising anybody. Everybody has their own yardstick of perfection. But what I think is that work should make one think, contemplate and realise that how much of effort, *taleem, riyaaz* has gone behind it. Work should not make anybody conclude, 'Oh, even I can do it.' You take my *Sufi* composition. I have 5000 compositions. Hardly any classical musician can claim that. Usually after five compositions one repeats oneself. I want to say that there is only the *Sopori gharana* of santoor players. This is history. Nobody can challenge it.

Interviewer:

How and why did you change the look of santoor? The gourd (*tumba)* of sitar is used, why?

Bhajan Sopori:

It is right and it happened because of the necessity. Earlier it was kept on *sahpaya*—triangular shaped three wooden pieces, two to three inches above the ground. This became difficult for me to carry. So I requested my santoor maker to make only one wooden plank on which the santoor could be kept. But it was not appealing to the eyes. So in 1963-64 I got a small *tumba* made. And this really helped my music too. Higher octaves became clearer and the instrument stopped tilting while playing *meend*. Still there was some discomfort, so I continued with my experiment. A stage came when I started using the *tumba* of the sarod. But even this wasn't comfortable. The corners used to break too often. So the instrument maker suggested using the sitar *tumba*. He redesigned the sitar's *tumba* for my santoor. And since then all *Sopori baaj* santoors have the sitar *tumba*. I am telling you the history of forty-five years.

Interviewer:

What is so different in your santoor from others?

Bhajan Sopori:

I'll talk about myself. Through the santoor I sing. This is my *shaili*. The other part of my *shaili* is *tantra ang*. What the others are doing, I leave it to the listeners. Let them decide. The basis of my style is vocal, in both *Sufiana* and Hindustani. And this *gayaki* should be explicit through the instrument. There's no point in announcing that my style is *gayaki ang* and the listeners do not even know whether it is the *bandish* or the *gat* that is being played.

Interviewer:

So can it be said that you brought changes on the santoor?

Bhajan Sopori:

My father initiated it in the 1930s. Unfortunately in the fire that broke out in Sopore in 1947 we had to shift. That santoor got destroyed in the fire. Only the sitar and a Sanskrit manuscript of my great grandfather could be saved. Otherwise that traditional santoor also would have been with us. I wasn't born then.

As I said, my father began initiating changes on the santoor in the 1930s. And till 1953–54 we had twenty-seven to twenty-eight bridges in the santoor only. Then in 1958–59 I made certain changes in the bridges and in the techniques. After reaching college level I began thinking about it more seriously—what do I want to say through my instrument? Then I started making other changes. And as I said earlier I personally used to monitor its making. Subsequently there was not only one santoor maker in Srinagar but I helped at least four or five santoor makers in Srinagar to expand their business. Later, here in Delhi also I personally took interest in its making. That's why I said fifty-eight years is not a small chapter of life.

Interviewer:

You learnt the sarod, the sitar and the piano too. How and why?

Bhajan Sopori:

Actually, it would not have been possible had I not been a child prodigy. With the blessings of God and my elders I was quick to grasp and was very sharp, infused with creativity. In addition to all this I was possessed with the urge to do everything. And there was one more thing. Because I had stayed with saints during my childhood, playing santoor for long hours, from midnight till dawn, having less sleep or no sleep, I could work non-stop for four to five days, without feeling tired or worn out. I developed stamina. I played the sitar, the Hawaiian guitar and with God's grace, I was reasonably good. Because of such rich experience, I could compose music that was different, unique.

Interviewer:

You also joined the graduate study course in Western Classical Music at the Washington University in 1973–74. Any specific reason?

Bhajan Sopori:

I was selected by them. I had sent one of my compositions and they liked it immensely. So, on that basis they admitted me and as I said earlier, by nature, I am always seeking knowledge. I wanted to learn the basic premise of composition. Here everybody thinks that he can become a composer. But real, actual composers are very few. Madan Mohan, Naushad, Khayyam—they are great composers. Through their compositions one can feel the emotions, their thinking, *shaili,* the structure of composition, their knowledge—their compositions are a grand edifice. So, I also wanted to give a systemic, scientific base to my compositions. That why I thought about joining Washington University.

Interviewer:

You are a poet, a *shayar* also.

Bhajan Sopori:

(*Laughs*) ... Actually what happened was that for compositions I used to write little bit. At that time there were no tape recorders; at home we did not even have a radio. When I used to go out and listen to film songs, often if I heard *sthaayi,* I would imagine the *antaraa* myself.

And this I used to base on the structure of the compositions, the way a composition was composed. Because every composition has a proper format, a base. So, it all began with imagination and gradually I started writing in English, as I was a student of English literature.

Interviewer:

Coming to the present scenario, one thing that is really perplexing is that why is the santoor not as popular as the sarod or the sitar. Why?

Bhajan Sopori:

Because its history is just about fifty-eight years old.

Interviewer:

Is that the only reason?

Bhajan Sopori:

Yes. What will happen to an instrument if there is nobody to teach it. In 1958 there was a huge music conference in Shalimar Garden. I exposed this instrument to the public for the first time. Then in 1959 I played it in Allahabad. It was a seven-day festival. And in front of all the musicians, I, a boy of eleven years, played this instrument. People had not even seen this instrument. They could not even think that classical music can be played on it. A very learned Mr Bhattacharya of Allahabad University decided to keep my programme in the university. It was then that this instrument was literally noticed. People who claim that they were playing santoor actually accompanied my father on the tabla. Life doesn't move according to claims. It is a matter of history and data. See I am the person who has brought the santoor back from Central Asia to Kashmir, although it was an instrument of Kashmir. Turn to the history of Jammu-Kashmir. My name is imprinted in the pages of history. You can't stop history. People might say that they have done three to four films. Here I've done three hundred telefilms (*says it in a slightly raised voice*).

Interviewer:

What do you like doing—films, tele-films or classical music?

Bhajan Sopori:

Both are different. Classical music is classical music. It requires a different bent of mind. Now when we talk about compositions, I've also composed for an oil advertisement. (*Chuckles*) I needed money at that time and needed it with honesty, so I did that advertisement. From advertisements in many languages, my compositions exist.

Interviewer:

In what languages?

Bhajan Sopori:

Like Kashmiri, Urdu, Hindi, Persian, Arabic, Dogri, Punjabi, Ladakhi, Rajasthani, Telugu, that is, in whatever language I got assignments, I completed it. There are many.

In *Sufi* tradition itself I've around 3,000 songs. I could do all this because I was focused and remained in the media for a very long time. I was the youngest Producer appointed by the All India Radio and when I left it, I was almost DDG (Deputy Director General). No performing musician has reached this level.

At AIR I got a lot of opportunity to experiment. I had a choir consisting of 7,000 people and we performed in front of a 15,000–16,000 strong audience. This is a reality, I am not bragging. Photographs, recording, invitation cards are all available. It's a different thing that I never boasted about all these achievements. I only wanted that my State should become a cultural hub.

Interviewer:

What prompted you to create ragas?

Bhajan Sopori:

In our classical music there's hardly any scope for creating ragas. It can be a combination only and after that if it attains a solo raga identity, well then it's God's gift.

Like I combined Madhuvanti and Patdeep and named it Patvanti. (*Sings to explain the raga structure*)

As for raga Nirmalranjini, there's a story. I was invited by Ma Nirmala Deviji to perform. The concert was at midnight. Just as I was going on stage I came to know that it was her birthday. So, I came back, requested the organisers to give me some more time. And I came up with this raga—a combination of raga Shivranjini and Malhar. I named it Nirmalranjini, after her name. This was my gift to her.

Interviewer:

Why do we not hear these ragas being played by other maestros?

Bhajan Sopori:

Because times have changed. We no longer appreciate the efforts of others. Now, we believe only in criticism.

Interviewer:

How much is your family responsible for your achievements?

Bhajan Sopori:

All the credit goes to them. Now it is my wife. Earlier it was my mother and in art it was my father. He taught me how to be focused in life. He taught me how not to be tempted by distractions. He gave me the example of water flowing in the pipe and how when holes are created in the pipe the water does not reach where it has to reach. And he explained how these holes are similar to the distractions in life. I do not know how much I understood these words then, at that young age, but I still remember them.

MOHAN VEENA

Music is the Language of Love
PANDIT VISHWA MOHAN BHATT
(27 July, 1950–)

We had been in touch with Salil Bhatt for quite sometime and had requested him to arrange an interview with his father and guru, Pandit Vishwa Mohan Bhatt, the creator of Mohan Veena and Vishwa Veena. But most of the time he was out on tour. Finally, we got a chance to interview him on 17 November, 2008, but the interview was conducted in parts stretching over a month.

Accompanied by his son, Salil Bhatt, he came to the studio. He had come to Delhi for a concert. Inviting us for the concert, he announced, 'There's a surprise element. I am going to unveil my new *discovery* (he does not like the word *creation*)–Vishwaranjini.'

Captivating audiences all over the world with his 'discoveries' and instruments–Vishwa Veena and Mohan Veena, Pandit Vishwa Mohan Bhatt, speaks softly, laughing about his teenage infatuation with a German girl and her guitar. 'But finally I chose guitar over her ...' and that infatuation soon became an obsession. He spent days and nights, thinking how to adapt the Hawaiian guitar to Hindustani classical music style. Initially his family members were a little doubtful about his obsession. 'They wanted me to learn the sitar, the family instrument. Only my mother saw the fire in my eyes. She completely believed in me and my belief.'

And after a few years of thinking and experimenting he finally introduced the Mohan Veena to the musical fraternity in Mumbai on 4 March, 1970. 'People accepted my instrument. In fact the very next day headline in the newspaper was, “Young artiste steals the limelight.” I still remember the headline and the sound of that applause still echoes in my ears.’

His eyes sparkled, remembering that first brush with fame.

And that of course was just the beginning of Pandit Vishwa Mohan Bhatt’s musical journey.

(17 and 18 December, 2008)

Interviewer:

How did your musical journey begin?

Vishwa Mohan Bhatt:

Our family has a musical lineage that goes back over 300 years. I started nearly forty years ago. My father used to teach classical music and while he would teach I used to watch him. Moreover in a family where music reverberates throughout the day from one corner or the other, your mind gets influenced.

In my family, music was always echoing from different corners of the house. My elder brothers, Shashi Mohanji, Mahendraji, my sister Manju, my nephew Krishna were all busy with their *riyaaz.* So, I was brought up in a musical environment and it influenced my growth.

Life was going on this way when one day a German girl came to learn from my father. She used to play the guitar and told my father that she would like to learn Indian classical music on the guitar. I was quite young, only fourteen years old. I liked both the girl and the guitar but finally I selected the guitar. (*Laughs aloud*)

Interviewer:

You played safe ...

Vishwa Mohan Bhatt:

(*Laughing*) ... Yes ... she went away but I took the instrument from her. And for the first time the guitar came into our lives. Till then there was only the sitar, violin or vocal music at our place. My elder brother late Shashi Mohanji was one of the first disciples of Pandit Ravi Shankarji. He became his disciple in 1957. Both my parents were vocalists. I had learnt sitar and whatever little musical notes I knew, I tried playing on the guitar.

But I found the guitar lacking in many aspects in terms of playing classical music; like, it did not have *tarab ke taar* or *chikari*. So I started making changes. But when it did not give the desired results, I took it to a sitar maker. I told him my requirements and he made certain changes.

Finally I made it a twenty-string instrument, with eight above and twelve below—*tarab ke taar*. It creates resonance, natural echo; so even when we change the *sur*, the musical note, the previous note keeps ringing. Gradually I started doing *riyaaz* on it with two fingers, just like we play the Vichitra Veena. Later on I brought in many other changes to create the *meend* and to give volume, depth and bass to the sound.

Interviewer:

How did you think about these changes? Were you not too young for it?

Vishwa Mohan Bhatt:

Actually, I just thought about it. And yes, I was young but the urge to do something was in me from the very beginning. I wanted to do something. It all began in 1966. And till 1983 I was experimenting on my own. Then in 1983 I became Pandit Ravi Shankar's disciple.

Interviewer:

Then in 2001 you created the Vishwa Veena, after a long gap. What prompted you to develop the Vishwa Veena?

Vishwa Mohan Bhatt:

I felt that I should do something more. An artiste should keep on inventing, creating. An artiste should not stagnate. He should always keep moving ahead, doing new experiments.

So Mohan Veena is more or less a modification of the Western Hawaiian Guitar, but I was still searching for an exciting vibrant tone that could attract a young boy of three as well as a ninety-year old.

I wanted to create an instrument that could give a continuous and sustained flow of music. So what I did was I took twenty strings of the Mohan Veena and added fifteen strings of the swarmandal at the side.

This way it would appear that two artistes were playing simultaneously while actually only one artiste was playing the instrument. And its shape is completely different from the guitar. It is made out of a single piece of wood capable of creating a fountain of music. So on 15 March, 2001 I introduced the Vishwa Veena to the musical world in Kamani Auditorium, New Delhi.

Interviewer:

But you give very few concerts on the Vishwa Veena. Why?

Vishwa Mohan Bhatt:

Yes, that's true. Why, because I am more attached to my Mohan Veena. I find the sound quality of Mohan Veena very good, in fact I find it perfect. It has tenderness, continuity of *meend*, there is boldness also. It has everything; moreover it is my first creation.

Interviewer:

What is the specialty of your *gharana* and music?

Vishwa Mohan Bhatt:

See, I am Pandit Ravi Shankar's disciple and in the Maihar gharana, *jod*, played after *alaap*, is completely based on *dhrupad*. It is *nom tom*. We play *jod* in *dhrupad* and *gamak* style. Systematic *badhat* is done. In most of my programmes I play *alaap, jod, jhala* for nearly forty-five minutes. Because Mohan Veena is best suitable for the *alaap, jod, jhala* part.

Interviewer:

So, in a way it can be said that to a large extent you bring the *dhrupad* element in your music.

Vishwa Mohan Bhatt:

Yes, definitely. It is particularly present in the *jod* part.

Interviewer:

Since your parents were vocalists did you also learn vocal music?

Vishwa Mohan Bhatt:

Yes, in the beginning. And while they were teaching others, I learnt it. And one day while doing *riyaaz,* I discovered that music was already there in me, in my blood. Ragas appeared very familiar to me. Gradually musical pieces started flowing out through my instrument, the Mohan Veena.

Interviewer:

How did you get your first international concert?

Vishwa Mohan Bhatt:

Our classical music is really respected abroad. They have such rare musical collections that it is impossible to get those pieces here. Two organisations from Los Angeles and San Francisco approached me in the early 1980s. They must have heard my music somewhere. They invited me and that was my first concert abroad. Then in 1985 I had gone with Pandit Ravi Shankar. He had done a fusion music show with Japanese musicians. I began to travel abroad from 1980, getting regular invitations to perform. In one tour I usually cover nearly twenty-seven cities. Then I give a gap of an year or two in between and then again go for an international tour, giving twenty-seven to thirty-two concerts.

Interviewer:

How did you get to collaborate with Ry Cooder?

Vishwa Mohan Bhatt:

During one such tour I met the guitar maker, Rick Turner of Los Angeles who was immediately drawn to my instrument. He helped me—took me to his shop, wrote down the dimensions of my instruments and finally made my instrument.

I think he was fond of my music as he had had my album and used to listen to it. It was he who later gave my album to Mr Alexander of Water Lily Acoustics for listening who in turn got in touch with me.

Perhaps Mr Alexander liked my music ... And I am talking about the times when there was no email or mobile facility. It was difficult to communicate. Even letters from abroad used to reach in fifteen to twenty days. Days passed without any news. But one day I received a letter from Alexander, expressing his interest in my music and that he wanted to record a fusion piece. I was happy but at the same time hesitant.

Interviewer:

Why such mixed feelings?

Vishwa Mohan Bhatt:

You see, till then I was following a straight traditional-purist line. His offer was completely new to me. But then my inner voice said, 'why not experiment?' I had my *guru* Pandit Ravi Shankar's example in front of me. So, I decided to follow in his footsteps. I took up the project.

My recording was scheduled with Ry Cooder, guitar player. We recorded and the album was titled *Meeting by the River*. The year was 1992 and it was my first international recording.

Not only this, we—Ry Cooder and I—had never met before. We met for the first time during the recording session only and had to complete the recording in one day, rather one night, because that was the only time I had in between my concert tours.

Interviewer:

Where was the recording done?

Vishwa Mohan Bhatt:

That is a very interesting story. The recording was done in a natural ambience. There's a beautiful mountainous place called Santa Barbara in America and on the hilltop there is a church. We recorded in this church because we wanted to have the best natural acoustic sound. We were having tea-coffee at midnight and suddenly a tune flashed through my mind. I told Ry Cooder to follow it and improvise.

Both of us never wanted to do any stiff, composed music. We wanted to make it an improvised musical piece, completely impromptu. Moreover, I thought it will be less strenuous (*laughs*) as I did not want to strain my mind by devising proper thought-out compositions and also because such compositions become mechanical.

In fact, our sound recordist was surprised to see that we completed the recording of the ten-minute piece in just thirty minutes. We had not even thought about the ending. We recorded it as we thought appropriate at that time.

Then we recorded three more pieces—one in raga Dhani, for the next piece I took *shuddh swars*, and Nat Bhairavi for the fourth piece. In this way we completed the recording by 5:00 am. As my flight was booked for 6:00 am, I left. Later when they saw the total duration, they were perturbed. The total duration had come to only forty minutes. And to bring out the CD one needs seventy minutes of musical pieces. But the recording company, Water Lily Acoustics, was so pleased with the musical pieces that it decided to go ahead with the release of the forty-minute album.

They took a chance, knowing that the buyer always wants seventy minutes of pieces in a CD. But fortunately when this CD—*Meeting by the River*—was released it remained at the top of Billboard charts for forty weeks running. And on 1 March, 1994, it won the Grammy award.

Interviewer:

You said that you composed the pieces on ragas but Ry Cooder had no knowledge about ragas then how did you both collaborate?

Vishwa Mohan Bhatt:

Of course I couldn't have played pure ragas in *vilambit* or *drut* gat. I changed it thinking how two streams of music can come together.

Interviewer:

What is the basic difference between Mohan Veena and Satvik Veena-- the instrument your son Salil Bhatt has created?

Vishwa Mohan Bhatt:

In Mohan Veena there are joints in between. Neck, body and fingerboard are made separately and then joined in between. So there's always a danger of it breaking up in transportation. We travel so much that this is the danger we face always. But in Satvik Veena there is no joint in between. It is just one wood piece and through carving, the fingerboard is included in it only. So there's no danger of joints getting feeble or breaking up. In Mohan Veena the pressure of the strings is also immense, approximately 500 pounds, joints are always in danger of weakening and breaking apart because of any jerk.

Interviewer:

But why has the Satvik Veena not got so much of acceptance and popularity?

Vishwa Mohan Bhatt:

Right now even Salil is new (*laughs*) ... but it will be accepted. People are accepting it.

Interviewer:

You have collaborated with almost all the top artistes of the world, so where is the place in all this for pure Hindustani Classical music?

Vishwa Mohan Bhatt:

I collaborate with them and it is completely different. If I wanted, I could have had the concert like Grammy-*Meeting by the River* show. But I didn't go into all that. I just concentrate on classical music. My concerts are always on classical music.

I never went on concert tours with any of my fusion music album artistes. It was only one day, one recording session.

However, I would like to say one thing, that we, Indian musicians, carry a heavy baggage of purity and tradition. A slight change and one's conscience is reminded and pricked about tradition and purity. We musicians have made classical music so heavy and frightening that people are even afraid to give us their opinion.

But I am not one of them. I strongly believe that within tradition, within purity, we have to develop our music. We have to move forward. How long can we keep on walking the age old line? We have to be progressive; we have to know and understand how to use our tradition in a new way.

The beauty of Indian classical music is improvisation. One has to make use of the knowledge, the rich tradition of our great maestros with the present scenario. One has to move forward with technology. We must analyse why classical music is unable to reach the masses?

Yes, I agree that film music will always have an edge over classical music because of so many enticing visuals whereas the purpose of Indian classical music is to purify the heart, body and soul. We, musicians have the responsibility of preserving our heritage by making our music attractive, interesting and to present it in a very glossy way. So that even a person who doesn't know anything about *sur* and *taal* gets interested in it.

I do not say that one should leave the framework or tradition or dilute the purity. No, that is not required for there is so much scope even within the framework. I remember Pandit Ravi Shankar's performance at Woodstock Festival. It became a lifetime experience for everybody present in the audience. The audience was completely mesmerised by his *taan, laya, tihayee, jhala*—it was an unforgettable experience. Indian classical music won the hearts of everybody.

In 2005, I was invited by Eric Clapton to the Crossroad Guitar Festival in America. I was given only twelve minutes. I played raga Bihag and I played *alaap, jod, vilambit, drut gat, sawal-jawab, jhala,* I played everything. There was a huge audience, nearly one lakh people, and they were completely spellbound.

Had I said 'no give me two hours, I want to do extensive *alaap* because only then the real essence of Hindustani classical music can be depicted,' the audience would have got bored. This is not possible. One must change as per the place and environment. One has to adapt and change. We, classical musicians cannot live in our ivory tower. The distance between the artiste and the audience must decrease.

Interviewer:

The general image of classical music is that it is very difficult and musicians have a holier than thou image ...

Vishwa Mohan Bhatt:

Yes, you are right. This has been created by the artistes themselves. Even when they come on stage it appears as if it is God Himself descending on the stage. This kind of an image creates distance with the audience. I do not like all this. I think we should try reducing such distance. There should be an instant connection with the audience.

Interviewer:

Talking about bringing classical music nearer to the masses, what do you say about the time-bound classification of ragas, like morning ragas, afternoon, evening, night? And now with changing times, how feasible is it to adhere to this categorisation?

Vishwa Mohan Bhatt:

To a certain extent I am in favour of this categorisation because I think this classification has been done in a scientific way. When we get up in the morning our state of mind is completely different. We do remember God in the morning and pray that everything goes well during the day. Our mood is different in the morning. We are not romantic in the morning. So, when morning ragas like Bhairav, Todi, Lalit, Bhairavi, etc. are played in the morning then we are automatically transported into a meditative and spiritual environment. These ragas have a meditative element in them. When we listen to Pandit Bhimsen Joshi's *Jo bhaje Hari Ko Sada,* then we experience the serenity of morning with those *surs* and we move an inch closer to the almighty, our mind becomes meditative.

While in the afternoon our mindset changes. It is worked-up, fast and agitated. So in the afternoon ragas with *teevra ma* are used. And in the evening, at the sunset, we feel nostalgic and at that time if we use *komal rishabh, teevra madhyam* and if we add *komal dhaivat* then the meaning changes. *Bhaav* and *ras* changes, even romanticism is heightened.

Similarly at night when everything gets over, there is stillness and there is beauty in stillness. For this feeling we have ragas like Malkauns, Bageshwari, Jog, etc. So I agree with the time classification theory.

But I also feel that the music of a good artiste can be heard anytime. If I want to listen to Todi at night, then I will listen to it but yes the raga may not have the same impact as it would when it is heard at the appropriate time.

Interviewer:

How has been your experience with films?

Vishwa Mohan Bhatt:

I don't like doing films because there's too much of interference. And the truth is that we classical musicians are very egotistical. Our ego gets hurt when there is too much of interference. Right now I am not able to control my ego but the day I conquer my ego, I'll do many more films.

Interviewer:

Despite all this you have given music for films like *Lagaan, Saathiya, Bawander, Ishqiya.*

Vishwa Mohan Bhatt:

(*Says it laughing*) ... Also for two Hollywood films—*Two days in the Valley* and *Dead Man walking.* But most of the time I have given music for just one or two songs in the films that you mentioned. And all those songs have been based on classical music.

Interviewer:

Recently you created a new raga—raga Vishwaranjini. How did you think about it and what is the special feature in it?

Vishwa Mohan Bhatt:

First of all I think 'create' is not the right word. I feel it would be better to say 'discover.' Because the thing is our classical music is rich and developed. There are so many ragas already existing with so many permutations and combinations that it is not right to say that one has 'created' a new raga.

Coming to Vishwaranjini, it is a combination of ragas Shivranjini, Madhuvanti and Dharmavathi raga from Carnatic music. It has *karuna ras*. Actually I was so disturbed, in fact all of us were, after the terrorist attack in Mumbai, that it came very naturally to me. And because I am a musician I could express my pain only through *swars*.

So, with the use of *komal gandhar*, which heightens up pathos and melancholy, I have tried bringing out *karuna ras*. In fact, I discovered this raga after the Mumbai Terrorist attack on 26 November, 2008. I never thought about it. It just happened; it was my way of reacting against terrorism and trying to promote peace, harmony and serenity in the world.

Interviewer:

Why have you named it raga Vishwaranjini?

Vishwa Mohan Bhatt:

Well, it was given by Salil. He took 'ranjini' from raga Shivranjini and the first portion of my name. So it became Vishwaranjini. I also liked it.

Interviewer:

What are your interests besides music?

Vishwa Mohan Bhatt:

I love travelling, seeing new places. I love to stay amidst nature. So far I have thirty-nine albums and most of them have been inspired by nature. Recently I had gone to Andaman & Nicobar Islands. I found the place so peaceful, serene and beautiful that for hours I kept sitting near the sea all alone, just watching it. The sunset looked so beautiful. While sitting there I created a musical piece and after returning to Jaipur I polished it. Now we have an album also. Besides this, I like watching movies, playing with kids; table tennis is my favourite sport.

Interviewer:

Whose music inspires you most?

Vishwa Mohan Bhatt:

The first name that comes to mind is of course that of my guruji, Pandit Ravi Shankar; I also like Pandit Nikhil Bannerjee, Ustad Vilayat Khan

Sahib; Ustad Amir Khan Sahib's *gayaki*. His *gayaki* takes me into a completely different world with its poise and control. Then Ustad Bade Ghulam Ali Khan Sahib's *gayaki*, the beauty in his singing, *murkiyan* in his *thumri gayaki*—that is so captivating. Hirabai, Mogubai, Kesarbai Kerkar—oh my God, all exemplary vocalists. In just three minutes Kesarbai Kerkar used to show her prowess.

Interviewer:

What is music to you?

Vishwa Mohan Bhatt:

Music is a vast ocean. It is in my blood. It will be with me as long as I live. But what I really want is that people should start understanding music in the true sense. I believe that music is the language of God, unfolded for the benefit of mankind. I think I am fortunate that I can understand a little bit about music and derive happiness from *sur* and *taal*. And these seven notes have no religion or language. They are alive all over the world. They can unite the world. Seven notes are present everywhere in the world.

So I think one should go into the depth of music, understand music and this is all the more important in present day life where people have become so mechanical, fast and ambitious. If one listens to music, classical music, then the mind will become calmer, negative thinking will disappear; terrorism will decrease, because classical music spreads love and understanding. I think music is the language of love. It can teach everybody to love.

Interviewer:

What would you like to tell young musicians?

Vishwa Mohan Bhatt:

A musician's life is very difficult. But I think if one controls one's desires, and remains focused then no matter what, things will fall into place. One will get what one wants. It is said that if you want something desperately then the universe joins hands to give you that. That goal also inches towards you. Determination is what matters.

When I made the Mohan Veena there were many critics, within family and outside as well. But I was determined. Only my mother believed in me. She was the one who said, 'You go ahead. I've seen the fire, the determination in your eyes. So go ahead with your experiment and after twenty-five years you will rule the world.' Her words came true. I worked really hard for it. I used to practise continuously for ten to twelve hours. And when I introduced it on stage in Mumbai, it was readily accepted by the people. This could happen because I had spent years and years with complete concentration and determination to make Mohan Veena. So, I think if there is determination then nobody can stop one from achieving one's goal. Thanks.

VOCAL

One Soul Two Bodies

PANDITS RAJAN & SAJAN MISHRA

(1 August, 1951–; 7 January, 1956–)

You don't expect such deep camaraderie between brothers in present times. But if you have to experience the beauty of friendship between brothers then meet Pandit Rajan Mishra and Pandit Sajan Mishra, vocalists from the Benaras *gharana.* There's no point of discord or disagreement. Pandit Rajan, elder by five years, begins the sentence and Pandit Sajan adds, supporting his elder brother's views. It is amazing to see so much love and understanding in the times of empty spaces and gestures.

We reached their double storey house in Ramesh Nagar, West Delhi, half an hour late, after getting lost several times in the congested lanes of the colony. There was no sign of annoyance at the delay. 'Yes, it is natural in Delhi. Traffic is so bad,' said Pandit Sajan, greeting us and making us feel comfortable. 'You people make yourselves comfortable, have tea. *Bhai Sahib* will be here in a few minutes.'

Having learnt from their father, the late Pandit Hanuman Prasad, their uncle Pandit Gopal Mishra and from late Pandit Bade Ramdasji, both the brothers moved on to developing their own unique style. Pandit Rajan usually begins the *bandish,* joined by Pandit Sajan in a few seconds. As in life, so in music, there's absolute understanding between the two. There's no space for disagreement or one trying to outdo the other. 'I am elder, I fulfil the duties of an elder brother, he is younger, he behaves like a younger brother.'

(26 June, 2004)

Interviewer:

Who was your first guru?

Sajan Mishra:

Our gurus were our father late Pandit Hanuman Mishraji and then our uncle, Pandit Gopal Mishraji. My elder brother Rajanji was fortunate to become the *gandabandh* disciple of Gyanacharya Pandit Bade Ramdasji also.

Rajan Mishra:

And we are very fortunate that we were born in a musical family and inherited a great tradition. Our family's musical lineage can be traced back to more than 300 years. Our grandfather, great grandfather, great great great grandfather, all of them were reputed musicians of their times.

Interviewer:

Since you started learning at a very young age, did you ever miss indulging in childhood pranks?

Rajan Mishra:

Oh, during childhood we were very naughty. Our parents were very considerate. They told us to do *riyaaz* for just one hour everyday. And we were fortunate to do *riyaaz* under their guidance. This really helped us a lot. Besides that one hour, we had complete freedom to do anything, play any game. We were really very naughty, played all games—cricket, *gulli-danda, kanche* and there was one game in which stones were to be hit by a ball.

Sajan Mishra:

Actually in this game the prize was the wrapper of cigarette boxes, instead of money. We used to feel so elated by winning particular brand wrappers. It was a very unique game.

Interviewer:

Did you ever attempt to smoke also?

Sajan Mishra:

No, we never smoked but yes we do take *paan*. And as you know *paan* in Benaras and in our culture is considered very auspicious. So we started eating *paan.*

Interviewer:

What kind of a guru was your father? Was he a better guru or a better father?

Rajan Mishra:

We were very fortunate to have a guru and a father like him. He was highly disciplined. He himself used to tell us not to do *riyaaz* for more than two hours. He did not believe in excess of anything. Once we got hooked on to cricket. We were either playing cricket or discussing about it. He noticed it. So he called us and politely asked us, 'Are you people interested in music or not? If both of you just want to play cricket then forget all about music.' We got the message. After that we started doing *riyaaz* regularly and played cricket only in our free time.

Interviewer:

When did you decide that you both will sing together and will do *jugalbandi* only?

Sajan Mishra:

See, from childhood we were taught together. My parents wanted us to sing together. As my elder brother is five years elder to me his *taleem* began earlier. As soon as I was five we started learning together. In our family *gandabandhan* ceremony is done when a child is five years old. So I was formally initiated into music when I was five. At that time various functions used to happen in temples on various days of the week like on Monday in Kashi Vishwanath temple and on Tuesday in Sankatmochan temple. We started performing together on such occasions. Since then we have been performing together with the blessings of the elders, our gurus and God.

Interviewer:

What is the specialty of the Benaras *gharana*?

Rajan Mishra:

Benaras is an ancient city. Since it is an ancient city, it has a rich ancient tradition. People from other *gharanas* also stayed there. So multi-dimensional vocal and instrumental styles developed in Benaras. In fact, Benaras is the only *gharana* where different forms of classical music like *dhrupad, dhamaar, tappa, tarana, khayal, thumri,* etc. are sung.

Interviewer:

Why is it that Pandits Rajan and Sajan Mishra are often categorised as *bhajan* singers, though you sing other forms too?

Rajan Mishra:

No, it is not like that. Basically we are *khayal* singers. Though we are from Benaras, we have never sung *thumri* on stage. And this is deliberate. People generally believe that in Benaras only *thumri* is sung. To dispel that notion, we decided never to sing *thumri* on stage; at home we often sing *thumri* but on stage we never do. As about singing *bhajan* and people appreciating us, it is because of *bhaav,* the emotions and feelings that we bring while presenting this form. Devoid of *bhaav* it cannot be called *bhajan* and if there's *bhaav* in singing even *khayal* can become a *bhajan.* So, *bhaav* is very important and *bhaav* is associated with Benaras which is not only a holy and pious place, but also a centre where literature has developed. In music, *sahitya* and *bhaav* are very important. Just singing the words of the *bhajan* is an exercise in futility. It does not become *bhajan*. Only when we are able to present it with *bhaav*, it touches the heart. Maybe because we are able to present *bhajans* with *bhaav*, our listeners appreciate our *bhajan* singing.

Sajan Mishra:

In addition to what *Bhai Sahib* has said, we give a lot of importance to pronunciation also. Because of our emphasis on *bhaav* listeners enjoy our *khayal gayaki.* And this is all thanks to the blessings of our gurus, God and our listeners.

Interviewer:

How is it that there's perfect understanding between both of you on stage in *sur, taal* and *laya?* Somewhere you had said, 'One soul in two bodies.' What exactly do you mean by it?

Rajan Mishra:

This is possible only if there's love between two people. We are two individuals. We sing together but we have never made our singing competitive. We are not envious or jealous of each other. We never compete with each other. We love each other; we appreciate each other's singing. When this (mutual appreciation and love) reaches its zenith, one soul emerges. Many music critics often say about our singing, '*Jugalbandi* as beautiful as solo.' I think this is the greatest compliment.

Sajan Mishra:

Yes, even I think so. And this is all because of the grace of God, the blessings of our parents and the values that we were taught. We are two different people with different voice texture, yet we reach out to listeners as one voice. We consider it our good fortune and again it is due to the well wishes of our elders and listeners.

Interviewer:

In your musical journey till now what changes have you noticed in the musical field?

Rajan Mishra:

There have been many changes. There's so much publicity and exposure now. The strength of listeners has also increased manifold. I am so happy to notice that young listeners have started attending concerts. They are trying to understand and get associated with classical music. While some forty odd years ago, only people above fifty used to come for concerts, now the scenario has changed. But, unfortunately in the recent past there has been a downfall in the spiritual value of classical music.

Interviewer:

Please elaborate ...

Rajan Mishra:

Now it has become a mere tool for entertainment and is no longer an offering to God. We believe that our music is an offering to God, it is a means of devotion. The peculiar thing is that our foreign audiences listen to classical music with a notion that it is spiritual. They seek solace in it. But the audience here, in India, is by and large not serious. The listeners sitting in the first few rows indulge in talking ... talking on the phones also. There's too much pretension here. All these things do not happen abroad. There, the listeners are disciplined.

Interviewer:

Don't you think ticketing is the remedy for such a problem?

Rajan Mishra:

To some extent. Even in a city like Delhi, there's no ticket for concerts. I think there should be a nominal ticket. It will improve the quality of listeners. Since it's free, listeners do not have any respect for classical music or for the artiste. They come along with their little children, who are either crying or playing in the auditorium. Scant attention is paid to what the artiste is singing. All this is quite distracting. But in Mumbai and Kolkata shows are often ticketed and the audience is much better.

Sajan Mishra:

In Delhi there's one more problem. If any high government official comes, then the seriousness of the concert and even the artiste is forgotten. The first row becomes a mini coffee house. Tea/coffee, snacks are also served to the official and his entourage. This is very painful. While abroad, if any VIP is late for the show, and if the show has begun, then even he/she is stopped at the gate.

Interviewer:

What kind of disciples do you have?

Rajan Mishra:

Now-a-days disciples want instant results. Immediately after joining they want to go on stage, they want to earn money and think that they are no less than their guru. This turns out to be the beginning of their downfall.

Soon their musical repertoire gets exhausted and their limitations stare back at them. Once this becomes evident, organisers shy away from inviting them for concerts. Very soon their downfall begins. They get frustrated. Yet it does not dawn upon them that it had happened because of their own shortcomings—not doing enough *riyaaz*, and having limited musical vocabulary. See, even in Bhagwad Gita it is written that one should keep on working without thinking about the outcome. I think the present generation should seriously start believing in it. First, they should work hard and this is applicable in all spheres of life, be it music, art, journalism or anything. First they should learn properly, work hard and have patience. If one has perseverance, God will definitely reward.

Interviewer:

Who is your most promising disciple?

Rajan Mishra:

There are many. Our sons-Ritesh and Rajnish, Viraj Amar of Ahmedabad, Mohan Singh and Sukhdev Singh from Ludhiana, Saarthi Chatterjee, and there are others also. I am very pleased with their progress and the amount of labour they put in.

Interviewer:

Did you force your sons to learn music?

Rajan Mishra:

No, we never forced them to become musicians. I just told them that they have inherited a great musical lineage; it's in their genes and the progress that they can make in music may not be possible in any other field. But yes, during their growing up period, like any other normal child, even they experimented in various fields. But with age they realised that music is their passion and that they wanted to make it their vocation. Now both of them—Ritesh and Rajnish, are very serious about music. They are working very hard.

Interviewer:

How many hours of *riyaaz* do you do. And your sons? How many hours do they do?

Rajan Mishra:

See, we used to do eight to ten hours. *Ab riyaaz to hota nahin hai* (Now we are not able to do *riyaaz*.) Now our *riyaaz* happens when we teach. Every third or fourth day we are participating in a concert, so now we formally do not do *riyaaz*. But yes, our children do it. They do it for three to four hours everyday. It is always better to do as much *riyaaz* as possible before one enters the concert platform. The more depth there is in your musical knowledge, the longer would you stay on the musical platform. Then for the next thirty to fifty years, it will be smooth sailing.

Interviewer:

When was your first public performance? How were you feeling at that time?

Sajan Mishra:

We have been very lucky. We started giving performances right from childhood, first in temples, and then later in concerts. The first major concert was in 1968 in Sankatmochan temple in Benaras, in front of 2000–2500 people. We were dressed up elegantly for the occasion and we went on stage very confidently. And this confidence emanated from the words of our guru who taught us to be a student while listening, but when on stage for a performance, be a teacher. This statement instilled in us confidence and with the blessings of our guru and elders, it went off well.

Interviewer:

At that time Sajanji must have been only twelve or thirteen years old?

Rajan Mishra:

Yes, and I can very proudly say that what Sajanji sang at that age was exceptionally brilliant.

Interviewer:

Which raga did you sing?

Rajan Mishra:

We sang a *bandish* in raga Malkauns, followed by a *tappa* and a *bhajan*. Mahant Amarnathji (head priest of the temple) was very pleased with our performance. He blessed us. That was the beginning of our musical journey together, and with the blessings of everyone it is still continuing.

Interviewer:

Which is your favourite raga?

Rajan Mishra:

See, earlier we used to carry a list of seven ragas which were very dear to us. This list included ragas like Malkauns, Darbari Kanhara, Puriya, Yaman, etc. But with age we realised that all ragas are grand. Earlier we used to find many ragas quite *niras* (dull), for instance raga Durga. But as we matured we discovered that we were wrong. Now we find *rasa* in each and every raga. So, all ragas are my favourite.

Sajan Mishra:

I agree with this but a few ragas are still very dear to me like Malkauns, Darbari, Marwa, Puriya and Bhairav.

Interviewer:

Which is your favourite *bhajan*?

Sajan Mishra:

Two *bhajans—Jagat mein jhoothi dekhi preet* and *Sadho Rachna Ram Banayi* became very popular. But we like all our *bhajans*.

Rajan Mishra:

Even I like both these *bhajans*. The words of both these *bhajans* are so simple that the message directly reaches the masses. Guru Nanak's words *Jagat mein jhoothi dekhi preet* really touches people's heart.

Interviewer:

You have started *gurukul* at Dehradun and Benaras. Why at these places and why not here, in Delhi, where you live?

Rajan Mishra:

We belong to Benaras, we were brought up there, so no better place could have been there than Benaras. It was but natural to start a *gurukul* at Benaras. And in Dehradun we started one because of the natural beauty, peace and quiet surroundings it offered. Even if one sings at 2:00 am or 3:00 am, nobody is disturbed. Natural beauty always enhances self-growth. On the other hand Delhi is a congested city; it is difficult to select peaceful surroundings here. And we have not taken any help from the government. We have never asked the government for any flat, any land, anything for ourselves. And since we never demanded anything from the government we have not got anything.

Interviewer:

You are busy artistes with conferences, seminars, concerts lined up. In between all this, how do you take out time for your family?

Rajan Mishra:

I really thank my profession. If we are not performing, then we are at home only. We do not have to go to office or anywhere. So if for twenty days in a month we are away on a concert tour then for next ten days we are at home for twenty-four hours. And this compensates for those twenty days. My wife, Bina (daughter of Pandit Damodar Mishra of Kolkata) and Sajanji's wife, Kavitha (daughter of Pandit Birju Maharaj), look after the house very well. They never complain. They have been our strength.

Interviewer:

Did your mother support your passion?

Rajan Mishra:

She definitely played a major role. She herself belonged to a musical family. Our maternal grandfather was a music guru in the court of the king of Nepal. While our great grandfather, Nankolal Mishraji, was a great musicologist, *vidwan,* pandit. So, we inherited music from the paternal as well as the maternal side. And I vividly remember that during childhood when we used to forget the *antaraa* of a *bandish* taught by our father, at night mother used to teach us while she was putting us to sleep. Next morning, we used to sing that in front of our father and in return we were appropriately rewarded. Quite often monetary bribe was given to us in return for learning *bandishes.* We used to calculate that if we learn this *bandish* four *annas* would be given to us which would help us buy a kite. In this way also we learnt many *bandishes.*

Interviewer:

Had you not been a musician what would you have become?

Rajan Mishra:

As far as I am concerned I would have become a professor in some college. I had done MA, Sociology and had joined as a research scholar. My professor had taken me as his student only on one condition. I was supposed to teach him music and in return he would guide me in Sociology (*laughs*). For sometime this give and take, this barter system, continued but then life changed and I had to come to Delhi from Benaras. So I couldn't complete my PhD.

Sajan Mishra:

I would have been either a music teacher or would have been in sports—a coach or somewhere in cricket. But God was very kind.

Interviewer:

Rajanji you mentioned about life taking a turn that prompted both of you to leave Benaras and come to Delhi. What was that turn?

Rajan Mishra:

Our uncle, Gopal Mishraji had come to Delhi. He called us in 1973 and arranged for our radio audition.

We cleared the audition and very soon our National Programme was broadcast.

At night when it was being broadcast, the Director General, All India Radio heard it. He liked it so much that he called us and said that our talent belongs to the nation. He gave us many other programmes, like Tuesday Night Concert, Radio Sangeet Sammelan and National Programme. During that time radio had prestige. It was highly respected and artistes used to get immediate popularity. So, with this began our musical journey on a wider scale.

Interviewer:

From that golden Radio era let's return to the present day where there's so much technological exposure. In present times, what advice would you like to give to youngsters?

Rajan Mishra:

I would like to say two things. First, to have patience, and secondly, to respect and completely believe in their gurus. If they can have these two qualities, I think they will be able to achieve their goal.

Sajan Mishra:

And also to be open to music and musicians from other *gharana*s. To respect other artistes. The more they respect other *gharanas'* music, the more enriched will be their own music.

Interviewer:

Can music be taken up as a source of livelihood?

Rajan Mishra:

Yes, why not? But one must be prepared for hard work, sincerity and patience. We have supported ourselves on music only. We do not have any other vocation or job or income.

Sajan Mishra:

Now there's a lot of scope in music. Listenership has increased, many cultural organisations have come up and they keep on organising concerts. There is more scope now in music than it ever was.

Interviewer:

How do you see classical music in the near future?

Rajan Mishra:

Our music is ancient. It has been with us since Vedic times. It is divine, spiritual and people should listen to it spiritually and enjoy it. Children should also be exposed to it. Musical values should be passed on to them, so that peace and harmony can blossom on this earth. Music can spread the message of peace and harmony.

Sajan Mishra:

Besides all this, I would also like to say that people should listen to Hindustani classical music with love and reverence and that they should encourage others also to do so. About the future of classical music, I can say that it is gaining popularity. Lot of youngsters are getting attached to it. Definitely the future is going to be very bright for Hindustani classical music.

Everyday is Different

VIDUSHI SHRUTI SADOLIKAR

(9 November, 1951–)

Jaipur-Atrauli *gharana* vocalist, Shruti Sadolikar-Katkar believes that in life it is not important to achieve success but it is satisfying to accept that one is walking towards it.

And quite early in life she realised her mission. When other kids were learning to walk, she started reciting *bandishes*, and learnt music while listening to her father teaching other students.

We interviewed Shrutiji in New Delhi while she was on her way back to Mumbai after the concert.

Short-statured and dressed in a cotton saree, she was amiable, cheerful and spoke without any hesitation while expressing her views. During the course of conversation she often looked at her painter husband, C. Katkar, who nodded understandingly.

Her formal training began when she was just a child, five or six years of age. Her father Pandit Wamanrao Sadolikar was her first guru. Later she learnt from Gulubhai Jasdanwala, known for his large collection of rare raga compositions.

Along with music she continued her studies and obtained a Master's degree from SNDT Women's University in Mumbai; she has also written a thesis on *Haveli Sangeet*. 'Education and performance go hand in hand. Education enlarges our vision and understanding.'

Shruti Sadolikar is the Vice Chancellor of the Bhatkhande Music Institute University, Lucknow, Uttar Pradesh.

The interview continued for more than an hour and she often explained her viewpoints by illustrating them with her singing. As we approached the end of the session, she took a deep breath and said, 'Oh, it was such an exhaustive interview. I am so happy that it covered so many aspects and was not one of those routine talks.'

(14 January, 2008)

Interviewer:

Shrutiji you began learning music quite early in life from your father, Pandit Wamanrao Sadolikar. At what age did you start learning and how did you take the transformation of your father into your guru?

Shruti Sadolikar:

(*Laughs*) I was the apple of his eye. So, all the time I was on his lap only. Whenever he used to teach others, I used to be there, listening attentively. As a result, though he was teaching others, I was learning. And whenever students were unable to deliver, I used to complete the *bandish*.

Interviewer:

What was your age at that time?

Shruti Sadolikar:

Just one and a half to two years. That was the time when I used to be with him all the time. In fact, I was more fond of my father than my mother. Wherever he used to go, be it to teach music, give performances or for doing theatre, I was always with him.

Interviewer:

It is quite surprising that at that age when normally children cling to their mothers you were hanging out with your father and correcting others also. Well, maybe this is what being a child prodigy is all about. And what about your siblings?

Shruti Sadolikar:

(*She smiles*). This is what my family members told me. Of course I don't remember it. Well, in my house my brother and all my sisters have a very good voice. But to pursue music, to have the tenacity to pursue it, to have the patience and above all to have an urge to present one's creativity to the outside world was seriously missing in all my other siblings. And till one has all these characteristics, it is impossible to become an artiste. I formally became my father's disciple at the age of six. At that time there was one other girl, slightly older than me, who was his disciple. The moment she used to make a mistake, she would become quiet. So, just to show her that she is not the only one who makes mistakes, my father put me along with her. In the beginning I really didn't like it because that was my playtime, but later on I started liking it.

Interviewer:

So, how was he as a guru?

Shruti Sadolikar:

Compared to his other students he was very strict with me. Like once he asked me to give *taal* through hands and sing. But I sang without giving *taal* with my hands. So when I completed the *rachna* father asked me, 'Have you finished?' I said, 'Yes.' Then he asked me, 'But what about giving *taal*?' I told him that I was giving it in my mind. 'But why not with your hand?' he reproached me. I replied, 'My hands are paining.' And after this he made me sit beside him and started giving *taal* with his hands on my thigh. First I thought he would stop after doing it once or twice. But when he didn't, I realised that he was punishing me for disobeying him. At that time I felt so humiliated. I thought my father, who always protected me, is hitting me and that too in front of the other girl. I was literally crying inside but had to control my tears from trickling down; otherwise it would have been worse.

After the class, angry, I just ran out to play. And when I returned, my thigh had turned jet black. My mother asked me whether she should put some ointment. Seething with anger and humiliation, I just refused any treatment. After that all of us took our dinner, except my father. At night, I heard my mother asking him why he had punished me so badly? He replied, 'Had I spared her, it would have given the wrong signal to the other students.' So as a guru, he was very firm, strict. His main principle was—never excuse yourself. The day one starts giving excuses for shortcomings, like 'I couldn't sing well because of so and so reason,' one would never be able to sing well.

Interviewer:

You say you were the apple of your father's eyes. Then didn't your brother and sisters ever envy you?

Shruti Sadolikar:

Luckily, they all were very lazy. (*Says it laughingly*) ... I should say. And to tell you frankly, I see my students doing long hours of *riyaaz*. But we lived in a very small house. And all the time there were so many people at home. So, to do *riyaaz* I used to get the tanpura once in a fortnight. I used to do more of mental *riyaaz*. For instance when I used to go downstairs to play, I would stand in a corner and recollect whatever I was taught. For a long time I continued doing this but then after some years my mother motivated me to find time for regular practical *riyaaz*. After this I started doing *riyaaz* early in the morning from 6:00 am till 11:00 am. And my mother saw to it that I was regular. She would not even let me get up in the middle, nor would she allow me to take some rest in between. She was also very strict.

Interviewer:

Was she also a musician?

Shruti Sadolikar:

Yes, for a long time she gave concerts, worked in the theatre and also in a film. But she was more interested in studies and wanted me to complete my graduation, before branching out into music as a professional.

Interviewer:

What was her name?

Shruti Sadolikar:

Leela ... Leela Sadolikar. She was very keen that all of us should be educated, to understand not only music and its finer points but to have knowledge about the world as well. She was very particular that I should be fully prepared to understand and answer any question related to my singing or style. And one can only be confident about things if one has theories and knowledge to support and substantiate it. She did not want me to be ignorant and say, 'I was doing it because my guru told me to do it.' She expected me to have my own reasons, research and theories to substantiate it and be able to convince the opposite party. She nurtured in me that thinking power. For my *riyaaz*, my father used to give me one or two *paltas*. Initially I used to wonder why I have to do the same thing for four to five hours everyday. But later I realised that regular *riyaaz* of the same *palta* for days really brought confidence and polished my singing. I realised it myself. And this realisation is the real *riyaaz*. Regular practice is not exactly physical labour, it enhances the imagination. That instant execution of your ideas and the freshness of your ideas can be maintained through research and thinking only. Otherwise if one just learns it by rote then it will become very mechanical; if you keep doing mathematical permutations and combinations, soon you will be exhausted. There is an end to everything.

Interviewer:

How is it that we do not have any album of your guru and father, Pandit Wamanrao Sadolikar?

Shruti Sadolikar:

Yes, that is right. No musical pieces of my father are available in the market. Maybe it was his fault. Many years ago there was an album in which he had sung raga Khambavati, Bhim and Tilang Bahar. But unfortunately today that record is not available. In 1972 in one of the concerts in Mumbai I had accompanied him on the tanpura. He sang for four hours so beautifully. At one place in Nayaki Kanhara, the *pancham* of *taar saptak* was sung so beautifully that people got up from their seats. We had that recording but somebody took it from him to listen to it and never returned it back to us. So we lost that too. Anyway, recently I have received a recording of his from New Jersey and will be releasing it shortly.

Interviewer:

What is so remarkable in the *gayaki* of Jaipur-Atrauli *gharana*?

Shruti Sadolikar:

Our *gharana gayaki* is of *shuddha akaar, jod* raga and in our *gayaki* with each *sur* there's an invisible bonding of *laya* and *taal* and this is very clearly depicted. Maybe that is not the point of emphasis in the *gayaki* of other *gharana*s. Even the *bandishe*s of our *gharana* are very unique. Some of them have been composed by *Gaan Samrat* (Emperor of Music), Ustad Alladiya Khan, the founder of the Jaipur-Atrauli *gharana*. And some bandishes have been included in our *gharana* from Vaishnav music like *Mero Piya Rasiya.*

Interviewer:

Who brought them?

Shruti Sadolikar:

Ustad Alladiya Khan; because many members of his family were stationed in Rajasthan. So, in the give and take between court musicians many *bandishes* reached our *gharana*, in fact not only our *gharana* but other *gharana*s also. Like the *bandish 'ban-than kahan chalen ho'* which we sing is actually a *dhrupad* about Lord Krishna.

Interviewer:

How has the style undergone changes from Ustad Alladiya Khan to your age?

Shruti Sadolikar:

See, his *taleem* from his family was in Nauhaar *bani*, Khandhaar *bani*, Gauhaar *bani*, Dagar *bani*—some from the paternal side and some from the maternal side or some came along with the daughters-in-law as part of their dowry. And Ustad Alladiya Khan's father Ustad Ahmed Khan was very knowledgeable. He remembered not less than 30,000 pieces of *dhrupad, dhamaar* and *khayal*. Even Ustad Alladiya Khan remembered many *bandish*es. And as state patronage declined, his repertoire of *dhrupad* pieces took the form of *khayal*. With his *dhrupad taleem* intact, he transformed those *bandish*es into the parameters of *khayal*. That's why you see that the *laya* of *bandish* in *vilambit* is not slow *vilambit teentaal or jhaptaal* in our *gharana*; our *vilambit laya* is in between *madhya* and *vilambit laya* (*sings to explain it*).

Interviewer:

Isn't this quite similar to the Gwalior *gharana gayaki*?

Shruti Sadolikar:

See, Gwalior *gharana gayaki* is the main source; it is *the source*, the Gangotri of music. There were many things in this *gayaki* that were taken in by different people, belonging to different *gharana*s. In earlier times communication or exposure was not as easy as it is today. So, it wasn't easy to copy. But we do see so many common things in so many different gharanas which have actually originated in different places, hundreds of miles away from each other. One has to understand this aspect. Every talented person and/or the pioneers of each *gharana* were united in a way. Music was the common thread that united them. They all saw it differently, from their respective places, interpreted it according to their vision and highlighted the beauty as per their understanding. So the *gharana*s are there, they are known by different names, each has its own tradition, but music, the base, is the same.

Nobody sings without *taal* or *sur*. And the *bandish*es are already there. So where is the difference?

Interviewer:

So, can we say that in today's times the uniqueness of each *gharana* has faded away?

Shruti Sadolikar:

This is the demand of the times. See even the Wall of Berlin had to be broken down; It is the call of history. We cannot flourish in isolation. The same has happened in music too. Each *gharana* maintained its sanctity but also borrowed things from other *gharana*s and changed and polished those things according to the parameters of their own *gharana*s. And then it appeared as if it was their own creation. The world moves on this premise. Americans get to eat idli-dosa in America and here in India we get to eat their pizza. (*Laughs*)

Interviewer:

What changes have you brought about in the music you inherited from your guru and father, Pandit Wamanrao Sadolikar?

Shruti Sadolikar:

To answer this question I have to go back a little. Ustad Alladiya Khan was trained in *dhrupad-dhamaar* and he extended that to *khayal gayaki*. And his *gayaki* had scintillating *taans*. But because he sang so much he lost his voice and for two years he could not sing. After a gap of two years when he started singing again, the texture of his voice had changed. A slight roughness had crept into his voice and because of this he faced difficulty in taking *meend*. So he changed his style of singing. And that became the stamp of my *gharana*. In my *gayaki* all those facets that I enumerated earlier are there but at the same time it has my signature on it as well. My father always told me never to learn music by rote. 'I am giving you the base. You build your own structure,' he advised me. So I stay within the framework of the Jaipur-Atrauli *gharana* but within that frame it is my choice how I expand the canvas. In fact all my gurus—my father, later Gulubhai Jasdanwala, disciple of Alladiya Khan and Manjhi Khan Sahib and Ustad Azizuddin Khan Sahib, grandson of Ustad Alladiya Khan—they all told me that they have showed me the way, but how to walk on it is my lookout. The way I used to sing earlier, say twenty or twenty-five years ago, is different from the way I sing now. With age I've come to understand the ragas better. I see every *sur* in a new form every time. The way I sang Yaman yesterday is different from the way I'll sing it today. Because every day is a new beginning for each raga, for each *sur,* for me too. Today I recognise the same raga differently. And it is this understanding that changes the style, the singing. This brings in the changes in presentation. Having said all this, as I explained before, the basic foundation remains same.

Interviewer:

What is the concept behind your twenty-*taal*s rendition?

Shruti Sadolikar:

There's one *rasik*, follower of music, very fond of different *taal*s more particularly odd number taals, like 11, 13, 15, 17 *matra taal*s. He had collected twelve *bhajan*s, each in different *taals,* twenty ragas in twenty *taals,* eighteen *thumri*s in different *taal*s and ten ghazals in different *taal*s. He was on the lookout for somebody who could make his concept come alive, breathe life into it so to say. Someone told him about me and he got in touch with me. That's how this project came about. It was a very difficult project. We practised for nearly three years every Saturday and Sunday. He was not bothered about the commercial viability of the project. He just wanted to leave something for posterity. Today I really thank God that I got an opportunity to sing so many *taal*s. I learnt quite a lot from this project.

Interviewer:

How is it doing in the market?

Shruti Sadolikar:

I've no idea. But when it was released in 1983–84 it was a chartbuster. it was very much in demand in universities abroad.

Interviewer:

You have done research on *Haveli Sangeet* as well. So what are your findings?

Shruti Sadolikar:

Once I heard from someone that Ustad Alladiya Khan Sahib taught one version of raga Bihagda to one disciple and a different version to another. So there are different *bandish*es circulating as Bihagda and they are based on different versions of the same raga. In that case which one is the authentic Bihagda? Some people said that Khan Sahib did this just to show his authority; and that basically *bigda hua* Bihag (distorted version of Bihag) is Bihagda. They would also question ragas like Basanti Kanhada saying that he just made it up on a whim. I was really disturbed after hearing such things. I wanted to know whether these people who are maligning Khan Sahib today have actually gone back to music history and verified whether there is any proof for all this or not! I asked my father and he said, 'Search for the answers. The same question had arisen in my mind and I had asked Khan Sahib.' I asked him what Khan Sahib's answer was and my father replied, 'I will not give you the answer. Go and search for it yourself, if you don't find the answer then I will tell you.' Then I got a fellowship and decided to take this up as the subject of my research.

Interviewer:

And did you find the answer?

Shruti Sadolikar:

I started with questions about why different versions of the same raga are circulating, where did *kanhada ke prakar* come from, why is it that the raga *swaroop* (form and shape) that we follow sometimes does not correspond with what people from other *gharana*s follow. Then I realised that in *pushti sangeet*, what we call *haveli sangeet* today, kirtans are sung for Lord Krishna at Nathdwara, and these same kirtans have been adapted into *bandish*es by people and that the raga *swaroop* is derived from that source.

Interviewer:

So how did the transformation actually take place?

Shruti Sadolikar:

See, in earlier times, about 500–600 years ago, musicians conceptualised ragas differently. At that time the tanpura was not very popular and veena was the main instrument. Therefore, the *andaz* of striking the *sur*, the placement of the notes are different from the *sur sthaana* followed today. The same raga would have sounded different in earlier times because the *chatusruti, trisurti* that can be articulated on veena is not there in the tanpura. So this has also affected the way we sing them vocally, *sa* and *pa* have become standing notes. All this history of music plays a major role in this case.

So, in *pushti sangeet*, the *swaroop* of many ragas is connected with their interpretation as it existed in the earlier times. And the people who used to sing those *kirtans* in the havelis or mansions were quite secluded and did not interact much with the outer world; they were immersed in their spiritualism. So, their music remained unaffected by the changes in the raga *shastra* and raga *swaroop* that were happening outside. Thus, the earliest form of ragas was preserved, safe with them.

So I started practising that and I realised that Bihagda is not *bigda hua* Bihag. Just as we call someone affectionately–say you address *kanha* as *kanhdu* or *sanwala* as *sanwalda*–similarly Bihag was lovingly called Bihagda. In the Vaishnavite interpretation, Bihagda is sung differently and there are many *bandishes*. That is exactly what Khan Sahib taught his disciples. So then I started getting very excited about *haveli sangeet*. I discovered that the depth of imagination and the richness of poetry in this form are unparalleled. It's a universe in itself.

Interviewer:

You sing *khayal, thumri, bhajan*. So, how do you prepare yourself for each genre? Is there any difference in preparation for each genre?

Shruti Sadolikar:

It is necessary to have a lightness in throat. Secondly in classical music, for *alaap, gamak* or *taan*, it is not necessary to have physical strength. It is the voice-throw that's very important. There's a way to take *murki*. It is not right to sing in a round-about way. In the throat there's a place for each *alankar* and that space has to be given to it. (*She sings to explain*). Actually it all depends on perception. And if the perception is not right then the presentation will also not be perfect.

Interviewer:

A school of musical thought considers *thumri* as semi-classical. But another school does not agree with it and would like to have it included in the category of pure classical. What is your take on this?

Shruti Sadolikar:

See, every form of singing is valid, correct. It is a different thing if one has prepared oneself for only one form. I think it can be compared to sour grapes. Take Ustad Faiyaz Khan Sahib. His voice was so powerful but when he sang '*banao batiyan,*' it seemed as if a woman is saying *hamse banao mat batiya.* He used to bring out the *ras,* the *bhaav* of the piece.

So, one should know what produces *ras.* It is not that classical music is lifeless or boring in comparison to light music. The important point is that we should know where is that *ras* and how to bring it out in renditions? We *should* know that.

And it is a fact that Begum Akhtarji, Rasoolan Baiji, Siddheshwari Deviji and our renowned present day vocalist Girija Deviji—they have all received *taleem* in classical music. Even Shobha Gurtuji was trained in classical music. Her mother, Manekabai Shirodkar, who was a rage during her time, had received training in classical music. She was the disciple of Ustad Bhurji Khan. And Shobhaji, belonging to a home where *taleem* was given in *jahan hamare saiyan* and *atar sugandh,* used to present breathtaking *thumri*s.

This was because, I do not know whether everybody will agree with me or not, but this is what I feel; that light music is the cream of classical music. *Thumri, chaiti, kajri,* all these forms are rich in content. Importance is given to words and the related emotions, the *bhaav*. *Raga shastra* takes a back seat. To highlight emotional content we do take liberties. However, some ragas are not very suitable for *thumri-dadra* because the *bhaav* in the sur of these ragas (like Hindol-Bahar) is not suitable for *thumri*. In fact, all our elders have said that one should have *chaumukhi vidya* (multi-pronged learning), otherwise the development of the artiste will be one-sided.

Interviewer:

Which is your favourite *thumri*?

Shruti Sadolikar:

This is quite a complicated question ... (*laughs*). In my childhood I had heard Begum Akhtar, Rasoolan Baiji, Siddheshwari Deviji and Girija Deviji. Somewhere I have been influenced by all of them, more by Begum Akhtar's *gayaki*. I used to listen to Begum Akhtar everywhere. The pain in her voice troubles me a lot. Somewhere it touches the deepest chord of my heart so much so that I am unable to control my emotions. It brings tears to my eyes. In *ek saptak* voice she has achieved what is so very difficult even in four *saptaks*. The way she highlighted the *bhaav* of words within the structure of *sur* is just unparalleled. She constructed a world of emotions, words, *sur* and it is this world that really inspired me a lot.

Interviewer:

You also met Begum Akhtar. So how did you meet her and what did she say after listening to your music?

Shruti Sadolikar:

I had met her many a time. But I met her as her friend Pandit Wamanrao's daughter and as her *bhakt,* a devotee. One day I had just returned home when the telephone bell rang. I picked up the phone. And the voice from the other end said, 'I am Begum Akhtar.' The moment I heard her voice the phone was about to slip out of my hands. And in my mind several thoughts passed by—it must be a wrong number, it can't be true, etc. Anyway the voice from the other end enquired about me and said that she would like to hear me sing. I was literally taken aback. Anyway, I told her perhaps after a day or two. And she replied, 'No, no, this evening, as I am going back tomorrow.' I was left with no option.

So she came in the evening. It was 4 June, 1971. It was raining and she came inside, completely drenched. She heard my singing and after the song said, 'You sing well, but tell me have you ever fallen in love?' I was embarrassed. My guru and other elderly people were sitting right in front of me. I didn't know what to say. But unmindful of the people sitting around, she continued, 'Fall in love ... at the most the heart will break ... let it break ... heartaches will generate pain and the more the pain the better will be your voice.' I haven't forgotten her advice till now.

Interviewer:

So, how many heartaches?

Shruti Sadolikar:

(Laughs) Well, I think I was lucky to have a friend who became my husband later on. But I think sometimes people's ego comes in between their liking and getting attached. The deeper meaning of all this is that to call somebody your own you have to forget yourself. It is this complete surrender that helps us grow as better human beings.

Interviewer:

And when the heart is broken, then?

Shruti Sadolikar:

Too, too, too painful. But then this pain can be channelised into creativity—through painting, writing, music, any creative outlet. And I think what she told me is a useful tip for everybody. One can bear the pain of heartbreak and make one's life richer, meaningful. After all it gives one an inner strength.

Interviewer:

Any other piece of advice you would like to give besides the journey of love-heartbreak-pain?

Shruti Sadolikar:

I would like to say that in today's technology, material happiness is easily available. But development of mankind is not only science and technology. It may make them successful but knowledge and art are equally important. We do everything to make our children score hundred per cent in examinations, but pay scant attention towards art. We are indifferent towards it. This outlook creates an imbalance in society and is painful. This urge for instant success becomes a hurdle in the longer run. Yes, we have a right to know the answers of why and what. But it is also necessary to know that it is not imperative to have answers to every question.

In life it is not important to achieve success, it is enough to accept that one is walking towards it. I think the happiness that one gets in striving towards success is much more than the happiness one gets on attaining success. One should never be defeated in life. One should not be frightened of failure and pain. If we accept defeat midway, we will never be able to reach our destination. And this can only happen when we follow any art form. Because it is in art that every day is different. One day the singing is impeccable but the very next day, on the very same stage, there's something missing. Every time we go on stage we seek the blessings of our elders and our guru. This humility is necessary. It is necessary to keep our feet firmly planted on the ground. It is art that makes us see life without the blinkers of ego or pride and infuses in us the finer qualities of life.

Interviewer:

Have you encouraged your children towards art?

Shruti Sadolikar:

Yes. I have one son. He is learning music and is a painter too.

Interviewer:

So he has taken after both of you–music from you and painting from your husband.

Shruti Sadolikar:

Yes.

Interviewer:

When both of you are not busy in your respective professional commitments then how do you relax?

Shruti Sadolikar:

Well, both of us are very fond of nature. We like to be amidst birds, trees; it is enough for us to just glance outside the window, to read books, to see films, particularly timeless films of Satyajit Ray, Japanese films and of course we listen to yesteryears' maestros and old film songs.

Interviewer:

When you look back on your life how do you feel? Do you have any regrets?

Shruti Sadolikar:

Oh, these mathematical calculations always go on in the mind. If I have reached here, what all have I lost in this journey. With my father passed away one age, an era. Death of a person is not a solitary happening. With one death passes away an entire age, a bundle of experience goes away. But what I have gained through this art is the immense love of people. When people suffering from terminal illnesses request to listen to Shruti Sadolikar's music, it is touching, heart-warming. It was my service to them; where I could not reach physically, my *sur* reached and made them happy. All this is due only because of the blessings of my elders and God almighty.

V O C A L

I am an Indian Musician

PANDIT AJOY CHAKRABARTY

(7 January, 1953–)

It was not easy to persuade Pandit Ajoy Chakrabarty to open up. He is reticent and laconic. Though unwell, he agreed to talk and gradually started sharing, making forthright statements. Having led a life of struggle, travelling between aspirations, dreams and reality, Pandit Ajoy Chakrabarty (Patiala *gharana)* somehow managed to strike a balance between studies and music. 'Credit for the first half of my life goes to my parents.' Both his parents were singers in their own right and encouraged their son to take up music seriously. Right from childhood, he wanted to carve his own destiny. He worked hard, working nearly sixteen to twenty hours daily, travelling nearly twenty kilometres everyday to his guru's place. His dream was to carve his name on the pages of the history of Hindustani classical music.

As a student he topped in both BA and MA. And later as a vocalist he became the first recipient of the Kumar Gandharva Award and the President's Award. He also received a Gold Medal from the Sangeet Research Academy (ITC-SRA, where he teaches now), Kolkata. In addition to all these accolades, Ajoy Chakrabarty was the first Indian classical vocalist to be invited by the government of Pakistan. To his remarkable similarity to the doyen of Patiala *gharana,* Ustad Bade Ghulam Ali Khan's *gayaki*, he promptly cuts in, 'I am not even equal to the dust off his feet. But yes, maybe because his philosophy of life is so dear to me, it reflects in my singing.'

(10 October, 2006)

Interviewer:

It is said about you that you started singing even before you learnt to speak. Is it true?

Ajoy Chakrabarty:

How can it be possible? It is true that some people have an inherent talent to listen to a note and reproduce it exactly. So, because of my parents' love for music, I could sing and reproduce exact notes at the age of two. That is what I've been told by my parents. I myself do not know about it.

Interviewer:

Did you start singing on your own or your mother sang lullabies ...

Ajoy Chakrabarty:

No, not lullabies, but both my parents were very good singers. They used to sing everyday and did *riyaaz* everyday, even before I was born. That was purely out of their love for music. They were not professional singers; they did not earn their livelihood through music. My father was a school teacher. I am talking about 1948 and after that.

Interviewer:

So, who were your gurus?

Ajoy Chakrabarty:

The first musical lesson that I got was from my father Ajit Chakrabarty and then I became Pannalal Samantji's disciple. I remained his disciple for two years. Later, I became the disciple of Kanai Das Bairagi who was a great vocalist. For ten years I learnt from him. He introduced me to the great guru Pandit Gyan Prakash Ghosh. When guruji, that is Pandit Gyan Prakashji, was appointed the Head of Asian Music Department in Philadelphia University, he sent me to Ustad Munnawar Ali Khan in 1969 and I became his *gandabandh shagird*. So I went to him and remained with him till his last breath, i.e., till 1989.

Interviewer:

One sees in your renditions a lot of influence of Ustad Bade Ghulam Ali Khan. In your concerts you also sing many of the *bandishe*s he composed.

Ajoy Chakrabarty:

I am not even equal to the dust off his feet. Artistes like Bade Ghulam Ali Khan Sahib are very rare to find. Even after 1000 years such artistes will not be born.

I only try to understand his philosophy, life, values, his attitude, the human aspect. I never learnt from him. I learnt from Ustad Munnawar Ali Khan Sahib, but I always try to follow the principles and philosophy of Ustad Bade Ghulam Ali Khan Sahib in my life. Since his philosophy is so dear to me, maybe that's why my music appears so very similar to his.

Interviewer:

What is that philosophy?

Ajoy Chakrabarty:

Philosophy is the key to music. Philosophy is how you think about music, what you think about music and how you like to present your music, how proud you are of your country, what kind of food, taste, education you have from different sources. Music is not only *sa re ga ma* but it reflects life itself.

Interviewer:

In your music there is a blend of tradition and improvisation. How do you bring this in your *gayaki*?

Ajoy Chakrabarty:

One cannot do without improvisation. Human beings always try to create, innovate. God created human beings and through us he created many things. So, we, human beings cannot live without improvisations, innovations or creating something.

Interviewer:

You have started a unique musical school–Shrutinandan. What is the philosophy behind it?

Ajoy Chakrabarty:

We are all musicians. In my opinion, howsoever great a musician might be, the greatest thing he or she can do is to prepare the next generation of performers.

This is what I personally feel. I am not going to pass any comment on anyone. The maestros who are no more with us were all time great classical maestros.

If I want that my music and I should stay alive even after my death, it can only be achieved through the next generation. Keeping this in mind, I thought that it would be irresponsible on my part if I keep my values, my music, my thinking, my country's different elements to myself. If I can't pass it on to the next generation then India will have no special value. So, I decided to do something, and decided to start an institution. God was kind enough to show me the way.

Interviewer:

What is the difference between Shrutinandan and other institutes?

Ajoy Chakrabarty:

Shrutinandan is an institution which tries to teach from *Sa* to *Ni.* The first alphabet of Shrutinandan, 'S' denotes *Sa* and the last alphabet is 'N', stands for *Ni.* And from *Sa* to *Ni* there are twelve notes; the word 'shrutinandan' also has twelve alphabets. So, in this institute we try to teach from *Sa* to *Ni*—not just the musical notes but also the philosophy of music and life.

Interviewer:

What is the general age of the children who come to this institute?

Ajoy Chakrabarty:

My aim is to inculcate values of music in young children. So, the lowest age is five and the maximum age at which I accept any student is eleven years.

Interviewer:

And how long can the child learn?

Ajoy Chakrabarty:

There's no age limit for that. One can be in this institute till s/he is fully prepared to sing.

It is not about getting the certificate after one or two years and leaving the institute. Giving a certificate is not my aim. My aim is to make that person a good musician.

Interviewer:

You say that 'music is neither heard nor sung in vacuum.' What do you mean by it?

Ajoy Chakrabarty:

Music is associated with life itself. It is an integral part of life, a turning point in life.

Music is like a painting, and the material for that painting is air. It is like drawing or sketching a painting in air. This means that the painting we try to create on air through breathing is music. So, music cannot be heard or sung in vacuum.

Interviewer:

What do you feel about the relevance of the concept of *gharana* today?

Ajoy Chakrabarty:

See, even earlier this concept of *gharana* was archaic. It had no meaning. Four artistes belonging to one *gharana* will sing differently. Music depends on one's individuality, thinking, values, culture and humanity. Of course, a basic line of thinking is maintained in a *gharana*. In that way *gharana*s are important.

But had Zakir *bhai* played like his father (Ustad Alla Rakha) only, he wouldn't have reached where he is now. He wouldn't have added anything new to the existing musical knowledge.

Then Allaudin Baba was such a great guru that today we have such great sarod and sitar players, like Ustad Ali Akbar Khan Sahib, Pandit Ravi Shankar and Pandit Nikhil Bannerjee—all great musicians. All three of them learnt from the same guru, yet all of them sound so different.

It is not that since all of them belong to Ustad Allaudin Khan's *gharana*, they should sound similar. Each one of them brought their own life, thinking and individuality into their music.

Interviewer:

What do you like singing?

Ajoy Chakrabarty:

I like everything. I am an Indian and like to sing all forms of Indian music. I am not a *khayal* or *thumri* or film music singer. I am an Indian musician.

Interviewer:

Why is it that you have not done too many *jugalbandis*?

Ajoy Chakrabarty:

I have only performed *jugalbandi* with Dr M Balamuralikrishnaji. And I have performed fifty times with him, all over the world. But I do not basically believe in *jugalbandi* performances because unless you have proper training under the same guru, it can never be successful. It becomes a competition in showmansip; it is no longer art.

Interviewer:

What are your views on the creation of *ragas*?

Ajoy Chakrabarty:

See, there so many existing ragas. I am too small to create any other raga. Many artistes have combined two ragas and called it a new raga. But to create ragas like Yaman, Bhoopali or Bageshwari is not possible. Nobody can create ragas.

Interviewer:

What do you think about present day music scenario?

Ajoy Chakrabarty:

If the so-called fusion music is created with honesty, it is good. There are some people who genuinely try to highlight the uniqueness of some instrument. That is good.

If it is made with honest intentions, sincerity and by keeping our 1000-year-old tradition intact, I don't have any issues with it. But most of the time fusion simply creates confusion.

Interviewer:

How about going back in time and remembering your first public performance?

Ajoy Chakrabarty:

My first public concert was at the age of four and a half years in *Jatra* and then at the age of eight I sang in front of 1000 people. My first concert was in Kolkata Indoor Stadium in 1968 at the age of sixteen. Then another really well-appreciated public concert was in Rabindra Sadan, Kolkata in 1974. I was twenty-two. It was a youth talent conference. I was not frightened or nervous. I just wanted to give my best, that's all.

Interviewer:

What do you think of today's young musicians?

Ajoy Chakrabarty:

Today's young musicians are much more intelligent, their understanding is better but most of the times they don't want to go into the deeper aspects of raga or music.

Feelings for raga, restlessness to understand a raga is missing. Very few people have it these days. But their overall presentation, connection with the virtual world, handling of technology, etc. is much more advanced.

Interviewer:

What you are saying is that their PR is much better. So, in this context can we say that today's music has become commercialised?

Ajoy Chakrabarty:

No, I would not say that. I know many young people who are loyal, devoted and are not at all commercialised. But the fact is that music has become a profession. It has become a means to earn money. It is good to see that commercial aspect but along with it if they give importance to *taleem*, education and training in music, it would be much better for classical music.

Interviewer:

What role has your wife played in making Ajoy Chakrabarty Pandit Ajoy Chakrabarty?

Ajoy Chakrabarty:

First of all I am not 'Pandit.' I am only a student of music, student Ajoy Chakrabarty. Credit for the first part of my life, up to the age of twenty-four or twenty-five goes to my parents. After that, till today, credit goes to my wife, my family and well wishers. Credit basically goes to my wife, because she has to take care of the way I dress, my travel and food, the homefront, children, everything. Earlier she also acted as my secretary. I am very grateful to her.

Interviewer:

What problems did you face in your growing-up years?

Ajoy Chakrabarty:

It is a like a film. See, my father was a primary school teacher and he used to sing so beautifully. But society at that time did not accept his singing within the fold of Brahmin tradition. He was not respected. So, in school and even in college, my budget was fifty paisa to one rupee per day. Often after music lessons I had to stay on the railway platform, without eating anything, just drinking tap water since the last train had already left and there was no money. Often we had to survive on a pinch of salt and a little mustard oil. My father used to get a salary of just ₹72/- per month as a school teacher. This was in the year 1964. I am telling you true facts. It is not a story. In these conditions, I was left with no option but to excel in studies, come first in class in order to get the National Scholarship and be able to continue my studies. I am the first recipient of Kumar Gandharva award and the youngest Sangeet Natak Akademi awardee as also the first classical musician to be invited to Pakistan.

Interviewer:

You mentioned that you often stayed at the platform. Why?

Ajoy Chakrabarty:

After my college I used to go to Ustad Munnawar Ali Khan's residence in Kolkata to take *taleem*. It was thirty kilometres away from my home in Shyam Nagar. *Taleem* used to continue till late night. After that when I used to reach the station, the last train had either gone or was just passing by. So I had to spend the night at the station.

Interviewer:

Now your daughter, Kaushiki Chakrabarty is also a musician. What do you think about her capabilities and how do you train her?

Ajoy Chakrabarty:

If she practises hard and does not have any personal burden then nobody can stop her from being one of the topmost female vocalists of her generation. She is the first Indian to receive the BBC World Music award. As for giving her *taleem*, I always try teaching her the uniqueness of all maestros, including that of light music, like Lata Mangeshkar, Asha Bhonsle and others, but of course she is a full-fledged *khayal* singer. To sing well, to earn a name and fame—all these things are not that difficult as to convert oneself from an ordinary to a great artiste, to make oneself touch the height of great standard.

Interviewer:

Why did your wife leave music?

Ajoy Chakrabarty:

She did not leave music as such; she just did not pursue it on the concert stage. She couldn't grind her talent to professional marketability. Moreover, had we both continued with our professional lives, then we would never have been able to groom Kaushiki into a successful musician. It is because of my wife that Kaushiki is where she is today.

Interviewer:

Who are the other torchbearers of the Patiala *gharana*?

Ajoy Chakrabarty:

There might be others, but I do not know.

Interviewer:

What advice would you like to give to youngsters?

Ajoy Chakrabarty:

Hard work pays. Practise eight to ten hours a day, at least, if not all the twenty four hours. And love it.

Interviewer:

How would you describe your musical journey?

Ajoy Chakrabarty:

Unique. When I remember all those years of struggle, I really find all those things very unique now. Meeting great masters and learning something or the other from them. Great artistes like Hirabaiji, Ustad Latafat Hussain Khan, Ustad Khadim Hussain Khan, Pandit K.G. Ginde, Ustad Ali Akbar Khan, Pandit Ravi Shankar, and I even got to learn so much from Zakir *bhai* about *taal* and *laya.* I always try to remember their uniqueness.

Interviewer:

What according to you is the connection between spirituality and classical music?

Ajoy Chakrabarty:

I think Indian music and Indian spirituality are not different. They are the same. And our success in life lies in its respect, belief, in preservation of our values and understanding the greatness of our culture.

In the Quest of Musical Knowledge

USTAD MASHKOOR ALI KHAN

(27 February, 1956–)

Vocalist Ustad Mashkoor Ali Khan of Kirana gharana is called *Bandish Nawaz.* This is the title that has been bestowed on him by the Salt Lake Cultural Association in 1998. Besides this he has been honoured with many awards.

He learnt music from his father, legendary sarangi maestro Ustad Shakoor Ali Khan and is presently teaching at SRA (Sangeet Research Academy), Kolkata.

A direct descendant of Ustad Abdul Karim Khan and *Sartaj-e-Mousiqui*, Ustad Abdul Waheed Khan—founders of the Kirana *gharana*, his search for musical knowledge continues.

He was barely five years old when his father, Ustad Shakoor Ali Khan brought him to Delhi from Kirana (a small town in Muzaffarnagar, Uttar Pradesh) and began to impart *gharana gayaki* to the young child.

Missing out on childhood fun, Ustad Mashkoor Ali Khan realised the importance of strict discipline and regular musical *taleem* with time, 'I am what I am because of my father; he completely concentrated on me, my musical training. Because he had struggled in his life, my father knew the worth of hard work and wanted his son to reach the stars. He loved me too much and in his own way he pampered me. I wish everybody gets a father like mine.'

Notwithstanding the rich musical lineage, he seems to feel that having talent is different from achieving immense popularity, 'I have seen luck betraying many talented people and supporting untalented people. To understand art, music and have talent is completely different from being "successful." This is the reality.'

We talked to Ustad Mashkoor Ali Khan just before his evening concert. With his sparkling white starched kurta and thin moustache, he is noticeable even in a dense crowd.

Constantly humming, even during the course of the interview, Mashkoor Ali Khan let his deep sonorous voice break into *sargam-taans* to explain a point. Music is his life. 'I cannot imagine doing anything else.'

(22 February, 2009)

Interviewer:

Your great grandfather was a *beenkar* and your father was a sarangi maestro but you became a vocalist. Why and how?

Mashkoor Ali Khan:

I did not learn the sarangi. My father, Ustad Shakoor Ali Khan, was both a sarangi maestro and a vocalist. In my family there was a tradition that a child who had a good voice was taught vocal music and if one's voice was not so good he was taught the sarangi. My great grandfather, Ustad Bande Ali Khan was a celebrated *beenkar*. He was an exceptionally fascinating *beenkar*. It is said that he prohibited anyone in the family from playing *been* after him. So after him nobody in the family played the *been*. Hence, after him, my family concentrated on vocal music and sarangi. My father had learnt vocal music from his maternal grandfather, Ustad Mehboob Baksh Khan and from his father, Ustad Abdul Ghafoor Khan Sahib and from his uncle, *Sartaj-e-Mousiqui* Ustad Abdul Waheed Khan Sahib. So from all these gurus he had learnt both vocal music and the sarangi.

Interviewer:

At what age did you begin to learn music?

Mashkoor Ali Khan:

I was only five years old when I started learning music. My father brought me to Delhi from Kirana, a tiny place situated in district Muzaffarnagar. He separated me from my mother and brought me to Delhi. As a child I used to sit in his lap and he would teach me *bandishes* in different ragas.

Interviewer:

But were you not too small to learn *bandishes*?

Mashkoor Ali Khan:

Yes I was, but the thing is that my father was determined to make me a vocalist. He just concentrated on me. In fact, my entire musical *taleem* has happened inside All India Radio, his workplace. Mr K.K. Mathur, Station Director, All India Radio, had granted special permission for me to go inside the radio station along with my father. A special pass was made for me. For nearly seven to ten years I regularly visited the radio station and got the opportunity to listen to many senior artistes. I am what I am because of my father; he completely concentrated on me, my musical training. For each raga my father knew at least twenty to twenty-five *bandishes* and he taught me all. At times I used to get irritated also because except music there was nothing else that I was allowed to do. I didn't even get time to play games. My training used to begin in the morning and finish only at night. Because he had struggled in his life, my father knew the worth of hard work and wanted his son to reach the stars. He loved me too much and in his own way he pampered me. I wish everybody gets a father like mine.

Interviewer:

But in this rigid training schedule didn't you ever miss childhood; also what about school? Did you go to school or not?

Mashkoor Ali Khan:

Of course, it was but natural for a child to miss the pranks of childhood, and as I said at times I really used to feel very agitated. But I did not have the guts to express my desires. He was very strict and I was frightened of him. Now I realise the worth of it for had I wasted my time in playing and childhood pranks, I wouldn't have reached where I am today. And school? Well, as we were staying in Chandni Mahal, old Delhi, I attended a school nearby—Shanta School. Before I joined this school I had a tutor who used to come home and teach. I think his name was Sir Thomas. He was a very good teacher.

Interviewer:

When did you give your first concert?

Mashkoor Ali Khan:

I started singing in private *baithaks* right from childhood, hardly six or seven years of age. In a way it can be said that my first big concert happened when I was ten years old and I sang a *bandish* in raga Bhatiyar. My father was sitting in the front row and after the concert he said, 'Work hard.' He never praised me, rather he always used to point out three to four shortcomings so that I did not grow complacent.

Interviewer:

As far as I know you have a huge treasure of rare ragas and that's why you are called *Bandish Nawaz*. Right?

Mashkoor Ali Khan:

Yes, you are right. And this treasure of rare ragas has been given to me not only by my father but also by other elders of the family. They all blessed me, 'Son, you take this *bandish*. I have become old but your singing will make it come alive once again.' So all my elders blessed me by gifting me special *bandishes*. This is the reason that today I have a wealth of unique, rare *bandishes* and ragas. You can also say that 85 per cent of *taleem* I have received from my father and 15 per cent has been imparted by the other elders of the family. And if today I have my own style, it is all because of my elders. They taught me how to present a *bandish* after exploring the raga. Today I hear so many maestros presenting *bandishes* without first exploring and expanding the raga. It is very important to have command over ragas. I am grateful to my elders that they taught me how to differentiate between various *prakaars* of one raga, like Shivmat Bhairav, Pratham Bhairav, Brahma Bhairav, Prabhat Bhairav and similarly for other *prakaars* of different ragas. Now time has come full circle. As I am teaching at SRA, I think and delineate each raga *prakaar* to my students so that they get their basics right.

Interviewer:

Why did you join an institute as a guru? Why did you not remain a full-time performing artiste?

Mashkoor Ali Khan:

My name was already well-known when I joined the SRA in 1981. I needed a place to stay and to continue my music without any obstruction for as you know now we do not have *darbars* and *nawabs* to support us. SRA provides the musical ambience and security that an artiste needs to fulfil his mission. An artiste here teaches music to young talents and has the freedom to pursue his or her own music also. There are no words to describe the beauty of this institute. I joined this institute as a musician-scholar. While staying in this institute I got the opportunity to understand the good points of other *gharanas* also. My musical horizon has widened. After knowing and understanding the various facets of different *gharanas*, I respect all *gharanas* and perhaps somewhere they have influenced my musical journey, too.

Interviewer:

Your recitals are marked with great imagination and vocal agility. In your *gayaki* there are numerous permutations of *khandmeru.* Why?

Mashkoor Ali Khan:

I was given *taleem* in it. It was because of Ustad Abdul Karim Khan Sahib and Ustad Abdul Waheed Khan Sahib that the very concept of *khayal gayaki* changed. They introduced the *vilambit* or the slow tempo method to delineate the raga note by note known as the *khandmeru.* My *gayaki* has taken birth from the sarangi, *been* and vocal music. I do *riyaaz* in *khandmeru,* that is *sargam*-singing and while on stage the combination and permutation of various *swar* patterns is all impromptu. I never pre-plan *khandmeru sargams* or flashy meteoric *taans.* It just happens on stage. And it happens because of the strict *taleem* and the complete synchronisation of heart, mind and voice. But above all God helps me. It is not that I think beforehand about it. But it is all within the fold of various *angs* (parts) of Kirana *gayaki*. (*He sings to explain the nuances of* khandmeru)

Interviewer:

You just mentioned that your *gayaki* has taken birth from sarangi, *been* and vocal. What is so special about Kirana *gayaki*?

Mashkoor Ali Khan:

See, my gharana, i.e., Kirana *gharana gayaki* is an amalgamation of various *ang* (parts) of the sarangi style of playing, the *been ang* and the *dhrupad ang.* The individual *swars* of the raga are considered not just random points in the scale but independent realms of music, capable of horizontal expansion. Emotional *pukars* in the higher octaves form a part of our music.

Another unique feature is the way we take intricate *taans*, *sargam taans*. And as I said earlier, this was improvised by Ustad Abdul Karim Khan Sahib. Then my *gharana* also has a vast repertoire of rarely heard *ragas* and *bandishes*.

And let me tell you. Many people say that we repeat ourselves. We sing just a few *ragas*. But the truth is that we have imprinted our mark on certain ragas so much that the audience likes to hear them from us repeatedly.

Interviewer:

Which are those ragas?

Mashkoor Ali Khan:

Ragas like Todi, Lalit, Multani, Patdeep, Puriya, Marwa, Shuddha Kalyan, Darbari Kanada. To tell you honestly, all these ragas have acquired new dimensions under the *Kirana gayaki*. I am not against any other *gharana*. I respect all *gharana*s and in fact, all *gharana*s have their specialities and a few favourite *raga*s and *bandishes*.

Interviewer:

You and your brother, Mubarak Ali Khan are vocalists. So was there any sibling rivalry?

Mashkoor Ali Khan:

Yes, there definitely was rivalry. We might be brothers but being in the same field, initially we did have many arguments. Just like all five fingers of the hand are not equal, so is it with children of the same parents. Our nature, attitude towards music and life is different. So, obviously some differences did occur.

Interviewer:

Do you believe in luck, *kismet*, destiny?

Mashkoor Ali Khan:

Luck, *kismet*, destiny whatever you may call it is different from having talent, creativity. I have seen luck betraying many talented people and supporting untalented people. Many people who are sitting at the top have scant knowledge about music. To understand art, music and have talent is completely different from being 'successful.' This is the reality. And the thing is when you do something different from the accepted practice, innumerable people are there to pull you down, criticise you. When Ustad Abdul Karim Khan used to sing *sargam* people used to criticise it and when he sang *Jamuna ke teer*, critics said, 'What's so new in it. It is so simple.' But when people sat down to sing it, they realised how difficult it was to sing that 'simple' *bandish*. Nobody could depict the pain and emotions the way Ustad Abdul Karim Khan had done. Nobody has been able to forget that till now. And that alone is true music. Had I been born during his time I would have just fallen at his feet and would have considered myself lucky to get even five paisa or ten paisa worth of knowledge from him. Oh, my God, what a time it must have been! Many a time my eyes become moist after listening to his *swar* combinations; it is all so unparalleled. I feel so restless after listening to Ustad Abdul Karim Khan Sahib, Ustad Waheed Khan Sahib, Hirabai and Pt Bhimsen Joshiji.

Interviewer:

How do you analyse your own music and see the road ahead?

Mashkoor Ali Khan:

Even after so many years of *riyaaz* I feel there is still a lot left to learn. I am still searching for musical techniques. Whenever I listen to legends like Ustad Abdul Karim Khan and Ustad Waheed Khan, I tell myself, 'See, this is the right way, *sur aise lagta hai'* (this is how the right note is struck). Music is a journey and I am walking on that journey in quest of that supreme knowledge.

Creating an Idealistic World

DR ARAWIND THATTE

(17 November, 1958–)

Thin, medium-height, harmonium maestro Dr Arawind Thatte doesn't belong to this world. Or so it appears. The moment I saw him, I knew he is temperamentally different.

In the recent past he has been refusing all accompanists' assignments. 'Earlier I used to give many concerts but since the last five to six years I have reduced accompanying. Right now I am focussing on solo concerts and on writing. I am trying to impart knowledge to my students, hoping that maybe with their understanding and hard work they would be able to do something good for the harmonium. That's why I've reduced the number of concerts and am just concentrating on writing, workshops, teaching and solo concerts. I want to concentrate on my work.'

'After working for over twenty years I realised that I have to give time to myself, to my thinking.' Dr Thatte explains, logically, about his refusal to take up invitations for *sangat* (accompaniment). But somewhere behind these words is also hidden the pain of worldly recognition eluding him, and of course the treatment that accompanying artists have to bear, 'Often I have been informed by the main artiste at the last minute of the change in accompanying artiste.'

The interview with him happened suddenly. He had come to Delhi for a concert and Pandit Madhup Mudgal called up saying, 'Why don't you interview Arawind Thatte. He has done so much for the harmonium.' It was a different thing that we were already planning to talk to him.

Passionate about his instrument, Dr Arawind Thatte is known for bringing harmonium on to the concert arena as a solo instrument. His *layakari* and fingering techniques changed the perspective of people about the harmonium.

'But still,' he says, 'a lot more has to be done for the harmonium, to take it to the level where it has the same respect as other instruments.'

Breaking sentences in between and speaking slowly and softly, he chatted with me for almost two hours.

(10 June, 2008)

Interviewer:

Dr Thatte you began your music *taleem* in vocal and then you took up harmonium seriously. Why this shift?

Arawind Thatte:

No, it was not a shift. Right from childhood I used to play the harmonium. My father and elder brother also used to play it. Later I started learning vocal; first I joined a music school and then became Pandit Jasraj's disciple.

Interviewer:

For how many years were you Pandit Jasraj's disciple?

Arawind Thatte:

Around twelve to fifteen years. And before that for five to six years I learnt vocal music in a music school. So actually I learnt vocal music only. In fact I did not learn the harmonium from anyone. My father had presented me a harmonium and I used to experiment with it. I was also a regular listener of natya sangeet and classical music on the radio.

Interviewer:

What you are saying is that you did not receive any formal training in harmonium, and learnt it while listening to it on the radio and also that there is nobody else in your family who can be called a professional musician?

Arawind Thatte:

Yes, that's right. My father used to take us for concerts and my mother exposed us to classical-music based film songs. So whatever songs I used to listen to on AIR or on records, I would try playing it on the harmonium. And then later on I started learning classical music in a music school.

Interviewer:

So, you learnt harmonium on your own! What problems did you face in this journey?

Arawind Thatte:

I did not face any problems. Right from the beginning I realised that the harmonium has great potential. People used to say that it has various limitations. I did notice those limitations but at the same time I felt that the instrument had immense potential which remained unexplored. I started getting this feeling that it had not been developed fully.

Interviewer:

So how did you bring about those changes? You are known for *layakari* on the harmonium but what about *meend* ?

Arawind Thatte:

(Smiles) At my place we all belong to the science stream and as a result all of us have that inbuilt analytical and mathematical habit. We are always trying to search basic principles and look at things scientifically. So I developed the habit of questioning. I saw the limitations but at the same time I also saw the potentiality. No doubt the harmonium has limitations. We cannot play *meend*. But I would like to ask, when one says that it has limitations then what are these limitations in comparison with? Limitation is always done in comparison with something. My next question is, why this one way comparison? If we are not able to copy vocalists, then it becomes our limitation. But that is a one way comparison. So I thought let me take out some music from the harmonium and ask whether other instruments or the human voice can reproduce it. I put it the other way round. First let me do it and then others should replicate it. In this way the limitations of the others will also come to the forefront. Comparison should be from both sides, isn't it? But it is not so. Comparison is always one way. Vocal comes first and if that cannot be reproduced on an instrument then it is said that the instrument is not good enough for classical music. So I questioned it and tried reversing it. Actually, there are many aspects like patterns, *layakari, jhala*, which can be produced on the harmonium but are difficult to reproduce on other instruments. So, right from the beginning I decided to focus on the plus points of my instrument, instead of just thinking about the negative aspects.

Interviewer:

What all modifications did you bring into the instrument?

Arawind Thatte:

Well, not much in its construction. Primarily I focused on the tuning. I always thought that the harmonium should be played according to each *sur* (note). And this required a proper study of *shruti-swar shastra*. But of course that does not mean blindly following everything written in *shastra*. I examined and questioned that too. In fact, I even question whether what we call *shastra* can be rightly considered *shastra*.

Interviewer:

For instance?

Arawind Thatte:

There is a difference between *shastras* and grammar. We cannot equate grammar with *shastras*, at least I wouldn't do so. So this *shruti-swar shastra* also has many loopholes. The concept is not well-defined and even the approach is not unified. People from different *gharanas* use *shrutis* (microtones) differently. For instance, if we take *rishabh* of raga Marwa, it is not necessary that people from all *gharanas* will use *rishabh* in a similar way. There is no unified theory in this. In fact there is much more space for *swars* in our music. So this number of twenty-two *shrutis* does not have much meaning. Even in our ancient texts there are many loopholes. Basically we refer to two texts—one by Bharata (*Natyashastra*) and the other by Saranga Deva (*Sangeet Ratnakar*). But there are lacunae in both these texts also. So, when I reflect on this and then come to the tuning of the harmonium, I imagine what possibilities could be created. I have been engaged in this kind of theoretical work.

Interviewer:

You have done research also. What was your research topic?

Arawind Thatte:

I have a doctorate in Mathematics but by profession I am a musician. And now I keep on thinking about various topics within music only, from basic level to practical aspects, about different methods of doing *riyaaz*, different angles of presentation, etc. Often we compartmentalise the style of playing an instrument. Like we say a particular instrumentalist's style is *gayaki ang* or *tantrakari ang*. I do not compartmentalise. I do not believe in this.

Interviewer:

You may not believe in this but ...

Arawind Thatte:

No, we cannot compartmentalise. Styles cannot be compartmentalised. I believe that form is classified according to the usage of musical ideas and how much is that idea being used. Presentation of forms can be infinite. There cannot be just two forms–*khayal style* or *alaap, jod, jhala*. Form is dependent on musical idea, its proportion and in what sequence it is being used. Form is dependent on these aspects. There cannot be a stamp of one particular style–*gayaki ang* or *tantrakari* ang. It can be a mixture of ideas and form of presentation is dependent on the thinking of the performer. There cannot be watertight compartments. See, otherwise, except *dhrupad*, the other forms are not that rigid in their approach. There is freedom to meander, according to your imagination, within *laya,* partially with *laya* and without *laya* also. It depends on performer's imagination. So, I try to do what I like and wherever my imagination takes me. I don't have to put a stamp on my creation that it is according to *khayal ang* or *tantrakari ang.* And when I think in the context of the harmonium then I feel that it has immense potentiality, but yes, it is not very much suitable for *ati vilambit.* One can work on the harmonium from *ati madhya laya* till *ati drut laya*, comfortably.

Interviewer:

Why is it not suitable for *ati vilambit laya*?

Arawind Thatte:

Because on the harmonium if I just strike one *swar* for a full half minute, it is not going to create an impact. People will feel that the artiste hasn't worked hard. On the contrary when a vocalist retains one *swar* for the same stretch of time, people appreciate his breath control. On the harmonium it will not create that impression in the listeners' minds. People will think that the artiste is just bellowing and putting pressure on one key. (*Laughs*). But let me tell you this. It is very difficult to retain one *swar* on the harmonium in the same frequency. But this hard work is not understood by people. They think what's so difficult about it? One just has to put pressure on a key. But the truth is, it is not so. Secondly, on the harmonium *meend* cannot be created. You can overlap notes, like if one has to go from *ni* to *sa* then (he sings to explain it) if I play *ni, sa* the continuity breaks but if I pull away my finger from *ni* only after playing *sa*, then continuity is maintained. Though both the notes will join, it is not *meend.* It just gives the impression of it. And then in Indian music we cannot play two-three *swars* together. On the other hand the short cut notes, which harmonium can produce, cannot be created by a vocalist. So this is the advantage of the harmonium.

Interviewer:

So when you thought about all these things and gave a solo concert with your thoughts and findings, what was the reaction then?

Arawind Thatte:

People liked it. That was nearly twenty-five years ago in one private *baithak.* And the first major public concert was nearly fifteen or twenty years ago. But the thought process that began so many years ago, about developing and refining presentation on the harmonium, still continues.

Interviewer:

Were you never frightened that whatever experiments you are doing on the harmonium may go waste as at that time the harmonium was not considered a solo instrument?

Arawind Thatte:

No, never. I was confident that what I am doing was worth it. And moreover, I do what I believe in. Because I believed in the potentiality of the harmonium, I continued doing experiments on it. I was not bothered about whether people will accept it or not.

Interviewer:

So you believed in your conviction that whatever you are doing is right for the instrument and you went ahead with it.

Arawind Thatte:

Yes.

Interviewer:

You mentioned that you became Pandit Jasraj's disciple. How did you become his disciple and how was your *taleem* under him?

Arawind Thatte:

My education, school and college happened in Pune. Along with my studies I was learning vocal music at Bharat Gyan Samaj. I was learning from Dattar Sir. The seed of classical music was sown in childhood itself. And I used to like the music of many maestros, like Rambhau Maratheji, Amir Khan Sahib, Bade Ghulam Ali Khan Sahib, Faiyaz Khan Sahib, Bhimsen Joshiji, Prabhaji, Kishoriji, Mallikarjun Mansurji, my guru, Jasrajji—I heard many maestros and liked them and even now I like them. I listen to maestros of all *gharana*s and try to analyse the specialty of each maestro. How many names should I take? In instrumental music also I heard all the great musicians. I try understanding their viewpoints, the beauty in their music, their good points and do self-grading. In fact I do a proper critical study of each and every artiste. We can learn a lot by listening to other artistes, critically studying the good and bad points of these artistes. I also study the shortcomings of artistes. Besides, we can also learn not only within music but from outside the music world, from any field. We can monitor the presentation styles, pick up the good points and try incorporating that in our styles. I was thoroughly impressed by the *layakari* and *taankari* of Pandit Rambhau Maratheji. As a child I felt that even I can do *layakari* and *taankari* but not *alaap*. I was a child so I thought that I could do it. But this was the thought that goaded me to approach guru Jasrajji. His contribution in *alaap* is so great that I thought I must learn it from him only.

Interviewer:

Did he take you as his disciple immediately?

Arawind Thatte:

I directly approached him. He asked me to sing something. I sang and he agreed to take me as his disciple.

Interviewer:

Did you stay with him?

Arawind Thatte:

No, I didn't stay with him. I used to come from Pune, once in a week or twice or thrice a month, depending on his time schedule. It is only a four-hour journey from Pune to Mumbai. At that time I was also doing my PhD in Mathematics. So after university I used to take the train to Mumbai, and at times I could just manage to squeeze myself between the two compartments or sit on the roof of the compartment. And at times I used to learn the whole night and then in the morning would directly go to the university. But at that time I was simply determined and I just wanted to do it, I had passion for music and the zeal to pursue it.

Interviewer:

Then how did you make the shift from vocal to instrumental music?

Arawind Thatte:

I was doing vocal since a long time but as I had some ENT problem I couldn't continue with it. I had sinus and septic tonsils. I did not go in for an operation as some people advised me against it. They said that after a tonsils operation the texture of my voice may change for worse. Consequently, every month or two months septic would develop in tonsils and I couldn't sing and ultimately I had to leave vocal music. Much later, at the age of thirty-five I did get the operation done but by then it was too late. I had already left singing. So I decided to concentrate on the harmonium, more so because there were many questions surrounding its suitability for classical music and also the way people were handling it. I used to get upset seeing all this. I wasn't satisfied with the way people used to play it. The fingering style was not appropriate. It used to create noise, not music. (*He sings to explain how it is noise and not music*). As that fingering style had been in existence for a long time, it had become an integral part of harmonium playing. I thought about challenging that style, which according to me was not music. I worked towards it.

Interviewer:

What are the changes that you brought about in harmonium playing?

Arawind Thatte:

It is difficult for me to say but if I have to list it then it is in tuning, in maintaining the clarity of notes even at high speed and developments in the fingering technique.

Interviewer:

And *layakari* on the harmonium Dr Thatte, for which you are widely known; and producing cross-rhythmic patterns.

Arawind Thatte:

(*He nods and smiles* gently)

Interviewer:

Dr Thatte, earlier, you mentioned the word shortcomings. So do you ever analyse your own music? What shortcomings do you see in your music?

Arawind Thatte:

Yes, shortcomings are there in my music too. I lack the 'killer instinct' which is very important for any performing artiste. The confidence level is amiss. I am nervous by temperament. Psychologically I am easy-going, not aggressive. Secondly, my mind runs faster than what I can execute physically, through voice or instrument. And in a performance there has to be a synergy between mind and hands or throat. Only when there is complete coordination between thought and practical execution, can the performance be smooth. And this uniformity is dependent on the psychological state at the time of the performance. If a phrase comes into my mind that I am unable to produce from my hands, then I'll flop. So, lesser the gap between thoughts and actions, the better an artiste you can be. At the time of the performance one should only think of what one can produce. In short, it is necessary to have complete control over one's mind. But it is quite difficult and partially I feel it is not in my hands. So, one should do meditation, and the like to overcome this hurdle.

Interviewer:

Do you enjoy giving harmonium accompaniment to artistes?

Arawind Thatte:

The first major programme that I did was when I was twenty-three or twenty-four years old. I accompanied Dr Vasantrao Deshpandeji. I was quite frightened. Before that I had accompanied other artistes but on a very small scale. This was for the first time that I was accompanying such a big artiste. And before the concert I had gone to his residence and asked him several questions. But he just encouraged me and told me not to get nervous. On the stage, he really controlled the situation. After him I accompanied many great artistes, like Malini Rajurkarji, Pandit Jasraj and thus began my journey. I started accompanying artistes. I started getting concerts one after the other.

Interviewer:

Do you like accompanying or playing solo?

Arawind Thatte:

This is a slightly difficult question. I like both. Accompanying is a challenge without responsibility but as a soloist it is a responsibility with a different kind of challenge. In accompanying one has to be in complete sync with the main artiste. At times the spirit of supporting and encouraging each other takes the form of competitiveness or one-upmanship. This should not happen.

Interviewer:

You have more or less brought the harmonium to the centre stage, so how do you see its future now?

Arawind Thatte:

The harmonium's future is still hazy, unclear. Till the negative points of the harmonium are addressed and answered, it will not be able to receive much respect from the listening public because audiences will not be able to know the cause of the shortcoming. They cannot analyse. They will just see the shortcoming and label the instrument or performance uninspiring. Secondly, we must tune the harmonium properly and then play it. And thirdly, it should be seen as an independent identity, i.e., not labelling presentations as playing *gayaki ang or tantrakari ang.* The main role of the soloist should be to play according to the potentiality of the harmonium. I am not saying that one should not take the good things of others. Surely one can and one should, but in the end, the harmonium should be played keeping its potentialities in mind. *Layakari* can be developed on the harmonium. I have created many compositions in different *laya—vilambit, drut, ati drut*—have made suitable compositions for all these. And I am writing a lot about music, not only about compositions but about various aspects of music in general, focusing on *riyaaz*, styles of presentations, vocal music and my views about *raga*, *sangeet*, and the like. I also think that there is some kind of a propaganda against the harmonium: that it is not suitable for classical music, it doesn't have *shrutis,* it cannot produce *meend*, etc, etc.

Interviewer:

A creative artiste's livelihood is insecure. Were you not frightened of insecurity? Was there any financial support from your family?

Arawind Thatte:

No, I was not frightened of insecurity. I was simply determined. And financially, my condition was not all that great but it wasn't bad either. I could take the decision because I had the moral support of my family. Even now I am like that only. I can eat anything. I lead a very simple life. And I am unmarried, so I do not even have family responsibilities. But of course my parents stay with me.

Interviewer:

What are your interests?

Arawind Thatte:

I like travelling, walking alone, staying amidst nature. I'll go to a place and then explore it on foot.

Interviewer:

How many concerts do you give in a year?

Arawind Thatte:

Earlier I used to give many concerts but since the last five to six years I have reduced accompanying. Right now I am focussing on solo concerts and on writing. I am trying to impart knowledge to my students, hoping that maybe with their understanding and hard work they would be able to do something good for the harmonium. I may not be able to witness this in my lifetime but my disciples may be able to carry forward my dream. That's why I've reduced the number of concerts and am just concentrating on writing, workshops, teaching and solo concerts.

Pain of the Prince
USTAD SHUJAAT KHAN
(14 August, 1960–)

We know Ustad Shujaat Khan as the son of the legendary sitar maestro, Ustad Vilayat Khan, who lived and created music history on his own terms, and went on to, create a niche for himself in the musical arena with his style known as *Vilayatkhani Baaj*. With six generations of music behind him, we thought Shujaat Khan would have all the tantrums of a musical 'prince,' but contrary to our imagination, he came dressed for the interview in an off-white kurta-pyjama, having no airs about his lineage. Modest and outspoken, he frankly narrated tales about his life, his relationship with his father and his sojourn with freedom, 'I ran away because my father was a very strong personality and I, being his son, was equally determined to carve my own future on my terms.'

His loud, cheerful humming signalled his arrival. Stoutly built, appearing more like a middleweight champion, he entered along with his young son, Azaan and announced, 'Sorry for the delay, but I had been recording whole night and am coming directly from the studios. Of course you can see that from my crumpled clothes and swollen eyes. I hope you don't mind my being dressed so ... should I call it shabbily...!' Breaking into loud laughter, he immediately erased any traces of mounting tension.

We soon realised that he is one of the few forthright musicians of present-day, who don't shy away from putting forth opinions on society, politics, government officials and music, '...Many musicians think like this but they don't say it openly. They are afraid that if they say anything against government officials they will forego their chance of going abroad or getting awards. But sorry, for me it just doesn't work.'

Quite frequently during the course of the interview, Ustad Shujaat Khan let his answers break into cascading laughter and punctuated answers with, 'I swear on my sitar.' Often he would slip into the alleys of his forgotten dreams and radical views, driving the conversation into some other terrain.

(17 June, 2008)

Interviewer:

You belong to a traditional family of musicians, with six generations behind you to guide and inspire. With names in the family tree like that of Ustad Imdad Khan, Ustad Inayat Khan, your father Ustad Vilayat Khan, were you ever scared, frightened? Did you ever wonder about your own capability and talent?

Shujaat Khan:

Oh, yes. Now, how do I explain it? See, on the one hand it's a matter of great honour and pride to be born in such a family with such lineage. But there is another side to this. There are advantages as well as disadvantages. Let me first tell you the advantages. The positive side is that I grew up with the aroma of music enveloping me from all sides. Every day stalwarts used to come to our house. Legends like Ustad Amir Khan and Ustad Hafiz Ali Sahib were our regular guests. They used to talk about music and often sang. Their conversation exposed me from childhood to the various facets of music, its complexities, and the like. I used to be completely engrossed in their conversations. And I'll be very frank; all this was as intimidating as it was enlightening, even at that young age. Later on, when I started performing, it was like getting a foot in the door. Sure, we do get a platform. Music is in our blood. And when I say music is in our blood, I mean we are exposed to music from childhood, in one way or the other. We are born with a silver spoon. But there's also another side to the picture. And without being morbid, it is a disadvantageous one. Few can understand our pain; I call it the 'pain of the prince', the difficulty of being a *Rajkumar.* That pain can only be experienced by a prince. Please don't misunderstand me, I am not calling myself a prince, I am just trying to explain the disadvantageous side through an example.

Interviewer:

Definitely. But can you expand it further?

Shujaat Khan:

Well, we—the sons and daughters of maestros—are under immense pressure from the very beginning. People have a lot of expectations from us. So the first thing is that of not having a choice, ever. Today, my son Azaan has a choice. He plays the guitar. He writes Sufi songs. He sings and it's his hobby. And I have never ever put pressure on him. He is free to follow his heart, free to make choices, But I didn't have the freedom to make a choice. It was clear to me from the beginning that I've inherited a great musical legacy, I will have to play the sitar and play it very well. I was never told so actually, in so many words, but I could feel it, I could sense it. I did not have a choice. On top of that, my very existence as well as the world at large would never let me forget whose son I was and their expectations from me.

Interviewer:

Sometimes, heirs of maestros have not followed the footsteps of their elders. What about the question of expectations in their case?

Shujaat Khan:

Not sometimes. Very often ... hahaha ... That's true. See, I would say forty-nine times out of fifty, children of maestros either run away from music or pursue some other vocation. Often they try but fail to live up to the expectations. In fact, these children enter the world of music because the maestros force them into it, 'Hey, listen to them, they are my children,' but it just doesn't work. See now, I don't want to take names but at present there are a few maestros whose children are doing really well in music; but they are only a handful. In the same breath I can name ten other maestros whose children tried but failed. There's so much pressure on these children that it becomes very easy for them to land up in rehabilitation centres; just like in the West, where children of great achievers end up in drug rehabilitation centres.

Interviewer:

Is it the frustration of not being able to achieve what their parents have achieved or are they victims of some kind of complexes?

Shujaat Khan:

You see, the expectations are high; fathers are never home, their protective cover is missing and even when the father is visible, he is a completely different entity, not a father figure. In these circumstances if the mother is also not at home, has the desire to go out, to party, then that's the end. It doesn't take much time for these children to be, swept away by the fame and glory of their father. The individuality of these children is soon shattered. There's a lot of money and adulation, but there's this other side of stark reality too. It's a very difficult world for us, children of maestros and legends. These are the two sides of this wonderful coin.

Interviewer:

What about you? How did you tackle this situation?

Shujaat Khan:

I have suffered a lot, have taken a lot of pain and even now, till today, people don't spare me. I am constantly compared to my legendary father, Ustad Vilayat Khan. But I take it as a challenge. I had two options—to live like a 'prince' or to capitalise on the opportunities and possibilities to overcome those hurdles and lead the life of a normal human being. Now I can say that one of my greatest successes in life is that my life is normal. My children are normal. I am normal. I pick up my own telephone, I drive myself, I shop myself because I don't want to become a slave of some kind of an image. If I buy vegetables it does not change my image. I am bothered about my image only when I am on the stage, performing. I've tried to retain normalcy in life.

Interviewer:

Who would you say is the most important person who helped you develop and retain such balanced views?

Shujaat khan:

See, it's very difficult to thank one person or give one reason for it. If I say, what I am today and the way I think is because of only one person then that will be incorrect. I have taken in something from everyone—my parents, brothers, relatives, wife, my children and friends. My wife has influenced me a lot. She is very graceful, charming and a very strong woman. From my father I learnt how to balance two things in life, although he himself was not always successful in balancing family and professional commitments. My kids, my friends, all of them have taught me something or the other. I feel blessed to have met such wonderful people who never allowed me to lose touch with reality. Like I said, money is not as intoxicating as fame and a lot of people get completely swayed by that. I am also human and it happens sometimes but my friends and family bring me back from that intoxicating glitz.

Interviewer:

As a teenager you ran away from home. Why?

Shujaat Khan:

I have always been open to different experiences in my life. Let me tell you what exactly happened. I was seventeen to eighteen years old. After finishing school, I wanted to live on my own.

Interviewer:

But didn't you think you were too young to be on your own?

Shujaat Khan:

No, I wanted to experience life. So, I told my father that I want to live separately. We had an argument, like any other father and son. But I was determined. And for the world it turned out to be shocking, scandalous. After moving out I really experienced life. I saw a lot of things, in fact the other side of life. I suffered and faced a lot of problems. I saw how people can treat you when you are not under the *pink umbrella* of Ustad Vilayat Khan. It was then that I realised the true value of fame, name and money. And I am very fond of fame, luxuries, comfort and beautiful things in life like costly shawls, jewellery, travelling. By the grace of god, today I live like a king, but I worked really hard for that and now I am enjoying it. While away from home and Ustad Vilayat Khan's shadow I also realised that our biggest asset is humanity. The other things—name, fame and money—one gets according to one's destiny. Honestly, I don't have any interest in being a Page 3 persona. I am not ready to pay ₹50,000 a month to a PR agency just to be there. I cannot let somebody tell me to go to a party in the evening and not to stay home to watch a football or cricket match on TV. Page 3 is important to those people who have no other achievement or success in life. For me, I have worked hard in life and by God's grace today whoever knows about Sitar knows Shujaat Khan. What bigger achievement can one have than this? Rest I am sitting with you here and anybody who sees me ... this crumpled kurta ... my condition... (*says jokingly and breaks into a loud laugh.*)

Interviewer:

Fine Shujaatji, just a few moments ago you mentioned about leaving home at the age of seventeen. So let's go back in time. I would like to ask you again what prompted you to move out of the 'pink umbrella'? Indeed it was a very bold decision.

Shujaat Khan:

Actually, it was a mixture of many things. One, Vilayat Khan Sahib was too strong a personality. Nobody around him was allowed to think. And even if they were given the freedom to think, they didn't. Now you'll ask why? Well, the truth is that why should you think when you are under such great patronage! Anyway, as for myself, being his child with his traits, I like to think ... think about myself, about my life, what I want. And it was he who instilled in me this burning desire to be myself and not to be a clone of Ustad Vilayat Khan Sahib. So that was one reason. Secondly, I was curious to see the world, to know and understand people from close quarters and not by sitting in a Mercedes or Rolls-Royce or by travelling in first class. I wanted to know the world outside five-star hotels, big buildings and palatial houses. Thirdly, because I wanted to have my own identity in music, separate from Ustad Vilayat Khan Sahib. Not that I wanted my posters or statues on streets or my name in history—it didn't matter then and even now it is not important to me. After death one can write my name infinite number of times but how will that affect me? But in truth, I wanted to contribute personally to this big world of music. Hence I felt, it was impossible to bloom or blossom under Vilayat Khan Sahib's shadow. He was so tall and strong that sunshine was not reaching me. So, finally I decided to go ahead with my (*emphatically*) dreams. At the end of it, of course I was young, I could earn money and I just wanted to be my own person.

Interviewer:

How did you earn money?

Shujaat Khan:

Oh! I washed dishes. I played background music when I was abroad. In India nobody will let you do that. But when I was abroad....

Interviewer:

You spent your childhood abroad or in India?

Shujaat khan:

In India, of course. I grew up studying in Shimla. But what I used to do is to go abroad for three to four months and do two to four programmes. If the money got finished I would go to Florida for fruit picking, and did all sorts of odd jobs. In those days as Mexicans were not allowed into America, labour was very difficult to get. So they used to pay a lot of money for fruit picking. Then sometimes I used to wash dishes. I am not trying to glorify this whole thing or romanticise it. It was great fun. I was meeting different people. I was meeting different musicians. I used to meet people in clubs and bars and exchanged opinions with them.

Interviewer:

Which countries did you visit and how did travelling influence your music?

Shujaat Khan:

Many ... America, South America, Russia ... since everybody goes to Russia, so I decided to go to Mongolia ... hahaha ... Anyway ... travelling, meeting people, left a mark on my thinking, on my music. I assimilated a lot of musical nuances from other genres. And to tell you frankly, more than anything else, travelling taught me that everything else is secondary in life; to be a good human being is the most important. I realised that I have to relate to people on this ground only, give the other person respect for being a human being and not on the basis of what he wears or where he lives. Unfortunately, I live in a society where material things are given importance. The moment you meet somebody, people ask you, 'where do you live?' And then they decide whether they want to talk to you or not. They scrutinise your dress ... so sometimes, just to spit on that narrow thinking, I purposely dress casually....

Interviewer:

For some time you stayed in Mumbai also. What did you do there? Did you dabble in films and if yes, how was your experience?

Shujaat Khan:

Yes, but for a very short time. I worked in films, gave background scores. It was easy money (*says with a mischievous grin*). In Mumbai, I suffered so much humiliation and poverty. There were times when there was no work. In India nobody would give me any other work apart from music, that too only sometimes. And in music also they hesitated in giving me work because they thought Vilayat Khan Sahib would get angry. On the other hand, apart from music if I went and asked for work, 'See, my name is Shujaat and please keep me as salesman in your shop.' They would promptly say, 'What are you saying, I see you on television everyday.' So you see, I didn't have a choice. You might have heard Gandhiji's verse '*Vaishnav jan to tene kahiye, je peer parayi jaane re*'. Actually people just sing it without understanding the meaning. And it's very true because nobody understands the pain of others. If one can understand the other person's woes, he will be a completely different person. God forbid anybody should experience such hardships that I had gone through. Helplessness ... and helplessness means no one to turn to; powerlessness where there was no way out and hunger, not having a morsel in my mouth for days. Above all, illness. I had nephritis. There was a problem in my kidney passage. My skin was coming off. And there was no one to turn to. Then I heard about a place in South India where treatment was available for nephritis. So I went there. Ultimately, it got treated. What I am trying to tell is that I worked hard to reach where I am today. I am very proud of having worked hard. Destiny has given me a lot, much more than I deserve or ever dreamt of. I was humiliated but I am not scarred. I laugh all the time (*and the guffaw follows*).

Interviewer:

But you could have gone to your father ...

Shujaat Khan:

And say, excuse me, please give me money ... no I couldn't. I just learnt music from him and kept learning till his death.

Interviewer:

What about your mother? Why didn't you seek her help?

Shujaat Khan:

See, my mother and father separated when I was eleven. That was also a part of my growing up. I was old enough to know what was going on but not old enough to know how to handle it. They separated but they were always very supportive towards me. I am sure they were always there for me. No parent can see their child in distress. But they can only help and support if they know where their child is.

Interviewer:

So one can say that despite being born with a silver spoon you orchestrated your own destiny.

Shujaat Khan:

Absolutely. In fact, I have often felt that I am a very ordinary person, living a very extraordinary destiny. And sometimes for an ordinary person living an extraordinary destiny it becomes difficult to live. As about myself, I feel as if I am in an alien world. But I've learnt how to swim in water and it is fine. It works.

Interviewer:

When did your *taleem* begin and who was your first guru? Was it your father or somebody else?

Shujaat Khan:

Quite young. I was only two and a half when I started learning from my father Ustad Vilayat Khan. There was a small sitar at home and I used to play it all the time. By the time I was four years old I started doing proper *riyaaz* for two to three hours daily. And at the age of six I gave my first solo concert at Ahmedabad.

Interviewer:

At the age of six! Are you saying that you gave a public concert at that age?

Shujaat Khan:

Yes at the age of six. Performed for forty-five minutes and the piece had *alaap*, *jod* and *gat*. And the credit goes to my father and guru for having all the patience, not to me.

Interviewer:

But even then going on stage at the age of six, facing people—it certainly requires some kind of nerve.

Shujaat Khan:

At that time it was very easy. It's difficult now. When one is young there is no reputation or prestige at stake. It is more like a game, something like childhood bravado. Today, it's difficult, because I know people have expectations of me and above all I have expectations from myself. So it's getting more and more difficult now. Soon after the concert my father shifted to Shimla and so did I with him. During daytime I used to go to school and at night practice for seven to eight hours.

Interviewer:

Was there any pressure?

Shujaat Khan:

No, no pressure. But yes after being declared a child prodigy and having given concerts I couldn't adopt a laidback attitude. Moreover, being Ustad Vilayat Khan's son, I couldn't afford to be called mediocre. Mediocrity is one of the ills of our society. But yes I do know that not everyone can be great but if one has faith, trust and belief in oneself, in his talent and is prepared to work hard then surely one can fulfil dreams and in fact, hard work is required in every field, why only music. You see for the ten to fifty odd seconds of glory, athletes put in ten years of rigorous training. So to say that hard work is required only in music is incorrect ... hard work is required in every field, but yes in music we are working on it both on the physical and emotional fronts simultaneously. So it makes it a little more dramatic.

Interviewer:

When did you decide that you have to come out of your father's shadow and create your kind of music, with your unique style?

Shujaat Khan:

I think it happened naturally. I never really thought about it seriously till of course I was sixteen or seventeen. But then I had already played a lot and even at that time it was not that I wanted to distance myself from Ustad Vilayat Khan.

Can you imagine anyone wanting to do that? Ustad Vilayat Khan has passed away but some people are taking mileage out of their casual acquaintance or association with him. Today, there are some people like his friends, children, daughter, brother, ... anyone who hardly knew him, just shook hands with him, claim that they spent so many years with him, learnt from him and somehow are taking mileage out of that simple handshake. That one is associated with Ustad Vilayat Khan is fine but if you ask me I think that to take his name to promote oneself, using his name as a crutch, is a cowardly act.

Interviewer:

You stayed with him, learnt from him. And now when you are on your own, can you tell us how is your *shaili* different from your father's?

Shujaat Khan:

See, if we don't go into too much technicalities then the first thing that strikes us is simplicity of musicality, of phrases. Earlier people shied away from playing straight phrases (*sings*) ... *pa re ga sa/pa sa ga re/ma dha pa dha sa* ... It was not considered to be a part of Indian music. So, one is this phraseology of straight notes that I started. Secondly, the use of harmonies in the sitar—I started this too. (*Breaks into singing again and further explains*) *Sa ga pa re/ma dha ma re pa/ni re ma dha pa* ... I started using harmony on the sitar besides playing *ulta jhala*—I think if the world will ever remember me, I say if, then they will remember me because of the intricacies of *ulta jhala*. My listeners wait for this and I am not boasting.

I am not even saying that I've done something greater than what my father Vilayat Khan Sahib had done. Whenever I listen to my father and people like Amir Khan Sahib, I feel ashamed that people nowadays have to live with musicians like me.

Interviewer:

I think you are being modest ...

Shujaat Khan:

Aah ... modesty at my age! Trust me, it's true. I am not saying that they were greater people than me ... ah ... we are all human beings but they had much more time to devote. They had so much dedication that they could put more finesse, more depth into their work. Of course, they were all genius. And now coming back to your query about differences between me and Vilayat Khan Sahib, you see, Vilayat Khan Sahib had put a lot of melody in *gat*. It wasn't there earlier. And to this I added space ... silences and spaces between notes and how much can we magnify it. This also people had not tried earlier. Earlier (*he sings*) 1, 2, 3, 4, 5, 6, 7, 8, 9, 10, 11 ... that's all but I developed it in three strokes only. So these are some of the innovations I had attempted. But believe me, I have no burning desire to tell the world about myself, my innovations.

Interviewer:

It was quite explanatory. Now when we are talking about innovations, what are your views on discovering or creating new ragas?

Shujaat Khan:

In my own opinion I disagree with these innovations. There are many great Ustads of our times who have created as many as fifty to sixty ragas. According to me, ragas have already been made. What we are doing or what these people are doing is joining the tail end of one raga with the head of other and the trunk of a third ... then they declare, 'Hey, listen, I have discovered a new raga...' Vilayat Khan Sahib also created a few ragas. He combined Hem, Bihag and Yaman, three ragas and called it Raga Sanjh Saravali. And before playing this raga in concerts he always used to say, 'I am going to play Raga Sanjh Saravali, a mixture of three ragas. It is not my discovery.' He always used to clarify this while playing the ragas that he had combined. And here we have somebody who is not even thirty or forty, proudly declaring that he is the creator of fifty ragas!

Interviewer:

But why would anybody do that?

Shujaat Khan:

Why are you asking me? Ask them ... The answer is simple. To gain importance, popularity. The truth is that when one feels what one is doing in life is not important enough then one resorts to such gimmicks. This is what I think and as I said earlier it's only my humble opinion ... opinion of a not very learned person. So you can say that it's an 'unlearned' opinion. I don't have to glorify my life.

Interviewer:

Fine, you are against creation of new ragas but what about fusion music?

Shujaat Khan:

I have no problems with fusion. In fact I have dabbled with fusion a lot. ... People say fusion is bad. But see, my album *Laajo Laajo* was released nearly ten years ago and till date people are buying it. At that time most of the artistes criticised me, but all of them have been proved wrong. People have liked it and are still buying it. Music is music—be it fusion or any other form. The problem today is that everybody is doing fusion music and that is killing fusion music. That is why it has become akin to cacophony. Listen to the fusion music of the great maestros Pandit Shiv Kumar Sharma and Pandit Hariprasad Chaurasia. So lyrical, so beautiful.

Interviewer:

Why are some people against it whereas others believe that it's a way to bring the younger generation closer to classical music? Let's not forget that even today not only the younger generation but a lot of older people too think that classical music is boring.

Shujaat Khan:

It's up to them. My question is we have a temple and we have a mosque, right in front of us yet we don't enter, till we feel the need. Similarly classical music too is there with us. No matter how I push or promote, people will come to listen to it, only if they feel the need to breathe in the beauty of our music. Our classical music is beautiful, meditative and enchanting. Those who call it boring are actually scared of it.

Interviewer:

Scared?

Shujaat Khan:

Yes. They are scared of themselves, of their reflection. *Alaap* in our music is such a thing that makes listeners peep inside their soul. It is a mirror of their past, of their memories and of the present. The reality is that a lot of people are frightened of seeing this image, their inner self, they are afraid, so they call it boring. Although, I must admit that some of the musicians do play very boring *alaaps* ... (*laughs*).

Interviewer:

How did *Laajo Laajo* happen? What inspired you to reach out to folk music?

Shujaat Khan:

Nothing specifically. My father used to do it. He just never thought of making an exclusive CD. In fact, my father was the first musician ever to play folk music on stage after a classical concert. So I thought when people like it so much then why not make an exclusive album with folk music. And like I said earlier it's probably the largest selling CD ever. Generally people forget an album in ten to twelve years but *Laajo Laajo* is still in demand.

Interviewer:

And then you came out with the album *Rain*. How did this Persian collaboration happen?

Shujaat Khan:

I met an artist from Iran. He used to play an instrument, similar to the sarangi, called kamancheh. We decided to join together and the outcome was the album *Rain*. This album was nominated for a Grammy.

Interviewer:

How important is getting nominated for awards or getting an award?

Shujaat Khan:

Music doesn't get bigger or smaller because of an award. If people like it, that is the biggest award. As for awards, state recognition, I would like to say that when my father refused a state honour, I asked him, 'Why are you refusing it?' And his answer was, 'Listen son, before accepting the award I would like to know what has been the criterion? If it is seniority then how is that people much younger have received it and if it is the popularity then how come artistes whose performances are marked by empty auditoriums get this award? And finally who are the judges? Do they have knowledge about music or are they politicians, bureaucrats, scientists, etc? The government is not in a position to judge Ustad Vilayat Khan's greatness.'

Interviewer:

Was that why he refused the state honour?

Shujaat Khan:

It was easy for him to say, 'I am sorry, maybe I am not worth it. Maybe I am taking someone else's award. Maybe there are people who deserve much more.' And he also said, 'While they are here if I take this award, it will be gross disrespect to them.' His answer made sense to me.

Interviewer:

What is your viewpoint regarding awards? Will you accept it or not?

Shujaat Khan:

Now, you are putting me in a tight corner. See ... how can people who know little about music decide about Shujaat Khan's talent? How will they know how well Shujaat Khan plays *gandhar* or *shadja* or *nishad*? Besides, what will an award give me, will I get a free ticket to travel or will I get money to buy a piece of land, produce wheat and survive?

Interviewer:

So, if tomorrow the state award is given to you, will you accept it or not?

Shujaat Khan:

Ah ... you have finally managed to corner me, haven't you! But as I said before, my father, who is like God to me in music, if he didn't, will it not be shameful for me to accept it. But yes, if you slip in a few crores with the award then probably I'll slip from my standpoint. As for medals (*laughs and says with a mischievous twinkle*) I can buy as many medals as I want from Chor Bazaar.

Interviewer:

Well, only Shujaat Khan can be so candid and good-humoured about this ... Tell me one thing, how do you rate your singing? You often sing in between your concerts. Is it a conscious decision?

Shujaat Khan:

No, please trust me. I have said this many times and I am saying it once again on record; I don't consider myself a singer from any angle. I don't even think I am in *sur* while singing. I have never practised singing in life. Not even for a second. I swear on my sitar. I think people like my singing probably because there is a rawness in my voice which appeals to everyone. When I go on stage, nine out of ten people request me to sing, 'Please sing a line...' It is because they ask me that I sing, not because I consider myself a great singer. Furthermore ... I only sing *bandish*es that have profound meaning. In my singing I have never used *gamak, taan* or *sapaat taan.* That is played on my sitar. Shujaat Khan will be known as a sitarist not as a vocalist. My singing is ... you can say ... just the icing on the cake.

Interviewer:

What is your vision about classical music and about yourself in the next few years?

Shujaat Khan:

What vision can I have about myself at this age ... I'll lose some more hair, will become lazier. My spondilitis will worsen. I will get tired faster ...

Interviewer:

You make it sound quite grim. I hope it is not that serious. But if I am not mistaken you are generally abroad—performing. You're leading quite a busy life as a performing artiste.

Shujaat Khan:

That's true. Right now I give nearly 100–150 concerts in a year. My effort is to reduce it. I've had enough. I am trying to bring it down to fifty to sixty programmes in a year. Secondly, now I see my music growing.

Interviewer:

What do you mean by music growing?

Shujaat Khan:

Ah! Depth, sincerity, old thoughts keep coming back into my music; things that I have heard and forgotten; put behind me in my march towards future, to become famous or rich or number one. In life one puts aside several things, while moving ahead with the times, in an effort to keep the audience intact. At that stage of life we generally play what we think the audience is going to like. But now, I've matured. And as about my future ... well, I just want to be able to go on stage and play for one and a half to two hours, continuously. To explore the raga fully, to go into each corner and crevice of the raga, to be able to catch each phrase of the raga and bring it out effectively. Apart from that truly, as I said, I don't see myself making any ragas. It will be similar to what my ancestors have done. I am a musician, so I don't see myself doing anything other than what I am doing presently. As for classical music, and/or its future, well ... it was always very bright and it will always be very bright. Unsuccessful people will always find complaints. Have you ever heard Ravi Shankarji, Vilayat Khan Sahib, Shiv Kumar Sharma, Hariprasad Chaurasia, Amjad Ali Khan complaining? No. Those who are not able to make their ends meet will complain. They keep sending twenty to thirty emails everyday to various organisers, saying I am coming that side so please schedule one programmes for me, begging for programmes. They have lost their pride and dignity. And my stand is that if you cannot perform music with pride and dignity then leave music alone. Go open a paan shop and run it with pride and dignity. But I can't give sermons here. The truth is that classical music is beautiful and popular. Just as the population has increased, listeners too have increased. If it was 100 earlier, it has become 150 now. But the problem is that we expect that we should get as much audience as Daler Mehndi gets and to be as famous or popular as Amitabh Bachchan or Shahrukh Khan. And I think that this can never happen in classical music. If you want that your name should be as popular and well-known as Shahrukh Khan and/or Amitabh Bachchan then you are in the wrong field. I am not saying that you can't do it but you are in the wrong field. In my field, may be in my concert I will have between 500 to 3000 people. I won't have crowds ranging between 30,000 to 80,000 people. Some years ago I brought out a pop album *Sukoon* with two videos. It remained at number two position for eight weeks in the popular album charts. But that was not what I wanted, it wasn't my line. I just did it to prove a point to myself. In fact, a classical artiste will have to understand that he is a classical artiste and not an entertainer of the masses. Those who understand it and love it will never die. Why go far, go to Sawai Gandharv Music Festival, one can see the strength of the audience, the admirers of classical music. Around fifteen to twenty thousand people sit and listen for three consecutive days. All said and done, I firmly believe that the future of Hindustani classical music is bright and beautiful. Everything is fine. We are just having a great time ... hahaha ... Have fun!

My Music is My Garden

USTAD WASIFUDDIN DAGAR

(Born 15 April, 1969–)

The grey coloured, vibrant apartment in Asiad Village, New Delhi, reflects its occupants. Music, life and the voices of many people echoing from various corners welcome us as we enter. This is the place where Ustad F. Wasifuddin Dagar, son of Ustad N. Faiyazuddin Dagar, nephew of Ustad N. Zahiruddin Dagar, grandson of Ustad Nasiruddin Dagar from paternal side and Ustad Hussainuddin Dagar from maternal side, lives. He represents the twentieth unbroken generation of *dhrupad* singers in the Dagar family. Just adjacent to the living room is the *riyaaz* room. We were taken inside, to be greeted by short-statured, stoutly built, Ustad Wasifuddin Dagar.

Wasifuddin's father passed away in 1989 and his uncle also left for his heavenly abode in 1994. After his uncle's demise Wasifuddin has been carrying on the family tradition. His rendition of *dhrupad* is a unique blend of his father's quality of voice and temperament and his own personality. His *alaap* is meditative and each *swar* is clearly delineated. His transition from one octave to the other is smooth. In addition to his supersonic *gamak*s, he decorates single phrases of *bandishe*s with innumerable variations and improvisations. During the course of the conversation, he often slipped into a reflective mood and answered questions philosophically. Two of his disciples kept sitting in the room, periodically nodding their heads in affirmation and promptly understanding their guru's cue for tea and snacks.

(29 July, 2005)

Interviewer:

Dhrupad has become synonymous with Dagar family. How and why did it happen?

Wasifuddin Dagar:

I am the twentieth generation of Dagar family. My ancestors were also *dhrupad* singers. Nearly two or three centuries earlier there were only *dhrupad* singers or musicians. After that *khayal* and other genres of music came into the limelight. But my family did not leave *dhrupad*. We continued to be *dhrupad* singers, unlike other families who left *dhrupad*. We gave our life, talent, time, soul, everything to *dhrupad*. Perhaps that's why our family has become synonymous with *dhrupad*.

Interviewer:

Dagar is a very peculiar surname. It is generally not heard. Why?

Wasifuddin Dagar:

There are four schools of *dhrupad—dagar bani, nauhaar bani, khandhaar bani* and *gauhaar bani*. As we have been following Dagar School of *dhrupad*, we call ourselves Dagars. But there is also a village in Haryana by this name. Now I do not know the exact relationship of my family with that village but if you go to Haryana many people use this surname. As for us, however, we use the surname because of its being a form of *dhrupad*.

Interviewer:

What is so special about *dagar bani*?

Wasifuddin Dagar:

As I said earlier there are four *banis* of *dhrupad* and in our *bani,* i.e., *dagar bani*, we give a lot of importance to the notes, our *alaap* is very long, emphasis is laid on the twelve basic principles, each word is pronounced clearly and emphatically. In fact, the moment anybody belonging to our tradition begins to sing, everybody comes to know that he belongs to the Dagar tradition.

Interviewer:

Are you saying that the other *gharanas* of *dhrupad* no longer exist?

Wasifuddin Dagar:

No, now they are being revived. As most of the followers of the other *gharanas* left *dhrupad*, their recitals were no longer heard when *khayal* gained prominence. The truth is that *dhrupad* is great. We all are *pujaris*, priests and *dhrupad* is the temple. Offering has to be made to the temple, not to the priest. We Dagars are devotees of *dhrupad* and our endeavour is to make *dhrupad* reach every nook and corner of the world. And we are not alone in this mission. There are other families also, like the Mallik family, and then there a few families in Bengal and Bihar, also. We never compromised with the changing times. We just concentrated on *dhrupad* and that's why you see the Dagar name being synonymous with dhrupad.

Interviewer:

So, it can be said that because the Dagars did not change with the changing times, Dagar and *dhrupad* have become synonymous.

Wasifuddin Dagar:

Yes. We worship *swar*, notes, the same way as we worship God even though we haven't seen Him. Let me give you an example. If I say music, it conjures up different images for different people. So music is not always M or music is not always M ... U ... S ... I ... C (*spells out the word*). Music is such a huge thing that it means different things to different people. Every note has the depth of an ocean. Music is an ocean, but every *swar* also has the depth of an ocean. So, you can experience many, many things through music. It can lead you to timelessness. Music is the only element that can control that restless beast, our mind. It is food for the soul.

Interviewer:

Why is *dhrupad* sung only in a few ragas?

Wasifuddin Dagar:

Now, that's not true. I'll talk specifically about the Dagar family. We prefer common ragas and we prefer those ragas that are complete in themselves with *shrutis*. We do not believe in creating new ragas. For us, ragas are not only the structure of musical notes in ascending and descending order. We believe that every raga has an aura. We try to understand that aura. We think that one raga cannot be constricted by a single *bandish* alone. In one raga we can compose several *bandishes*. Like one is recognised by one's thoughts, voice, looks and even nails, so are ragas. We sing only those ragas that are complete in themselves.

Interviewer:

Why is it generally believed that *dhrupad* is difficult to understand?

Wasifuddin Dagar:

This depends on the perspective of those people who spread such ideas. A few days ago I was asked this question in a lecture. I just asked that person—is *khayal* easy? Is *thumri* easy? He replied 'No.' So I asked him if so, then why do you say that *dhrupad* is difficult. He had no answer. I do not understand why people spread such misconceptions. Tell me, isn't everything in life difficult? It is very easy to buy one hotshot camera but if one has to go into the depth of photography, one has got to learn about focus, about sensitivity of film, speed, frame, aperture and so many other things. So, nothing is easy. Everything is difficult if one has to learn anything seriously.

Nowadays, if one has to log off or delete any file from the computer, even the computer asks so many questions. At times these are very confusing and difficult. This being the case, why is the adjective 'difficult' used only for *dhrupad*?

Yes, we cannot entertain people in five minutes, like film songs, but if somebody is ready to give us fifteen minutes then definitely they will benefit from *dhrupad* renditions. What has happened is that we think rhythm alone is music, whereas the truth is that there is rhythm in music. It is a serious misconception that *dhrupad* is difficult to understand. As I explained above, though many things in this world are difficult, yet we try learning about them, we attempt them, right? It is just a mental block we have that makes us feel we cannot understand classical music or that *dhrupad* is extremely difficult.

Interviewer:

Our classical music is said to be *bhaav pradhan* ...

Wasifuddin Dagar:

True. Mere words and/or phrases have no meaning or depth. It is the *bhaav* that gives meaning or depth to words or phrases, otherwise they remain mere words. We try presenting those words in different ways, with different emotions. There is no such thing as 'perfect.' Nothing is perfect. Only He–God, is perfect. In India we have started believing 'I am perfect.' It is a Western concept. The westerners think they are perfect, not we Indians. But now everybody has become Western in thought. They believe that they are perfect. The truth is that we can only try to be perfect. And we spend all our lives in search of that perfection, that happiness. It is music that can take us nearer to that bliss, that elusive happiness.

Interviewer:

Why are most of the *bandishes* in *dhrupad* devotional? Is it not constricting the freedom of *dhrupad* as a genre?

Wasifuddin Dagar:

Yes, mostly. But there are other *rasas* also. *Shringar rasa* is also there. *Dhrupad* is limitless. We are limited; our thinking is limited; Are we not free? Yet, don't we stay in a house that has a boundary? Even our country has a boundary. Are we not independent within that very boundary? Actually, it all depends on the person whether he sees things as a drop in the ocean or an ocean in the drop.

Interviewer:

How many concerts do you give in a year?

Wasifuddin Dagar:

It differs. At times sixty or seventy; sometimes even hundred, including concerts happening abroad. It is not fixed. It varies. At times I've also done three concerts in a day, with just an hour's gap in between.

Interviewer:

Presently how many hours of *riyaaz* do you do?

Wasifuddin Dagar:

Minimum four hours. At times I sit for *riyaaz* at 8:00 am, only to be forced by my mother to take a break for meals around 3:00 pm. Then again I sit in the evening with my students. Actually music to me is like nature. As we never get tired of seeing the sunrise or the sunset, music is also always new and fresh for me. Everyday I find something new in a raga. It is a dialogue to me. I take it as a means of communication and try to establish my identity with that raga. See, we are given our identity by our parents, by the elders of the family. Initially we are introduced to people as somebody's child or a relative of somebody or a friend of somebody. For sometime that reference is taken. But when we meet that person for the umpteenth time we expect them to recognise us as an individual in our own right. This is human nature. As we all have different personalities, ragas are also imbued with many shades and hues. Raga gives to the person whatever he or she asks, be it in the form of *khayal, thumri, ghazal, dhrupad.*

Interviewer:

What syllables do you take in *alaap*?

Wasifuddin Dagar:

Dhrupad has the unique meditational quality. We take syllables of *om anant tam, taran tarini tum—hai ishwar hum na khatam hone wale andhkar mein hain. Aap taran tarak hain, hari om narayan, hari om narayan*—we expand it in the notes of a raga. Each *swar* is touched. And *swar* is very delicate. A long time ago my great grandfather asked his grandfather, 'What is the truth of *swar*?' And the answer given to him was, '*jitna jiska imaan saccha, utna uska swar saccha*.' (Your notes will be as true and pure as your integrity is).

Interviewer:

You belong to a musical family. How was your childhood?

Wasifuddin Dagar:

I had a very normal childhood. I was quite naughty. I think music was all around me even before I was born. But it is not necessary that one would become a musician just because one is born in a musical family. One has to have talent. Even in our family there are some who did not take up music. I started learning quite early and whenever some guests were there, I was asked to sing. My *tauji*, Ustad Zahiruddin Dagar, had taught me four or five compositions. I liked being the centre of attraction. After all what does a child need? Just a little attention. Everybody in the family and all my friends supported me. So, I pursued music seriously and after school completely devoted my time to music. I didn't go to college.

Interviewer:

Who were your gurus?

Wasifuddin Dagar:

My *tauji,* Ustad Zahiruddin Dagar and my father, Ustad Faiyazuddin Dagar, commonly known as the Junior Dagar brothers. In 1989 my father died and in 1994 *tauji* too passed away.

Interviewer:

After your father's death you must have felt a sudden vacuum. You must have thought who would teach me now?

Wasifuddin Dagar:

I always called my *tauji* as *bade abba* (big father). His younger brother died, not my father. Not only me, my sisters also never felt father's absence. *Tauji* never let us feel that way. I also performed with him.

Interviewer:

He was your *guru* and *tauji*. So did you ever feel nervous about being on stage with him?

Wasifuddin Dagar:

Yes, always. When he told me to sing with him for the first time, I nervously asked him, 'Can I sing with you?' He promptly replied, 'Yes, why not? Do you think I've gone crazy to ask you to sit beside me here, on stage?' For me this was another learning process. With him, on stage, I learnt how to present myself on stage. You see, my music is my garden and my concert is my bouquet. I know the best flowers of my garden. I select those flowers that make a beautiful bouquet and present that bouquet on stage. What to select and how beautifully to present it on stage, I learnt with *tauji.* It was a good experience.

Interviewer:

We had senior Dagar brothers, then junior Dagar brothers presenting *jugalbandi* but you shifted your focus away from that form. Why?

Wasifuddin Dagar:

I have seen the pain and anguish that one person undergoes after the partner dies or the pair breaks away. When Moinuddin *tauji* passed away, Aminuddin *tauji* missed him throughout his life. For thirty years he felt his absence and similarly when my father passed away, Zahiruddin *tauji* often used to take his name on stage. He missed my father till his last days. It becomes very lonely for the living partner. So I decided to break away from that tradition and started presenting solo concerts.

Interviewer:

How many disciples do you have?

Wasifuddin Dagar:

I have three performing students and around ten or eleven who are learning.

Interviewer:

What kind of a future do you foresee for *dhrupad*?

Wasifuddin Dagar:

I like saying that the glass is half full; not half empty. Nearly twenty years ago, the condition of *dhrupad* was quite bad. Now it is reaching people and the audience is coming for concerts. There was a time when it was declared that *dhrupad* was dead. Critics went ahead and wrote the obituary for *dhrupad*. But after a lull of a few years it revived itself. And today, *dhrupad* is reaching the masses. It is full of all the *rasa*s that are there in any other *gayaki* form.

Interviewer:

Why is it that there are very few women *dhrupad* singers?

Wasifuddin Dagar:

No, I do not agree with you on that. The percentage is the same. Just count how many *dhrupad* performers are there. After that if you take out the percentage, it will be equal. These days women are there in every field and are doing well.

Interviewer:

Why did your sisters not learn music?

Wasifuddin Dagar:

Because of family tradition. Maybe it will change in the coming years. (*laughs*).

GLOSSARY

A

Aabhog: Dhrupad (a genre of Hindustani Classical music) composition's fourth part.

Aakaar: To sing the melodic structure by using 'aa' only. Words of the text are not used.

Aap: Respectfully used for elders. The pronoun 'you' has three variations in Indian languages, registering varying degrees of respect or familiarity. In Hindi the variants are *tu, tum* and *aap*

Abba: Father. In Muslim culture father is often addressed as Abba.

Achha: Exclamatory form of expression, meaning 'oh, oh yes, okay, right, all right, is that so, etc.' depending on the context.

Ajji: In Kannada grandmother is addressed as 'Ajji.'

Akhada: In common parlance akhada is the training hall or ground where wrestlers learn and practise the art.

Alaap/Alaapchari: The beginning of the composition where the singer explores the raga without any musical accompaniment.

Alankar: Musical ornamentation.

Ammi: Mother is commonly referred to as ammi in Muslim households.

Amrut: Manna or nectar. Drink that grants immortality according to Hindu scriptures.

Andaz: Style, attitude.

Andolan: In musical parlance, slow development of a singing note, a kind of melodic ornamentation. Common meaning is a protest or revolutionary movement.

Anna: In Tamil, Telugu and Kannada anna means elder brother.

Antar: Difference.

Antaraa: The second section of the composition. Here the singer sings the notes of the composition in upper register or octave.

Antardhwani: Name of the raga. It means sound from within. It is a raga created by Pandit Shiv Kumar Sharma. According to him it means 'the sound of the inner self.'

Anurag: Affection.

Arre: Exclamation of surprise.

Asht: Eight.

Ashtaang: Eight fold style of singing. Gwalior gharana gayaki is known for it.

Ashtapadi: The literal meaning is 'eight steps.' In music, it signifies eight steps or lines within each composition.
Ati drut laya: Fast tempo of a composition.
Ati Madhya laya: Medium tempo of a composition.
Ati vilambit: Very slow tempo of a composition.
Atma: Soul.

B

Baaj: Instrument; style of playing, frequently used for instrumental music.
Baant: Division.
Bada: Big.
Bade Abba: Father's elder brother.
Badh: Limitation.
Badhat: Progression or exposition of a raga with metric cycle.
Badshah: King.
Badtameezee: Ill-mannered, uncouth behaviour.
Baiji: Courtesans.
Baithak: In the music world, a small gathering of people to listen to music.
Bajaana: To play.
Banaav: The complete word is *Bol Banaav.* It means expressive usage of words to convey emotions; largely used in *thumri.*
Bandish: Composition.
Bansuri: Flute.
Baramasa: Genre of a classical music, like *thumri, dadra,* etc.
Beej: Seed.
Been: Veena or Rudra Veena. (Though now commonly the word *been* is used for the instrument played by snake charmers). In the text it specifically signifies Veena as Ustad Bande Ali Khan was a Veena player.
Beenkar: String instrument player.
Behlava: Using words of the composition in Alaap to describe the mood of the composition.
Benaras/Banaras: City in Uttar Pradesh from where many singers flourished.
Bepard: Shameless.
Bhaav: Emotions.
Bhabhi: Elder brother's wife.
Bhai: Brother.
Bhairav: Name of a morning raga.
Bhajan: Devotional songs.
Bhakt: Devotee.
Bhakti: Devotion.
Bhavana: Sentiments, emotions, spirit.
Bhed: Mystery, difference, distinction.
Bheda: Distinction or difference.
Bhor: Morning.
Bhyanak: Frightening.
Bigda hua Bihag: Distorted version of Raga Bihag.
Bitiya: Affectionate form of addressing the daughter.

Bol: Words of the song.

Bol-baant: It literally means division of words. In music it means breaking the text into various forms and then regrouping them and thereby creating different musical rhythmical patterns.

Bol Banaav: Expressive usage of words to convey emotions; largely used in *thumri.*

Bolo: Speak out, Say it.

Braj bhasha: A dialect of Hindi common in Mathura and Vrindavan areas. Along with Awadhi, it was a predominant literary language till the 19th century.

C

Carnatic: South Indian Classical music.

Chaiti: Form of singing.

Chandra sarangi: String instrument.

Chatusruti: Notes or swars in classical music; R2 is Chatusruti.

Chaturmukhi: All round development.

Chaumukhi vidya: All round education.

Chhand-prabhand: Chhand means a metrical pattern and prabhand is a form of music that was prevalent before the advent of dhrupad genre. Prabhand was the closed category of music (Nibaddha sangeet), very pointedly divided into four categories—opening part, exposition part, fixed part and the concluding part.

Chikari: Literally meaning high pitched. On instrument it means high drone string, primarily used for rhythmic clarity.

Chota: Small.

Churidar: Tight fitting lowers.

D

Dadra: A rhythmic beat of six *matras.* A form of classical music.

Dagar bani: Gharana of Dhrupad genre of Hindustani music.

Darbar: King's court.

Darbari: Name of a raga.

Dhaivat: The sixth note, *Dha.*

Dhamaar: Genre of Hindustani Classical music; A *taal* of fourteen beats.

Dharini: Derived from the Sanskrit word which means hold or maintain. Means the carrier or bearer. Used for goddess Saraswati. *Pustak dharini* means one who holds a book in her hand.

Dhrupad: Genre of Hindustani Classical music.

Dhwani: Sound.

Dohe: Couplets (two-lined verses).

Drut: Fast tempo.

Drut-gat: Fast tempo composition.

Dupatta: Simple, soft cloth piece worn by women on the upper part of their body over a salwar-kurta or churidar kurta.

E

Eeshwar: God.

Ekalavya: Character from the Epic Mahabharata who learnt the art of archery by watching his guru, Dronacharaya teaching other disciples.
Esraj: String instrument.

F
Farsi: Persian language.

G
Gaan Samrat: Emperor of music.
Gaanewala: Male singer.
Gaanewali: Female singer.
Gamak: Ornamentation in singing.
Gamakas: Plural of gamak
Gandabandh/ Gandabandhan: Knot tying ceremony marking the formal acceptance of a disciple by the guru.
Gandhar: The third note, *Ga*.
Garara: Loose lower apparel worn by women.
Gatkari: Ornamentation.
Gauhaar bani: Form or school of Dhrupad gayaki. There are four schools of Dhrupad—Nauhaar Bani, Gauhaar Bani, Khandhaar Bani and Dagar Bani.
Gayaki: Singing style.
Gayan: Singing or song.
Geet: Light music.
Ghar ke log: Family.
Gharana: A school or family of music, having certain characteristics unique to the school.
Ghazal: Form of music where lyrics are largely derived from Urdu poetry.
Gopi: Cowherdess or milkmaid. Originally they were Krishna's companions when he resided in Brajbhumi or Vrindavan.
Gulli-danda: Game popular with rural kids.
Gurukul: In the present day context, traditional music school. Earlier all education was imparted in India in gurukuls where the disciples stayed with the guru at his place, learning the art, craft and technique.
Gurumukhi vidya: Knowledge orally imparted by the guru.

H
Hamdard: Well-wisher.
Harkat: Waves of the voice. The voice suddenly travels from high to low or vice versa.
Haveli sangeet: A form of Hindustani Classical Music, primarily sung in palaces or mansions.
Hori: Form of music where lyrics relate to Holi, the Hindu festival of colours.

J
Jalsa: Celebration.

Jaltarang: One of the most rarely heard instruments today but one of the oldest instruments in the world. It consists of china bowls filled with water and struck by two wooden sticks. Earlier artists used to play this instrument with metal bowls. Each bowl can be tuned to the desired frequency by varying the quantity of water in it. These bowls are placed in a semi-circle around the artist and played.

Jatra: Folk theatre form of Bengal.

Javali: Love Songs.

Jhala: Fast paced conclusion of a classical rendition.

Jhap taal: 10-beat pattern used in raga exposition.

Jhoola: Folk songs of Uttar Pradesh, describing swings.

Jod: Also written as Jor. The four sections of classical music are alaap, jod, gat and jhala. Jod is the portion of instrumental piece in which the rhythm begins. Since it does not have a fully developed cycle, it is not accompanied by tabla.

Jugalbandi: Duet.

K

Kalakaar: Artist.

Kaansen: One who is not a singer but has deep understanding of musical notes.

Kajri: Form of classical music. Primarily sung in Uttar Pradesh. Lyrics often describe the longing of a woman for her beloved.

Kaku: Intonation.

Kala: Art.

Kamancheh: Iranian bowed string instrument.

Kan swara: Notes that are linked with the preceding or succeeding notes are called grace notes or kan swaras. Its intensity is either above or below the decorated pitch.

Kancha: Glass marbles.

Kanhada ke Prakar: Various forms of Raga Kanhada

Karuna rasa: Pathos.

Khaal: Outer skin.

Khandhaar bani: School of Dhrupad genre.

Khandmeru: An improvisational style, marked by combination of fixed set of notes, broken up in fragments (*Khands*). However, emphasis is maintained on that particular raga notes. Ustad Amir Khan's *gayaki* was known for this technique.

Kharaj: The lower octave – 2.

Khatke: An ornamentation while singing. It often involves a faster attack on the principal note.

Khayal: A vocal genre. It literally means imagination, fancy, thought.

Khichdi: Originally a recipe, where rice, lentils and spices are cooked together. In common non-culinary usage it means dishing out a mixed-up version of two or more distinct original forms.

Kirtan: Devotional song.

Komal: Soft note.

Kothewali: Courtesan.

Kriti: Format of a musical composition in Carnatic music.
Krodh: Anger.
Kurta: Loosely stitched shirt-like garment worn by men and/or women.

L

Ladki: Girl.
Laya: Rhythm.
Layakari: Manipulation of rhythm in mathematical pattern.

M

Madhya: Medium.
Madhya laya: Medium tempo.
Madhyam: The fourth note of the *Saptak*, *Ma.*
Mandra: Lower octave.
Manka: A precious stone.
Matra: Single beat. Basic time measurement unit in Hindustani Classical Music.
Meend: Slow glide that connects two notes.
Mehfil: Gathering of music connoisseurs.
Mizaaj: Mood or temperament.
Mishri: Sugar candy or crystal sugar.
Mukh: Mouth.
Muqam: Set of melodic formulas.
Murchhana: The sequential order of the seven notes, used for melodic presentation of the composition.
Murki: Fast ornamentation around the main note.
Murkiyan: Plural of Murki.

N

Nagma: Song.
Namaz: Daily prayers of Muslims.
Natya: Classical Indian dance.
Natyashastra: Ancient Indian treatise on the performing arts.
Nauhaar bani: Form or school of Dhrupad music.
Niras: Dull.
Nishad: The seventh note, *Ni.*
Nom tom: Alaap performed in Dhrupad. It gives emphasis on rhythm and repeat words like nom, tom, na, re, de, ne, etc.

O

Om anant tam, taran tarini tu: Lyrics. It means God we are surrounded by never ending darkness. You are our saviour ...

P

Paan: Betel leaf.
Pakhawaj: A double headed barrel shaped percussion instrument. A drum primarily used in dhrupad recitals.

Palta: Scale exercises.
Pancham: The fifth note of the *Saptak, Pa.*
Pandit: Title given to a learned singer.
Parampara: Culture, tradition.
Payo: To get, receive.
Pitamah: Character from the epic, Mahabharata—Bhishma Pitamah, the patriarch of the Kurus, grand uncle of Kauravas and Pandavas. Pitamah by itself refers to the doyen in any field, the patriarch or grand-old-man in colloquial terms.
Pradhan: Chief. In verb form it means 'to give emphasis.'
Prakaar: Forms.
Pranam: Greetings.
Prarthana: Prayer.
Pratha: Tradition.
Pujari: Priest.
Pukar: A musical intonation using higher notes.
Purab-ang: Form of singing. As this style emerged from Varanasi, which is to the east of Lucknow, it came to be known as Purab ang. It is largely used for *thumri gayaki.*
Purdah: Veil or screen. Also refers to the practice of Muslim women not appearing before outsiders, especially menfolk not from the family, without a burqa.
Purvi: Name of a raga.
Pushti/Pushti-marg /Pushti Sangeet: The word Pushti-marg means the path of grace. It is a Vaishanav sect of Hinduism. It means selfless love for Lord Krishna. While Pushti Sangeet means devotional music sung in praise of Lord Krishna.
Pustaka: Books, denoting literature.

Q

Qawwali: A form of Sufi devotional music.

R

Rabab: Type of bowed string instrument.
Rachna: Composition.
Raga: The melodic modes used in classical music, consisting of particular scale notes. The literal meaning is colour, hue or shade. Figuratively it means something that colours our emotions.
Ragadari: To follow the modes of classical music.
Ragini: Female raga according to the classification of ragas into male and female types.
Ras: Essence. Figuratively used for beauty.
Rasa: An aesthetic theory that defines sentiments into nine categories, like love, humour, pathos, violence, etc.
Rasik: A person who has feelings or passion.
Rasika: Connoisseurs of art.
Rishab/Rishabh: Second note of the *Saptak, Re* or *Ri.*

Rishi-muni: Saint; spiritual person, ascetic.
Riyaaz: Practice.
Rudraksh: Precious seeds used for prayer beads. 108 beads are strung together and worn around the neck and used for meditation.
Rupak: Seven count beats.

S

Saaz: Instrument.
Sachha: Truthful.
Sadhna: Meditation.
Sadra: A vocal genre in Hindustani classical music. The compositions are set to 10-beat Jhaptaal.
Sahiba: A honorific like Sir. A respectful title used for a woman.
Sahitya: Literature.
Sahpaya: Triangular shaped three wooden pieces used for keeping instruments.
Samaroh: Musical gathering.
Samajik vyavastha: Social system.
Sammelan: Conference.
Sanchari: Third subsection of a musical composition; a meandering melodic movement.
Sangat: Accompaniment.
Sangeet: Music.
Sangeet Martand: Title given to a musician. It means radiant Sun of Indian classical music. Pandit Jasraj has been given this title. Earlier, Pandit Omkarnath Thakur was also given this title.
Santoor: String musical instrument.
Sapaat taan: The notes are placed in an order in one or more octaves.
Sapt suran teen gram ikkees murchhana: Song lyrics
Saptak: A group of seven notes.
Sarangi: A string instrument played with a bow.
Sargam: Term for the seven notes of the *saptak*.
Sarod: A fretless string instrument played by plucking the strings. It has evolved from *rabab*.
Sarood: Persian word that means music.
Sartaj-e-Mousiqui: Title given to musicians, meaning master of music.
Sau-rangi: In earlier times Sarangi was called Sau-rangi, meaning having 100-colours.
Sawal-jawab: Question-answers.
Shadja: The first note, *Sa* of the *saptak.*
Shaili: Style, form.
Shant: One of the rasas, meaning peace.
Shastra: The word is generally used as a suffix in the context of technical or specialised knowledge in a defined area of practice. E.g. Natya Shastra relating to dance, Artha Shastra relating to Economics and so on.

Shastras: Plural form of shastra.
Shastriya: Classical.
Shata-tantri: Original name of the santoor. It literally means a veena of 100-strings.
Shayar: Poet.
Shehenshah: Emperor.
Shehnai: Double reed wind instrument.
Shagird: Disciple.
Shishya: Student.
Shloka: Sanskrit couplets.
Shringar: One of the rasas, meaning love or amour.
Shruti-swar: Shruti is a microtone in the Indian classical scale that has twelve notes and twenty-two shrutis.
Shuddha madhyam: Used in the context of notes.
Sthaayi: Beginning or initial phrase of a fixed melodic structure in Indian classical music.
Sur/Swar: Note or pitch.
Sur sthaana: Placement of a note.
Surbahar: String instrument, quite similar to the sitar. It has a larger resonance box.
Swarmandal: String instrument. It is used by vocalists to give pitch support.
Swaroop: Appearance; form and shape of a raga.
Swar siddhi: Practice of music.

T

Taal: The rhythmic metric cycle used in Indian Classical music.
Taleem: Education or training.
Taan: A rapid series of notes used in vocal and instrumental music.
Taankari: The craft and artistry in using taan.
Taar Saptak: Higher octave.
Tabla: The pair of drums used in Hindustani Classical music. It consists of the bayan, left hand drum and dayan, the right hand drum.
Tanpura: A long-necked string instrument, played by continuously plucking the strings. It is used for providing the drone notes.
Tantra ang: Instrumental style.
Tantrakari: A masterly innovative technique or style, largely used in solo instrumental performances by maestros.
Tapasya: Penance.
Tap-khayal/ Tapp-khayal: Tappa like *khayal*.
Tappa: One of the genres of classical music. The lyrics are in Punjabi language, as its origin is traced to the folk songs of camel-drivers of Punjab-Sindh area. It was popularised by Ghulam Nabi Shori (Shori Miyan), who was the court singer of Nawab Asaf Ud-Daullah of Lucknow (1776-1797).
Tarab ki taar: Sitar strings. Besides main strings, there are *tarab ki taar*, meaning sympathetic strings.

Tarana: Genre of classical music that uses vocables or drum syllables. It is performed in a medium or fast tempo.
Tarannum: Melody.
Tauji: Father's elder brother or cousin. The word is also used as a form of respectful address for elders in the village or community in some parts of North India.
Teen taal: A beat of sixteen counts.
Teevra madhyam: Sharp note, *Ma*
Tehzeeb: Manners.
Thum-khayal: A new genre in *Khayal* which has lot of *thumri* expressions.
Thumri: Genre of Indian classical music. The text is often romantic.
Tigalbandi: Three musicians performing together.
Tihayee: Musical pattern repeated three times in succession and ends on the *sam*.
Tillana: Rhythmic piece that is widely used in dance performances.
Trisruti: Sruti is the smallest interval of pitch in classical music. There are three sruti intervals between *Sa and Re.* Trisruti is the third.
Todi: Name of a morning raga.
Tu: You. Refer Aap for details.
Tumba: Gourd. The lower portion of the sitar.

U
Uchhal-khood: Horseplay, showmanship, upstart behaviour.
Ulta jhala: The melodic pattern of a jhala (explained above) are completely reversed in this style of singing.
Upnishad: Ancient scriptures.
Ustad: Maestro; learned musician. Title used for Muslim maestros.

V
Vani: Vocal music.
Venu: Flute and wind/reed instruments.
Vidwan: Learned.
Vilambit: Slow tempo setting of a composition with rhythmic accompaniment.
Vistaar: Development of a raga; exposition of a raga.

Z
Zamzama: A series of murkiyan (explained above) taken in quick succession that makes the musical canvas develop a zig-zag rhythm or pattern.
Zenana: Women.

INDEX

A

Abbasi, Ishtiaq Ahmed, 121
Akhtar, Begum, 117–118, 120–124, 127–130, 249
Amonkar, Kishori, 49, 55
Atre, Dr Prabha, 97–98
- academic work, 105–106
- as an avant-garde artiste, 114
- contributions of, 113
- on critics and criticism, 106
- on different types of music, 110
- doctoral thesis *sargam,* 106
- experience at All India Radio, 105
- future of classical music, 109
- *gharana* system, 100, 102–103
- gurus, 99–100
- *guru-shishya parampara,* 108
- influence of Carnatic music, 101–102
- inspiration for writing poetry, 111–112
- interest in musician, 101
- international concerts, 109–110
- interpretation of raga, 104
- job at SNDT University, 106–107
- *khayal* performance, 114
- music as a career for women, 112
- music composing, 110–111
- music style, 103–104
- personality of, 99
- public performance, 101
- raga compositions, 115–116
- raga-*rasa* and raga-time theories, 115
- *riyaaz,* 99
- standardisation in content-structure and teaching methods of music, 107–108
- *thumri* style, 101
- unpopularity of classical music, 109

B

Bai, Zohra, 32
Bakre, Shrikant, 100
Balamuralikrishna, Dr. M., 258
Bannerjee, Nikhil, 222, 257
Barodekar, Hirabai, 100
Begum, Roshanara, 43, 101
Bhatt, Mahendra, 213
Bhatt, Salil, 211, 218
Bhatt, Shashi Mohan, 213
Bhatt, Vishwa Mohan, 211–212
- advice to young musicians, 223–224
- beginning of musical journey, 213
- collaboration with Ry Cooder, 216–218
- compositions for films, 221
- difference between Mohan Veena and Satvik Veena, 218
- first international concert, 215–216
- *gharana* system, 215
- guitar and classical music, 213
- interests besides music, 222
- Mohan Veena, 214–215
- people perception about classical music, 220–221
- perception about music, 223
- pure Hindustani Classical music, 218–220
- raga *Vishwaranjini,* 221–222
- *riyaaz,* 214
- Vishwa Veena, 214

C

Chakrabarty, Ajoy, 253
- advice to youngsters, 261
- beginning of musical journey, 254
- childhood, 260
- commercialisation of music, 259
- connection between spirituality and classical music, 262
- daughter Kaushiki, 260–261
- first public performance, 258–259
- *gharana* system, 257
- gurus, 254
- improvisation in music, 255
- influence of Bade Ghulam Ali Khan, 255
- *jugalbandis,* 258

perception about music, 257
philosophy of music, 255
present day music scenario, 258
ragas, 258
Shrutinandan school, 255–256
views on young musicians, 259
wife, 261
Chakraborty, Kaushiki, 260
Chatterjee, Bimla Nandan, 178
Chaudhuri, Devabrata (a.k.a Debu), 141–142
advice to youngsters, 156
awards and recognition, 151
classical music in school curriculum, 146
Delhi life, 150
experiences as a teacher, 146–148
family, 152–154
foreign tours, 151
'get the concert,' 143–145
gharana system, 149
guru-shishya parampara, 148
innovations in ragas, 149
media and popularity of artistes, 155–156
musical journey and experience with audiences, 155
number of concerts in a year, 143
promising disciples, 154
raga and *bandish*es, 151
role of music in society, 143
sitar training, 150
support to newcomers, 145–146
Chaurasia, Hariprasad, 33, 160, 165–166
advice to people, 174
audience analysis, 171–172
becoming a musician, 168–169
childhood, 167
contribution to music, 172
disciples, 172–173
establishing *gurukul*s, 169
favourite raga, 170
flute introduction into classical music, 167
guru, 167–168
Hindustani Classical Music, 173–174
*jugalbandi*s, 171
music in films, 170–171
opinion about music schools, 170

D

Dagar, Aminuddin, 55
Dagar, F. Wasifuddin, 301
*bandish*es in *dhrupad,* 305
childhood, 306
concerts, 305
dagar bani, 302
dhrupad renditions, 302–304
disciples, 308
future for *dhrupad,* 308
gurus, 307
perception about classical music, 304–305
riyaaz, 305–306
solo concerts, 307–308
syllables in *alaap,* 306
women *dhrupad* singers, 308
Dagar, Moinuddin, 55
Dagar, N. Faiyazuddin, 301
Dagar, N. Zahiruddin, 301
Desai, Dattopant, 20
Deshpande, Dr Vasantrao, 280
Devi, Annapurna, 168
Devi, Girija, 67
advice for youngsters, 71–72
beginning of *taleem,* 68
changing demographic patterns of listenership, 70
gurus, 68
honours, 72
musical journey, 71
Purab Ang gayaki, 69
thumri and *khayal,* 69–70
Devi, Savita, 175
bandishes, 176
children, 182
father's influence, 180
first public concert, 178
formal training, 176
guru, 176
jugalbandi, 176
as a lecturer at Daulat Ram College, 179
Maa—Siddheshwari, 176, 180
marriage and separation, 179–180
music as a subject, 178
perception about music, 182
riyaaz, 176
Siddheshwari Devi Academy of Indian Music, 181–182
thumri styles, 181
Devi, Siddheshwari, 68, 175
Devidayal, Namita, 65
Dr Gangubai Hangal Music and Performing Arts University, 18

G

Gandharva, Kumar, 17–18, 24
Gandharva, Sawai, 20
Gandhi, Mahatma, 20
gharana system, 36–37
Gopalakrishnan, M. S., 78, 80

H

Hangal, Gangubai, 17–18
- about mother, 19
- on Bhimsen Joshi, 21
- childhood, 19
- at a Congress session in Belgaum, 1920s, 20
- daughter Krishna, 26
- favourite ragas and theory of ragas, 24
- first concert, 22
- as Honorary Music Professor, 18
- learning of Carnatic music, 19
- marriage, 25–26
- on name, 23–24
- rapport with musicians, 24–25
- on restrictions and prejudices regarding caste, 20
- Sawai Gandharva's teaching, 21
- *The Song of My Life,* 18
- voice quality post tonsillitis operation, 22–23

Hindustani classical music, 11–12
- areas receptive and appreciative of, 35
- *Gharana* (musical style), 12
- vocal and instrumental styles, 11

Hiranand, Shanti, 117–118
- artistic freedom, 127
- as Begum Akhtar's disciple, 120–124, 128
- challenges to women pursuing music life-long, 132
- disciples, 125
- family, 125, 131
- *ghazal* and *thumri,* 130–131
- music training, 119–120
- passion in music, 119
- programmes on All India Radio, 120
- *riyaaz,* 124
- singing for films, 126–127
- solo concerts, 125
- *The Story of my Ammi,* 129
- teaching method, 128–129
- *thumri-dadra,* 128– 129
- vision about classical music, 129

I

Iyer, Parur Sundaram, 78

J

Jaan, Gauhar, 31

Jadhav, Lakshmibai, 61

Jasraj, Pandit, 87–88, 273
- advice to followers, 96
- childhood, 92
- disciples, 96
- first guru, 92–93
- *gayaki* power of, 89
- *gharana* system, 91
- *guru-shishya parampara,* 94–95
- *Haveli Sangeet,* 92
- Hindustani classical music, 95
- Jasrangi Jugalbandi, 90
- mentor, 92
- miracles, 93–94
- musical journey, 92
- present times music schools, 95
- ragas, 90–91
- rendition of bhajan *Om Namo bhagwate,* 89
- singing of *shlokas* at concert, 89
- teaching methods, 96

Joshi, Bhimsen, 17, 21

Joshi, Nirmala, 47

K

Kabra, Brij Bhushan, 160

Kala, 76

Karanth, B. V., 47

Karnad, Girish, 65

Karnad, Vasant, 65

Katkar, C., 237

Kelkarji, L. R., 77

Kerkar, Kesarbai, 25, 57, 61–65, 68

Khan, Abdul Karim, 21–22

Khan, Ahmed, 243

Khan, Ali Akbar, 24, 257

Khan, Alladiya, 57, 59, 61, 64, 242, 244

Khan, Allaudin, 257

Khan, Amir, 49, 55, 101, 169, 223

Khan, Amjad Ali, 183–184
- awards and recognition, 185
- Bangash Music, 197
- beginning of musical journey, 186–187
- childhood, 186–187
- composition of ragas, 195–196
- disciples, 197
- family, 188, 198
- favourite raga, 195
- formal education, 191
- fusion music, 196
- future of Hindustani classical music, 196
- innovations in playing style, 193
- *khayal gayaki ang,* 193–194
- lecture-demonstrations, 192
- music profession, 188
- parents, 185–186
- perception about music, 188–189, 198
- *riyaaz,* 192
- source of inspiration, 190
- unpopularity of sarod, 194

Khan, Azizuddin, 57, 61, 63
Khan, Baba Allaudin, 29–30
Khan, Bade Ghulam Ali, 49, 55, 101, 128, 223, 253–255
Khan, Bande Ali, 265
Khan, Bhurji, 60–61
Khan, Bismillah, 24, 176
Khan, Chhajju, 51–52
Khan, Faiyaz, 31, 68, 151
Khan, Ghulam Sabir, 50, 56
Khan, Hafiz Ali, 183
Khan, Haji Mohammad, 51–52
Khan, Halim Jaffer, 140
Khan, Laddan, 52
Khan, Manjhi, 60
Khan, Mashkoor Ali, 263–264
  *bandish*es, 265–266
  beginning of musical journey, 265
  belief in luck and destiny, 269–270
  childhood, 266
  first concert, 266
  future of music, 270
  gayaki, 268
  gharana system, 267
  Kirana *gharana gayaki,* 268
  rare ragas, 267
Khan, Mubarak Ali, 269
Khan, Munawar Ali, 128, 255
Khan, Mushtaq Ali, 145, 150, 152
Khan, Mushtaq Hussain, 47–48
Khan, Nasiruddin, 60
Khan, Nathan, 59–60
Khan, Rahimuddin, 55
Khan, Sabri, 49–50
  All India Radio service, 54–55
  becoming a professional musician, 53
  becoming a sarangi player, 51
  childhood years, 51
  disciples, 56
  evolution of musicians and music, 56
  gharana system, 52
  on Ghulam Sahib, 56
  international sarangi concerts, 53
  kinds of sarangi, 54
  requirement of an accompanying artiste, 55
Khan, Shakoor Ali, 265
Khan, Shujaat, 283–284
  experiences in life, 288–290
  fusion music, 295–296
  future of music, 299–300
  Laajo Laajo, 296–297
  lineage and expectations, 285–287
  perception about classical music, 296
  Persian collaboration, 297
  public concert, 292–293
  shaili of music, 294
  taleem, 292
  travelling experiences and its influence in music, 290
  viewpoint regarding awards, 297–298
  views on creating new ragas, 295
  vision about classical music, 299
Khan, Suhail, 49
Khan, Sultan, 33
Khan, Vilayat, 222, 283, 289, 295
Khote, Durga, 60
Khurana, Shanno, 39–40
  alaap style, 43–44
  as an actress, 44
  disciples, 45
  early years of musical journey, 39–40
  family support to learning music, 41–42
  festival on rare ragas, 46
  *gharana*s, 43–44
  musical education, 43
  on organising a festival of women musicians, 46–47
  reason for being aggressive, 48
  riyaaz, 45
  tappa singing, 45–46
Kohli, Indira, 120
Krishnan, T. N., 76
Krishnaswamy, 54
Kulkarni, Dhondutai, 57–58
  advice for young musicians, 66
  as Bhurji Khan's disciple, 60–61
  father's influence, 59
  gharana system, 59
  as Kesarbai's disciple, 61–64
  at Mumbai, 63
  teaching style of Bhurji Khan and Kesarbai Kerkar, 64
  voice culture technique, 64
  working at All India Radio, 60

M

Maharaj, Kishan, 175, 179
Maneji, Sureshbabu, 100
Maniram, Pandit, 87
Manju, 213
Mansur, Mallikarjun, 17, 24, 49, 55
Mattoo, Jeevan Lal, 42
Menuhin, Yehudi, 194
Mishra, Gopal, 225
Mishra, Rajan, 225
  All India Radio experience, 234–235
  Benaras *gharana* system, 227
  categorisation as *bhajan* singers, 228
  changes in musical field, 229–230

  childhood, 226
  disciples, 230–231
  education, 234
  family support, 233–234
  father's influence, 227
  favourite *bhajan,* 233
  favourite raga, 232
  future of classical music, 236
  gurukul at Dehradun and Benaras, 233
  gurus, 226
  jugalbandi, 227–229
  music as a source of livelihood, 235
  riyaaz, 231
Mishra, Sajan, 225
  Benaras *gharana* system, 227
  categorisation as *bhajan* singers, 228
  changes in musical field, 230
  father's influence, 227
  favourite *bhajan,* 233
  favourite raga, 232
  first public performance, 232
  future of classical music, 236
  gurus, 226
  jugalbandi, 227–229
  music as a source of livelihood, 235
Mishra, Sarju Prasad, 68
Mishra, Shrichandra, 68
Mohan Veena, 211
Motiram, Pandit, 87
Mudgal, Justice Mukul, 87
Mudgal, Madhup, 271

P

Pandit, Laxman Krishnarao, 133
  advice to younsters, 140
  bandishes, 139
  changes in musical scenario, 134
  concerts during 1940s and 1950s, 138
  condition of classical music and musicians, 136–137
  contribution to Gwalior *gharana,* 134–135
  disciples, 137
  first public concert, 138
  gayaki, 135
  gharana system, 135–136
  guru, 138
  ragas, 137, 139
  riyaaz, 137
  status of classical music in society, 136
  tappa and *thumri,* 139
Pandit, Meeta, 133, 140
Prasad, Dr. Rajendra, 186
Prasad, Hanuman, 225
Prasad, Mani, 175

R

Radio Gandharv, 15
ragadari system, 42
Rai, Ramdeo, 67
Rajam, Dr. N., 73–74
  becoming a performer, 83
  concerts, 75
  as disciple of Omkarnath Thakurji, 77–78
  disciples, 84–85
  Emeritus Professorship, 84
  family support, 84
  father's influence, 76
  fusion music, 82–83
  gayaki ang on violin, 79
  grandmother as guru, 75
  Hindustani Classical music training, 76–77
  hobbies, 85
  preparation for stage, 83–84
  raga *vistaar* (raga expansion) in Carnatic music, 82
  research on north Indian and south Indian styles, 79–81
  riyaaz, 76
  taans technique, 80
  time classification theory, 81–82
  views about young, upcoming practitioners, 85–86
Rajam, Ṅ., 13–14
Rajguru, Basavaraj, 17
Rakhaji, Alla, 33
Ramanna, 20
Ramdas, Bade, 225
Ramji, Raja, 167
Rasoolanbai, 68
Ravi Shankar Centre, Chanakyapuri, New Delhi, 27

S

Sabri, Gulfam, 49
Sabri, Jamal, 49
Sabri, Kamal, 49
Sabri, Sarvar, 49
Sadolikar, Leela, 241
Sadolikar, Wamanrao, 242, 244
Sadolikar-Katkar, Shruti, 237–238
  advice to younsters, 250–251
  beginning of musical journey, 239
  changes in style of singing, 244–245
  father's influence, 240
  guru, 239–240
  Gwalior *gharana gayaki,* 243
  Haveli Sangeet, 246
  Jaipur-Atrauli *gharana* system, 242–243

love-heartbreak-pain, 249–250
mother's influence, 241–242
preparation for different genre, 247
riyaaz, 240–241
son, 251
thumris, 248–249
transformation of ragas, 246–247
twenty-*taals* rendition, 245

Sangeeta, 76
Satvik Veena, 218
Shankar, Lakshmi, 33
Shankar, Ravi, 24, 27–28, 213–216, 219, 222, 257
about Western audience, 37–38
advice to aspiring young musicians, 38
criticisms, 35
daughter Anoushka's music, 38
as disciple of Baba Allaudin Khan, 29–30
first solo public concert, 30–31
on fusion music, 34
with George Harrison, 33
on *gharana* system, 36–37
on Hindustani classical music, 35–36
jugalbandi concerts with Ali Akbar Khan, 32
mother's influence, 31–32
music for Indian films, 34
role in Uday Shankar's troupe, 31
with Sir Yehudi Menuhin, 33
teaching style, 37
as 'the cultural ambassador' of India, 34

Shankar, Uday, 27, 29
Sharma, Shiv Kumar, 33, 157
accompanying artists with, 163–164
compositions in ragas, 161
early perceptions on santoor, 158
gharana system, 162
innovations in santoor, 159
introduction of santoor in classical music, 158
jugalbandi, 163
modifications in playing santoor, 159
music therapy, 162
ragas, 161
riyaaz, 160
solo album, 160
thematic albums, 160

Sharma, Umadutt, 158
Shirodkar, Menakabai, 22, 60
Sopori, Bhajan, 199–200
association with saints, 202–203
balancing music and studies, 201
changes on the santoor, 206
composition of ragas, 209
dhrupad ang, 204
family support, 210
film compositions, 208–209
gayaki ang, 206
gourd (*tumba*) look of santoor, 205–206
knowledge of sitar and piano, 206
music as a profession, 202
parents, 201
as a poet, 207–208
Sopori baaj, 204–205
sound therapy, 202
Sufiana tradition, 203
unpopularity of santoor, 208
Western Classical Music, 207

Sopori, S. C., 199
Sopori, S. N., 199
Sriram, 76
Subbulakshmi, M. S., 77
Subhalakshmi, 184
Subramaniam, L., 33

T

Thakur, Omkarnath, 31, 68, 74, 77–78
Thakur, Prerna Behen, 89
Thatte, Dr Arawind, 271–272
ati vilambit laya, 276–277
changes in harmonium playing, 279–280
compartmentalisation of music, 276
concerts, 282
family support, 282
future of harmonium, 281–282
harmonium as accompaniment to artistes, 280–281
harmonium training, 273
layakari, 274
modifications on harmonium, 274–275
as Pandit Jasraj's disciple, 273, 278–279
presentation of forms, 276
research in music, 275
shift from vocal to instrumental music, 273, 279
shortcomings in music, 280
solo concert, 277

Turner, Rick, 216

V

Vatsyayan, Kapila, 47
Viji, 76
Vishwa Veena, 211

W

Waghela, Maharaja Jaiwant Singhji, 88